THE DELTA ANOMALY

by Rick Barba

Simon Spotlight
New York London Toronto Sydney

4
Bar

This book is a work of fiction. Any references to historical events, real people, or real locales are used fictitiously. Other names, characters, places, and incidents are the product of the author's imagination, and any resemblance to actual events or locales or persons, living or dead, is entirely coincidental. SIMON SPOTLIGHT An imprint of Simon & Schuster Children's Publishing Division 1230 Avenue of the Americas, New York, New York 10020 © 2010 Paramount Pictures Corporation. ® & © 2010 CBS Studios, Inc. STAR TREK and related marks are trademarks of CBS Studios Inc. All Rights Reserved. All rights reserved, including the right of reproduction in whole or in part in any form. SIMON SPOTLIGHT and colophon are registered trademarks of Simon & Schuster, Inc. For information about special discounts for bulk purchases, please contact Simon & Schuster Special Sales at 1-866-506-1949 or business@simonandschuster.com. Manufactured in the United States of America First Edition 10 9 8 7 6 5 4 3 2 1 ISBN 978-1-4424-1409-9 (hc) ISBN 978-1-4424-1241-5 (pbk) ISBN 978-1-4424-1425-9 (eBook) Library of Congress Control Number: 2010935106

2/11
Bet

Contents

CH.1.12
Fogbound

In the summer of 2255, the San Francisco fog was like a living entity. Pushed ashore by ocean winds, it would creep and crawl over the city's famous hills like a great white leviathan. Most nights that July, the city was smothered in the fog's wet hide. Twirling white tendrils drifted down streets and alleys.

But if you could get *above* the fog layer, it was a breathtaking view.

At eight hundred fifty feet aboveground, the woman bound and gagged in the beacon cone at the top of the Transamerica Pyramid was *well* above the fog.

It was a breathtaking experience—quite literally.

● · .+ .· ◆ · .+ ·•. .

Jacqueline Madkins—Jackie to her friends—was a tough gal. From her sensible shoes to her sensible haircut, she radiated a no-nonsense air that had served her well in her career. She'd been running security operations in the famous 286-year-old pyramid, the crown jewel of the San Francisco skyline, for almost ten years. She was one of only four people in the world with unrestricted access to the beacon cone.

So when SecureCam Omega went offline earlier that night, she'd groaned in disbelief.

Jackie was alone in the security control center on the thirtieth floor. Her security team, a crew of twenty guards, was making its regular rounds. It was quite an operation. She sat at a bank of monitors flickering live feeds from the building's one hundred sixty surveillance cameras. She started tapping SecureCam Omega's feed button on the camera control console.

Blank screen. It was as if the camera went dead, but Jackie knew that couldn't happen. She shuddered involuntarily as a strange chill ran down her spine.

The top two hundred twelve feet of the Transamerica Pyramid was a hollow, translucent lumenite spire. Inside the spire, a steep staircase zigzagged up to the cone that housed the one-thousand-watt LED aviation warning light, a flashing red strobe. SecureCam Omega—the one that was apparently on the blink—surveyed the beacon chamber. Getting to it was a long, hard climb.

Jackie thought about that climb and looked down ruefully at her feet. "It's not that I don't like fabulous shoes," she'd recently explained to her sister, Dawn, "it's just that they are not exactly practical in my line of work!"

Suddenly, her comlink buzzed. She hit a button on her belt unit.

"Talk to me, Will," she said.

"Did you just *see* that?" blurted the voice of Will Rosen, one of her night-team guards. He was just a teenager, and he sounded shaken.

"See what?" asked Jackie.

"The flash!" cried Will.

Jackie swiveled her chair to another console and checked what she called "the big board," a full schematic of the entire building. Blue glowing icons marked the real-time locations of all twenty team members. Each icon was numbered.

"Okay, I got you marked up on forty-eight," she said. "Is that right?"

The Transamerica Pyramid's entire forty-eighth floor was a single, spectacular conference room. It offered a full 360-degree view of the city.

"Confirmed," said Will. "It was, like, right outside the window." His breathing was short and shallow. "Very bright, like an explosion."

"I didn't hear anything," replied Jackie.

"Neither did I," said Will.

"This is getting really weird," Jackie muttered.

"What's that?" asked Will.

Now her red line was ringing. This was a direct emergency hotline to SFPD. "Nothing. Sit tight, Will. I'll be right up," she said, and cut off the comlink. Then she picked up the red receiver on the console. "Pyramid security, this is Madkins." She spoke with professional calm.

"Yo, Jackie, you okay over there?" said a voice on the line.

"Hey, Sam," she said. It was Sergeant Sam Kalar at SFPD's central district station, just down the street. "What's up?"

"We got people reporting a big lightning strike on the pyramid," replied the voice. "Calls coming in left and right."

"One of my guys saw a flash, but no sound," said Jackie. "I think we're fine. I've got power, all systems running. But we'll check it out."

"Okay," said Sergeant Kalar. "Let me know."

"Roger," she said, and hung up.

Time for my workout, she thought grimly.

Fifteen minutes later, Jackie was still lumbering up the spire staircase. She was in good shape, but this was the equivalent of climbing a twenty-one-story spiraling fire escape. After a few rest stops, she finally reached the landing that supports the final twenty-foot ladder leading up to the beacon platform.

"Going in," she said into her comlink.

"I got you marked, boss," came the voice of Will.

Jackie slowly hauled herself up the ladder through a narrow opening into the small cone-shaped room. A glass pyramid cap at the top housed the Halo3000 aviation warning beacon. The red strobe flashed forty times per minute with an intensity of twenty thousand candelas, bright enough to cause retinal damage. But a shield platform underneath the beacon let Jackie scan the chamber without danger.

"No damage up here," she said over the comlink, an obvious note of relief in her voice.

"Copy that," said Will.

Then Jackie spotted the malfunctioning camera near the floor. With a simple twist, the unit clicked off of its base. She tucked it into a side pouch she'd worn for just this purpose.

Nothing to worry about, she told herself, allowing relief to wash over her. She mentally chastised herself for having felt so worried over nothing.

As she approached the ladder for descent, a slight hissing sound from above caught her attention. She glanced up at the beacon's shield platform. Wisps of black were slowly drifting downward.

"What the . . . ," she said.

"What's that, boss?" called Will.

"I see smoke up here," she said, puzzled. "Up in the beacon housing."

She listened to crackling silence over the comlink. Will was as perplexed as she was. "We'd better get a repair guy up here ASAP," she said. "There's a number in the database for Aviation Safety Systems. Call right now and, oh my god . . ."

Black smoke was now pouring into the chamber from above. It shot down in three long plumes. Each plume started circling Jackie and tightening its spiral. She could feel the smoke slithering over her bare arms, face, and throat. The last things she felt before falling unconscious were the distinct sensation of a powerful pressure strapping her arms to her sides, and a thin film spreading across her mouth, sealing it shut.

"Jackie, do you read me?" called Will over the comlink. "Jackie?"

Jackie couldn't reply. Moments later, she lost consciousness.

CH.2.12
The Delta Quadrant

Starfleet Academy life was grueling.

Weeks of rigorous, unending study. Physical and mental training that no sport could prepare you for. Brutal hours in the tactical simulators, followed by humiliating debriefing sessions filled with failure analyses. And then there was the competition—the finest minds and bodies in the entire galaxy, pitted against one another daily, *hourly*. It took a toll.

The Starfleet cadets needed to blow off steam.

Chestnut Street in San Francisco—where the beautiful people and aliens prowled, mated, and dated—was a favorite hangout. Tonight the city's infamous fog swirled like a pale fluid. James T. Kirk, Leonard "Bones" McCoy, and a Tellarite cadet named Glorak strolled down Chestnut Street looking for fun while trying to avoid collisions. Visibility was low. The fog was so thick that bodies appeared and disappeared like ghosts—for example, that Chinese lady carrying a huge, live lobster.

"Good god!" said McCoy, jumping out of the way.

Kirk laughed and watched the woman pass. The lobster was waving its rubber-banded claws like a symphony conductor. Kirk pointed at the crustacean. "I'll see you at dinner, Bernstein!" he called. A few steps later the apparition melted back into the white mist and disappeared.

Glorak wrinkled his piglike snout and said, "Your oceans produce such strange creatures!"

"Don't get me started on oceans," grumbled McCoy.

Kirk turned to Glorak. "Bones hates oceans worse than he hates space," he explained.

"You . . . hate space?" asked Glorak.

"Yes, I hate space," said McCoy.

"Interesting that you've chosen a career with Starfleet, Dr. McCoy," said Glorak.

"Oh, *is it?*" said McCoy testily.

Kirk slung an arm around McCoy's shoulders. "'Space is disease and danger wrapped in darkness and silence.' I believe that's an exact quote." Kirk blinked up at a neon sign glowing in the fog. "First words you ever spoke to me, Bones. Kinda makes me nostalgic."

McCoy glared at Kirk. "Nostalgic for *what?*"

"For simpler days," said Kirk. "For . . . innocence."

"One thing you've *never* been, Jim," said McCoy, "is innocent."

Kirk whacked McCoy on the back. "Speaking of which . . . let's find girls. I hear they tend to flock in this vicinity."

McCoy shook his head. "I can't even find the damned sidewalk."

"I warned you about that Andorian ale, my friend," said Glorak darkly.

"I'm talking about the *fog*, for god's sake," said McCoy.

"Oh," said Glorak.

"Come on," said Kirk. "Let's find that new club."

Word around campus was that a holo-karaoke bar had just opened off Chestnut. It was called the Delta Quadrant, and rumor had it that some female cadets were planning a birthday outing there that evening. Kirk despised karaoke, especially this new version where you could sing your song surrounded by holographic projections of the actual band. But, Kirk loved female cadets. So it was an acceptable trade-off, tactically speaking.

The three cadets continued up Chestnut, dodging loud groups of bar-hopping pedestrians. Kirk stopped a few people to ask directions to the Delta Quadrant, but everyone he encountered was either a little too drunk—or too eager to get home with that evening's conquest—to stop and give clear directions. So the trio kept getting lost down side streets. As usual, Kirk pushed ahead of the others.

"I'm making poor command decisions," he muttered to himself. Glancing down a dark alley, he spotted several dark entities twirling in the whitish fog. He stopped to watch, mesmerized. Their jerky movements seemed inhuman. Odd, hissing voices wafted toward Kirk, and a chill seized him. But then the entities suddenly evaporated. The figures literally melted away into the fog.

When the others caught up, Kirk pointed down the alley. "Did you see that?"

"See what?" asked McCoy.

"Creepy people dancing and, like, . . . hissing," said Kirk.

Glorak snorted loudly. "You sure they were *dancing*, Kirk?"

McCoy glared at Glorak. "I hate it when you suck in your snout like that," he said.

Glorak smiled at McCoy and sucked in his snout a few more times.

"Yes, that's it exactly," McCoy said, disgusted.

Kirk stared into the fog. The vision had been unsettling. After a few more seconds, he shrugged. "Whatever."

Kirk, McCoy, and Glorak pushed ahead through the night's white shroud. As they turned the next corner they heard loud music pulsing from an open doorway just ahead. Above the door, a 3-D holograph of the Greek letter delta hovered in the air, spinning eerily in the fog.

"Ah, that must be it!" cried Glorak.

As Kirk rolled into the club, he expertly scoped out the room. Within moments, his eyes settled on the lovely Cadet Uhura, sitting at a corner table with the voluptuous, red-haired, green-skinned Gaila. Kirk smiled—this was a triple score. First, like all good Orion girls, Cadet Gaila *loved* men. Second, Gaila was a computer lab tech, and it always paid to be on good terms with someone who had access to Starfleet guts. And third . . . well, one of Kirk's favorite pastimes was trying to make the straight-laced Cadet Uhura uncomfortable. She was absolutely adorable when she squirmed.

"Gentlemen, lock your targets," said Kirk.

"Right," said McCoy. "Every man for himself."

"Standard rules of engagement?" asked Glorak.

"Correct, Mr. Glorak," replied Kirk. "Rendezvous here at 2200 hours."

"But Mr. Kirk, that's curfew!" said Glorak.

Kirk nodded. "Good point, Mr. Glorak," he said. "Make it 2155."

"That leaves little room for error."

Kirk glanced over at Uhura and Gaila. "I don't anticipate errors," he said, grinning.

• · ·: :. ✦ . ✦ ·. ·

Kirk moved across the room like a man with a mission. He passed the club stage where a wobbly Andorian girl with white hair and fishnet tights was making a fool of herself singing an ancient Madonna song. She blew Kirk a kiss as he passed. As he approached Uhura, Kirk was disappointed to see that his fun had been compromised: She looked to be already uncomfortable, and it wasn't because of him. Next to her, Gaila loudly ordered another drink that she clearly didn't need.

"Hello, Cadets!" said Kirk brightly.

"Jim Kirk!" shrieked Gaila. She pointed at him. "Look! It's that Jim Kirk!"

Uhura nodded. "So it is."

"He's hot!" she whisper-yelled to Uhura. Gaila then exploded into a honking laugh that sounded like alarmed waterfowl rising from a lake. The noise was so frightening that Kirk nearly backed away.

"Wow," said Kirk, nodding. "Impressive *levity* there."

"S'my birthday," slurred Gaila. She attempted to lean seductively toward Kirk and almost fell off her stool. "Where's my gift, Jim Kirk?" She grabbed a handful of his shirt. "Is it in your pocket?"

"Oh, well, see, I didn't . . . ," " began Kirk, but Gaila cut him off by waving wildly at a passing cocktail waitress.

"One more!" she screamed over the thumping music.

"Right here! Green drink for green girl!" She pointed at herself, laughing hysterically.

The waitress glided in close. She said, "I already *got* your order, hon. But are you sure you want it?"

"I think it's a poor decision, Gaila," said Uhura.

"Excellent!" said Gaila. She looked up at Kirk. "I'm excellent."

"I can see that."

"You're a little *too* excellent, Gaila," said Uhura.

Nearby, the bartender slung a slushy green drink onto the service stand. As the waitress hustled off to snag it, Gaila suddenly slid off her chair and onto the floor at Kirk's feet. She started giggling uncontrollably.

"Whoooops!" she howled.

People at the next table laughed, but looked a little uneasy.

"Wow," said Kirk. "You're *really* hammered."

"Thank you!"

As Kirk helped Gaila back onto her chair, she flung her arms tightly around his neck. Kirk was momentarily tempted, but then he caught a look from Uhura—a cross between "Don't you dare!" and "Please god, help me!" So he unlocked himself from Gaila's grip and shot off to intercept the cocktail waitress.

"I've got this," he said, dropping money on her tray and snagging the drink.

"Don't give it to green girl," said the waitress wearily.

Kirk nodded and quickly slipped the drink to a stocky, jovial Xannon cadet named Braxim at the next table.

"On the house," said Kirk.

Braxim smiled broadly. "Thank you, Mr. Kirk," he said.

"Don't mention it." Kirk leaned down. "And I mean that literally."

Braxim laughed heartily. "I have been watching the Orion girl," he said, beating his chest for emphasis as Xannons do. "You will need assistance, I am sure. Orion girls can be *most* unruly. Trust me—I know firsthand."

"Thanks, friend," said Kirk, making a mental note to ask for more information on that firsthand knowledge sometime.

When Kirk returned to the table, Uhura was trying to convince Gaila to head back to the Presidio, the site of the Starfleet Academy campus. But the Orion girl abruptly jumped to her feet and, without a word, staggered off to the restroom.

Uhura gave Kirk a dark look. "As much as it pains me to say this to you, of all people," she said, "I need some help."

"Okay," said Kirk.

"I doubt this girl can walk all the way back to campus," said Uhura. "Let's drag her to the Powell Street shuttle. It's just a few blocks."

Kirk nodded. "For a price," he said.

Uhura narrowed her eyes. "Are you kidding?"

"Just tell me your first name," said Kirk, smiling at her in a way that made most girls swoon.

Annoyingly, Uhura just stared at him.

"So . . . no deal?" asked Kirk. Uhura rolled her eyes and started after Gaila. "Okay, well, I'll help you anyway," called Kirk as she hurried away, "whatever your name is." As Uhura ducked into the restroom without responding, he added: "I'll be waiting right here, sweetheart."

Kirk spotted McCoy nearby and quickly pulled the doctor away from a few prospective "patients." "We need to escort Uhura and Gaila to the shuttle landing," he said quickly.

"Why?" asked McCoy. "It's just four blocks away. And you're kind of interrupting something here," he said, motioning discreetly to a cute blonde sipping a pink drink.

Kirk winked at her. She winked back. *Focus,* he told himself.

"It's foggy out," replied Kirk. "Dangerous."

"Are you joking?" exclaimed McCoy. "These women are Starfleet-trained in self-defense, Jim! They can handle themselves just fine."

"I know that," says Kirk. "But Gaila is messed up, bad. Uhura needs help getting her back to the dorm."

"Good god, Jim, I'm a doctor, not a babysitter," said

McCoy, his eyes returning to linger on the blonde.

"Some medical skills *might* be useful here," said Kirk.

"That girl doesn't need my skills."

Kirk grabbed McCoy's jacket. "Look, I need you, Bones," he said. "This Orion woman scares the hell out of me."

McCoy grinned. "Well, *that's* a first."

"And I think we'll need a couple more guys," said Kirk, scanning the club.

Ten minutes later, Glorak and Braxim stood with Kirk and McCoy near the door to the women's restroom.

Tellarites and Xannons were both stout, strong races, so this duo was a nice addition to the escort detail. And Braxim, like most Xannons, was a fun-loving fellow who loved company. With his big barrel chest and bony forehead protrusion, he seemed to be forever leaning forward.

"I love nights such as tonight!" he exclaimed, giving his chest a quick thump. "I find coastal fog to be most bracing and romantic, particularly when it lacks a methane component!"

McCoy nodded. "Yes, methane fog does put a damper on romance," he agreed.

Suddenly Uhura burst from the women's room, alone. "Did she come out?" she asked, frowning.

"Gaila?" asked Kirk. "No."

"Are you sure?"

Kirk looked around. "We've been here ten minutes or so," he said. "When did you see her last?"

"Just a minute ago," she said. "She was in a stall. I went out to wash my hands, and then she was gone." Uhura ducked back into the restroom, then popped back out.

"The window's open!" she said angrily.

"Crap. Let's go," said Kirk.

The five cadets hustled to the club entrance. "Bones, you check any alleys around the club with Glorak," said Kirk quickly. "Braxxy and I will head up to Chestnut. She can't be far." He turned to Uhura. "You should stay here in case she comes back looking for you."

"Oh, she won't," said Uhura with irritation, stepping outside and scanning the foggy sidewalk. "She's on the prowl. I've seen Gaila like this before. She's *relentless*."

"I fear for the men of this city," muttered McCoy.

"She is *quite* inebriated," said Braxim, squinting out at the fog. "How far could she go?"

Kirk looked at McCoy.

"Pretty far," they said simultaneously.

The cadets split into two search parties—the result of good Starfleet away-team tactical training. McCoy, Uhura, and

Glorak deployed toward the Powell Street shuttle landing, four blocks up Russian Hill—a steep climb. Meanwhile, Kirk and the brawny Braxim started tracking up and down Marina District streets. A sudden inland gust churned up the milky fog around them. It drifted in jagged tendrils, seeming almost alive.

"Still like the fog, Braxxy?" asked Kirk, wiping his eyes.

Braxim smiled wryly. "It does seem unfriendly now," he admitted.

Kirk pointed to an old-fashioned neon sign, PAK's GROCERY, glimmering on the corner just ahead. "Your turn," he said. "I'll scout ahead a bit."

As Braxim ducked into the store to search for Gaila, Kirk moved along the street looking for alleys.

Suddenly, he heard Gaila. She was singing.

"Gaila!" he called out. "Yo, girl!"

Kirk followed the sound to the entrance of an alley running behind some classic row houses. Abruptly, the singing stopped . . . replaced by a hissing metallic voice. Now Kirk heard Gaila gasping. He ran up the alley until he could see a vague outline of Gaila with another murky figure, dark in the pale fog, wrapped like a black cloak around her. He hesitated for a brief moment, wondering if he was interrupting something. Was Gaila gasping or *choking*?

Kirk decided she was probably not enjoying the

encounter. She sounded like she was convulsing. If he was wrong, he'd deal with it. He had to make sure Gaila wasn't in trouble.

"Hey!" shouted Kirk. "Hey, *you!*"

As Kirk shouted, the figure that had been all over Gaila reared up—huge now, maybe seven feet tall. The hissing morphed into a familiar sound, but Kirk couldn't place it. Kirk shouted again, using his "command voice" (learned in Fleet Command and Control Methods) but the dark entity did not move.

Then Gaila groaned in agony. Now Kirk was pissed.

He dropped low, lunged, then sidestepped and unleashed a jab kick. He was sure he had a clean, easy shot at the attacker, but his foot struck nothing but air. Suddenly he was locked in a vise grip. The guy was incredibly strong. Kirk couldn't move his arms. Then it got worse— fast. He felt a sticky sheet being pulled over his head. The sheet tightened across his face. He couldn't move, and he couldn't breathe.

Then Braxim burst through the fog.

"I called the police!" he shouted at the attacker, holding up his open hand-held communicator. "I called 911!"

Suddenly the sheet peeled off of Kirk's face. He fell to the ground, gasping for air, and looked up to see the fog rolling toward Braxim's feet.

In an impossibly deep voice, the entity spoke a phrase in a language that Kirk did not recognize. He seemed to be speaking to Braxim.

Then the attacker completely melted away into the thick fog.

CH.3.12
Two Exams

The next day at Starfleet Medical College, the Academy's chief medical officer, Dr. Charles Griffin, ordered a team of top cadet physicians, including Leonard McCoy, to assist in a full examination of Cadet Gaila. Although the San Francisco police participated in the initial crime scene investigation, conducted interviews with Cadets Kirk and Braxim, and filed an official report, the incident was considered a Starfleet matter now, under military jurisdiction.

The Orion girl, unconscious following the attack, woke up with no memory of the incident. Other than a lingering dry cough, she seemed largely unaffected. In fact, she was in remarkably good spirits; Gaila found young male doctors like McCoy so *interesting*.

"*Please*, don't move while the doctor is conducting a scan," McCoy said for the third time.

Gaila glanced around the small exam prep room. "What

doctor are you talking about?" she asked, confused.

McCoy held up the scanning attachment of his medical tricorder.

"Me!" he said, exasperated.

"Oh," said Gaila. "Do doctors always refer to themselves in the third person?"

"I have no idea," said McCoy. "Stop moving."

He activated the scanner and moved it slowly upward in front of Gaila to conduct preliminary imaging and analysis of her torso.

"It's hard to sit still," whispered Gaila.

"Why?" asked McCoy. "Are you in pain?"

"No," replied Gaila.

McCoy frowned at the tricorder read-out screen. "Then what is your problem, woman?"

She wriggled on the examining table. "This hospital gown is like . . . it's like sitting on sandpaper."

"So take it off."

Gaila widened her eyes as McCoy punched a few buttons and held the medical device out for a second scan of Gaila's body. When he looked up, she gave him a sly look.

"Is that a Code Seven medical directive, Doctor?" she asked, lowering her gown off her shoulders.

But McCoy simply looked back down at the device in his hands. As his eyes followed the tricorder upward, he saw something just below Gaila's chin. The doctor reached out and ran his index finger across the nape of Gaila's neck.

She shivered under his touch. "Mmm, that's nice," she said.

"Cadet, when did you bathe last?" asked McCoy, gazing at his finger.

"Yesterday," she said.

"You're sure?"

"Yes, I'm sure," she said, a little indignantly. She pulled up her gown, realizing her seduction attempt might be a lost cause. "And I *would* have showered this morning, but I woke up in an intensive care unit connected to a bunch of tubes."

McCoy held up his finger. It was smudged black.

Gaila looked confused. "What's that?"

McCoy stepped to a nearby console. He tapped another button and began recording a report:

"*Preliminary physical exam reveals a chalky black residue on Cadet Gaila's skin,*" said McCoy. "*Medical tricorder imaging scans also indicate internal traces of a microscopic contaminant, with hot spots concentrated in two internal organs.*" He paused, then added: "*Including one unique to females of the Orion race.*"

Now Gaila was frowning too.

"Dr.. McCoy, are you talking about an infection?" she asked.

"Possibly," said McCoy. "Or maybe an injected substance. The medical tricorder analysis is inconclusive, which is odd." He held up the device and glanced at the readings again. "Very odd."

Now Gaila looked worried. "You think this guy *infected* me? With what?"

McCoy's voice softened a bit. "Hard to say," he said. "But 1 wouldn't worry, Cadet. Your vital signs are perfect, and my scans show no toxins, nothing malignant or invasive attacking you. You seem perfectly healthy. And your friends stopped the attacker before anything serious happened, thank god."

Gaila started to reach toward her neck but McCoy quickly grabbed her hand.

"I'm sorry," he said. "I'm going to need samples of that for lab work."

Gaila nodded, looking uneasy.

"So what happens next?" she asked.

McCoy pulled on sterile gloves, ripped open a sampling kit, and took out the swab. As he dabbed it on Gaila's neck, he said, "The chief medical officer of the college, Dr. Griffin, will supervise a comprehensive full-body scan. Then we'll take some fluid samples—blood, saliva, urine—and send them off to pathology for testing." He smiled reassuringly at Gaila. "Just to make sure you're okay."

Gaila nodded again. She said, "I wish I could remember what happened last night."

McCoy's reassuring smile disappeared, and he grew serious again. "Young lady, the Marina District is upscale, but it's still urban," he said. "Running off alone into the city night is not a tactically sound plan of action. Especially when impaired."

"Doctor, are you suggesting that I was *asking* to get attacked?" said Gaila, her nostrils flaring a bit.

"No!" said McCoy. "Of course not." He cleared his throat. "But still ..."

"Listen, Doctor," said Gaila in a lowered voice.

Now McCoy looked nervous. "Yes, Cadet?"

Gaila leaned toward him. "You may be cute, but you need to work on your bedside manner," she said, shaking her head. "It's not very good."

Everybody knew that Starfleet Academy's Command College was where the hardcore competitive juices flowed. It was where Starfleet's best and brightest—the future flight commanders and bridge officers—were chosen. And those lacking the "right stuff" were weeded out. It was the theory of natural selection in action.

It was James T. Kirk's favorite place on campus.

Except for today. Today, Kirk was getting his butt kicked by his Team Alpha nemesis, Cadet Viktor Tikhonov.

Worse, the butt-kicking was being administered in one of Kirk's favorite activities—Advanced Tactical Training, or ATT.

Well-trained tactical away teams, i.e., landing parties, were critical to the success of the overall Starfleet mission. The training was very physical but also called for creative decision-making in extreme situations—the kind of command skills Starfleet wanted in its future leaders.

Only top-performing Academy students were invited to ATT, and fewer than half of those actually passed the course. Cadets were divided into teams of five and put through six hard months of intensive training and competition. The best two teams then entered a final testing round, a series of three tactical scenarios. Each scenario focused on one of the three primary away-team mission types: Security, Science, and First Contact.

"First Contact" was the Starfleet term for encountering a new race and conducting initial Federation diplomacy in the field.

The two remaining cadet teams were dubbed Alpha and Delta. Each team was required to select a leader for the final testing round: Kirk was elected Team Delta captain, while Team Alpha chose Tikhonov. The Academy faculty had already noted Kirk's bold, intuitive leadership qualities, and his teammates liked and respected him. Two weeks earlier, Kirk had led Delta to the highest score in the First Contact mission final.

But Kirk's rival, Tikhonov, was as good as he was arrogant. And he was *very* arrogant.

Now the Alpha captain was leading a devastating romp over Kirk's crew.

That Monday's exercise, called the Derelict Cairo scenario, was the Security mission final. It was an exhausting, dangerous test that pitted two away teams directly against each other aboard an abandoned, powerless, Constitution-class heavy starship cruiser, the USS *Cairo*.

Armed with phasers locked on light-stun setting, the two cadet teams were simultaneously shuttled into separate hangar bays in the *Cairo*'s cylinder-shaped secondary hull. Each team's objective was to race up the ship's connecting pylon onto the eleven-deck, saucer-shaped primary hull.

There, the goal was to secure the *Cairo*'s main bridge and hold it against the opposing team for two uninterrupted hours. A timer was installed on the helm console in front of the command chair; it had a red Delta button and a blue Alpha button. To secure the bridge, any cadet could press his or her team's button to start the timer. If that person's team's button remained pressed for two consecutive hours, they won. If the other team managed to press their own button, the timer reset to zero.

Thus the Derelict Cairo scenario could go on for many hours. One infamous battle back in 2249 had gone on for two full days.

The task was complicated by the *Cairo*'s zero-gravity, low-oxygen environment. Cadets wore infinite rebreather masks that reduced visibility, and because they were weightless, cadets had to kick off walls and other surfaces to maneuver.

That morning, Tikhonov had been efficient and relentless. The Russian's physical skills were unmatched at the Academy and perfectly suited to the setting of a powered-down starship. His team had secured the bridge in record time.

Now Kirk was desperately trying to rally his crew.

"Mr. Glorak!" he hissed into his communicator as he floated along a silver air duct. "Do you read me, over?"

A phaser bolt suddenly ricocheted down the duct. Luckily, it missed him. In a panic move, Kirk punched out a duct grate just below his face, heaved through the opening, and floated down into a dimly lit room full of sofas.

"Glorak?" he said. "Anybody? Is anybody out there, over?"

Glorak's voice crackled from the communicator. "Captain Kirk," he snorted. "I've lost the squad, over."

"What?"

"The squad, Captain!" replied Glorak, sounding tense and frazzled. "Gone. I've got Mr. Raynor and Mr. Marcus both down, unconscious, and . . . Yes—yes, it looks like Simmons has been taken prisoner."

Kirk couldn't believe it. "Are you kidding me?"

More phaser bolts ripped across the room.

Kirk caught a glimpse of two hostiles in their blue Alpha vests; Delta wore red vests. He clipped his utility belt to a nearby wall rung to keep from floating out into the open, and then quickly reviewed the situation.

Kirk had assumed that Tikhonov would take advantage of his superior strength and pull himself through the ventilation system on a beeline run to the main bridge, deploying the rest of Team Alpha to cover his trail. So Kirk had chosen to mirror that tactic. He'd sent his full Delta team, led by Glorak, along the most obvious route to the primary hull—straight up the torpedo exhaust vents. This way they would engage and occupy the Alpha squad. Meanwhile, Kirk would take a roundabout route via a series of forward observation decks. He'd scoot along air ducts to the Sickbay Complex and then veer up through five decks of crew quarters into the docking port directly behind the main bridge.

From there, Kirk planned to surprise Tikhonov, maybe gun him down in a classic duel, and hold the bridge. By himself. Kirk thought this was a great plan—in theory. He was now realizing this was not such a great plan in execution.

"I'm taking heavy fire here, Captain," called Glorak. "Where are you?"

"I . . . don't know," whispered Kirk. "This looks like a recreation area. I think I took a wrong turn."

"Nice," said Glorak.

"How'd you lose so many guys, man?" asked Kirk, his voice rising a bit.

"Ambush," replied Glorak. "Mr. Tikhonov nailed Raynor and Marcus from a torpedo launch tube! Very impressive accuracy, I must say."

"Tikhonov is *there?*" exclaimed Kirk. "Then who's on the bridge?"

"I have no idea, Captain," said Glorak. "But I can't . . . *unh.*"

Kirk looked at his communicator. "Glorak?"

"No, Mr. Kirk," replied a familiar Russian accent. "This is not Glorak. This is the voice of your humiliating defeat."

"Hey, Viktor," said Kirk, trying for nonchalance.

"Your entire team is incapacitated, comrade."

"Except me."

"Yes, except you."

"Then I see you've fallen right into my trap," said Kirk.

The Russian chuckled. "You will make a fine third officer on my ship's bridge someday, Mr. Kirk."

"Speaking of the bridge, I'll see you there, Vik," said Kirk.

"Bring all your guys, though. I want a fair fight."

Tikhonov laughed again. "I like you, Kirk," he said. "I'm pulling back my scouts from the Officers' Lounge so you can surrender with dignity."

"I'm in the Officers' Lounge?" asked Kirk, looking around.

"Yes, Mr. Kirk."

"Oh."

Sure enough, the phaser fire stopped. Kirk cautiously lifted his head above the console. The room was now deserted. No blue Alpha vests.

"Gosh, thanks, Viktor," he said.

"Do you wish to negotiate terms of surrender?" asked Tikhonov.

Kirk smiled and clicked off his communicator.

"Kirk out," he said to himself.

He pulled his tricorder from his belt. Dialing up a schematic of the *Cairo* air duct system, Kirk plotted a course to the bridge, setting waypoints—something he should have done before. He was surprised to discover that this room was on C Deck, just two decks directly below the bridge.

Kirk unclipped his utility belt and kicked upward off the console, toward the open ventilation duct just above him.

"This should be fun," he said.

• · ·⁚ ✦ · ✦ ·· ·

McCoy couldn't believe what he was seeing. He rapidly tapped the digital pads on the quantum molecular microscope, making focus and scan adjustments.

"I told you," said a man in a white lab coat. He gazed excitedly over McCoy's shoulder. "See? I am not crazy."

McCoy squinted into the microscope again. He made some more adjustments. Then he looked up.

"They're moving," he said.

"They are so much more than *moving*, Dr. McCoy!"

"That's true," agreed McCoy.

The man in the lab coat was Dr. Naamba Reyjik, director of the pathology lab at the medical college. His smile revealed two rows of gleaming white teeth that seemed illuminated against his dark skin. He slapped McCoy on the back.

"This is undoubtedly a First Contact!" said Dr. Reyjik, jabbing a finger upward to punctuate his point. "There is nothing like this in our experience, my friend. Nothing in the Starfleet database even comes close. Believe me, I checked. I spent the last two hours checking. I have my whole *staff* checking. There is no precedent in the medical or scientific literature."

McCoy nodded. He felt a pang of excitement too. Then a realization hit him like a concussion grenade.

"Good god, my patient!" he blurted.

McCoy burst from the lab, nearly running over a group of research interns. He made a full sprint down the corridor to the turbo lift, which was open and unoccupied. McCoy dived inside, fist-punched a button, and rode the lift down to the diagnostic ward. There, he leaped out and continued his sprint past two concerned nurses at the ward station.

When he arrived in Gaila's room, she was in a fitful sleep.

McCoy hurried to her side. He knelt there and gently shook her awake. She sat bolt upright . . . then started vigorously scratching her abdomen.

"Dr. McCoy," she murmured sleepily, smiling, "have you been watching me dream about you?"

McCoy watched Gaila claw at her ribs a few seconds, then she suddenly stopped and looked at her hands.

"Wow," she said. She touched her abdomen in several places. "It went away."

"What went away?" asked McCoy.

"The itching inside," replied Gaila. "Just like that. Huh. Guess it was . . . just the dream."

"Tell me about your dream," said McCoy. He reached for the medical tricorder on the stand next to the bed and activated its scanner.

Misunderstanding why he was asking, Gaila fluffed

her hair and adjusted her gown. "It was weird, Leonard," she began in a breathy voice. McCoy winced at her use of his first name, but he didn't interrupt her. "I was walking in the fog, like, on a city street. The fog was heavy, but it wasn't wet like fog. It was dry and scratchy. It was sticking to me, getting in my eyes." She waved a hand in front of her face for emphasis. "Very unpleasant."

McCoy said, "Hold still, please." He started a new tricorder scan of Gaila, starting at her feet. "So what happened, Cadet?"

"Please, call me Gaila," she said, batting her eyelashes.

"I prefer 'cadet,'" said McCoy. "Right now I'm a doctor, not your friend."

Gaila rolled her eyes. "Whatever." The breathy voice was gone. "So then I started itching all over. It felt like the fog was under my skin, in my mouth and nose, even inside me. But I started crying, and it all changed."

McCoy pressed a tricorder button. "How so?" he asked.

"I don't know, exactly," said Gaila, frowning. "I just remember wiping my eyes. My hands were black."

"Black?" asked McCoy.

"Yes."

Now McCoy reached out and touched two fingers under Gaila's chin. He lifted her head gently.

"Cadet, we asked you not to bathe yet," he said.

"I didn't," she said.

There was no sign of the chalky black residue on Gaila's neck. McCoy looked at the tricorder readout.

"Well, I'll be damned," he said.

The room's door suddenly swung open. It was Dr. Reyjik. He nodded at Gaila and turned to McCoy.

"It's gone, isn't it, Dr. McCoy?" he said.

McCoy arched an eyebrow. "How did you know?"

Reyjik widened his eyes. "Because the . . . *substance* is trying to escape our quantum containment chamber, even as we speak," he said. "I've been watching it for several minutes. Remarkable. But since the particulate matter would have to be subatomic in size to egress, it is failing in its attempt."

"My god," said McCoy, shaking his head.

Gaila looked from one doctor to the other.

"Can somebody please tell me what's going on?" she asked.

McCoy held up the medical tricorder. "According to these readings, the microscopic contaminant, whatever it was, has fled your body. It is completely and utterly gone."

"Where did it go?" asked Gaila.

McCoy and Reyjik exchanged a look. Then McCoy shrugged.

"Home, I guess," he said.

Five Alpha males, led by Viktor Tikhonov, would soon con-
verge on the main bridge of the USS *Cairo*. Floating in the
turbo-lift shaft behind the bridge, Kirk surveyed the situation. It didn't look good.

After scooting up air ducts, Kirk had arrived to find
the bridge deserted. The two Alpha scouts he'd engaged
in the Officers' Lounge had most likely secured the
bridge earlier—their blue Alpha button on the timer
was pressed when he'd arrived. But now the two were
nowhere to be seen.

Kirk had already slapped the red Team Delta button to
start the timer in his favor. After that he found a crowbar
in the bridge toolkit, and pried the turbo-lift doors halfway
open—not an easy task in a weightless environment—and
pulled himself into the open shaft. Three floors below, the
disabled turbo-lift car blocked the shaft. Now all he had
to do was defend the bridge for two hours while outnumbered seven to one.

Kirk didn't believe in no-win scenarios. But he was real-
istic. The odds were stacked against him.

*Gotta take out Tikhonov at least, maybe one or two other
guys too,* he thought. That way, even in defeat he could
emerge from this disaster with some shred of dignity.

So Kirk waited patiently.

He listened carefully.

And what he heard was . . . perfect silence for sixty-eight excruciating minutes.

What is Viktor doing? he wondered.

The whole time Kirk had his phaser pointed at the main air duct on the bridge's ceiling because he fully expected a Team Alpha rush from the ceiling. It was the best way for Tikhonov to leverage his superior numbers.

Sure enough, at the seventy-minute mark a loud rattling came from the ceiling duct. Kirk slowed his breathing and aimed. Suddenly, pulsing phaser blasts began pouring out of the duct. Kirk held his fire. He could tell that the Alpha shooters had no idea where he was.

Glittering bolts of energy flew from the open duct in all directions, ricocheting off consoles and chairs. *No doubt they're laying down a cover fire*, thought Kirk as he held his aim through the half-open turbo-lift doors, ready for the rush.

The noise and flashing phaser fire from the ceiling duct was distracting. So distracting that Kirk didn't notice the temperature rising in the turbo-lift shaft until it was too late.

The last thing he heard before drifting into stunned sleep was the sound of Viktor Tikhonov and another Alpha cadet peeling back the melted roof of the turbo-lift car directly beneath him.

Kirk maintained consciousness long enough for one last thought: *I just got skunked.*

CH.4.12
Black Bits

Cadet Uhura flipped pages of a so-called "women's magazine" as she sat in the visitors' lounge of the medical college hospital. She stopped at an article entitled "Ten Good Reasons to Date an Older Man." A sardonic smile spread across her lips.

The phone at the ward station trilled. As the nurse picked it up, Uhura tossed down the magazine. She stood up and started pacing.

"Diagnostic ward," said the nurse.

Gaila had called Uhura that morning sounding completely healthy and even happy. "Don't bother to visit, I'll be out of here soon, *unfortunately*," the Orion girl had said. "Some of these doctors are crazy hot, girl. I've got my eye on one, and I think he's totally into me!"

But a few hours later Gaila had called back, sounding confused. "They found something on me, or in me, or whatever, so they have to run tests," she'd said. "Plus something happened. They won't tell me what. But now everybody is all business around here." So Uhura had promised to visit. Gaila was easily her closest friend at the Academy. They'd even talked about rooming together in the future.

"Are you Cadet Uhura?" asked the ward nurse suddenly.

"Yes, ma'am," said Uhura.

The nurse held out the phone. "For you," she said.

Uhura frowned. Nobody knew she was here except Gaila. She took the phone and said, "This is Cadet Uhura."

A deep voice rumbled on the other end. "Cadet, this is Vice Admiral Tullsey."

Uhura's eyes grew big. Admiral Tullsey was Starfleet Academy's commandant of midshipmen.

"Yes, sir?" she said, reflexively straightening her back.

"I need you to report to my office immediately," he said.

"Yes, sir," replied Uhura. "Can I ask what—?"

The phone clicked as the admiral hung up.

"I guess not," said Uhura.

She handed the phone back to the ward nurse. "Nurse, could you please tell Cadet Gaila that I got called away unexpectedly?" she asked. "Tell her I'll try to come back later this evening."

"Sure," said the nurse.

"Will I need an after-hours pass?" asked Uhura, unclipping an ID badge from her hip and holding it up. "Here's my security clearance, level C."

The nurse nodded. "I can tell you're a by-the-book kind of gal," she said.

Uhura gave a wry smile. "Some people like that about me," she said. "And some don't."

The ward nurse laughed. "Well, I'm sure your instructors appreciate it," she said, scribbling on a slip of paper and handing it to Uhura.

"Mmm . . . one of them does," said Uhura.

After the post-mission debriefing session for Derelict Cairo, a humbled and dejected Cadet Kirk limped along a dormitory corridor toward his quarters. It seemed that Tikhonov's phasers had been *poorly calibrated*. At least that was the excuse they used to explain why their light-stun setting had an extra kick that left most Team Delta members with pounding headaches and nasty bruises.

A hatchet-faced cadet named Vanderlick thrust his head through a doorway.

"Hello, Custer," he said with a nasty grin.

Kirk pointed at him. "I held the bridge for seventy minutes," he said.

"Most of that time, Team Alpha was playing magnetic dominoes in the Officers' Lounge," said Vanderlick.

"Who told you that?"

"Tikhonov," said Vanderlick.

"And you *believe* that guy?"

"He uploaded the video," said Vanderlick, flipping open a PDA. "Good stuff." He held out the screen toward Kirk. "Check it out. You drool like a baby when stunned by a phaser."

Kirk pushed past Vanderlick to his room and dropped onto his bunk. He wanted to sleep for a week. But all he could do was stare at the ceiling and replay the painful mind-movie of his *Cairo* debacle, over and over.

After an hour of that, he tried to look ahead.

Teams Alpha and Delta were now deadlocked at one win apiece in the final round of ATT testing. The only remaining test—the Science mission final, called the Tanika Station scenario—was set for the following week. It was considered the most challenging and important away-team exercise. After all, the official Starfleet Academy motto was *Ex astris, scientia:* "From the stars, knowledge."

Kirk was so deep in thought that when his room phone rang, he started and bolted upright.

● · ·∴ ✦ · ✦ · ✦ ·· ·

Ten minutes later a dazed Kirk was walking across campus toward the commandant of midshipmen's office. Other cadets who tried to greet him were stopped short by the look on his face.

Maybe I lost so bad, they're kicking me out of Starfleet, he was thinking. It was a plausible thought. In the debriefing session the senior staff officer noted that this was the first skunk in the history of the Derelict Cairo scenario—a "skunk" being the winning team lost nobody while the losing team lost everybody. This brought cheers from Team Alpha and admiring looks from the faculty overseeing the test—all aimed at Tikhonov.

And why else would Tullsey himself call? The admiral had been particularly blunt and humorless on the phone.

When Kirk entered the commandant's waiting room, he was surprised to find Cadet Uhura sitting there.

"Cadet," he said.

Uhura looked up, then did a double take. "Kirk," she said. "You look terrible."

"Thanks," he replied. "You look great, as usual."

Uhura ignored the compliment. "Seriously, Cadet. What's wrong?"

"Nothing," said Kirk, plopping heavily into a chair. "Why are you here? You getting kicked out too?"

Uhura couldn't suppress a laugh. "Yeah, right," she said.

"I don't think Starfleet kicks out its favorite hotshots."

Kirk looked at her. "You think you're a hotshot?" he asked, confused. *I always thought she was so humble,* he thought.

"No, I think *you're* a hotshot." She crossed her hands on her lap. "Let me rephrase that. *Starfleet* . . . thinks you're a hotshot."

"Not anymore," said Kirk with a bitter laugh. "I just set a new record for worst performance on Derelict Cairo."

Uhura's perfect little nose wrinkled in an expression of irritation that Kirk found adorable. "Oh, spare me, will you?"

Kirk leaned toward her. "What do you mean?" he asked.

"Kirk, *everybody* knows that the two cadets chosen as team captains of the finalists in the ATT series are the favorites of the Command College," she said. "So spare me your pity party."

A thin smile spread across Kirk's face. He sat back in his chair and didn't speak.

Then a door opened. A scary-looking woman with arched eyebrows leaned into the waiting room. This was the commandant's adjutant, Lieutenant Commander Judy Renfield.

Kirk and Uhura stood at attention.

"The admiral will see you now," she said crisply.

Uhura stood up even straighter. "Yes, uh . . . which one of us?"

"Both of you, Cadets," answered Renfield.

Kirk and Uhura exchanged a look, then shrugged and stood up.

Admiral Tullsey was speaking to a tough-looking older man in a rumpled suit as the cadets entered his office. The man acknowledged Kirk with a weary nod, and Kirk flashed to a memory from the previous night. This man had been one of the SFPD cops on the scene after the ambulance arrived for Cadet Gaila.

As Admiral Tullsey rose to his feet, Kirk and Uhura both snapped to attention with crisp salutes.

"At ease, Cadets," said Tullsey, returning the salute. "Have a seat." As the cadets slid into two chairs obviously arranged for them, Admiral Tullsey gestured to the older man. "This is Detective Harve Bogenn, SFPD Homicide."

"You were at the crime scene last night," said Kirk.

Detective Bogenn nodded. "I was," he said.

"Actually, Detective Bogenn was at *two* crime scenes last night," rumbled the admiral with a severe look.

"Oh, no," said Uhura. "Was there another attack?"

Bogenn pulled out a small electronic notepad. "I'm afraid there was," he said.

"Another one of ours," said Tullsey, shaking his head.

"She worked in Starfleet Orbital Operations. Another Orion gal."

Uhura looked sick. "Worked? You mean . . ."

"As I said, Cadet, the detective works in Homicide," said Tullsey.

"Was it the same guy?" asked Kirk, stunned.

Bogenn nodded. "Just an hour later, across town." He glanced down at something on his notepad.

Kirk looked over at Uhura, who was clearly upset.

She said, "This guy's a *murderer?*"

Detective Bogenn sighed. "It's worse than that." He looked at Uhura, then at Kirk. "You're both new to the city, correct?"

Uhura and Kirk both nodded.

"So you've never heard of the Doctor?" said Bogenn.

Kirk shook his head no, but Uhura frowned in concentration. After a second, she said, "Wasn't there a serial killer in San Francisco that they called the Doctor? Like, twenty years ago or something?"

"That's right," said Bogenn.

"And you think this is the same guy?" she asked.

"Without a doubt," he said.

Detective Bogenn gave them a quick rundown of the case history. Eighteen years ago, during the dense summer fogs of 2237, a string of seven disturbing murders rattled

San Francisco like a series of aftershocks. The killer was dubbed the Doctor because each victim was found intact—no trauma, no incisions—yet missing entire internal organs, as if they'd been surgically removed. The Doctor struck only on foggy nights. Nobody ever saw him. After the last murder in August of that year, the killings stopped. The Doctor never struck again.

"But he's back now," said Bogenn.

"How do you know?" asked Uhura.

Bogenn brought up the medical examiner's report.

"Postmortem scans show the Orion woman missing two organs," he said. "Yet not a mark on her body, anywhere." He turned to Admiral Tullsey. "Your Cadet Gaila is a lucky girl."

"I guess we have Mr. Kirk to thank for that," said the admiral.

"And Braxim, sir," said Kirk. "The attacker didn't really back off until Braxxy showed up, yelling about calling for help."

Now Bogenn smiled. It looked more like a grimace, but he was clearly pleased about something. He turned to Uhura.

"That leads us to the reason *you're* here, Cadet," he said.

"I was wondering about that, Detective," said Uhura carefully.

Detective Bogenn stood up.

"Listen, I've been in Homicide eighteen years," he said. "Started back in thirty-seven. Yeah, the Doctor was my first case. What a way to start, right? I was a junior-grade detective then. The old guys, the veterans, they all said they'd never seen a case with so little physical evidence. No witnesses, no prints, no residues, no scent for the dogs, not so much as a shoe scuff at any of the scenes. Nothing. Just the bodies, lying there, organ-farmed."

Now Bogenn turned to Kirk. "But by sheer dumb luck, we've got something on the bastard now."

He tapped a button on his electronic notepad and held it up.

An audio recording played. It was Braxim's voice shouting out: *"I called the police!"* That was followed by a pause . . . and then came the sound of a deep, chilling, inhuman-sounding voice. It spoke a phrase that sounded clear and precise . . . and yet also entirely unintelligible.

"This was pulled from our police emergency data bank," explained Bogenn.

"That sounds like an old-fashioned robotic voice," said Uhura.

"Yes," said Detective Bogenn. "We think it's a voice filter mask, although unlike any we've heard before."

"Can I hear it again?" she asked.

"Of course," said Bogenn. "But first, listen to this. The second attack occurred just fifty-three minutes later, outside a gallery in the Soma District. The Orion woman managed to call for help too. Unfortunately, she didn't have rescuers like your friend did. But she left us this."

A second recording played. Kirk and Uhura listened to a few disturbing seconds of gasping breath, then a strange, metallic humming. After that, the same voice resonated in a deep bass register, speaking a somewhat different phrase but equally unintelligible. And then . . . silence.

Uhura said, "When you really listen, it sounds like multiple voices speaking in unison."

Bogenn nodded. "We noticed that as well. We think that's an effect rendered by a voice-filter mask," he said. "These masks are very popular with criminals these days. The good ones totally deconstruct voice patterns in ways that make it impossible to find matches in our VOX database."

Now Admiral Tullsey looked at Uhura and said, "Does that language sound familiar to you, Cadet?"

Uhura asked for a playback, and Bogenn obliged. She listened with intense concentration, blinking her eyes rapidly.

After the recordings ended, she said, *"Fascinating."*

"How so?" asked Bogenn.

"It's no language I know," she replied. "But something in the phrasing sounds oddly familiar."

Admiral Tullsey said, "Since last night, this recording has been analyzed by the SFPD, the FBI, the United Earth Security Agency, and three interplanetary intelligence organizations. So far, nobody can make sense of it. So now it's in our hands." The admiral opened a dossier on his desk. "We're the best at alien languages. And according to Cadet Uhura's instructor, she is the most gifted xenolinguistic analyst in Starfleet."

Kirk looked at Uhura, impressed. Not bad for a first-year cadet.

Detective Bogenn handed Uhura a data stick. "Anything you can tell us about this would help," he says.

"I'll do what I can, Detective," said Uhura.

"Your instructor couldn't say enough good things about you," added Bogenn.

Now Uhura looked oddly uneasy.

Kirk decided to intervene. "Uh, you mentioned organ-farming, Detective," he said. "Do you think that's what this guy's doing? Harvesting and selling organs?"

"Maybe," said Bogenn. "But then the question would be, how is he extracting them? Like I said—no incisions in the body. No trauma. Just empty cavities where the organs used to be."

"Wow," said Kirk. "That's just . . . gross."

"Yeah, it is," said Bogenn.

The meeting ended with Kirk, at Bogenn's request, presenting a thorough recollection of his encounter with the Doctor.

Later, as they left the commandant's office together, Kirk leaned close to Uhura and whispered, "Teacher's pet."

Uhura blushed a bright red.

"Shut up, Kirk," she said.

She's so cute when she's embarrassed, Kirk thought.

McCoy glanced around the pathology lab.

A truly impressive brain trust was gathering here, and growing by the hour. At the whiteboard, a Nobel Prize winner from Starfleet Academy's biotechnology lab named Dr. Dat Nguyen was chatting with Dr. Reyjik. Nguyen was drawing diagrams that looked like a child's scribbling to McCoy. Dr. Nguyen had done groundbreaking work on plasmids, viral vectors, and horizontal gene transfer . . . topics that McCoy knew absolutely nothing about. At least Dr. Reyjik seemed to know what Nguyen was talking about.

Meanwhile, the left eye socket of Dr. Wallace Marston, one of the Federation's leading experts in alien life-forms, was glued to the quantum microscope's viewing piece. His eyeglasses were pushed up onto his huge, shiny forehead in classic scientist-geek fashion. A very large man with a naturally booming voice, Marston was known to speak his mind in tactless outbursts that intimidated colleagues. McCoy liked him.

"I hesitate to call this an *organism*," boomed Dr. Marston.

Dr. Nguyen stepped toward the microscope at the head of the class.

He said, "Actually, I tend to agree with you, Wally."

Marston adjusted the scope settings. "Granted, this substance *seems* to be alive . . . in a sense. But there is no recognizable organic structure in the individual cell units, or whatever they are. Not like any I've ever seen, anyway."

"They certainly move in a highly organized manner," said Dr. Nguyen.

"Like a flock of birds." Dr. Marston nodded. "Or better yet, bees. As if there's a controlling hive mind."

"But look at that amazing structure!" said Dr. Nguyen, almost bouncing like an excited kid. "Each one is a perfect twelve-sided polyhedron, yet less than half a micron in diameter."

Across the room, Dr. Reyjik began to root around in a neatly divided specimen drawer.

"Gentlemen," he called out. "I would like to try something."

He pulled out a small vial of fluid. Then he approached the microscope.

"We have a fairly large sample of the alien *substance*— whatever it is—in the microcontainment chamber," he said. "I'm going to dock another chamber and split the sample in half. Then I'll introduce a unicellular intruder to one chamber." He held up the vial. "A good old-fashioned *amoeba proteus.*"

"Excellent!" said Dr. Marston, rubbing his hands together.

"Most exciting," said Dr. Nguyen, his head bobbing in agreement.

McCoy tried not to laugh at their nerdish enthusiasm as Dr. Reyjik prepared the specimen. The pathologist flicked a switch and a big viewscreen lowered from the ceiling. Inside the microscope's viewer, a microcamera began to record the image and project it onto the screen.

"Okay, inserting the monster now," said Reyjik.

All four doctors turned to watch the big screen. The amoeba was indeed a monster by comparison—at more than two hundred microns wide, it was four hundred times bigger than each of the tiny alien bits. Reyjik had to zoom back the view so the full amoeba could be seen on-screen. All of the creature's organelles could be studied clearly in the remarkable quantum field view. As the big organism pushed out a pseudopod (a blobby sort of arm) toward the swarm of polyhedral bits, the particles began to swirl in a lazy cloud around the big guy.

"It's beautiful, isn't it?" said Dr. Marston in his foghorn of a voice.

"It'll try to eat them, right?" asked McCoy. "I mean, like, suck them in and ingest them."

"Oh, most certainly," said Dr. Reyjik.

For a few seconds, that appeared to be exactly what was happening. The amoeba would extend toward a cluster of bits and engulf them into its jellylike interior. But very quickly, the situation changed.

The scientists' facial expressions changed as quickly as the state of affairs in the sample chamber.

"Good . . . *lord!*" exclaimed Dr. Nguyen.

As if triggered by a flipped switch, the alien bits suddenly burst into a roiling frenzy. They seemed to be replicating rapidly too; within seconds, the entire screen was blackened by particles. The foglike swirl was so thick that it blocked any view of the big amoeba. And then—again, as if suddenly switched off—the wild blur of motion ceased. And there was the amoeba.

McCoy took a step toward the screen. "Those *things* are attached to every bit of it," he said.

Dr. Reyjik stared in awe. "It's completely coated!"

Reyjik zoomed in the view for a closer look. As he did so, the amoeba began to pulsate. Moments later it exploded. McCoy knew the event he viewed was microscopic, but it truly looked like a bomb detonation.

"The amoeba is gone!" cried Dr. Nguyen.

"Unbelievable!" boomed Dr. Marston.

But the craziness wasn't over yet. For a few seconds the black bits drifted apart like dissipating smoke. Then the outward movement stopped, and the particles slowly began to drift back together.

In less than a minute they had recreated the shape of the amoeba.

McCoy stared in amazement.

"Those crazy things were smeared on my patient's neck," he murmured. "My god, some of them were *inside* her."

Then came one last surprise. The black particles lightened in color, then became translucent. Inside, the stunned viewers could see every organelle of the original amoeba, perfectly recreated.

"My god, they learned its shape and structure," said Dr. Marston in a hushed voice.

"Perhaps its function, too," added Dr. Nguyen.

"Yes," said McCoy. "And they killed it in the process."

CH.5.12
Stalked

Uhura, eager to help in any way she could with the investigation, wasted no time in getting started. Within thirty minutes of the meeting in Admiral Tullsey's office, she was in the Academy's xenolinguistics lab running language recognition scans on the emergency recordings.

"Computer," she said, speaking distinctly to the console panel in the lab's sound booth. "Run module Tella-dot-zero-one on both samples."

"Acknowledged," responded the console.

This routine would scan both recordings of the voice for any known strands or fragments of the primary Tellarite language dialect. The computer's quantum drive began to hum.

Earlier, Uhura had re-listened to the killer's "words" a number of times. As spoken phrases, they remained odd and unrecognizable. But something in them tapped at her memory. She had a large personal database of knowledge. Language was Uhura's lifelong passion; she'd first tinkered with language recognition software when she was twelve. These particular modules that she ran on the emergency recordings were her own custom programs.

"No matches found," reported the console.

"Log the result in the master chart," said Uhura as she typed notes.

"Result logged," said the console.

"Please run subroutine Tella-dot-zero-two with the same samples," said Uhura.

"Acknowledged," replied the console.

She'd grown up speaking English and two Eurasian languages plus two separate Swahili dialects. Uhura had always loved the music of spoken words, the way different languages across the galactic quadrant constructed similar and familiar sounds to express the same things. It amazed her that gusts of air—exhaled from lungs, oscillating the vocal cords, shaped by throat, tongue, lips, and jaw into vibrations of sound—could convey such a stunningly complex range of meaning. Thus she loved not just the words themselves, but the way they were spoken.

"No matches found," reported the console.

"Log the result, please."

"Result logged."

Uhura lowered her head. A long night likely lay ahead. Normally she enjoyed immersing herself in her work. But tonight she felt an immense loneliness. She knew this project was hitting close to home.

She glanced at the data stick from Detective Bogenn inserted in the computer console.

A killer's voice, she thought.

Then she heard the lab's exterior door open and close.

Uhura swiveled her chair toward the door of the sound booth. The lab, like all campus buildings, was highly secure. But as she heard footsteps approach, she tensed and stood up to face the door. When the booth door whooshed open and she saw who it was, she felt so relieved she almost laughed.

"I hope I didn't burden you with my recommendation, Cadet," said the figure in the doorway.

"No, sir," said Uhura, smiling. "I was . . . I am . . . honored."

Her instructor nodded. "Good," he said. "You were, of course, the only logical choice."

"Really?" said Uhura in a slightly teasing voice. "You mean you didn't just pull my name out of a hat?"

He looked confused. "That wouldn't be logical."

Uhura sighed, sat back down, and swiveled back to face the console. Then she said, "Would you like to review my findings?"

Uhura's instructor stepped up behind her. He placed one hand on the back of her chair and leaned in close.

"Yes," he said.

Uhura nodded, warmth spreading inside her at his closeness. "Computer," she said, "please bring up the results log for Commander Spock."

"Acknowledged," said the computer.

Kirk's favorite low-key off-campus hangout was Brewsky's.

Just a ten-minute walk from the Academy's campus, Brewsky's was a classic San Francisco Beat-era coffeehouse at the corner of Union and Fillmore. Kirk liked the smoky espresso and the low-key jazz. He *really* liked the laid-back baristas in their short skirts and black berets. Holiday lights were strung up year round. Something about that relaxed him. It eased the stress of being a fleet officer candidate at the most demanding school in the known galaxy.

The night was clear and the west winds had died down, keeping the fog offshore. But on the way to Brewsky's, Kirk still glanced down every alley he passed, and he eyed a huge hooded alien leaning against a LiquiLED light box. On a whim, Kirk decided to see if he spoke using a voice filter mask.

"Hey pal, I'm lost," he said to the towering creature. "Is

Fisherman's Wharf that way?" He pointed up Russian Hill in the wrong direction.

The cowed head turned slowly toward Kirk. Then the fellow reached up and slid off the hood. It was a dour, wrinkle-faced Hupyrian.

"Oh, sorry, man," said Kirk. Hupyrians were a servant race that typically swore a vow of silence. They spoke only to their Ferengi masters.

The Hupyrian pointed toward the bay.

"Thanks. You have a good night, sir," said Kirk. He clapped the big fellow on the arm and continued down Union Street.

At Brewsky's, Kirk stepped to the counter.

"Triple espresso," he said.

The girl behind the counter was new. She looked at him and said, "Triple espresso what?"

Kirk eyed her. She wore a name tag: HANNAH.

"Please?" he added, flashing a smile.

She turned to measure out beans and scoop them into the grinder.

Kirk watched her work for a second, enjoying the view. Her hair was dyed blue and hung all the way down to her waist. She was dressed in classic beatnik style: tight black turtleneck, a very mini black miniskirt, and black boots. Her bright blue eyes had an exotic curve under the sexy fringe of her bangs, and suddenly they were looking right at him.

"Anything else?" she asked.

"No," said Kirk.

"Okay." She stared straight at him until he shrugged and started toward his favorite table in the corner.

"I'll be right over there, Hannah," he called over his shoulder.

"How do you know my name?" she asked.

"Your name tag," said Kirk. He pointed at it. "See? There it is."

She looked down at it and blushed. "Right," she said.

"When you wear a name tag, Hannah, it gives people the legal right to call you by your name," said Kirk, his confidence boosted by her telltale blush.

She looked him over. "You're a Starfleet cadet, aren't you?"

"Why, yes I am," said Kirk. He glanced down at himself. "How can you tell?"

"I dated a cadet last year," said the girl.

"Ah, so you're an *expert* on cadets."

She nodded. "Unfortunately."

"Okay, well, I'll be at the corner table, Hannah. Just give me a holler when that delicious brew is ready."

"I'll call your name," she said.

"Good plan," said Kirk, walking away.

"Of course it would help if I knew what it was," said Hannah.

"Come join me and I'll tell you," he said.

Hannah laughed. "How about I just call 'cadet'?" she replied with a wink.

An hour later, Kirk was hip-deep in his studies.

It felt good, even therapeutic. With Starfleet's science directives open on his reading pad, he highlighted and dragged key passages over onto his linked notepad, then scribbled notes furiously. Pondering the core purpose of Starfleet's mission was finally wiping his mind clean of Team Delta's loss to Tikhonov's Alpha, and of his surreal brush with a serial killer the night before.

Kirk was suddenly aware of a black-clad figure to his left—the new barista, Hannah. She was wiping down a table.

"What are you studying, Cadet?" she asked without looking at him.

Kirk tilted up the reading pad. "Science," he said.

"What kind of science?" she asked.

"Cadet science," replied Kirk.

Hannah turned to face him. She put her hands on her hips. "You're funny," she said with a dry look.

"I'm hilarious."

"Maybe I can help you," she said. "I like science. In fact ... I'm a scientist."

Kirk nodded. "What kind of scientist?" he asked.

"I'm a botanist," she said with pride.

Kirk tilted his reading pad back down on the table. Suddenly he didn't want to study anymore. "Hmm ... a botanist." He was impressed. *Gorgeous and smart,* he thought.

"Well," she said, shrugging, "actually, I'm a graduate student."

"Ah, so you're a near-botanist," said Kirk. "Where at?"

"San Francisco State," she replied.

"Cool," said Kirk.

Hannah looked at him again for a few seconds without speaking. Her gaze drove him crazy. If she continued looking at him like that, he was going to need a cold shower. Then she turned and started wiping down another table.

Kirk opened his mouth to speak several times as she polished the old-fashioned linoleum surface, but he reconsidered each time. This girl did something to him that no girl ever did—she made him nervous.

Finally he tried, "So I've got this big science test Monday."

Hannah kept working on the table, but she was listening.

"Most important exam of my entire career," said Kirk. "Much at stake. All hangs in the balance."

She picked up a wadded napkin. "Over one test?"

Kirk smiled, happy to have her attention again. "It's a simulation, actually."

Then he described what little he knew of the Tanika Station scenario. It was a competition, but not head-to-head. The two away teams, Alpha and Delta, would deploy into the same alien environment at different times. The task was to carry out basic science directives that every Starfleet officer and enlisted man was expected to execute in any "discovery setting."

"Basic science," said Kirk. "Observation. Run a few scans. Take samples. That sort of thing."

"You're supposed to *discover* things," said Hannah.

"I guess," said Kirk. He shrugged. "What do you think? As a scientist, what's your take? Any advice?"

Hannah eyed him and bit her lip as she thought. Kirk tried not to squirm.

"Okay," she said. "First off, I despise the term 'discovery setting.'"

Kirk's eyes widened. "Why?" he asked.

"When a botanist goes out in the field," she said, "it's like being invited into someone's house, except you're not really invited. That's the first thing to remember."

Kirk nodded. "That makes sense," he said, kicking out the other chair at his table, inviting her to sit down.

Hannah tossed her towel onto the table. "You're intruding, uninvited, into somebody's home, the place they've lived their whole lives, the place they love. It means *everything* to them, this place." She looked at Kirk and sat down. "So are you *discovering* it? It's been there a long time. Centuries. Longer, maybe. But now your very presence is changing it. Maybe just by walking through a discovery setting you are disturbing things, altering them permanently. Maybe you're even destroying something. Something beloved and sacred to somebody else." Her cheeks glowed as she spoke. She was clearly very passionate about the subject.

"I see what you're saying," Kirk said. "But you know, Starfleet doesn't just pull on the heavy boots and stomp around in every habitat we find."

"Right," said Hannah, rolling her eyes. She stood up from the table.

"Look, Starfleet General Order Number One," Kirk said, speaking quickly, "generally known as the Prime Directive, puts us under the strictest orders to make no attempt to alter the natural course of any prewarp society. I assume you're familiar with the Prime Directive?"

A dark look passed over Hannah's face.

"The Prime Directive is a joke," she said.

"Why?" he asked.

"It's a smoke screen," she said.

Kirk was perplexed. "How so?"

She sighed and began to wipe down another table.

"Let's just say that I'm pretty cynical about Starfleet's so-called *mission*," she said wearily.

Kirk got the feeling he'd just tapped in to a vein of conversation that Hannah had already deeply mined . . . perhaps in her previous relationship with the Starfleet cadet. But Kirk couldn't just drop the subject. Despite his blatant disregard for many Starfleet rules and regulations (especially those governing a cadet's personal life), he was actually a true believer. He believed in Starfleet's core mission of exploration, discovery, and peaceful contact. And right now he felt very compelled to garner Hannah's approval and respect.

"You think we're just a bunch of gun-toting thugs, right?" he asked.

Hannah folded her arms. "You're taking this a little too personally, Cadet," she said.

"The name is Jim," he said.

"Okay, Jim," she said. And then she finally smiled at him, and the tension was gone. When she smiled, Hannah was absolutely stunning.

"Jim Kirk," said Kirk, dazzled. He was blatantly staring now.

"Listen, Kirk, I'm sure you believe in your mission," she said. "I'm not cynical about Starfleet cadets. Most of you, anyway."

Kirk braced himself for criticism. "So what's the objection?" he asked.

"I think you're tools," she said.

"Ouch," said Kirk.

Hannah sighed. "The United Federation of Planets was formed as a result of a brutal, bloody war that almost wiped out two civilizations," she said. She pointed at the sky outside the coffeehouse window. "The Romulans are out there, just one light-year beyond Federation space. The Neutral Zone is *nothing* to them. They're building up, biding their time. You *know* they are. They'll come at us again soon. Meanwhile, we're in a race for allies and resources. We want our side bigger and stronger than their side when the time comes. Thus Starfleet was born."

"So you're saying Starfleet is all about alliance and conquest?" said Kirk.

Hannah sat down across from him and leaned forward, an intense look on her beautiful face. "You *know* it is," she said.

Kirk broke her gaze. He looked down at his reading pad.

"And so these science directives are just . . . some sort of sham," he said.

Hannah noted Kirk's reaction. She sat back and took a deep breath.

"Sorry," she said. "I'm passionate about this issue. Obviously."

Kirk waved a hand. "Hey, it's cool," he said. "It's good to get perspective. You know, see how regular people think."

Hannah laughed. "So you think I'm *regular?*" she said in mock horror.

Kirk grinned. "Compared to the people I'm surrounded by every day, you are, like . . . *extra*regular."

"My mother would be so proud," she said.

Kirk pointed over at the counter. Two ratty guys in leather were examining pastries in the display case.

"Customers," he said.

"Oh, yeah, I have a job," said Hannah. She stood up. "I haven't fully gotten my mind around that yet."

"I can tell," said Kirk.

"Funny, Kirk," she said.

As Hannah went back to the counter, Kirk thought about what she'd said.

The United Federation of Planets was originally formed in 2161 as a peaceful alliance between Humans, Vulcans, Andorians, and Tellarites. It had grown since to include many more star systems. But she was right: Interstellar unity didn't happen because scientists wanted to hold hands and explore stuff together. The impetus for the Federation Charter was the Battle of Cheron, a nuclear exchange that capped four brutal years of war between Earth and the Romulan Star Empire that nearly decimated both sides. The original members certainly joined together for security purposes—defensive, military purposes—with an eye on the expansionist Romulans, and, later, the Klingon Empire.

But did that mean Starfleet's mandate for peaceful exploration was just a clever cover story for darker goals?

Wasn't the acquisition of knowledge a good thing?

Or was Starfleet just a tool for conquest and economic expansion?

Kirk gazed down at the science directive document open on his reading pad.

2.1 The primary role of all Starfleet personnel is that of ambassador. A secondary purpose is field research.

2.2 When encountering new life-forms, regardless of their level of sentience, the default Starfleet posture is one of benign greeting.

2.3 Once trust is established, scientific research may begin.

2.4 In the case of a hostile response, all Starfleet scientific activity will be suspended until diplomacy establishes or re-establishes trust.

2.5 Trust between observer and observed is the bedrock of good science.

Trust, he thought. Interesting.

He looked over at Hannah. Yes, she had a few sharp edges. But like a good botanist, she was treating the two specimens at her counter with total respect.

To kill time until she returned, Kirk grabbed his notepad, inserted earbuds, and punched up some old media accounts of the Doctor killings from eighteen years ago. They described him as cold, clinical, calculating, and relentless. Speculation ranged from rumors that he was everything from a surgeon to an unknown alien to a vampire. The SFPD was very tight-lipped about crime scene details and autopsy results, so reporters were frustrated. They spent their time whipping up dread. One favorite angle was: *He could be any-body! That nice guy sitting next to you on the shuttle? Maybe that's him. Maybe he's your neighbor. Your real-estate guy. Your accountant—yes, even your accountant fits the profile.*

Fear of the unknown always drives us to create a profile, thought Kirk. *But in all that profiling, none of the experts ever suggested the Doctor might be a seven-foot-tall dude wearing a voice-filter mask.*

Kirk clicked a button on his reading pad and watched a few man-on-the-street interviews. People had been really afraid. Restaurant and club owners complained about empty floors on foggy nights. Nobody was going out. Home-security companies made a killing.

Kirk wondered, *Are we in for another summer of this insanity?*

Out of curiosity, he checked the latest news. Interestingly, he found no report on last night's attacks. SFPD and Starfleet were locked down, for now. Earlier, as Kirk and Uhura had left the commandant of midshipmen's office, the admiral issued a direct order in no uncertain terms: Speak to nobody—not family, not friends, *not anybody*— about the incident. Of course, Detective Bogenn briefed the Starfleet medical team treating Gaila, so Kirk had already discussed the matter with McCoy. But nobody else was in the loop.

Kirk knew it was only a matter of time before word leaked out.

He looked over at Hannah again. When did she get off work? Would she walk home alone through the district?

Word *had* to get out soon. You didn't want public panic, of course, but then again you didn't want drunken fools stumbling down dark, foggy alleys like Gaila had done last night.

Finally Kirk clicked on a news link that brought up a cheesy special report, aired in July of 2247, ten years after the "Summer of the Doctor," as the report garishly called it. It was standard media melodrama, but Kirk was struck by some of the facts—in particular, the wide variety of victims. The Doctor didn't appear to have a preferred type. One of them was a young woman, Emily Karcher, a student at USF. She was walking back to her dorm late from her work-study job in the campus sandwich shop when she was attacked. . . .

Hannah suddenly appeared at his side.

"Have you studied the Starfleet directive about pillaging yet?" she asked, grinning and trying to peek at his screen.

Kirk jumped. He popped out his earbuds and closed down the screen.

"Whoa," said Hannah, holding up her hands. "Sorry."

"I didn't hear you coming," said Kirk.

"I tend to move silently," she replied. "I'm kind of like a cat. Well, except I don't like fish parts."

Kirk clicked off the video report. "Hey, listen," he said. "What time do you get off work?"

"You don't waste any time, do you?" she asked.

Kirk was flustered. "No, uh, that's not . . . I'm not . . . this isn't, like, asking because . . . uh," he said, and then stopped.

Hannah's teasing smile reappeared. "Smooth recovery, Jim."

"Look, just never mind, okay?" he said.

"I don't get off until after your curfew," she said simply.

"Okay, well, it's not foggy tonight anyway."

She looked quizzically at Kirk and was about to speak when his communicator beeped. He looked at the incoming number. It was McCoy.

"I should take this," he said.

Hannah gestured to go ahead. She grabbed a nearby spray bottle and started squirting the front window.

"Kirk here," he said into his communicator.

"Jim, get your tail over here to the pathology lab at Medical, immediately," said McCoy with urgency. "And I mean *right* now. We got some very interesting results on Gaila's samples."

"On my way," said Kirk. He turned to Hannah at the window. "Big, big meeting," he said, pointing at his communicator. "Very important."

"See ya," she said quickly.

"Hannah, there's something I need to tell you," said Kirk. "But I can't yet because I'm . . . under orders not to."

"Right," she said.

"Listen, just … be careful tonight," he said. "Going home, I mean."

"I'm always careful," she said. Behind her, newly sprayed cleaning solution was smeared in a translucent sheen on the window. It looked like a weird aura behind her.

Kirk quickly packed his things and headed for the door. On the way out, he said, "I'll be back."

Hannah glanced over at him from the window. "*That* is a vintage Starfleet cadet line," she said.

Kirk smiled and pointed at her. "I mean it," he said. "I'll be back. When do you work next?"

"Thursday," she said with a nonchalance that pierced Kirk's heart.

Kirk kept pointing at her as he stepped through the doorway out onto Union Street. "I'll be back," he said again.

"Whatever," she said.

This girl is gonna kill me, he thought.

Starfleet's medical college complex was an adjunct of the main academy, and was located in the northeast corner of the sprawling campus. On the way, Kirk jogged past the gorgeous but eerie Palace of Fine Arts. In the dark, it looked like a haunted castle. The cypress trees that clumped around the glimmering palace pond looked stately and graceful by day, but now they just looked spooky.

Then he saw it: a tall, dark figure.

It seemed to float through the shadows of the big stone arches lining the palace walkway near the pond. Kirk slid to a halt. The figure halted. Kirk started to jog again. The figure started moving again.

He's following me, thought Kirk.

"Hey, you!" he yelled. He started running toward the figure. Kirk had no weapons of any kind. But he had a feeling about this guy.

And he was right. The dark figure darted around a stone pillar, then bent down to duck under an arch. When Kirk reached the arch, his head cleared it with two feet to spare.

Okay, he's huge, thought Kirk, sprinting hard.

But he stayed on the figure's tail as the big guy glided past the palace and onto the dark streets north of the parking lot. Then Kirk saw him duck between two rows of houses.

Great, another alley, he thought.

He skidded to a halt at the alley entrance. The figure stood stock-still just thirty feet away, facing him. Instinctively Kirk flipped his communicator open and punched the record button. He held it up.

Go ahead, he thought. *Speak, fool.*

And the figure spoke. It was the same creepy, low-pitched metallic voice. But this time, Kirk had no problem deciphering the phrase.

The voice simply said: "James T. Kirk."

Then he turned away, moved impossibly fast down the alley, and darted lightly up the street.

By the time Kirk got through the alley, the Doctor was long gone.

CH.6.12
Smart Dust

In 2255, Mount Zion Hospital boasted the best Level-1 cardiopulmonary center in the Bay Area. So when the paramedic team found a woman in the Transamerica Pyramid suffering from acute respiratory failure, Mount Zion was the logical choice for delivery. It was close by, and it was a good place to take someone whose lungs were ripped to shreds.

In the ICU, Jackie Madkins was heavily sedated, so getting a coherent story would have been difficult. In any case, the endotracheal tube running from the ventilator down her throat into her ravaged lungs made it impossible to conduct any interviews just yet.

The on-duty physician, Dr. Joseph Revier, spoke into a diagnostic console microphone near her bed.

"Smoke inhalation likely, based on multiple factors," he reported. *"Initial call indicated a smoke influx, reported to the caller by the patient . . . although the emergency response team*

found none at the scene. Other primary evidence: heavy concentrations of black particulate residue found in patient's nose, mouth, and respiratory passages." He glanced over at the resting woman and frowned. *"However, lung scan results are contradictory. Tricorder molecular scans also remain unresolved."*

His med-com beeped. He flipped it open.

"Revier here," he answered.

"What's with the sample, Joey?"

Revier frowned again. "What do you mean?"

The voice on the other end laughed. "Dude, the sample vial you sent us is empty," he said. "You been diverting again, bro?" "Diverting" was a hospital term for stealing prescription drugs for personal use.

"What? I packed that thing full," Revier said, sitting up straight. "That vial was black."

"Well, it's crystal clear now."

"Crap," said Revier. "Something got switched up in delivery, maybe. Whatever. I'll get you another one right away."

"Cool," said the lab tech. "You joining us for the game tonight?"

"Hell yes," said Revier.

A passing nurse tapped his shoulder and pointed over at the bed.

"What's that?" asked the nurse.

Dr. Revier turned to look, then blinked rapidly.

A black, smoky haze hung in the air just above Jackie Madkins.

Uhura wasn't sure if her Aunt Uhnu actually butted heads with a rhinoceros—she kind of doubted it, although Uhnu was certainly crazy enough to do such a thing. More likely Uhnu had simply fallen and hit her head, or suffered a small stroke. But the rhino story was the family's exotic way of explaining Uhnu's strange babbling.

Later, med-scans would reveal severe damage to key language centers in Uhnu's brain, the areas of her cerebral cortex associated with word order and meaning. Uhura already knew this intuitively, however. From a very young age, Uhura was the only one in her family who could understand Aunt Uhnu during these episodes.

The reason: Uhura would listen more to how Uhnu was speaking than to what she was saying.

This experience of "translating" Uhnu's gibberish was an early lesson in the importance of *prosody*—the rhythm, loudness, pitch, and intonation of speech . . . or, as Uhura explained it as a child, "the talking music." The brain's prosody functions are clustered in the opposite brain hemisphere from the word-meaning functions, and they were undamaged in Uhnu's brain. So the music of her expression was precise, but the actual words themselves were chopped up in odd ways.

Uhura had discussed this issue with her instructor, Commander Spock, several times over the past year.

"When translating languages," she told him, "I find that sometimes it isn't enough to listen precisely. Sometimes you have to listen . . . differently. Like listening to music." She laughed and said, "That probably sounds lame."

"I find perfect logic in what you're saying," Spock had replied.

And that's how Uhura made her first breakthrough on the Doctor.

The nagging familiarity she heard in the killer's voice had to do with the rhythm of his phrasing. Uhura was a master of all three Romulan dialects—they were her best alien languages. After one particular replay of the recordings it hit her: She was listening to Romulan rhythms, if not Romulan words exactly.

Of course, the samples were so brief that it was difficult to verify. She created a spectrogram for each 911 sample—a digital picture of the phrase—and ran it through a stress-inflections module she'd created for her Romulan translation software. This turned up a number of Romulan phrase matches. A few too many, in fact.

"Computer, how many matches do we have at ninety percent likelihood and above?" she asked the console.

"Sixty-two," replied the console.

"*Sixty-two?*" exclaimed Uhura. "Are you sure?"

"Checking now," said the computer. "Yes, sixty-two confirmed."

"Great," said Uhura.

The computer had a sophisticated speech recognition database and was quite familiar with Uhura's speech patterns. So its internal analysis of Uhura's response correctly identified her tone.

"You are displeased with the result," said the computer.

Uhura always found it somewhat amusing when the computer tried to analyze and identify her state of mind.

"No, I'm thrilled," she said.

After a pause, the computer said, "You are being ironic."

"Very good, computer," said Uhura. "I'm proud of you."

The console did not respond. Uhura grinned. *Praise does not compute,* she thought. This computer was starting to assume her personality. "Give me a printout of all sixty-two Romulan prosodic phrase matches and their translations, please," she said. She rubbed her temples. "And please note that I'd kill for a cup of coffee right now."

"Request is printing," replied the console, and the laser printer across the room clicked to life.

"And my coffee?" asked Uhura.

Another pause. Then the computer said, "I've sent a warning to the on-campus cafeteria."

Uhura started laughing loudly.

Not far from Uhura, in the next building, Dr. McCoy was poking a finger at Kirk.

"You *chased* him?" said McCoy incredulously.

Kirk shrugged. "He was following me."

"Do you have a death wish?" bellowed McCoy.

"I don't like being followed," replied Kirk.

"For the love of all things holy!" exclaimed McCoy.

He dragged Kirk by the arm over to one of the lab's console monitors. "Come here, friend. Let me show you what we learned about this *guy* you just chased."

McCoy punched up the video of Dr. Reyjik's amoeba experiment and briefed Kirk on the unsettling characteristics of the residue found on Gaila's skin and her internal tissue samples.

"That's just . . . creepy," said Kirk, watching the black bits swarm the amoeba.

"Even though it acts like a biological entity, its structure just seems a little too . . . *perfect*, doesn't it?" said McCoy. "I mean, look at it, Jim." He froze the screen and clicked in for a close-up of just a few bits. "Every one of these submicron bits looks precision engineered."

He clicked the play button and the microscope video continued. Kirk watched with intense fascination. When the amoeba exploded, Kirk flinched. When the swarm re-created a translucent amoeba, his mouth dropped open. When the video ended, he just stared at the blank screen.

"Wow," he said quietly.

"Yes, exactly," said McCoy.

"So what is that stuff, Bones?" asked Kirk. "And how did the Doctor get it?"

"I don't know, Jim, but that damned nickname really angers me," said McCoy. "Why would they call him that? *I'm* a doctor. He's not."

Kirk was surprised. "It's not like you to get so angry, Bones," he said.

"Anyway," said McCoy, waving it off, "that perfect poly-hedral structure convinced me to walk our dust sample over to the materials science lab."

"And what did they say?" asked Kirk.

"Hang on," said McCoy, flipping open his communicator. "Let's get an expert in here."

● · · ● ✦ ● ✦ ● ·

Ten minutes later, Dr. Parag Chandar knocked on the door. He looked far too young to be running any lab, let alone one of the most advanced nanotechnology centers in Federation space. He was a good friend of McCoy's; they played squash twice a week together.

"Ah, James Kirk, the man himself," said Dr. Chandar amiably as he shook Kirk's hand. "We meet, finally. Leonard tells me much about you. It's *remarkable* how much money you owe him, Jim."

Kirk laughed. "Yeah, well, I pay him back by keeping Starfleet away from his Ole Miss transcripts."

"Gosh, I'm *so* glad I finally got you two jokers together," said McCoy.

Dr. Chandar pulled a small silver cube from his pocket and plugged it into a data port on the lab's main console. "Let's take a look at our little guy, shall we?" he said. A few windows popped up on-screen. He tapped the touch screen to open one. "Here's a good place to start."

The window displayed a slowly spinning 3-D schematic of a single black particle.

"Amazing, isn't it?" said Chandar. "Like a cut gem."

"Incredible," said McCoy.

"So what is it?" asked Kirk.

"Let's call it a nanite," said Chandar. "We *could* call it a nanorobot, or nanobot for short, but that term seems clunky and doesn't do it justice. Nothing does, really. This guy is *amazing*. He's technically a machine with substantial computing power, but he acts like a living organism."

"Interesting," said Kirk. "If it's a machine, who built it, and for what purpose?"

"Excellent questions, Cadet," said Chandar, smiling.

"Got any answers yet?"

"None whatsoever."

"We just found the damn things last night, Jim," said McCoy.

"I know." As Kirk watched the particle on-screen, the side with the white etching rotated into view. "What's that white mark?"

Chandar shrugged. "No idea," he said. "That exact same glyph is on every nanite we examined. Some of the guys think it might be the manufacturer's ID, like a logo or something. Others suggest it's a time-date stamp, or maybe a code or message." He shrugged again. "We had fun with that one."

McCoy looked at Dr. Chandar. "So how does this thing work, Parag?"

Chandar tapped open another window on the monitor screen. In this video, several nanites swirled around one another, then locked together to form a larger entity.

"Each speck is smart," he replied. "Each likely has many

gigabytes of computing power. It moves effortlessly."

Dr. Chandar opened a third window. This one showed nanites swarming to coat the amoeba's cell wall, locking together into a deadly blanket.

"And there's clearly communication *between* nanites," continued Dr. Chandar. "Each likely has a built-in receiver, because of the way the whole swarm acts as an intelligent superentity." He gestured at the on-screen image. "Look at it, gentlemen! All those bits moving with one purpose, one mind. Like hive insects."

McCoy didn't even try to hide his disgust.

"I hate insects," he said.

"Sorry," said Dr. Chandar.

"Are they following internal programming," asked McCoy, "or just doing what they're told by somebody else? I mean, does the swarm *think*, or just follow orders?"

Chandar shook his head sheepishly. He raised his palms.

Kirk scratched his face. "Hmm. So these things can get *inside* of people?"

McCoy fielded this one. "They're subcellular, Jim," he said. "Unbelievably tiny. Built at the molecular level. Small enough that they can easily penetrate skin or other membranes and migrate to targeted organs."

Kirk pointed at a nanite. "Say, what are those little nubs and pockmarks on each side?"

Parag enlarged the window to full-screen size and zoomed in.

"Universal connectors," said Parag. "Pins and ports." As two nanites locked together on-screen he added, "See how they match up perfectly? This brilliant design allows the swarm to form an infinite array of shapes and functions. You saw an example: First, it physically scanned and analyzed the structure of the amoeba. Next, it self-replicated to create the approximate number of bits it needed. Finally it linked into a perfect model of the amoeba, including internal structure, organelles. All in a matter of seconds!"

"That is impressive," agreed Kirk.

"But that's not the only advantage of the design," continued Chandar. "Since each nanite is essentially a self-contained computer, the connectors also let them link into a distributed computing network!" He stared at McCoy, his eyes blinking with delight, clearly expecting a reaction.

"Parag, I'm a doctor, not a computer scientist," growled McCoy. "Can you explain, please?"

"Well, think of Einstein's brain," said Chandar.

McCoy glanced at Kirk. "Do I have to?"

"Listen, what exactly *was* Einstein's brain?" said Chandar. "We'd all agree it was a remarkable organ. Every brain is. But it was merely a collection of neurons, right? Cells.

Individually, each neuron is not that smart. But when they work together, twenty or thirty billion of them, well, they can think the way Einstein thought."

Dr. Chandar pointed at the slow-motion replay of nanites linking into a chain, then into a solid figure.

"The swarm," he said, "when connected by these links, becomes an immensely powerful supercomputer. The level of its artificial intelligence must be very high."

He gazed at the screen. "Little Jack and his brothers are more sophisticated than any nanotech we've ever developed or even put on our dream board."

"Dream board?" asked Kirk.

Chandar adjusted settings on the console touch screen.

"That's where we log all our nuttiest ideas," he said. "You know, the ones that nobody thinks are possible." He grinned. "And of course they eventually become our gold-priority projects."

"Clarke's Second Law," said Kirk, nodding.

Chandar was delighted. "Precisely!" he said.

McCoy looked annoyed. "What the hell are you two talking about?"

"Arthur C. Clarke, my friend," said Chandar. "A great writer who happened to be a visionary man of science. He stated his famous laws of prediction nearly three hundred years ago: 'The only way of discovering the limits of the possible is to venture a little way past them into the impossible.'"

Kirk watched the rotating model of the single nanite with an amused grin. "So you named it ... Jack?" he asked.

McCoy rolled his eyes. "They name *everything* over there," he said. "Lab equipment, specimens, vehicles. Vending machines."

"Well, *this* fellow deserves a name," said Chandar, eyeing the screen with near reverence. "It's a miraculous technological achievement. Almost magical." He gave Kirk a sly glance.

Kirk nodded. "Clarke's Third Law," he said. "Even you know this one, Bones. 'Any sufficiently advanced technology is indistinguishable from magic.'"

"Well, gentlemen, maybe it *is* magic," said McCoy darkly. "But we've seen what this magic dust can do to a living organism. Sorry, but I'm a doctor, and that disturbs me."

Kirk nodded. "Good point, Bones," he said.

"And one other thing, Parag," said McCoy to Chandar. "You said it underwent self-replication. How could it do that?"

Chandar opened another window on the screen. This showed the sequence in which the frenzied swarm imploded the amoeba.

"This swarm appears to scavenge organic materials for

its building blocks," said Chandar. "Then, with remarkable efficiency, it generates a sort of factory that pumps out new nanites."

"It scavenges organic materials?" repeated McCoy.

"Yes, Leonard," replied Chandar.

"Don't you mean, it crushed the amoeba and then used amoeba guts to build nanite babies?"

At this, Chandar lost a little of his enthusiasm. "Well, yes," he said. "That would not be an inaccurate statement."

McCoy gestured abruptly at the screen. "Okay, so let's start asking some obvious questions," he said, his voice rising. "Like, why is some lunatic out on the streets of San Francisco using a smart dust swarm to liquidate the organs of perfectly innocent people?"

Kirk nodded. "And where did he get it? How does he control it?"

"Maybe he doesn't!" said McCoy. "Would you look at that stuff? Maybe the damned *swarm* calls the shots!"

A grim admiration crept across Kirk's face. He could always count on McCoy to look at the Human side of any equation. The tone in the room had certainly changed. He said, "Whatever this stuff is, we need to get your new information into the hands of the authorities investigating this case."

Chandar smiled and nodded toward the console. "I'll

leave the data cube with you," he said. Then he turned to McCoy. "I must go now, Leonard," he said. "There is so much more to do. We've really just started."

McCoy grabbed Chandar's hand and shook it. "Thanks for the lesson, Parag. It was most enlightening."

After Dr. Chandar left, McCoy sat down at the console and gave Kirk a sharp look. "Do you see now why you shouldn't try to confront huge killers just because they're following you?"

Kirk sat in a chair next to McCoy. "Hey, I chased him off," he said.

"Are you sure about that?" asked McCoy. "You probably just led him to the campus."

"He ran away."

"That doesn't mean he stopped following you."

Kirk sighed. "You just want to argue now, don't you?"

McCoy slumped wearily. "No, I'll pass on that," he said. "Let's just get this cube to the admiral and call it a night."

An hour later in the xenolinguistics lab, Uhura pored over the laser printout of all sixty-two common Romulan phrases that matched the rhythms of the killer's phrasing. As she worked quickly through their translations, she found that most were easy to discard.

"Computer, I think we can drop this one too," she said to the console. She read the phrase in Romulan: "'Your sand fleas have already been ionized.'"

"Phrase thirty-one, confirmed as rejected," said the console.

"Do you agree that a brutal serial killer would not say this to the potential rescuers of his victim?" she asked.

The computer whirred, then said, "I cannot respond to speculative queries."

Uhura nodded. "That's because you're a computer," she said.

She'd now winnowed the list to just twenty or so likely candidates. Fifteen of those were variations of the same phrase:

"'Your [NOUN] has already been [PAST TENSE VERB].'"

Uhura glanced at the time. It was almost nine p.m. She smiled.

When Commander Spock left after his brief visit earlier, he'd promised to return before nine, giving them enough time to review any new findings before her ten o'clock hall curfew. One thing she'd learned about her Vulcan instructor: He was always on time. It was a trait she found most agreeable.

Another thing she found agreeable: Commander Spock's high opinion of her abilities. When downloading the 911 call recordings from the SFPD data stick she'd gotten from Detective Bogenn, Uhura also found some background files that included a copy of Spock's note to the commandant of midshipmen:

Admiral:

Cadet Nyota Uhura has my highest recommendation. Without a doubt, she is perfectly suited for this assignment.

Nyota is unmatched in xenolinguistics and has displayed an unparalleled ability to identify sonic anomalies in subspace transmission tests, a critically important trait for any Starfleet bridge communications officer. Given the requirements of this assignment, her skill set would seem to be a perfect match.

I shall endeavor to assist Cadet Uhura in whatever she needs. Be assured that I will give her investigation my highest priority attention.

Commander Spock

Yes, this was agreeable, all of it: Spock's deep well of knowledge; his uncompromising personal and professional integrity; his careful attention to her academic progress and training. And now the wording of this recommendation seemed to validate all of her secret hopes for the future. Bridge communications officer on an expeditionary starship! This had been Uhura's dream job since she was a precocious little girl.

She checked the time again: 8:56 p.m.

"Okay, where is he?" she asked aloud.

"More parameters required," replied the console.

Uhura applied a quick coat of lip gloss. "That was a rhetorical question, computer," she said.

"Rhetorical question," repeated the console. "A question posed for dramatic effect without the expectation of a reply."

"Correct," said Uhura.

"You do not require knowledge of the subject's location?" replied the console.

Uhura thought about this. "Okay, so maybe it wasn't quite rhetorical," she said.

"Please input parameters for the subject," said the computer. "Once target is identified, I will run a search subroutine scan."

Uhura was amused again.

"Computer, you are becoming my most entertaining companion," she said. Then she frowned a bit. "I guess that says something about my personal life."

As the computer processed this confusing information, Uhura's communicator beeped. She flipped it open.

"Hello?" she answered.

"This is Commander Spock," replied Spock.

Uhura smiled. "Hello, Commander."

A short pause. "I apologize for the late call. I've had meetings in Admiral Tullsey's office. Starfleet Medical has presented some new and very fascinating information about the attack on Cadet Gaila. I'll brief you when I arrive in approximately fourteen minutes."

"Yes, sir," said Uhura.

"Are you making progress, Cadet?" asked Spock.

"Good progress, sir." Uhura nodded.

"Excellent," said Spock. "Well, then. I'll see you shortly."

"Yes, Commander," said Uhura. She listened as Spock clicked off the connection.

Uhura flipped the communicator shut. She smiled to herself, and then turned to the computer console.

"Please cancel the search," she said.

"Search canceled," replied the computer.

Uhura made sure things were in order at the console. She checked her hair in the mirror. With thirteen more minutes to kill, she got back to work, thinking she'd be thirteen minutes more prepared when Spock arrived.

She ran a search string on Romulan sonic fragments.

As she did so, a thin trail of black smoke slowly drifted through the window behind her.

Oddly enough, the window was closed tight.

CH.7.12
Shadow Hours

At 9:10 p.m., Kirk and McCoy were walking into the campus residence plaza. They could hear laughter drifting out of open dorm windows on this unusually clear, warm summer night. A full moon, rarely seen, cast its pale glow on the main quad.

"What a long day," said Kirk.

Three dark figures crept past in the hydrangea bushes along the plaza walkway. One carried a live, flapping chicken by the feet. All three wore green, glowing skull masks.

"Apparently, it's not over yet," said McCoy, watching them.

"Kirk!" hissed one of the figures. "Over here!"

Kirk rolled his eyes. He walked over to the bushes.

"Nice chicken," he said.

"Yes, I'm convinced it's a good one," said the figure.

"Ah, Rodriguez," said Kirk. He gave McCoy a look. "I'd know that voice anywhere. What's going on?"

"We need your help," said Rodriguez. "We're trying to chicken this dude over in Nimitz Hall but his window's locked." Rodriguez pulled off his skull mask. "What kind of idiot would lock his window on a beautiful night like tonight?"

Kirk smiled. "Think, Rodriguez," he said. "Why would a guy lock himself in his room?"

As Rodriguez rubbed his chin, thinking, the chicken began to squawk and flap wildly.

"It's pecking my hands!" cried the skull-face holding it.

"I told you to bring the Kevlar gloves," said the third skull. He looked at Kirk and shrugged. "I told him. The guy never listens."

Kirk nodded. "Sure you did, Sweeney," he said.

"Whoa, you know my voice?" asked Sweeney. He pulled off his mask.

"Deaf guys know your voice," said Kirk. "When you talk, dogs run away. Ever notice that?" He turned back to Rodriguez. "You got an answer for me yet, genius?"

Rodriguez grinned big. "He's got a *girl* in there," he said.

"Bingo," said Kirk. "You can graduate now."

"Wow," said Rodriguez with moonlight glinting in his eye. "It's too perfect. But man, how do we get in?"

Kirk turned to McCoy. "Is it like this over in the medical wing?"

"Worse," said McCoy.

"Worse?" said Kirk. "Really? But you guys are so much older."

"Exactly," said McCoy. "We've had more practice."

Students in the medical college had already earned MDs before beginning their Starfleet training. Thus they were typically four to five years older than cadets in the Academy's other colleges.

"So can you give us a hand, Kirk?" asked Rodriguez.

"Guys, I've had a long, hard day," replied Kirk. "Sorry."

Rodriguez nodded and pulled the skull back over his face. "Okay, let's move out, squad," he said to the others. "Don't drop that chicken, Bartley!"

"It's pecking my hands!" cried Bartley.

Kirk turned away but asked, "Who's getting this chicken?"

"Tikhonov," said Rodriguez.

Kirk stopped in his tracks. He turned back.

"*Viktor* Tikhonov?" he asked.

"Yeah," said Rodriguez. "I hate that guy."

McCoy stepped up beside Kirk. "Jim, you're getting that look in your eye," he said.

"What look?" asked Kirk, grinning at Rodriguez.

"The one where you end up in front of the Cadet

Oversight Committee and plead for one more chance to stay in Starfleet," said McCoy.

Kirk nodded, still grinning.

On-campus social life often had a commando-like, competitive edge to it. Plots were hatched. Strike teams formed. Alliances made, then shifted. Coveted objects were stolen, recovered, and then stolen again. Unwanted objects delivered.

One example: A holo-bust of the infamous twenty-second century naval commander Rear Admiral Carleton Schiller had been trading hands for the past fifteen years. Originally nabbed from a nook in the Academy library as a prank, Schiller was subsequently stolen by another cadet squad in a daring daylight raid. Since then, Admiral Schiller was considered an object of immense value in the Academy residence halls. Even the briefest possession would bestow great prestige on the holder. He often made dramatic appearances at public events, usually followed by a power blackout. This led to the traditional shout of "Schiller!" and a mad scramble to track him down. Insane amounts of logistical planning went into these appearances. Some said Schiller was responsible for training many of the brightest tactical minds in Starfleet.

Many such activities occurred during what Academy cadets traditionally called "shadow hours." These were the two hours every weeknight between 8:00 p.m., when all formal activities ended, and 10:00 p.m., when curfew went into effect. They were supposed to be study hours. Sometimes they were; sometimes they weren't.

Cadet residence halls were not like typical college dorms. Codes of conduct were strictly enforced. Weeknight curfew was 10 p.m., with lights out by midnight. Formal rules of behavior applied—at least in the settings of training, assembly, and classroom. Rank was respected. Cadets also generally ate and exercised together in what Academy literature called "an enhanced morale and team-building atmosphere."

But smart cadets figured out creative ways to have fun inside the margins. Shadow-hours activities frequently stretched outside the bounds of Academy rules and regulations. Cadet James T. Kirk embraced this tradition, and usually pushed it to its limits.

It should be noted that Starfleet cadets had more personal freedom than typical military cadets—after all, Starfleet did see exploration and pursuit of knowledge as its primary missions, not war. Inventiveness, intellectual curiosity, and original thinking were valued traits in Starfleet cadets.

And it was no Spartan bunkhouse existence, either. Upperclassmen lived in roomy, well-appointed apartment quarters. First- and second-year cadet quarters were more dormitory style, but the residents were free to personalize their spaces. All residence halls were coed; male and female cadets would soon be spending months or even years at a stretch as shipmates on expeditionary voyages, so it made sense to get everyone used to it now.

Kirk sauntered down the corridor, whistling. This was the second floor of Nimitz Hall. He'd never been here before, as far as he knew.

A girl wrapped in a towel stepped from her room into the hallway. She stopped when she saw him.

"Jim?" she said.

Uh-oh, thought Kirk.

"Hey there," he said. *Tara. Teran? Taysha. Starts with a T...?*

"Where've you been?" she asked.

"Trying to stay afloat," he said. "You know." *Tracey, maybe?*

She gave him a look. "I don't know how you do it," she said.

"Neither do I," said Kirk. He had no clue what she was talking about. "Say, I'm looking for Viktor Tikhonov. I think his room is somewhere on this floor, right?"

Now she smiled. "What do you want from *that* idiot?" she asked. "Another beating?"

Kirk smiled wryly back.

"Ouch," he said. He mimicked a knife jab into his heart, then twisted it.

She turned and strolled down the hall. "You're at his door," she said.

Kirk turned to the door next to him. "Ah, thanks," he said. "Thought it looked familiar."

The girl snickered as she stepped into the women's shower room.

"I'm Holly, by the way," she called as the door closed.

Ah, now I remember, he thought with a smile. "You look good in that towel, Holly!" he called back.

The door clunked shut behind her.

He glanced up and down the corridor. Deserted. Odd for Nimitz, a notoriously crazy hall, but whatever, he'd take it. He put his ear to Tikhonov's door. Good old-fashioned American metal thrash-rock was throbbing loudly in the room.

Real romantic there, Viktor, thought Kirk, amused.

He pulled a sealed envelope from his pocket and slid it into the side doorjamb. Then he pounded loudly on the door and hurried down the corridor to the men's restroom. He peeked out to see Tikhonov's door hiss open; the shirtless Russian emerged, flushed and angry. The envelope fluttered to the floor in front of him. He picked it up, tore it open, and read the note inside. Then he withdrew into the room.

As the door hissed shut, Kirk started counting: *Ten, nine, eight* . . .

Before Kirk could get to five, Viktor burst out of the room fully dressed and obviously pissed. He turned back and said, "Just *relax*! I'll be back in ten minutes." As his door hissed shut again Tikhonov pounded down the corridor to the stairwell.

Kirk waited a few seconds. Then he strolled down the hall and tapped on Tikhonov's door.

"Yes?" called a female voice.

"Campus security, ma'am," replied Kirk.

When the door opened, he flashed a phony badge. The girl inside wore a skimpy white robe and was very attractive. Kirk nodded in approval.

"You're not Cadet Tikhonov," he said.

"What's wrong?" asked the girl.

"Just a seal check," said Kirk. "Routine."

"A *seal* check?"

"Window seal, ma'am."

The girl's face twisted a bit. "Why now?" she asked.

"We wait until shadow hours to increase the likelihood that cadets are in their rooms," said Kirk, trying to sound authoritative. "We try to avoid unauthorized keyless entry whenever possible so as to respect the privacy of the cadet corps, as it were."

The girl rolled her eyes. "Whatever," she said.

She stepped aside and Kirk walked to the room's only window. He unlatched it, then started opening and closing it loudly, again and again. Each time he lowered the sash to the sill he slammed it with gusto.

He looked back at the girl, who was busy examining her manicure. Kirk raised the sash and pretended to examine the side jambs. He ran his finger along the sill.

"Looks good!" he bellowed.

He closed the window, neglecting to relock the latches. Then he strode back through the doorway into the corridor and spun smartly to face the girl.

"Thank you, Cadet," said Kirk. He snapped a salute and held it, gazing at the girl.

After a few seconds, she shook her head in disbelief and saluted back.

Kirk whipped down his hand and marched off down the hallway.

• · ·⁚·✦·⁺✦ ·• ·

Outside Nimitz, Kirk walked toward a clucking tree.

"Load the chicken," he said to the tree.

"Do we have a clear launch vector?" asked a voice in the tree.

Kirk looked around.

"Yes," he said.

"My hands are totally pecked," whined a second voice.

Kirk patted a lower branch.

"Good luck, gentlemen," he said. "I want reports on my desk at 0700 hours."

"Roger that," said voices in the tree.

Kirk walked toward his dorm, Farragut Hall, with an extra bounce in his step.

In Kirk's room, McCoy took a swig from his miniflask and then held it out. Kirk nabbed it and took a swallow, then grimaced.

"My god, Bones, what is this swill?" he asked.

McCoy nodded at the flask, grinning. "A little home recipe from Mississippi."

Kirk stared at it. "I'm drinking moonshine?"

McCoy grinned. "You're a lucky man," he said. "So let's think ahead for once, shall we, Jim? What if Mr. Tikhonov finds out about your window caper?"

Kirk took another swig and started coughing.

"It is my fervent hope," he said between gasps, "that he comes looking for me."

McCoy frowned. "Are you kidding?" he exclaimed. "He's not only an animal, he's feral."

Kirk wiped his mouth and handed back the flask, which McCoy stashed in his hip pocket.

"Listen, Bones, let me tell you something about Viktor Tikhonov," he said. "He's a damned good cadet, and if I ever get jumped by a squadron of cloaked Romulan birds of prey, Viktor's the guy I want leading my security team."

McCoy nodded. "But . . . ?" he asked.

"But he's under the mistaken impression that he'd be a good starship commander," said Kirk.

"He's doing quite well in the ATT testing," said McCoy.

"Yes, he is," said Kirk. "He's an excellent away-team leader. His tactical thinking is sharp. Better than mine, Bones. I admit it."

McCoy smiled. "Again, but . . . ?"

"But that's different from commanding a *Constitution*-class heavy cruiser with a crew of hundreds and a mandate to make peaceful contact with whoever or whatever you meet out there," said Kirk gesturing toward the sky.

"Yes, that's true," said McCoy. "And I have no doubt you're destined to be that starship commander, Jim, and maybe Viktor Tikhonov isn't. But that doesn't explain to me why you want him to come looking for you."

Kirk folded his arms.

"So Viktor and I can have a little heart-to-heart talk about . . . the qualities of leadership," he said.

McCoy laughed. "I don't think that's what will happen, my friend," he said. "Not if he comes after you with boiling blood and a pair of chicken-scratched hands."

"Bones," said Kirk, leaning toward McCoy for emphasis, "I can take care of myself."

"I know," said McCoy. "But just in case . . . well"—he pulled out the flask again—"I suppose I've got your back, you crazy Iowa pig farmer."

Kirk grinned. "We grew wheat," he said.

"Whatever," said McCoy.

Kirk's communicator beeped. He flipped it open: an incoming text. As he read it, he frowned.

"It's Glorak," he said. "There's something going down across campus."

"What is it?" asked McCoy.

"'Emergency vehicles incoming,' he says."

"For who?"

Kirk shrugged. "He didn't say."

Several fire department hovercrafts, halo-lights flashing, had already settled on the central quad by the time Kirk and McCoy arrived. The focus was the Institute of Xenology building. It was sealed off, and a crowd had gathered on its front lawn.

Kirk approached a tall Betelgeusian cadet and asked, "What's up, Beeker?"

The cadet shrugged his avian shoulders and opened his speaking mouth. "Fire, I guess," he said with a tongue snap. "Not really sure yet."

Kirk spotted Admiral Tullsey's adjutant, Lieutenant Commander Renfield, standing just inside the yellow barrier tape. As he started toward her, an SFPD police cruiser glided in for a landing nearby.

The adjutant spotted Kirk and waved him over. "She's okay, Cadet," she called as Kirk approached.

"Who's okay?" asked Kirk.

"Your friend," replied Renfield.

"My friend?"

"Cadet Uhura."

"What!?" exclaimed Kirk. "Where is she?"

Lieutenant Commander Renfield lifted up the yellow tape and Kirk ducked under.

"ICU at the medical college," she said.

"What happened?" asked Kirk.

"Reports are sketchy," said Renfield, arching one of her scary eyebrows. "Apparently there was a fire in the xeno-linguistics lab. A particulate detector set off the building alarm."

"Uhura was working on those 911 recordings, no doubt," said Kirk.

"No doubt," said Renfield. "Two students evacuating the library heard her coughing. They found her in a research pod filled with smoke. Thank god they managed to drag her out. All three suffered serious smoke inhalation, it seems."

Kirk nodded. "I take it they put out the fire," he said, gesturing toward the firefighters.

"Well," said Renfield, "that's just the thing."

Kirk frowned. "What?"

"The emergency responders found no fire," she said. She gave Kirk a look. "In fact, they found no smoke whatsoever."

Kirk was confused. "You said they suffered smoke inhalation," he said.

Lieutenant Commander Renfield shrugged. Then she said, "Well, we did find a black residue on all three of them. So I suppose that—"

Kirk immediately spun around to look for McCoy. "Bones!" he yelled. "Bones!"

McCoy pushed through the crowd to join them. Kirk gave him a quick summary of the situation.

"Did you see this residue, Lieutenant Commander?" asked McCoy.

"Yes," she answered.

"It was black and chalky, correct?" said McCoy.

"Yes, it was."

McCoy's emergency pager suddenly went off. He checked its message, then looked at Kirk. "It's Dr. Griffin," said McCoy. "He wants me to report to ICU immediately."

"Good god, Bones," said Kirk.

"I know, Jim," said McCoy.

"You gotta get that stuff out of her," said Kirk urgently. "Before it . . ."

"I *know*, Jim," repeated McCoy.

They both ducked back under the yellow tape and began to sprint toward the hospital wing of the medical college.

CH.8.12
City Lights

Spock stood in the ICU waiting room, hands clasped behind his back. He didn't pace or fidget, despite his unsettled emotions. This was due to the calming techniques he'd learned as a boy from his mother. Ironic that a Human woman so often guided by deep feeling could teach a Vulcan male to find such peaceful, meditative corridors in his consciousness.

One of his older colleagues on the science faculty, Dr. John Telemark, stepped up beside him.

"I'm sure they'll be fine, Commander," he said.

Spock nodded. "Yes, the medical team took both male cadets off their ventilators almost immediately. I was told they're alert and doing well."

"Good news!" said Telemark. "And the girl?"

"Stable but still unconscious, according to the last report," replied Spock, quickly glancing toward the double doors leading into the care unit where Uhura was.

Telemark gestured in the opposite direction, down the corridor to the hospital's main lobby.

"Quite a few cadets keeping vigil out there," he said.

Spock allowed himself a thin smile. "The cadet corps has an intriguing social psychology," he said.

"How so, Spock?" asked the older professor.

"Cadets spend an inordinate amount of time devising ways to humiliate one another," he said. "It is a most peculiar practice. And yet when one of their own is imperiled, they become as protective as a Hyborian mite colony."

Telemark smiled. "Well, as a distinguished recent graduate, I guess you'd know," he said.

"Cadet training was an interesting time," said Spock.

Dr. Telemark glanced toward the lobby again. "That Delta team captain is out there, I forget his name. They say he's an impulsive fellow. I don't expect he'll fare well in Tanika Station next week."

Spock bowed respectfully, but said, "I'm learning that Human decision-making is often a curious process. In certain subjects, decisions that may seem illogical at first often turn out to be tactically sound." He frowned. "The Human brain seems to be a mystery to itself. It makes what appear to be snap judgments and rash choices that, as it turns out, have in fact been sufficiently processed subconsciously." He looked at his colleague. "I believe you call it intuition."

Telemark smiled again. "I call it flying by the seat of your pants," he said.

Spock raised an eyebrow. "An interesting metaphor, Doctor," he said.

"Well, that young cadet from Iowa thinks he's ready for your Kobayashi Maru scenario." Telemark chuckled. "But frankly, I don't think he'll get past Tanika Station on Monday."

As Spock began to reply, Dr. Griffin burst through the ICU doors and approached with his shock of white hair and a crooked smile.

"Hello, gentlemen," he said.

"How are they, Doctor?" asked Spock quickly.

"Hard to say definitively," said Dr. Griffin. "They certainly *seem* well enough. Cadet Uhura suffered the worst inhalation trauma, but there's no thermal damage to her airway passages. Most of the problem seems to be the metabolic acidosis, and a bit too much tissue-level oxygen debt."

Spock and Telemark looked at each other.

Dr. Griffin smiled. "Sorry," he said. "Ah, her blood's a little out of whack. But we're fixing it. In any case, she's resting comfortably on a ventilator and her vitals look good."

Spock felt his face release tension.

"So she's out of the woods, Charlie?" asked Telemark.

"I think so," replied Griffin. "But I've got a young doctor in there who thinks the carbon residue on Cadet Uhura is somehow active."

Spock's eyebrow arched again. "Active?" he asked.

Griffin bobbed his great white head. "Yes."

"In what way, Doctor?" asked Spock.

"Not sure, Commander, but he's taking soot samples from her nose and mouth right now," replied Griffin. "He's also planning a bronchoscopy to examine her airways and to suction debris. Dr. McCoy seems to believe that this smoke is . . . well, more than smoke, I guess."

Spock considered that. "It is indeed curious that no residual smoke was found in the lab."

"Well, gentlemen, I have a police report to make," said Dr. Griffin. He nodded toward a grizzled-looking man in a rumpled coat approaching from the lobby. "Hello, Detective Bogenn," he called. "Let's meet in my office, shall we?"

As Dr. Griffin and the detective walked off, Spock's eyebrows furrowed.

"Active smoke residue," he said. "Curious."

Dr. Telemark sat down in a lounge chair and sighed.

"Well, Spock, perhaps we should go over the holodeck calibrations again for next Monday's simulation," he said.

"We want Tanika Station's mysteries to remain impenetrable for our cadets."

Spock sat down next to him.

"Since I expect to be here quite a while, Doctor," he
said, "I believe that's an excellent plan."

Dr. McCoy barely had time to order a bronchoscope unit
to ICU before observing an event that he fully expected to
see. The critical care nurse assisting him with Cadet Uhura
suddenly backed away from the bed.

"Uh, Doctor?" he said.

McCoy turned to see what appeared to be a smoking
body.

"Yep, there it goes," he said.

"Is she . . . burning?" asked the nurse, looking panicked.

"No," said McCoy. "Relax, Harmon." He pointed at the bedside console. "Do you have the observation cameras rolling?"

"Yes, sir," replied Nurse Harmon.

McCoy watched intently as the hazy smoke slowly
rose from Uhura's body and gathered into a black,
doughnut-shaped cloud. It hovered a few moments
directly above her, then suddenly shot to the ceiling and
disappeared.

It left no trace behind.

"She's clean now," said McCoy. He grabbed a tricorder scanner on the nearby stand. "But we need an organ scan, stat. If her organs are intact, I expect she'll wake up soon, so let's remove that tracheal tube too. And Harmon?"

"Yes, Doctor?" said the nurse, still staring at the ceiling.

"Call pulmonary and cancel that bronchoscope," he said.

The next two days proceeded in a relatively uneventful fashion at Starfleet Academy. Students went about their business by day, and schemed, commando-raided, partied, and coupled up by night. Meanwhile, the Academy's medical and scientific staff were comparing notes and conducting more studies on the mysterious black substance.

As Kirk tried desperately to prepare for the upcoming Science mission final, nagging questions kept popping into his head:

How does the Doctor control the swarm?

Why did the swarm target Uhura? Why did it spare her? What are its operating protocols?

Did I lead it to her somehow? Did it follow me to campus?

How does the killer know my name?

It sometimes seemed as if he'd imagined the encounter at the Palace of Fine Arts; it was so surreal. When he'd run into Detective Bogenn that night in the hospital lobby and finally reported the incident, Kirk got the impression that the detective was skeptical. But then he whipped out his communicator and there it was—"James T. Kirk"—in all its creepy, voice-filtered eeriness. Uhura wouldn't have to translate that.

So Kirk spent two days trying to put the Doctor and the swarm out of his mind in order to focus on Tanika Station. He studied his Starfleet science directives for hours. He met with his Delta teammates each day to review Science mission protocols, brainstorm possible scenarios, and then game-plan and role-play a response to each one.

Unfortunately, one other thing made full concentration difficult as well.

He couldn't stop thinking about the stunning girl from Brewsky's.

So when Thursday evening finally came, Kirk found himself jogging down Union Street and bursting into occasional adrenaline-fueled sprints. Meeting girls rarely made Kirk feel jittery, but Hannah was unlike any he'd ever met. He kept retracking their first conversation. She made him think. He liked that.

When he arrived at Brewsky's, a line of five had formed at the order counter. Hannah gave him a quick glance and took orders with a sly smile. Kirk eavesdropped on her banter with the customers in front of him. She was good with people.

"What can I get you?" she asked him.

He slapped down his payment chip. "Triple espresso," he said.

She just looked at him.

"*Please*," he added.

After paying, Kirk moved to his usual corner table and set up his e-pad. That morning, Thursday, all of the participants in next Monday's Science mission final had received a single page of instructions on what to expect. Kirk had read it carefully several times, each time amazed at how little they would know going in. He scrolled through it one more time, looking for subtle hints or hidden clues between the lines.

"Cadet?" called out Hannah loudly from the counter. "Is there a 'Cadet' here?"

Kirk looked up. She was gazing around the room.

"Your espresso is ready, Cadet," she called sweetly.

Kirk grinned. He went up to the counter.

"Sorry," he said. "Didn't hear my name. I was too engrossed in my studies of fascism."

"It's a good major," she said.

Kirk picked up the espresso cup. "Yes, plenty of job opportunities."

Another girl behind Hannah was tying on an apron. She said, "Have a good night, girl."

"Thanks, Jen," said Hannah. She started untying her own apron.

Kirk frowned. "You're off?" he said, glancing at his watch. "It's only seven."

"Yes, I'm off," she said.

"You said you'd be working tonight," said Kirk.

"I did work," she replied. "Now I'm off."

"Oh," he said, disappointed.

Hannah turned to the new girl. "Can I get a short mocha?" she asked. "No whipped cream. For here." She pointed over at Kirk's table.

Kirk slowly brightened. "Ah," he said.

Jen, the other girl, smiled. "Who's that?" she asked, nodding at Kirk.

"That's Jim," said Hannah. "He's a Starfleet cadet. Jim, this is Jen. She's a poet. I'm sure you guys have a *lot* in common."

Jen waved. "Hi, Jim," she said.

Kirk waved back.

Jen looked him up and down. "Cute," she told Hannah.

"You think so?" replied Hannah, feigning surprise.

She ducked under the counter and sauntered over to Kirk's table. Almost glassy-eyed, Kirk followed. As he sat down he flipped his e-pad shut.

"Hey, don't let me interrupt your studies," she said.

Kirk just laughed.

Some things Kirk learned about Hannah:

She was born and raised in Fresno.

Her father was a botanist. Her mother? A botanist.

She loved plants.

She hiked in the Marin Hills north of the city every weekend.

She broke up with her cadet boyfriend in part because of his addiction to holodeck games.

Another reason: He was a self-centered jerk.

The best reason: He didn't like the movie *Casablanca*.

She loved San Francisco bookstores.

And although she was fond of flowering plants, she had a special affinity for mosses and liverworts.

Some things Hannah learned about Kirk:

He hated Iowa.

He loved Iowa.

He had a police record in Iowa.

He missed Iowa.

He never wanted to go back to Iowa. At least he vowed

never to return until his stepfather, Frank, left the state.

He was born in Medical Shuttle 37.

He loved his mother.

He loved everything he knew about his father.

His father had saved the lives of more than eight hundred people—including Jim's—while giving his own life to do so, and Jim wanted to do at least that much good during his own career.

And he liked to go fast.

They'd been talking for more than an hour when Hannah suddenly said, "Let's walk."

"Sure." Kirk grabbed his jacket.

"Nights like this are rare," she said.

Kirk glanced at her. "True," he said.

Hannah was wrapping a green silk scarf around her neck. She grabbed her jacket too and said, "We just don't get much *summer* here in summer."

"No kidding," he said. He glanced out the window. It was the second clear, fogless night this week.

They stashed their bags behind the counter with Jen and headed out onto Union Street.

"Where to?" asked Kirk.

"How about a cable-car ride?" she replied.

"Let's do it," said Kirk.

It was a short stroll up to Hyde Street where they hopped aboard a car on the Powell-Hyde line. They rode it downhill to the turntable on Market Street, where cars were spun for the return trip. There they transferred to the Powell-Mason line that ran back north over both Nob Hill and Russian Hill toward the wharf. As the car clanked out of the turntable and rolled uphill on Powell, Hannah suddenly grabbed Kirk's hand.

"Look," she said, "I appreciate tonight. I think it's great that you like me."

Amused, Kirk looked at her. "Gosh, and here I thought I was so subtle," he said.

Hannah waved her hand. "My point is," she said, "I appreciate your interest in my life. But don't avoid talking about the Academy. I know it's important to you, and I will try not to judge. Okay?"

Kirk shrugged. "I don't want to bore you," he said. "Or say something militaristic that makes you jump off the cable car."

Hannah laughed. "Hey, I know it's intense at the Academy," she said. "I get that. It's all-consuming. And it should be. I mean, space isn't grad school; it's life and death. The Romulans are coming. I get how you have to pour yourself into it . . . or else you don't make the grade."

"Ah, let me guess," he said. "That cadet you dated, all he talked about was the Academy. And himself."

Hannah looked down, and Kirk knew he had hit a nerve.

"I'm not that guy," said Kirk. "Okay?"

"Okay," she said.

They both held tight to the grip poles as the car lurched around a turn on Jackson.

"Of course, I do have a pretty high opinion of myself," said Kirk. "And I need someone like you to help keep that in check." He squeezed her hand. "You're doing a good job."

She smiled her amazing smile, and Kirk felt his heart skip a beat.

"Okay, so what's up with your Science test on Monday?" she asked.

Kirk squinted. "You really want to hear about it?"

Hannah nodded. "Yeah, I'm all ears."

Spock stood at the window of Uhura's hospital room. He faced north toward the Golden Gate Bridge, which stretched away at a sharp angle less than a mile away. A towering fog bank was beginning to roll over the span like a massive tidal wave.

"The inland wind is ruining our perfect night," said Spock, turning to the bed.

Uhura burst into a coughing fit. Spock took a step toward the paging button in concern, but she waved him away.

"No, no, I'm okay," she said, clearing her throat. "Really. I'm good."

"Maybe you should try another round of supplemental oxygen," said Spock. "Dr. Griffin said the pulmonary irritation could flare up again."

"Thank you, Commander, but that won't be necessary," she said.

Spock took a deep calming breath. Then he said, "I fear I am on the verge of annoying you, Cadet."

Uhura laughed, which triggered a cough. Then she said, "And I worry that I'm keeping you from more important things."

Spock's eyes widened. He was still learning Human inflections and connotations, and he wondered, *Is Nyota signaling a desire that I should go?*

"Perhaps I should let you rest?" he said, unsure of how to proceed.

"No!" She answered a bit too emphatically, and covered by quickly adding, "I mean, I think we still have some issues to review. From my lab work."

Spock nodded. "I do feel somewhat responsible for this incident," he said.

"Why?" asked Uhura, puzzled.

"A simple logic string," he replied. "You would not have been in the lab so late if I had not recommended you to the commandant for this task."

"Really?" she replied, almost indignant. "Commander, I thought you knew me better than that."

Spock turned back to the window. "Why do you say that, Cadet?" he asked.

"I'm in that lab almost *every* night," she said.

"Oh," said Spock. "I was not aware of your evening routine."

Uhura looked him in the eye and smiled. "You will be eventually," she said.

Spock raised an eyebrow. He gazed down at neat rows of white gravestones. The medical college grounds sat adjacent to the San Francisco National Cemetery, a military burial site. Just to the right sat the Officers' Lounge, a well-lit place where Starfleet royalty liked to sip debilitating concoctions and tell war stories. Spock avoided it religiously.

Uhura wondered if she had gone too far. She pressed a button on her bed rail to lower her head a bit. "I've only been your student a short while," she said.

"Yes, true," he said.

"In another six months you'll probably wish you'd never met me," she said.

Spock allowed himself a smile. "You are relentless in your pursuit of knowledge," he said. "However, I find that to be a most admirable trait, Cadet. One of many you possess."

Uhura breathed a sigh of relief.

The fog's gloomy front rank was pushing through the Presidio now. Above, the lights of the Golden Gate were blinking out of view, one by one. Spock watched the murk spread like surging water across the perfect military rows of grave markers below him. He almost flinched as a ragged fog specter, pushed hard by the sea wind, flew straight into the window. It broke apart on the pane like a boiling white fluid.

Spock closed his eyes. Then he opened them and turned to Cadet Uhura.

"So let us work," he said.

"Yes, let's," she replied.

● · · ⠅ ⠄ ✦ · ✦ ·· ·

Kirk gave Hannah the latest update on the Tanika Station scenario. It wasn't much; all Kirk knew was that Team Delta would be shuttled into an enclosed environment and (according to the prep sheet) "carry out Starfleet science directives in a First-Contact setting."

"An enclosed environment?" she repeated.

"Correct," said Kirk.

"So you're not planet-side?" she asked.

"Doesn't sound like it," replied Kirk. "And we already did the First Contact mission final, so we're assuming Tanika Station will be uninhabited."

"So your job is to explore, observe, then acquire and analyze science samples," she said.

"Yes," said Kirk. "But these exercises are designed to be unpredictable. So, any advice?"

"Just don't kill anything, soldier," replied Hannah. Then she impulsively leaned over and kissed him.

"If I promise not to kill anything, will you do that again?" Kirk asked, pulling her closer. The air seemed to crackle with electricity. Kirk went in for another kiss, when suddenly the cable-car bell rang. "Columbus Avenue, hang on, half left!" called out the conductor, shattering the moment.

"Hey, you ever been to City Lights?" asked Hannah with sudden excitement.

Kirk said, "No. What is it?"

"What is it?" she repeated. "Are you kidding?"

"No."

Hannah turned to the grip man at the car controls. "Next stop!" she called. As the car rounded the half-turn onto Columbus and braked to a halt, Hannah checked her watch. "It's getting late," she said to Kirk. "What about your curfew?"

"I'll be fine," he replied.

City Lights was a bookstore, and it was generally

considered the birthplace of the 1950s Beat generation. Two years prior it had celebrated its three-hundredth birthday, a remarkable achievement in an age where bookstores didn't much exist anymore as actual, nonvirtual places. True, City Lights was as much a museum as anything. But it was still a cool place to hang out, look over old-fashioned printed books, and have a cup of good old-fashioned slow-brewed coffee.

Kirk and Hannah hopped off the car at Columbus Avenue and started walking toward the famous bookstore. Kirk grabbed Hannah's hand. She snuggled closer to him, and he wrapped his arm around her.

Columbus slashed the city at an angle, running from the North Beach waterfront all the way to the soaring towers of the Financial District. It dead-ended right into the Transamerica Pyramid. As they crested the hill near the park at Washington Square, the glittering skyline was etched sharply against the darkening sky. A few blocks later, the great pyramid loomed directly ahead of them.

Hannah pointed at it.

"Hard to believe that was one of the five tallest buildings in the world when it was built," she said. "Now it's the runt of the skyline."

This was true. In 2255, many skyscrapers in the district

towered far above the Transamerica Pyramid. Some were nearly twice its 850-foot height.

"Well, it's still the only pyramid, I guess," said Kirk.

"Right," said Hannah. "The sacred shape."

"What do you mean?" he asked, thinking, *This girl can make anything sound sexy.*

Absently Kirk noticed the first tendrils of fog creeping through buildings up ahead. As he crossed Green Street, he turned to see streetlights being blotted from view in the distance as the fog advanced. The wind was picking up. He zipped up his jacket.

Hannah formed a shape with her hands. "Many ancient cultures saw the pyramid as some kind of mystical shape," she said. "Some still do."

Kirk was amused. "Well, they make great tombs and casinos," he said.

Hannah nodded. "The pyramid's geometry is supposed to intensify electromagnetic frequencies that create a perfect scalar resonance."

"Yes," said Kirk. "I understand this effect whitens whites and brightens colors. It also kills germs that can cause bad breath," he said, leaning in for a quick kiss.

Hannah laughed and kissed him back.

A brilliant flare of white light suddenly flashed in the sky up ahead, near the tip of the Transamerica Pyramid.

"How'd you do that?" Hannah asked after a moment. "Do you control lightning, too?"

Kirk was alert. He listened for a few seconds. "No thunder," he said. "Hey, I grew up in Iowa. Where there's lightning, thunder follows."

Three more blinding flashes lit the sky in rapid succession, like a pulsing strobe.

"Definitely not lightning," said Kirk.

"Maybe it's some kind of aircraft warning," said Hannah. "'Cause, wow, look at the fog!"

Heavy fog suddenly poured across the street from right to left, coming from the seaward direction. The wet chill felt like a sudden freeze.

"Yikes," said Hannah. "Let's get to the bookstore."

They picked up the pace down Columbus. Kirk felt a sudden sense of dread. His peripheral vision had caught a glimpse of movement directly behind them. Now he spun around, and nudged Hannah behind him.

A tall, hooded figure seemed to hover in the air just up the sidewalk, about ten feet in front of them.

Kirk's jaw clenched so hard, it popped. Then his tactical training kicked in. He took a deep breath and cleared his head.

"Hannah," he whispered over his shoulder. "Get ready to run."

Kirk kept his eyes on the dark figure. It moved toward

them. Kirk backed up, forcing Hannah backward too.

"Listen carefully," he said quietly. "If you see any sign of black smoke, any sign at all . . . run. Do you hear me? Run like hell."

"I hear you," said Hannah calmly.

"Don't let it catch you."

"Right."

A second dark figure coalesced in the fog next to the first. Kirk blinked and looked again.

"Great," he said.

Hannah peered around him.

"You're *Starfleet*, Kirk," Hannah whispered. "Kick some ass!"

CH.9.12
Delta Origins

Starfleet Academy's cryptology lab was the best code-breaking unit in the known galaxy, and its Cheetah3000 massively parallel quantum processor was custom-made for extracting meaning from something like a single white glyph etched on a black bit.

Yet McCoy was still stunned at how quickly the super-computer cracked the code. Less than twenty-four hours after he'd submitted the white marking for cryptoanalysis, the machine spit out a result with an estimated 99.9999997 percent probability of being accurate.

As McCoy sat in Dr. Chandar's nanotech lab in Hawking Hall, the Academy's science center, watching live video of a nanite swarm, he reviewed the results with his friend.

"The *category* of meaning is not surprising or mysterious at all, Parag," said McCoy, scrolling down the document. "It's a date and origin stamp."

"Just as we suspected," replied Chandar. "It was so clearly a simple ID mark."

"Ah, but wait," said McCoy. "Here's where it gets interesting." He turned the pad toward Chandar. The screen displayed a swirling mass of stars. "The white glyph is actually an embedded strand of numerical data that, when plotted in 3-D, produces this stunning holo-image. It's our galaxy, Parag! The Milky Way! Re-created in *remarkable* detail."

Dr. Chandar stared in amazement. "A star map," he said.

"Exactly," said McCoy.

"And does it display travel waypoints so we can see where the swarm has been?" asked Chandar.

"Unfortunately, no," replied McCoy. "Each nanite's galactic map has only two sets of spatial coordinates marked. One is Earth, as you would expect—the swarm's destination marker."

He tapped on his pad's screen, and the view zoomed through star clusters until it centered on the solar system and zoomed in on blue Earth. The planet was highlighted by a glowing aura.

"Now here's the other marker," McCoy continued. "We have to assume that this set of coordinates marks the swarm's place of origin."

He tapped the screen again. This time the view

careened through the star systems of the galaxy's Alpha Quadrant and zoomed clear out of known space.

Dr. Chandar's head jerked at an angle in bewilderment. "That is no region of galactic space I'm familiar with," he said.

"Yes," said McCoy. "You are not familiar with this region because nobody is."

The view settled on a glittering region that appeared to be a mass of swirling debris—comets and asteroids, perhaps, and other planetary fragments.

McCoy looked gravely at Chandar. "Parag, this is a core ward sector of the Delta Quadrant."

"What?" cried Chandar in disbelief.

"Unknown space," said McCoy, nodding. "We don't even have sensors there."

"But our nearest border with Delta is thirty thousand light-years away," said Chandar. He whipped out a calc-pad and did some quick figuring. "A Constitution-class starship traveling at its maximum velocity of Warp Six would take, let's see . . . more than *138* full Earth years just to reach the edge of that quadrant."

"Precisely," said McCoy. "And that's why the date stamp is so interesting."

Dr. Chandar's face lit up with an involuntary smile—all his neurons were firing.

"The date stamp," said McCoy, "based on standard

galactic time computation, indicates the swarm was created or activated just two months ago, standard Earth time. So either it was created en route from the Delta Quadrant . . . or it got here unbelievably fast."

Chandar nodded. "Perhaps via some sort of transwarp corridor?"

"Well, I'm not a physicist," said McCoy.

"No, you're a doctor," said Chandar. He pointed at his monitor, where a nanite swarm swirled lazily in live video on-screen. "And that's why I think you'll find this fascinating."

McCoy rolled his chair closer to the monitor.

"Oh, wait," McCoy said. "There's one more thing about the glyph." He punched up the Cryptology report again, then scrolled to a section, enlarged it, and held it up for Dr. Chandar. "Does this number mean anything to you, Parag?" he asked. "Anything particular in the world of, say, nano-technology?"

Chandar stared at the pad's screen: *5618.*

"'Five-six-one-eight,'" he read. "Hmm. No, not right off-hand."

McCoy looked at the pad. "Because this simple number forms the entire bottom quarter of the glyph, according to the cryptoanalysis."

"That would suggest it is important," said Chandar.

McCoy gave the on-screen number another look, then

shook his head and closed up his digital pad. "I guess we'll run it past some of the other labs," he said. "It must mean something."

Dr. Chandar rubbed his hands together and scooted his chair to the microscope.

"Okay!" he said. "Now watch. This is fun!"

Kirk had an idea.

"Take off your jacket!" he said to Hannah.

"What?"

"Your jacket," he said, pulling off his own.

The two dark figures stood unmoving as the fog thickened. It was cold and wet, and now Kirk and Hannah shivered without coats on.

"If you see anything that looks like black smoke, start fanning as fast as you can," whispered Kirk. "Like this!" He started flapping his jacket up and down.

Hannah gave him a sideways glance. "Have you lost your mind?"

Kirk took a step toward the figures, wildly flapping his jacket. As he did so, a third dark figure appeared between the other two. In a deep voice, this middle figure spoke.

"What the hell are you doing, mate?"

Kirk stopped flapping.

"Who's there?" he called. "Show yourself!"

The three figures moved slowly forward until their facial features were vaguely visible. It was clearly three Human males, all tall, all dressed in dark, hooded jackets. All three had heavily tattooed faces.

"What are you guys, a basketball team?" asked Hannah. Still shivering, she slipped her jacket back on.

The two fellows on the outside laughed, but the guy in the middle just leered dangerously at Hannah. He had a mouth full of silver-carbonate teeth filed to gleaming points. He pulled off his hood to reveal a shaved, tattooed head. A row of razor-sharp skull studs ran down the middle of his scalp to form a very painful-looking mohawk.

Kirk knew the branding. These guys were part of the Mongol Saints, the most violent gang in the Bay Area. Based in Oakland, Saints often traveled in threes, looking for easy marks.

Kirk smiled and relaxed.

"Sorry, guys," he said. "Whew! Thought you were some-one else."

Hannah, also having realized who was standing oppo-site them, stared at him, mouth open.

Kirk, still holding his jacket, draped his other arm across Hannah's shoulders.

"Did any of you fools see the bright flashing lights on

the pyramid?" he conversationally asked them.

The hoodless guy in the middle stopped leering. The way the other two flanked him, it was clear that he was the leader.

"No," he said. "Say, that thing with the jacket—that was really funny."

Kirk sighed. "Thanks," he said. "Hey, listen, it's cold. Care to join us in the bookstore? It's just down the block." He grinned and looked the stud-head in the eye. "I'll buy you a peppermint latté."

He was not amused. "No thanks, mate," he said. "We'll take your girl, though."

"No, I don't think you will," Kirk said calmly. His arm was still around Hannah. He reached down with his free hand, flipped the communicator open on his hip, punched in a quick code, and flipped it shut. Then he spun Hannah away from the trio and started walking away from them.

"Good luck with the surgery, guys," he called back.

Behind him he heard one of the wingmen say, "What surgery?"

"Jim, what are you doing?" asked Hannah, twisting to look over her shoulder. "They're coming!"

"I know." Kirk smiled. "Just walk."

A small group of people popped out of the fog and passed them heading the other direction, but Kirk knew it wouldn't matter to the Saints. They enjoyed brutal public beatings.

"Jim, I'm scared," whispered Hannah.

"Don't be," he said. "You are safe with me. I promise." He tightened his grip around her slender shoulders.

Behind him, he heard the metallic *ssshing!* of razor-knives sliding open.

Dr. Chandar adjusted the microscope. The live camera feed shuddered on the monitor. On-screen, the nanite-filled containment chamber slid sideways until the micro-camera centered on what looked like a hazy gray wall. It split the screen in half.

"See that?" said Chandar, pointing at the wall on the monitor. "That's the containment field boundary."

McCoy nodded. "The nanites can't pass through it," he said.

"Correct," said Chandar. "Yet *somehow*, via some sort of subatomic microsensor array perhaps, the nanite is able to get readings on things that lie *beyond* the impenetrable boundary."

"How do you know?" asked McCoy.

"Watch!"

Dr. Chandar picked up a long needle. He moved its tip to the edge of the nanite containment chamber locked in the microscope's specimen tray.

"This a sterile, chrome-plated teasing needle used for dissection," said Chandar. "Look, there it is."

On-screen, the needle's microfilament tip appeared as a massive, blocky figure just outside the containment wall. The nanites continued their lazy swirl.

"They're not too curious about it," said Chandar. "In fact, they ignore it, even if I tap the chamber." He smiled. "Now watch."

Chandar scraped the needle's sterile tip back and forth lightly across the back of his hand. "Let's add some Human epidermal cells, shall we?" Then he moved the needle tip back to the edge of the containment wall.

"Holy cow!" said McCoy.

The swarm was in a frenzy now. Bits gathered at the boundary, moving so rapidly that they blurred. In just seconds the swarm had blackened the screen as thousands of nanites pushed frantically against the barrier.

"Amazing," said Chandar. "There's clearly some kind of marker in my biology that triggers the swarm's curiosity."

"Have you tried this with other biological specimens?" asked McCoy.

"Dozens," said Chandar.

"And?"

"Well, the swarm finds them interesting at first," said Chandar. "But it seems that when its sensors determine that the sample isn't Human biology, the swarm deactivates."

"What about alien biology?"

Chandar set down the needle. "Same thing. Initial interest, then it drops away."

"So the swarm is particularly curious about Human cells," said McCoy.

"It seems so."

McCoy stared at the screen. With the skin sample gone, the swarm's frenzy had ended quickly. Nanites were drifting around the solution chamber again.

"Deactivates," repeated McCoy.

"What *are* they?" asked Dr. Chandar. "I wish we had our own swarm of these guys."

"Why?" asked McCoy.

"I tell you, Leonard," he said, "if we could tap into their telemetry and figure out how they tick, then maybe we could control them and turn them loose on themselves."

"Yeah, swarm and antiswarm," grumbled McCoy. "They could tear one another to subcellular bits. Then we could get on with our damned lives."

Chandar laughed. "No, Leonard, that's not what I mean," he said. "They could study themselves, model themselves, *learn* themselves, and then report to us what the hell they are."

McCoy glared at the monitor.

"I'd rather they just tore themselves apart," McCoy said.

"I understand," said Chandar. "It is dangerous, this swarm. And god only knows what it could do if turned completely loose. We could have a gray-goo scenario on our hands."

"What the hell is that?" asked McCoy.

"Gray goo?" said Chandar. "A self-replicating neural swarm that basically goes out of control and eats entire planets."

McCoy swiveled to face his friend. *"What?"*

"Don't worry, it's not a *likely* scenario, but it is possible," said Chandar.

"Explain," said McCoy.

"Gray goo is a term coined in the early days of nano-technology research," said Chandar. "It starts with a swarm of nanomachines, just like our nanites here. They're pro-grammed to self-replicate—to scavenge matter from an ecosystem, tear it apart at the cellular level, and then use the pieces to build copies of itself."

McCoy stared at the screen.

"In the gray-goo scenario, something goes wrong," continued Chandar. "Could be an error—an accidental mutation, say, or maybe a coding glitch. Or it could be deliberate—sabotage, or a doomsday war device. In any case, the swarm kicks into a frenzy of nonstop replication.

It attacks and breaks down every bit of matter it finds. It turns everything into a gray chemical soup of elemental pieces. Then the swarm's internal nanofactories use the soup to build nanite copies."

"Hence, gray goo," said McCoy.

"Frightening, isn't it?"

"It's the most frightening thing I've ever heard, Parag."

Dr. Chandar held out his hands. "Like I said, only *theoretically* possible," he said. "When you think about it, viruses are nearly perfect nano-entities. And yet they don't run amok, eating everything, breaking everything down into goo. Our planet's ecosystem has remarkable defense mechanisms that can fend off even the most aggressive viral attack, over time."

McCoy groaned. "Well, I feel *much* safer now," he said.

Chandar laughed. "I'm glad, Leonard." He gazed at the monitor again. "But the thing is, a nanoswarm could be an unprecedented research tool, if used properly."

"Right," said McCoy. "As long as it doesn't eat us first."

His pager suddenly beeped.

"Hmm," he said, checking it. "It seems I'm wanted in the shuttle hangar transporter room immediately." He looked up at Dr. Chandar. "It says . . . *on the double.*"

Chandar gestured toward the door.

"Run like the wind, Dr. McCoy!" he said with a smile.

Kirk pushed up his shirtsleeve, revealing a medallion strapped to his upper forearm. He tore it off and fastened it around Hannah's arm.

"What's this?" asked Hannah.

"See you in twenty minutes," said Kirk, giving her a quick kiss.

Behind them, the three Saints howled. Kirk looked back at them. They were huge.

"Okay, maybe thirty," he said.

"Jim?"

He flipped up a crystalline cover on the medallion and punched the inset red button. Targeting scanners got an instant coordinate lock on Hannah. Her molecular structure was scanned on a quantum level, her body was disassembled into a matter stream of subatomic particles, dumped into a pattern buffer, then transmitted via subspace frequency to the shuttle hangar at Starfleet Academy and finally reassembled on the transporter pad.

To the Saints, it just looked like she had just dissolved before them.

"What the *hell?*" shouted one Saint. "Where'd she go?"

Kirk shrugged. "I sent her home," he said. "I didn't want an unfair advantage over you."

Mongol Saints were famed street fighters—dirty and deadly. But Starfleet close-combat training was based on the brutally aggressive, efficient, no-nonsense principles of Krav Maga, originally the old Israeli Defense Force combat system. The fight was over in fourteen seconds. Kirk suffered a superficial razor-knife slash to his left forearm. The Saints suffered two dislocated elbows, one broken hand, one collapsed cheekbone, and three broken noses. And for Hannah, as well as all the other women in the neighborhood, Kirk inflicted a few additional nasty blows that promised to keep them out of commission for a little while.

When Hannah stepped off the shuttle hanger transporter pad in a daze, the console was unmanned. But most Starfleet transporter stations were preset to receive emergency transports at any time. She looked at the armband strapped around her bicep.

A uniformed man rushed in. When he saw her, he halted and folded his arms.

"I should have known," he said. What he thought was, *Where does he find these girls?*

Hannah looked at him. "Where am I?" she asked.

"This is the hunting ground of Cadet James T. Kirk," said the man. "I don't suppose you know him?"

Hannah looked around. "He's in trouble!" she blurted. Then with a hint of annoyance she added: "Who are you?"

"My name is McCoy, Leonard McCoy." He gave her a sharp look. "What do you mean, trouble?"

"Three guys were about to jump us," she said.

McCoy glanced at her arm. "So he slapped that thing on your arm and zapped you here," he said. "Tell me about the three guys. Where was this?"

"Big gangbangers," she said. "Like, *biker* big. Huge. Three of them. We were on Columbus Avenue."

"On the street?"

"Yes."

McCoy smiled. "Well, Jim should be here any minute."

Hannah frowned in disbelief. "Did I mention that there were three of them?" she asked. "*Three* guys?"

McCoy nodded. "Yes, you did," he said.

Hannah pulled the emergency transporter band off her arm and tossed it abruptly to McCoy.

"Why aren't you worried?" she asked sharply.

McCoy stepped toward her.

"I *am* worried," he said. He glanced at his watch. "Right about now, those three guys need a top-notch trauma center, and I'm not sure there's a good one in that neighborhood."

CH.10.12
Tanika Station

The following Monday morning, Dr. McCoy huddled with Team Delta in the ready room of Shuttle Hangar 1. He was there at Kirk's request to run preflight checkups before the five-man team boarded the *Gilliam*, a Class F-shuttle bound for the top-secret location of Tanika Station. The cadets wore the compression biosuits they'd been issued, an indication that their destination was in space.

Everyone was tense and silent. A burly crew-cut cadet named Raynor seemed to be even more tense than everyone else, and he paced back and forth.

"What's the delay?" he asked in irritation. "We've been here two hours, waiting."

As McCoy packed up his medical tricorder, he glanced around the room.

"You men are *unbelievably* ugly," he said. "That might have something to do with it."

"Really?" replied Glorak from a window overlooking the cargo bay. "You think so?"

"Yes," said McCoy. "You especially."

Glorak snorted a laugh. His Tellarite snout popped in and out.

"See?" said McCoy. He shook his head.

"He's right," said Marcus, a skinny cadet from Seattle. He pointed at Glorak. "You should be shot and processed in salt."

Glorak nodded back. "Along with your mother," he said politely.

Marcus, grinning, acknowledged defeat and held up his palm. Glorak reached over and high-fived him.

Kirk shot McCoy a grateful grin.

It had been a long weekend. On Saturday the team lost a member, a cadet named Simmons, who, despite his stellar Academy record—or maybe because of it—suddenly packed up and fled home to Omaha. To replace him Kirk had recommended Braxim, the Academy's only Xannon cadet. Kirk knew that his easygoing demeanor would be a plus for team chemistry. He needed someone to offset Raynor, who Kirk feared had a tendency to be a loose cannon. And he didn't need that on his team. Braxxy was strong and smart and had performed well with his own ATT team, which got ousted in the semifinal round of testing.

Across the room, Braxim stood up and tried to stretch. His micro-elastic biosuit clung to him like a second skin.

"These are decidedly uncomfortable for a man of my girth," he said. "But I guess it's better than bloating up like a week-old corpse." The biosuit's purpose was to maintain counterpressure in the vacuum of space, where decompression caused Humanoid flesh to swell up to twice its normal size.

Kirk grinned over at McCoy. "Sure you don't want to join us up there, Bones?" he said.

"People should just stay on their planets," muttered McCoy.

Braxim laughed his foghorn laugh.

"Doctor, I'm tempted to agree with you," he said. "My Xanno ancestors emigrated from rock to rock for four hundred and fifty years. We planet-hopped across two quadrants, finding nothing but pestilence and racist rejection. We crossed mountains, deserts, oceans, voids, and asteroid belts looking for a home. My people camped on countless miserable way-station planets until we found New Xannon."

Suddenly a red light flashed over the ready-room door.

"Team Delta," called a voice over the speakers. "Your shuttle is ready. Prepare to board."

Raynor punched the air. "Yes!" he said.

"Please proceed to Pad Fourteen," added the voice.

As the five cadets began to gather up their gear, McCoy approached Kirk looking a bit embarrassed. Seeing this, Kirk asked, "What's up, Bones?"

"I'm supposed to give you this," said McCoy.

He slipped a small felt bag tied with green ribbon into Kirk's hands. Kirk untied and opened it. Inside was a botanist's eyepiece on a lanyard, and a note.

The note read:

Always check for glands on the underside of leaves. Look for growth patterns and try to figure out, "Why?" Never assume the plant you see is all there is. You are damn sexy when you're about to kick some ass. I'm off at seven.   Hannah xo

Smiling, Kirk folded the note and slipped it with the eyepiece into a hip pouch on his biosuit.

"And let me add, Jim, this girl is a *something else*," said McCoy, widening his eyes.

Kirk grinned. "She's a good one," he said.

McCoy nodded. "I like her," he said.

"Me too."

"Although she does remind me a bit of my ex-wife," said McCoy with a dark look.

Kirk clapped McCoy on the shoulder. "Friend, not every bright, beautiful girl is out to tear the flesh from your bones," he said.

"I hope not," replied McCoy. "I'll walk out with you."

The team walked single file between the rows of support craft lining the walls of Shuttle Hangar 1. Behind Kirk and McCoy, Braxim was still talking about his home world.

"New Xannon is a *beautiful* place, my friends, much like your Earth!" he exclaimed. "Yet it is thirty-two thousand light-years from our planet of origin, and that makes me sad." He shook his head. "I sometimes wonder if the tales are fantastic myths."

Up ahead, McCoy could see the sign marking LANDING PAD 14. There, red landing lights flashed on the *Gilliam* as the nacelles that housed the twin ion-impulse engines began to whine.

At the shuttle door, McCoy grabbed Kirk's hand and gave it a firm shake.

"Good luck, Captain," he said.

"Thanks, Doctor," said Kirk.

As Kirk hopped aboard, Braxim stepped up behind him, eyes twinkling. "By winning today, I honor my ancestors, Dr. McCoy," he said.

"Yes, I'm sure word will spread clear back to your origin world, wherever that is," said McCoy.

"Perhaps so," said Braxim. "But it would take many years to reach the core ward sectors of the Delta Quadrant."

Frowning, McCoy watched the big Xanno duck into the passenger compartment.

"Delta Quadrant?" he repeated.

Uhura's heels clicked sharply on the pavement as she walked across campus toward the Institute of Xenology building. The irritation in her throat and chest had subsided considerably, with only a mild tickle remaining.

At the institute's entry checkpoint she put her eye to the iris scanner. The device beeped and said: "Nyota Uhura, cadet first." When the door hissed open, she stepped to the reception desk and flashed her security badge.

"Hi, Jerry," she said.

"Hey, Nyota!" said the big security guard sitting at the desk. "Where you been?"

"Trust me, you don't want to know," she replied.

Jerry pointed at the sign-in sheet. "You got visitors waiting for you in the lab," he said. "Couple of doctors."

"What? I just left a full physical exam," said Uhura with annoyance. She read the names on the sheet and frowned. "Yep, that one's on my medical team. I don't know this other guy."

"I bet they just like checking your pulse," said Jerry with a wink.

Uhura gave him a look. He put his hands up.

"I'm just saying," he said with a grin.

When she reached the lab, Dr. McCoy rose from his chair and said, "Hello, Cadet." Another young man in a lab coat stood and nodded.

"Doctor, your interns just checked my lungs twenty minutes ago," she said.

"I'm not here about your lungs," replied McCoy. "It's about your translations."

Uhura looked surprised. "What about them?"

McCoy gestured to the man next to him. "Cadet Uhura, this is Dr. Parag Chandar," he said. "He runs the nanotech lab over in Hawking Hall."

"A pleasure," said Chandar, shaking Uhura's hand and bowing.

Uhura smiled. "So what's up?"

Chandar smiled brightly. "We have some information that might be useful for you," he said.

Orbiting Earth at an altitude of two hundred fifty miles above the equator, the shuttle *Gilliam* fired a small side thruster, starting a gentle spin. Its nose pointed toward the center of a massive rotating space platform; the shuttle's rotation soon synched with the platform's spin. Then the *Gilliam* nudged forward into a large rectangular docking bay.

"Helmets on," called the pilot. "Prepare for EVA."

Team Delta exchanged looks. EVA: extravehicular activity. A spacewalk.

"Wow," said Raynor.

"This is it," Braxim added.

Kirk reached down and pulled a pressurized helmet out of the compartment under his seat.

"Let's do it," Kirk said.

The lightweight helmet slid over Kirk's head then locked under a foamed neoprene flap in his biosuit's neckline for a tight seal. He connected the helmet's air tube to a small dual-purpose backpack; the pack held three hours' worth of breathable air plus a set of small ion thruster-jets for spacewalk maneuvers. ATT program cadets got lots of training in biosuits, so Team Delta was ready to go in less than a minute.

On the flight up, the team had received a live video briefing from a simulated Mission Control. The dour-looking flight controller, Commander Jack Stetmann, appeared on-screen and reported the following sequence of "events" to brief them:

- Three days ago, Starfleet Intelligence intercepted a signal from a deep-space object of substantial mass.
- A patrol craft had tracked the coordinates to an active space platform of advanced design.
- Attempts to communicate with the facility got no response.
- A security recon team discovered a simple airlock, then entered and established an outpost.
- Preliminary visual and sensor scans revealed what appeared to be a vast alien ecosystem.

"A floating greenhouse," the commander had called it. "We've designated it Tanika Station. Captain Kirk, your team is being deployed as a science unit for observation and sampling. Questions?"

Kirk said, "Any sentient life-forms? Inhabitants?"

"Negative."

"Anything moving?" asked Kirk.

"Negative. Other than water."

Kirk checked his notes. "Breathable atmosphere?"

"It appears so," answered Commander Stetmann. "No

noxious gases, just oxygen-based gases. However, the security team conducted no tests for microcontaminants."

"Noted," said Kirk. "Aside from the airlock, any other mechanical systems evident?"

"None visible, Captain."

Kirk noted his phrasing, and checked his notes again. "Artificial gravity?"

Stetmann nodded. "There is gravity plating in the hull."

Kirk smiled. "So we're looking at a walk in the park."

Stetmann's face remained inscrutable. "Not sure what you mean, Captain."

"Tanika Station appears to be an uninhabited alien conservatory of sorts," said Kirk. "Like an arboretum. A park."

"So it seems," replied Commander Stetmann.

Glorak leaned toward the screen. "Do you recommend side arms at the ready, Commander?"

"Phasers are *always* recommended in alien settings, Cadet," said Stetmann.

The EVA was simple and uneventful.

A few quick bursts of the backpack jets propelled all five cadets to the airlock at the far end of the docking bay. A single handle opened the door to the interior chamber, which was big enough for a platoon of twenty cadets. Inside, another handle closed and pressurized the airlock. Kirk immediately found himself standing on the floor.

"Ah, the graviton plate automatically activates," said Glorak.

Seconds later, the team stepped out into Tanika Station. None of them were quite prepared for what they saw.

"Mother of god," said Cadet Marcus.

Nobody else spoke.

The small clearing just beyond the airlock doorway was a like an elevated platform. It offered a panoramic view of the station's interior, which was shaped like a vast oval bowl. The space was at least a mile long, three football fields wide, and as tall as a fifteen-story building. It dropped in toward the center, where a silver lake glittered at the bottom of the bowl.

Kirk raised a digital optics scope to his visor and surveyed the terrain. Around the oval, about a dozen narrow streams flowed down the sides of the landscape bowl— the water originated from spouts low in the station wall at the top. The streams wound through lush jungle vegetation before emptying into the central lake. A system of narrow walking trails crisscrossed over the streams and one another. Above, two wide solar strips ran the length of the ceiling, casting a full-spectrum glow. The colors were remarkably vibrant.

"This is . . . beyond words," he murmured.

One of the spouts gushed from the wall just thirty yards from the airlock door. A dirtlike path led from the airlock down a gentle slope, then curved along the running stream.

"Is that actually water?" asked Glorak.

"My scanner says yes," said Braxim, holding up his tricorder. "No surprise, really. Water is one of the most abundant molecules in the universe and seems essential for any living system."

"These all flow into that central lake," said Kirk, pointing.

"Incredible," said Glorak.

Kirk took in the stunning panorama one more time, then turned his mind to the action plan. "Let's keep the helmets on for now, gentlemen," he said. "Mr. Raynor, take some air readings, please."

"Right, Captain." Raynor unpacked his tricorder, added an attachment, and started running scans.

Braxim gazed around in wonder.

"This place is rich with life!" he exclaimed. "You can just *feel* it!"

Kirk said, "It feels you too, Mr. Braxim. And it might not *like* you."

Braxim held up his arms and turned around in a circle. "I am no threat!" he called out.

Kirk had to smile at that.

Tanika Station did indeed teem with life, albeit strange life. A cool, humid breeze blew through the landscape. It felt like an English garden—natural and a bit wild, not the orderly rows of foliage found in a typical greenhouse.

"Sensors indicate good air composition, no sign of microbial pathogens," called Raynor. "Nothing bad to breathe, Captain."

"Okay, I'll give it a go," said Kirk.

He unlocked his helmet and lifted it an inch or so, breathing in the Tanika Station air. It was moist, pungent, and fragrant. After inhaling shallowly twenty times and feeling no dizziness or other effects, Kirk removed the helmet and tried a few deep breaths.

"I think it's good," he said. "Raynor, keep your hat on for a while, just in case."

"Aye, Captain," replied Raynor.

Glorak, Marcus, and Braxim pulled off their helmets and clipped them to their utility belts. The team spent the next twenty minutes setting up a rudimentary base camp with lab equipment near the airlock door. When they finished that task, Raynor popped off his helmet too.

Kirk slung a pack over his shoulders. He stepped to the trailhead. Ahead, the colors were so vivid, Kirk was reminded of a Matisse watercolor.

"Okay, gentlemen," he said. "Let's move to Phase One recon."

Uhura stared in horror at the monitor on her lab workstation. On-screen, a black swarm was imploding an amoeba proteus.

"Those . . . *things* were in my nose and throat?" she said in disgust.

"Yes," said McCoy.

"And you say they can go *anywhere?*" she said.

"Almost," said McCoy.

"We were able to contain these specimens in a quantum field chamber," said Chandar.

"Well *that's* nice," said Uhura.

McCoy nodded. "I find them just as disturbing and creepy as you do, Cadet," he said. "But now you can see how the Doctor, damn his name, could remove Human internal organs without incisions or any other sign of trauma. See, he didn't actually *remove* the organs. He directed these little bastards to enter the victim's body and *eat* them."

Uhura just stared at the monitor. A flash of anger lit her dark eyes.

"That's beyond evil," she said.

"I fully agree," said McCoy.

"But how, exactly, does this information help my translation research?" asked Uhura.

Dr. Chandar froze the video screen.

He said, "Data extracted from the nanite swarm indicates that its place of origin is deep in the Delta Quadrant. No doubt this mysterious serial killer is a Delta alien as well."

Uhura considered this for a moment. Then she said, "You're suggesting that the killer might be speaking in some language indigenous to the Delta Quadrant?"

"Correct," said Chandar.

She shook her head. "Doctor, the Federation has never had *any* contact, direct or indirect, with any Delta race or entity. Thus I've had absolutely no experience with any Delta language."

"Actually, you have," said Chandar, smiling.

Uhura frowned. "What do you mean?"

"The Xanno emigrated from Delta space," said Chandar.

Uhura gave him a skeptical look. "I've heard that, but I assumed it was just folklore," she said. "A creation myth."

"Tell that to a Xanno," said McCoy.

He pulled a sheet of paper from a folder and set it on the console in front of Uhura.

"What's this?" she asked.

"It's a highly classified, Priority Three level study of Xanno history compiled by Starfleet Intelligence prior to admission of New Xannon into the United Federation of Planets in 2229," said McCoy. "You'll find that the evidence for the Delta origin of the Xannon race is pretty definitive."

Uhura scanned the document.

"Okay," she said. "But I still don't get how that helps me. There must be hundreds of thousands of Delta Quadrant languages. Why would this alien killer know Xanno, especially if the Xanno left that quadrant more than four hundred fifty years ago? Seems like a long shot."

"It does, doesn't it?" said McCoy. He pulled another sheet of paper from his folder and handed it to Uhura.

"And what's this?" she asked.

"Eyewitness accounts of the attack on Cadet Gaila from the police report," said McCoy. "Note the parts I highlighted. Both Jim Kirk and Braxim describe the same thing: the odd behavior of the so-called 'black fog' that suddenly rose up around Braxxy. That was *undoubtedly* a nanite swarm. And both cadets believed that the killer was speaking to Braxim when he made the statement recorded in the 911 call."

Uhura's eyes widened. "Yes, that *is* very interesting."

Dr. Chandar nodded vigorously. "And I find it quite interesting that the swarm rejected Cadet Braxim."

"Rejected?" said Uhura.

"Yes!" said Chandar excitedly. "Given what we know of the swarm's inquisitive tendencies, it seems most unusual that it made no attempt to enter our Xannon friend and ... well, conduct its *research*, as it were."

"Yes, it looks like the good Doctor gave Braxxy a quick scan and then *spoke* to him," said McCoy.

"As if in recognition!" cried Chandar, rubbing his hands.

"Possibly," said Uhura. "Of course, Braxim didn't recognize the spoken language either. So it wasn't Xanno." Her eyes lit up. "Or at least, not Xanno as it's usually spoken."

McCoy noted her sudden enthusiasm.

"What do you mean?" he asked.

Uhura started punching buttons on the console. She said, "My last scan for Romulan sonic fragments produced some match results. It seems possible that the recorded phrases are actually scrambled bits of Romulan, at least in part. But we could only match fragments to about sixty percent of the first phrase. And of course, they made no sense in the order they were spoken."

"But now you'll scan for Xanno fragments too?" said Dr. Chandar, grasping what she was thinking.

"Computer," said Uhura to the console. "Let's look for fragments in Sample One again. This time run it with subroutine XAX-zero-one, please."

"Acknowledged," said the computer.

The console made a rapid series of *ping!* sounds. Uhura smiled big at McCoy and Chandar.

"Each ping is a match," she said.

"Thirty-one matches found," said the console.

"Okay, show us the original spectrogram, please," said Uhura.

A graph filled with jagged white lines popped up on-screen. It was the digital sound-picture Uhura had created from the 911 recordings of the killer's spoken words.

"Those white frequency bands are the killer's words to Cadet Braxim," she said. "Computer, superimpose the Romulan sonic fragment matches onto this graph, please."

About two-thirds of the white bands turned red.

"The red bands are the parts that appear to be fragments of Romulan words," said Uhura. "Computer, now superimpose the Xanno matches as well."

All of the remaining white bands turned blue, and many of the red bands turned purple where the red and blue overlapped.

"Wow," said McCoy.

"Okay," said Uhura, looking at the spectrogram. "As

you can see, the Romulan and Xanno speech is not only fragmented, but also scrambled together in overlapping tracks." She shook her head in frustration. "Unscrambling that mess would be like decrypting a coded military communiqué. I just don't have the computing power to do that."

McCoy and Chandar exchanged a look.

"Cadet," said McCoy. "I think it's time you met the Cheetah."

Team Delta's Phase One game plan was to simply explore, observe, and record. The original consensus had been to allot just one hour for this activity. But the team quickly tripled that time based on the sheer size of the specimen collection field.

Those first few hours in Tanika Station flew by fast. As Kirk jotted notes on his e-pad near a stand of spiraling lemon-yellow shoots that curled upward into spectacular interlocking patterns, he glanced over at Braxim. The big Xanno sat raptly next to a low murmuring waterfall.

"I could live here, Jim," he said, watching water flow over a stacked jumble of smooth rocks.

Kirk closed the e-pad. "Maybe that's possible," he said.

Braxim smiled. "How so, my friend?"

Kirk gazed up at the spiraling yellow plants.

"Braxxy, this platform doesn't exist just to test a handful of lowly Starfleet cadets once a year," he said. "It's clearly some sort of advanced bioscience facility."

"It is a *magnificent* space!" Braxim boomed. He pounded his great barrel chest a couple of times for emphasis. "If I could work here every day, I would consider life a daily blessing."

Kirk smiled, thinking about Hannah. "Yeah, I know someone else who'd share that sentiment." It wasn't the first time that Hannah had popped into his head. It seemed he couldn't stop thinking about her.

Nearby, Marcus was snapping holo-photos of a patch of what looked like nubby red ice plant growing on the stream's bank. The camera flashes were as bright as lightning, and Kirk winced. Not far from Marcus, Glorak stood calf-deep in the rushing stream.

"I've never seen such dense moss colonies," called Glorak. "Look at those finely articulated sporophytes over there." He pointed toward a cluster of moss capsules, all brilliant orange and fire red. "Look at the colors!"

Kirk glanced over at Marcus. "What's your take on this place, Marcus?"

Marcus adjusted his camera lens. "I grew up near the Olympic peninsula, west of Seattle," he said. "It's a temperate rain forest—a jungle, but cool, not tropical." He aimed at the spiraling yellow plants. "This place is a temperate rain forest on steroids."

Just up the trail, Raynor waved his tricorder scanner around the paddlelike fronds of a bright green fern shuddering in the breeze.

Kirk called to him. "What about you, Raynor?"

"I don't know, man," replied Raynor. "Something about this place feels weird."

Kirk had the same feeling, especially as they'd explored lower into the bowl and gotten closer to the central lake. A basin of sediment surrounded it, and the air smelled more pungent the closer they got to the silvery water.

"It does feel different here," grunted Glorak from the stream.

"Yeah," whispered Marcus loudly. "It feels like we're being watched."

Kirk agreed. Somewhere, fifteen or twenty vigilant test administrators and Starfleet senior officers were observing and logging their every move and spoken word. But this feeling was more than that. To Kirk, it almost felt as if the *environment* of Tanika Station was watching them.

After three hours of careful observing, imaging, and note-taking—all the while following Starfleet science directives to the letter—Team Delta climbed back to base camp to prepare for their Phase Two specimen-collection activities. As the cadets unpacked their science kits, Kirk remembered Hannah's gift, the botanist's eyepiece. He pulled it from his hip pouch and slung the lanyard around his neck.

"We Tellarites are deeply fond of nature," said Glorak as he loaded items into a pack.

"Yes, it's an excellent place to root for truffles," said Marcus.

Glorak laughed. He was always good-natured about the endless pig jokes people tossed his way.

"Well," he replied, "speaking of that, I suggest we start by rooting in that central basin around the lake. The growth patterns there are unusual, and the specimens promise to be quite curious."

"Yeah, there's some wacky stuff down there," agreed Marcus.

"Good plan," said Kirk. "That basin is clearly the nexus of this environment."

The team set off down the path. As Kirk trekked between rows of bizarre periwinkle horsetails waving in the artificial breeze, he felt Hannah's eyepiece swinging on his neck. He wondered how she would be running this show. As they descended into the basin surrounding the lake, Kirk noticed that the pungent, almost metallic smell was now stronger.

Up ahead, Glorak suddenly stopped, looking confused.

"What are these?" he asked. He turned to Kirk.

Glorak stood next to a pair of shaggy plants, gnarled with yellow vines and hung with multicolored, fruitlike pods. They grew from a mound of black, sludgy silt on the stream bank. Each stood about three feet tall and spread equally wide. Each was a remarkably complex coil of shapes and colors.

"Wow," said Marcus, unpacking his camera.

"Those weren't here before," said Raynor, rubbing his crew-cut hair in a move Kirk had come to recognize as a stress tick. He glanced off to the left. "Look, there's more."

Sure enough, several dozen of the bright, twisted plants grew along the lakeshore. Some were bigger and more colorful, featuring more knots of tissue, bulb, and vine—clearly in a more advanced state of growth. But others were no bigger than small houseplants.

"They're beautiful," said Braxim.

"Yes!" said Glorak, excited. He slung off his pack and slid a sterile plant trowel from a side sleeve. "They obviously grow with great speed. If we can get one of the smaller samples under the microscope at base camp immediately, we may be able to record some of the cellular growth."

Kirk just stared at the nearest organism. He took a few steps closer to it.

Meanwhile, the others were following the Delta game plan. Marcus locked his camera atop a titanium tripod and opened its legs wide.

"I'll overlay the collection grid while you guys snip samples," he said.

Meanwhile, Raynor was checking his plan notes. "Okay, we'll need images and samples of primary organ structures from a healthy, mature specimen," he said. He unsheathed his laser pruning shears and stepped toward one of the taller plants. "This one looks good and strong."

Next to him, Braxim began to pull out plastic specimen bags. "You snip, I'll collect," he said to Raynor.

As all of this was going on around Kirk, he watched silently. His mind was racing.

"Hey, stop!" he said suddenly.

All four of his team members stopped and looked at him.

Kirk stepped toward the mature plant that Raynor had been about to cut a sample from. "This plant looks familiar," he said.

Raynor shrugged. "So?"

Kirk pulled out his e-pad and tapped the screen a few times. He held it out toward Raynor.

"Check it out, man," he said.

Four windows were opened on-screen. Each displayed an image of a different plant specimen they'd studied higher up in the Tanika Station bowl. All four species were now visible as organ systems integrated on the new plant growing on the bank.

The other cadets examined the images.

"Wow," said Marcus. "This is a superplant."

"These other species must be migrating downstream and combining somehow," said Glorak.

"Yes," said Braxim. "They're definitely merging together into more complex structures."

"I don't like the word *structures*," said Kirk. "Let's call them bodies with organs, shall we? Because that's what they are."

"What a discovery!" said Glorak. He held up his trowel. "We *must* dig out a sample." Then he leaned closer to Kirk and whispered, "Dissection and learning its recombinant mechanisms could be the key to winning this scenario, Jim."

Kirk shook his head. "No. Wait," he said. "All we did was follow a path. Any fool could make that so-called discovery. If the Science mission final is that simple, I'm sure even Viktor Tikhonov passes with flying colors."

"So what are you saying?" asked Raynor. "You think these plants are intelligent? Because they sure don't look like it."

"Neither do you," said Kirk, "but we don't just chop *you* up into lab samples."

"Jim, it's just a plant," protested Glorak. "You eat vegetables, do you not?"

"Guys, look around," said Kirk. "What's the basic dynamic of this ecosystem? So far it's entities of lower complexity combining into entities of higher complexity." Kirk gestured toward the big, complex plant. "Does that look like a vegetable? And do you think all this recombinant magic stops with him? We've only been here three hours! In three more hours, this plant might evolve into Viktor Tikhonov."

The group continued to look skeptical.

"But then it would be a vegetable," said Marcus, breaking the tension.

Kirk laughed. "Look, all I'm saying is this: If we take our samples, what further development have we stopped? And what are we killing in the process of collecting samples?"

Raynor just stared at his laser shears with intensity. He was itching to collect samples.

"I know your story, Kirk," he said. "We all do."

Kirk turned to Raynor. This was it, he knew: The moment your crew goes with you or not. There are moments where command is won or lost. Kirk felt it here. And there was no formula to follow. Just your gut.

"What's up, Raynor?" he asked.

"Most of your life, Starfleet was the last place you wanted to be," said Raynor. "But me, I've wanted to be a starship bridge officer since I was six years old." He glanced over at the others. "What if he's wrong, guys? What if that's just a dumb plant, and we fail our Science mission final because of some ridiculous tree-hugging theory?" Raynor rubbed furiously at his head. He was getting very agitated.

Kirk looked at the lake; it was as smooth as a mirror. He took a deep breath. He knew he was right and Raynor was wrong. But Raynor's point was valid, and he needed to be dealt with in a way that wouldn't alienate him. He tried to think from Raynor's perspective. What did he know about him? The guy was obsessive about detail in lab sciences. Cadets hated being his partner for lab work because he was never satisfied with results. Kirk knew how to proceed.

"What are you trying to say?" Kirk asked, looking him straight in the eyes.

"I'm not saying anything, Captain," said Raynor.

Kirk nodded. "I just don't want to be a sloppy scientist. I don't want to make critical mistakes because I hurried when I didn't have to. Let's just take a step back here, okay?"

Raynor's eyes widened, but he didn't speak.

"This basin down here," said Kirk, "this silt, the lake—it's different. It's special. We all feel it. It's some kind of broth of life." He held out his arm. "But it's still outside our normal frame of reference."

Braxim folded his arms. "Maybe we should stop thinking of this place as a science test," he said.

Kirk nodded. "See, 1 think we unconsciously assume that whoever built Tanika Station must be guys who look like us," he said, gesturing around him. "But if this was an actual alien worldlet, maybe they wouldn't. Maybe they'd look like *him*." He pointed at the plant. "This guy might be the creator, for all we'd know right now. Or at least a link to the creator's mind."

Raynor stepped up to the gnarled plant. "1 guess 1 just don't see it," he said.

"Look, I'm not saying you're wrong, Jack," said Kirk. "I'm just saying, no careless science. Let's stick with nonintrusive methods for a while . . . you know, before we start cutting up our hosts right here in their living room."

Raynor thought, and finally nodded. "Yeah, okay."

"Cool," said Kirk.

It was then that Kirk had his first insight into the mind of the Doctor prowling the city fog miles below.

He's an alien in a place he doesn't understand yet.

He's a scientist.

And his research is sloppy.

Meanwhile, Marcus resumed his photography. He rotated the camera thirty degrees at a time atop the tall, slender tripod to lock in images of the surrounding specimen grid. As the strobe flashed rapidly, Kirk squinted again at its dazzling brightness. He noted the tall, slender shape formed by the three tripod legs: an elongated pyramid with lightning pulsing at the top. He'd seen it before, walking down Columbus Avenue with Hannah.

Those flashes atop the Transamerica Pyramid were alien imaging scans of the city.

Somebody was up there shooting a grid overlay of San Francisco, he thought. *For their specimen-collection activity.*

Suddenly the interior of Tanika Station was pierced by the loud, throbbing, intermittent wail of a siren. All activity froze as Team Delta gazed up at the sound source somewhere on the station ceiling.

Kirk's communicator beeped. He flipped it open.

"Kirk here," he said.

"Delta, this is Mission Control," replied the voice of Commander Stetmann. There was an edge to his voice that hadn't been present in the mission briefing. "We have a situation."

Now a deep, metallic groan echoed from the far wall of the bowl. It overwhelmed the pulsing wail of the siren.

"What's going on, Commander?" Kirk shouted over the noise.

"Sensors indicate a station hull breach," replied Stetmann.

Kirk hesitated. Was this real . . . or part of the simulation? He looked in the direction of the sound. It didn't sound simulated.

"Roger that, Control," said Kirk. "Is it reparable?"

"Negative on that, Delta," replied Stetmann. "We estimate total hull integrity failure in less than sixty minutes." There was a pause. Then: "Get your team out of there, Captain. Fast."

"Acknowledged," said Kirk. "Kirk out."

He flipped the communicator shut and turned to his away team.

"Helmets on, gentlemen!" he yelled.

CH.11.12
Pyramid Scheme

As the *Gilliam*'s retro-thrusters pushed it backward out of Tanika Station's docking bay, Kirk's gaze was glued to the shuttle window. He was anxious to see the platform's exterior hull. He was still unsure what was real and what was simulation.

But before the *Gilliam* could clear the bay walls, duranium blast shutters slid down over all windows in the shuttle's passenger cabin.

Impulsively Kirk pulled off his harness and rushed forward into the cockpit. But he arrived just in time to see blast shutters slide down over the cockpit windows as well.

"You might want to buckle up, Captain," said the pilot.

"Do you know what's going on out there?" asked Kirk.

"I've got orders to get clear fast, so that's what I'm doing," said the pilot.

Kirk nodded. He returned to his aisle seat and yanked down the seat harness.

The pilot's voice came over the cabin speakers.

"Welcome back to the *Gilliam*," he said. "This is Captain Spruce, your pilot. Due to the possibility of an imminent explosive decompression of massive force, we're going to raise our deflector shields. I hope you're buckled up, gentlemen. If it comes, it will be off the scale. We'll be accelerating away *very* fast. Full-scale acceleration coming in five . . . four . . . three . . . two . . . one."

And then a g-force of 6.7 plastered Kirk into his seat.

His vision went gray for a few seconds, then black. He felt himself creep up to the very edge of consciousness, but the acceleration halted after about ten seconds. Kirk was disoriented at first, but recovered quickly, as did the other cadets. Then the blast shutters slid open all around the cabin.

Kirk and Raynor, who was buckled into the window seat, both leaned to look out. But Tanika Station was not visible from their angle.

Kirk sank back into his seat. So did Raynor.

"Do you think it really exploded?" asked Kirk.

Raynor shrugged.

"If that station had a catastrophic decompression, they're going to have a *big* debris problem downstairs," said Kirk.

Raynor just looked at him.

Kirk nodded. "Never mind," he said.

Then they all sat in silence for a long while.

Kirk had plenty of time to wonder if Team Delta would get another shot at a Science mission final. Or had they already failed? Their Phase One observation, mapping, and site-recording activity had been good at least. Or . . . well, maybe not. He had no way to compare Delta's performance to that of Tikhonov's Alpha squad.

All Kirk could do was sit and wait.

Uhura entered the office of Dr. Patricia Park, a well-known mathematician and head of the cryptology lab at the college. Dr. Park was sitting at her desk, shuffling papers and muttering to herself. When she spotted Uhura she jumped up and stuck out her hand.

"Patty Park!" she announced.

Uhura stepped forward and shook hands. "Cadet Uhura, Professor," she said. "It's an honor."

"Yes, I've heard about you from Spock," she said loudly.

Uhura was taken aback, but managed to say, "Oh. Well, good things, I hope."

"Are you kidding me?" blurted Dr. Park. She started laughing. Then she waved a hand. "Anyway, let's get down to it." She suddenly ducked out of sight behind her desk.

Uhura stood there, smiling awkwardly. After almost a full minute she said, "Professor?"

Park popped up so quickly Uhura almost screamed.

"Yes, Cadet?"

"Sorry," said Uhura, bringing a hand to her mouth. "I thought you . . . might need some help."

"Oh, we *all* need help," said Dr. Park.

She looked at Uhura for several seconds.

Uhura smiled uneasily. She was about to speak to break the awkward silence when Dr. Park snapped her fingers and pointed at her.

"Ah, right, you're the Romulan project," she said. "Right. I knew that!" There was a knock on the door. "Come in!" she called absently.

Dr. McCoy opened the door and entered the office. As he was about to introduce himself, Dr. Park suddenly dropped out of sight again. McCoy stopped short and frowned at Uhura, who shrugged. But this time Park popped right back up with a folder.

Reaching out his hand, McCoy said, "Professor Park, I'm Dr. Leonard McCoy from the medical college." Dr. Park shook hands with such great vigor that McCoy almost burst out laughing. He managed to say, "Sorry I'm late. I was in the commandant's office." He glanced over at Uhura. "Cadet, your friend Detective Bogenn from SFPD was there with some new developments in the case."

"We'll talk later," said Uhura, nodding.

Dr. Park plucked a sheet of paper from the folder and held it up.

"Here's your first decryption," she announced.

McCoy looked at it. "The whole thing? This soon?"

Park smiled. "Doctor, would you call a family into surgery and say, 'Folks, I'm about halfway done with that triple heart bypass, I just wanted to chat about my progress'?"

McCoy was amused. "No," he said. Then he added, "I like your style, Professor."

"Grade-grubbing doesn't work in this office, mister," said Dr. Park with a sly look. She turned to Uhura. "Well, the Romulan part was easy. Almost beneath us, I must say. The phonic scrambling is an old Romulan military code, one that United Earth Intelligence Agency cracked almost a hundred years ago, not long after the war kicked into full gear."

"A hundred years ago?" repeated McCoy. "How the hell does a guy get a code like that?"

"Good question," said Dr. Park. "The Romulans stopped using this basic encryption method long before the war ended, and it's never been seen since. Once we tapped into the archives, Cheetah nailed the Romulan bits in about two minutes. The Xanno bits weren't much tougher, because the encryption pattern was the same. The user simply applied the scramble to the Xanno language."

She slapped the paper onto the desk. Uhura pulled a

pencil from her case and looked at the breakdown.

"I don't know Xanno well enough yet," she said. "But there's enough overlap that I can probably get most of this." She penciled in a translation quickly. "Okay, this is the first phrase, the one spoken to Cadet Braxim," she said.

McCoy stepped up beside her to read it.

Your species has already been absorbed.

"Absorbed?" asked McCoy. "What does that mean?"

Uhura looked down at the Romulan version again.

"The Romulan verb translating to *absorbed* may also be interpreted in a slightly more aggressive way, depending on context," she said. "Something that in English might be more like *incorporated* . . . or *assimilated*."

"Your species has already been assimilated," said McCoy with a wry grin. "Sounds like Xannon anatomy is old news to the Doctor."

"Maybe because of their shared roots in the Delta Quadrant," said Uhura. "They've encountered each other before."

"Exactly what I was thinking," said McCoy. "The Doctor is only interested in organs he hasn't eaten before."

Uhura looked up at Dr. Park, who had been listening carefully and had a funny look on her face. "What is it, Professor?"

"Doesn't it strike you as *odd* that this person you recorded is speaking directly to folks using a Romulan military code scramble?" she asked. "I mean, this speech is coming right out of his mouth, right? Or is he wearing some sort of scrambler device, like a voice-filter mask that also encrypts speech? And if so, why? Doesn't he want to actually *communicate* with the people he's speaking to? Why speak in a code they cannot possibly understand? Or is he just an idiot?"

Uhura and McCoy looked at each other for a second. Then McCoy scratched his chin.

"Good questions," he said.

"I'm sure the SFPD is wondering the same thing," said Uhura. "Although, of course, they don't have the benefit of our decrypted translations yet."

Dr. Park brightened. "Ah yes," she said. She pulled a second sheet of paper from the folder and put it on the desk. "This one had the same parameters, although the third language complicated things enough that Cheetah really chugged and took an extra forty-seven seconds to decode it."

Uhura's scans had found Romulan, Xanno, and English phonic fragments scrambled onto three overlapping tracks on the second recording, the one made from the Orion woman's emergency call.

Dr. Park smiled at Uhura. "And I have a surprise for you on this one," she said.

Uhura was intrigued. "This is the recording that ended with all that static?" she said.

"Yes and no," said Dr. Park. "It ended with what might *sound* like static to the untrained ear. But my people are trained."

McCoy and Uhura exchanged a look.

Dr. Park continued. "That static is actually a holo-image data transmission. Again, kind of old school, and kind of strange. Who speaks in binary file-transfer language?"

Once again, Uhura put pencil to paper and came up with a translation. "With the language overlaps, we have different shades of meaning on some of the words," she said. "Again, the static is at the end. So that's where I left a placeholder for the image data transfer."

The translation she wrote down:

Species unknown to us. Acquire/assimilate samples that contrast with 5618. Reassemble/regroup at base [IMAGE DATA].

McCoy read it and shook his head.

"He spoke this, and then the cold-blooded bastard released his nanite swarm," he said, "to model her liver, heart, and an organ unique to Orion women called the pherol gland. And in the course of modeling them, it destroyed them."

Uhura pointed at the number. "What does five-six-one-eight refer to?" she asked.

"I don't know," said McCoy. "That same number is part of each nanite's ID stamp."

Uhura turned to Dr. Park. "So what's the surprise?" she asked.

"This," said the professor.

She opened a drawer and pulled out a small holo-projection disc the size of a coaster. It was the kind of disc that people put on their desks to display favorite holo-images. You could plug a data cube full of images into the device. The 3-D images projected up from the disk and cycled every few seconds.

"It was easy to decode the raw data—it's just numbers, after all," said Dr. Park. "The harder step was to find archival programs that could read the old code and project the image," said Dr. Park. "But we found them. Then we just popped it all onto this cube."

She plugged a cube into the projector disk.

"So based on the translation," said McCoy, "this image we're about to see is the base where, apparently, a regroup was supposed to happen."

Dr. Park pressed the on/off button on the back of the holo-disc.

Up rose an old-fashioned, greenish hologram of the Transamerica Pyramid.

"Good god," said McCoy.

At the very tip of its spire, a red bead of light flashed brightly.

Kirk couldn't take much more introspection, so he tried daydreaming about Hannah.

It was a ninety-minute shuttle flight back to Starfleet Academy, and the first hour was spent in utter silence. The guys were spent. Marcus and Glorak fell asleep sitting up. Raynor just stared out his window. Only Braxim seemed to have any energy. He spent it reading through his notes, prepping for the post-mission debriefing session.

Suddenly the cabin viewscreen crackled to life.

"Team Delta to attention, please," called Commander Stetmann.

Glorak awoke with a piercing snort. Everyone sat up at attention.

"I'm turning Mission Control over to Admiral Miller," said Stetmann.

Stetmann slid off-camera and was replaced by

the large, fleshy face of Rear Admiral Ben Miller, the Academy's chief of testing services.

"At ease, Cadets," said Admiral Miller. "Gentlemen, I'm here with the test administrators and the assessment team." His eyes turned to Kirk's side of the cabin. "Team Captain Kirk, I presume you will act as team spokesman?"

Kirk glanced across the aisle. Everyone nodded. Then he turned to Raynor. Raynor nodded too.

"Yes, sir," replied Kirk.

"Good," said Miller. He looked down at something just below camera view. "I have your final assessment here. Given your performance, it was remarkably easy to compile." He paused. "I don't recall a summary assessment coming together quite this quickly before." He looked toward Kirk. "Ever."

The admiral likes rubbing salt in the wound, thought Kirk. He resolved to maintain perfect composure and give nobody the pleasure of seeing him squirm.

"Yes, sir," he replied coolly.

"Now, I've been administering Tanika Station for almost seventeen years now," he said. "As in most of our simulations, there is no black or white, wrong or right answer. Teams can follow many courses of action and achieve varying degrees of success. Our grading methodology is very flexible."

Kirk thought: *And here it comes.*

"But, Cadet, this is the only time we've seen a team take *your* course of action," he continued. "First off, do you have any questions?"

"Yes, Admiral," said Kirk. "Was the hull breach real or simulated?"

"Simulated," said Admiral Miller. "We like to see how cadets react to uncertainty and the possibility of real danger." He smiled. "Your team evacuated the station with calm, sharp attention to detail. Very impressive."

"Yes, we retreated well, sir," said Kirk.

Kirk heard group laughter offscreen. The admiral was amused as well.

"We have a new simulation programming chief here at the Academy," said Admiral Miller. "He's a recent graduate, and he's given some of our traditional scenarios a thoughtful overhaul, including Tanika Station. In this testing, we seek to assess how your group decision-making and command judgments reflect the Starfleet mission. His insight is quite keen on these issues." The admiral punched a button on his desktop. "I'm going to read his summary of your performance because I think it speaks for the entire assessment team."

Kirk braced himself. He glanced over at Raynor, who looked like a prisoner at sentencing.

"'Tanika Station,'" read Admiral Miller, "'is a dormant

alien world, reawakening. As such it presents a unique challenge for Starfleet science personnel. Its ecosystem offers much that is familiar to cadets, yet functions in a way that is entirely unfamiliar. Team Delta correctly recognized this meta-reality. The team's decision to refrain from standard specimen collection was the most correct and most logical response possible.'"

Kirk turned to look at his teammates across the aisle. All three were grinning back like jackpot winners. Glorak even gave him a thumbs-up, which from a Tellarite is a sight to see.

Then he felt a big hand on his shoulder.

It was Raynor, next to him. He gave Kirk's back a quick whack. Then he folded his arms, unable to suppress a goofy smile.

Admiral Miller read on: "'Sampling would have harmed Tanika Station's highly intelligent inhabitants, whose complex biological systems—body tissues; organs including a distributed brain structure, appendages, and connective tissue—are formed via organic synthesis reactions that are extremely rare on planets with carbon-based life forms, but do in fact exist. Taking specimen samples would disrupt the delicate processes and, in essence, kill inhabitants.'"

Like, say, somebody "researching" Humans by removing their organs, thought Kirk.

Half an hour later, Kirk stepped off the *Gilliam* with his Delta teammates onto Landing Pad 14. It had been nearly twelve hours since they'd reported for duty that morning to Shuttle Hangar 1. Now the sun melted into the Pacific horizon, invisible behind the columns of fog advancing on the city.

McCoy stood at the landing pad. He had a large backpack on one shoulder and held another one in his arms.

"Hey, Bones," called Kirk. "We passed."

"Of course you did!" said McCoy, raising his arm for a high five. "But I hope you're not tired."

"I'm exhausted," said Kirk.

"Then you'll have to rest up in the police cruiser," said McCoy.

"What?"

"Follow me," said McCoy. He tossed the backpack he held to Kirk. "I'll brief you on the way."

Kirk could see the fire in McCoy's eyes. "What's up, Bones? On the way to where?"

"The Doctor's lair!" said McCoy with a wicked grin. "We're going to nail the bastard tonight."

Kirk was stunned. "You know where he is?"

"More or less," said McCoy, jogging ahead. "C'mon, man, speed it up. The fog's rolling in!"

Kirk swung the backpack onto his shoulders and started jogging to keep up. "What's in the backpack?" he called.

"A vacuum cleaner," said McCoy.

Kirk started laughing. "It feels like it. This pack is heavy. What's really in it?"

But McCoy wasn't kidding.

Ten minutes later Kirk found himself in the backseat of an SFPD hovercraft. He was crammed between two people: McCoy and Cadet Uhura. Kirk was almost too tired to enjoy being in such a tight space with Uhura. Almost.

"This is cozy," he said to Uhura.

She rolled her eyes. "I think you're still feeling the effects of zero-g there, Cadet," she said.

"Could be," said Kirk. He glanced down at the laptop case on her lap. "Mind if I check my e-mail?"

Uhura gave McCoy an exasperated look.

"Jim, let's go over the plan," said McCoy.

"What plan?"

"The one we hastily devised with no real thought given to any contingencies," replied McCoy.

"I know that plan," said Kirk. "I use it a lot."

On the jog across Shuttle Hangar 1 to the policecraft, McCoy had brought Kirk up to date on Uhura's translations and the Transamerica Pyramid hologram. Now he opened a side pouch on the backpack that sat on his lap.

"Jim, the Doctor may be a tough guy, or not—nobody really knows," he said. "But we do know that his nanite swarm is lethal and almost unstoppable if it decides to come after you. So Parag and I did a little testing in his lab this afternoon."

McCoy pulled a standard type-two phaser pistol from the side pouch.

"First, we have this baby," he said. "It's slightly modified. When you fire a wide-field spread shot in this setting, you vaporize all nanites within the primary area of effect. The problem, of course, is that any surviving bits self-replicate so quickly that the swarm can just keep coming at you."

Kirk pulled another phaser pistol from his backpack. "It's preset to disruptor effect?" he asked.

"Right," answered McCoy. "Now, it only takes a few thousand nanites, enough to fill a grain of sand, to create a microfactory that produces more nanites. If just that many get inside you, they can start tearing apart your flesh at the cellular level and then use the molecular debris to crank out more nanites. In less than a minute you'd be consumed from the inside out."

"Wow," said Kirk, his smile fading. "That sounds unpleasant."

"But Starfleet doesn't recruit geniuses like Parag Chandar for nothing," said McCoy. "Remember that a nanite is a computerized machine. It relies on a data stream for instructions and operation. Parag ran a few tests and learned that very high-frequency sound disrupts that data stream in these nasty buggers."

McCoy opened the backpack's other side pouch and pulled out a small device about the size of a wallet.

"This is an ultrasonic sound emitter," he said. "It's set to a specific frequency that—in the lab, anyway—seems to freeze any nanite within its wave radius. The frequency is about fifty kilohertz, too high for our ears, so you won't hear anything when you activate it. But the sound is there."

"Like a dog whistle," said Kirk.

"Exactly," said McCoy.

Finally, McCoy opened the backpack's main compartment and pulled out a flexible rubber hose.

"The spire of the Transamerica Pyramid is an enclosed space that gets smaller the higher you go," said McCoy. "Phaser fire might be dangerous up high in the spire. I wasn't joking about the vacuum cleaner," he added. "Your pack holds a portable vacuum unit used for collecting hazardous gases and microwaste at industrial or biomedical accident sites. It's *very* powerful, so watch where you aim, pal."

Kirk stared at the hose.

"We're going to *vacuum* the guy?" he asked.

McCoy gave him a look. "Look, Parag coated the dust bags inside the canisters with a medical polymeric matrix sealant, permeable enough to let air molecules pass through but impermeable enough to contain half-micron nanites . . . for a while, at least." He grimaced. "We think."

"You think?" said Kirk.

"Well, a plastic bag is not quite like a quantum containment chamber, which is virtually unbreakable," said McCoy. "Parag can foresee a scenario where a smart swarm analyzes its predicament, bonds into a solid state— like, say, a metal fist—and just punches through the bag."

"That's . . . almost funny," said Kirk.

"Yeah, hilarious," said McCoy.

Kirk turned to Uhura.

"Hi," he said.

She just rolled her eyes.

"So what's with the laptop?" asked Kirk.

Uhura slid a slim tablet computer from its sleeve. "This is our translator," she said.

"I thought *you* were the translator," said Kirk.

"Well, if the Doctor speaks, I record it and run a spectrographic analysis here," said Uhura. "Then a subroutine scan unscrambles and translates anything he says almost instantaneously. This assumes he'll use the same outdated Romulan military code, and also scramble known languages like Romulan, Xanno, and English. I have their databases in here."

McCoy nodded admiringly. "She put this together herself, Jim, in about two hours," he said.

"And you coordinated this with Detective Bogenn?" asked Kirk.

"Yes," said McCoy. "He was skeptical until he learned of another 'smoke inhalation' incident the other night. Get this: It attacked security personnel up in the pyramid's spire."

"Wow, in the spire itself?" exclaimed Kirk.

The Transamerica Pyramid loomed up ahead. On the building's north side, the blue police cruiser lowered through the fog to Washington Street. The SFPD had the perimeter locked down, with streets barricaded two blocks in every direction. Police vehicles clustered in the intersections with lights flashing.

"Don't you think all this activity will scare him away?" asked Uhura, glancing around as she stepped through the cruiser's rear hatch.

"I hope so," said Kirk. "'Cause I'm going into battle with a serial killer armed with a vacuum cleaner."

Detective Bogenn approached them from the main entrance of the building.

"Hello, Starfleet," he said grimly.

• · ·ᵏᵏ ᵏᵏ ✦ ·ᵏ✦ ··ᵏ

The pyramid's security control center on the thirtieth floor was an armed camp of SWAT units and regular cops hauling heavy weaponry. As they entered, Detective Bogenn, McCoy, and Kirk glanced around at all the hardware.

"Look at these jokers," muttered McCoy.

Detective Bogenn led them toward an old-fashioned bank of elevators.

"Bigger guns make them feel better," said the detective. "Especially when they have no idea what they're facing. But then again, neither do I."

A self-important-looking SWAT captain stood with his team blocking access to the elevators. They projected a studied air of military menace.

As Detective Bogenn moved toward the nearest elevator, the SWAT captain stepped in his way. Bogenn regarded him. "Yes, Captain Detroit?" he said.

Kirk burst out laughing. "Is that really your name?"

"Who are these kids, Detective?" growled the captain, ignoring Kirk.

Kirk whipped out the vacuum cleaner hose and said, "Starfleet maintenance. We're here to clean up the mess, Captain."

Bogenn turned to look at Kirk.

Kirk reached down and flicked on his vacuum unit. After a few seconds of loud whooshing, he turned it back off. Then he put a finger to the earpiece of his headset and spoke quietly.

"Hotel Bravo, this is Go Team Alpha, vacuum unit is operational, repeat, operational," he said. Then he smiled at the SWAT guys.

Bogenn turned wearily back to the SWAT captain. "This is Starfleet jurisdiction, Captain," he said. "Stand down, please."

Captain Detroit and his men exchanged a few looks, but then the captain took a smart step backward.

"Thank you, Captain," said Detective Bogenn.

As they rode the elevator up to its topmost floor, forty-eight, Bogenn looked over at McCoy.

"Doctor, I understand Starfleet wants me posted in the command center," he said.

"That's right, Detective," said McCoy.

"Why?" he asked bluntly.

Kirk spoke up. "Because it's unsafe."

Bogenn turned sharply to him.

"Cadet, I've been hunting this son of a bitch for eighteen years," he said. "He's brutally murdered eight people, and there's a ninth, a fine woman, fighting for her life on a breathing machine right now. I just saw her tonight. She's dying. Only a double lung transplant could save her."

Kirk nodded. "I understand, Detective," he said.

"Do you?"

"Yes, I do," said Kirk. "But with all due respect, this one's not like anything you've ever seen, not at SFPD Homicide."

Bogenn sneered. "You wouldn't know what I've seen, son."

Kirk nodded. "That's true," he said. "But this guy is so alien. . . . Well, he doesn't think like anything you can relate to, not even in a twisted way." Kirk pulled out his phaser and flicked off the safety. "To him, we're like plants. We're specimens. And he doesn't fear us. Because his weapons are better than ours."

Detective Bogenn pulled back his jacket and unsnapped the holster flap over his laser pistol.

"Well, in my book," he said, "a killer is a killer. Period."

Kirk shook his head. "If you try to fight him with that weapon, you'll be dead in forty-five seconds."

"Jim's right, Detective," said McCoy quietly.

Bogenn glanced up at the floor readout just as it hit forty-eight and the arrival bell dinged. "Fine. At least tell me who we're looking at," he said.

"Sir?"

"Who is he?" asked Bogenn. "What's his motivation?"

"Ah," said Kirk. He looked at McCoy.

"Hard to say," said McCoy. "He may be a lone-wolf scientist, or hell, a scout for an advanced civilization. We just have no clue."

"A scientist?" repeated Bogenn with raised eyebrows.

"Yeah, an evil scientist," said Kirk.

Detective Bogenn thought about this for a few seconds. Then he said, "I can't believe I'm letting two goofy cadets take point on this." He shook his head. "We're usually tossing kids like you into overnight detox."

Kirk grinned. "The night is still young, Detective."

The Doctor was ready for them.

The moment Kirk and McCoy stepped inside the towering spire an angry-looking cloud of churning black smoke descended on them from above. Here, on the spire's lowest level, two thousand square feet of open space was spread around a central staircase. So it was fine for phaser fire.

"I'll freeze them, you shoot!" shouted McCoy.

He had entered the atrium holding the sound emitter and quickly flicked it on. Above them, the smoke froze in place.

"It works!" cried Kirk.

"Of course it works!" yelled McCoy. "It's lab tested! Now shoot the bastards, will you?"

Kirk raised his phaser and squeezed off a shot. The widespread discharge of nadium particles instantly incinerated the swarm. Charred bits dropped from the sky in a shower of ashes. Kirk and McCoy were coated in dusty gray and started coughing.

"Great jumping goats!" said McCoy, brushing ash out of his eyes and hair. "It gets you even when it's dead."

"Let's move, Bones!" said Kirk. "He knows we're here now."

The two cadets started up the spiral staircase. The higher they climbed, the narrower and steeper the stairs grew. Both wore hands-free, voice-activated headsets to keep contact with Bogenn and Uhura at the command desk. About a hundred feet up, Kirk spotted another tendril of black haze dropping rapidly toward them from the top of the spire. It was narrower, so getting a good phaser shot would be tricky.

"Here it comes," called Kirk, pointing at the plume.

McCoy, just below him, wielded the sound emitter. Again, the jagged cloud froze. Kirk aimed carefully, but couldn't find a shot angle where he'd miss the stairs above.

"I'll have to climb up and shoot out away from the staircase," said Kirk as he clambered up the steps.

When he reached the same height as the quivering black cloud, he narrowed the phaser's spread and aimed carefully. Before he fired, he heard the swarm's noise—an eerie cross between a vibrating hum and a hiss. When he pulled the trigger, the blast vaporized the swarm . . . and melted a gaping hole about ten feet wide in the clear lumenite spire.

"Crap," he said.

"Don't worry about it. Let's go!" called McCoy, pounding up the stairs from below.

They continued their climb. Another fifty feet up, Kirk suddenly stopped.

"Listen," he said. "Do you hear that?"

McCoy listened. "I hear a hum," he said, looking down at his feet. "Right there."

Kirk's eyes widened in alarm. He aimed the phaser at McCoy's feet.

"Jump!" he shouted. "Jump down! Quick!"

Just as McCoy leaped, a black hissing swarm rose from the spot where he'd just been standing. It was an ambush. Kirk held his fire; the nanites were too close. McCoy quickly activated the sound emitter just as strands of oily smoke surged around him like the tentacles of a black octopus. The cloud froze again, but a few smears of black dust stained McCoy's clothing.

"Damn!" he said, looking down. "It's *on* me."

Kirk reached in his backpack, pulled out the hose, and turned on the vacuum. He waved it around McCoy, and its powerful suction cleaned the air of black bits in just seconds. Then he carefully dabbed it at the dark smudges on McCoy's clothes. It sucked up the nanites but also tore off two patches of the doctor's Starfleet jumpsuit.

"Ouch. I *told* you it was powerful," said McCoy, examining a reddened patch of now-exposed skin on his arm.

They continued upward, stopping every few steps to listen for signs of another ambush. The spiral of the stairs grew tighter and steeper, and the lumenite glass angled in closer on all sides as they climbed. Finally Kirk could see the landing at the bottom of the twenty-foot ladder that ran up into the beacon chamber at the top of the spire.

"Almost there, Bones," he called down.

"Yeah, and then what?" asked McCoy.

Kirk had no answer. But he got one soon enough. As Kirk rounded the last curve of stairs and stepped onto the ladder landing, he heard a deep, metallic murmur and a hissing directly above. He looked up to see the hooded head of a dark figure looking down through the opening at the top of the ladder.

McCoy stepped up next to Kirk.

"It's him," hissed Kirk.

McCoy nodded. He raised his phaser and pointed it at the figure.

"Come on down, mister," he called. "You're now a prisoner of the United Federation of Planets."

A second hooded head appeared in the opening, then a third. The odd metallic moan grew louder.

Kirk sighed. "This feels vaguely familiar," he muttered.

All three figures remained motionless. The metallic moan intensified.

"Okay, so all *three* of you are under arrest," called McCoy. "Are you gonna just stare at us and moan? Come on down!"

As if prompted by McCoy's invitation, all three figures moved down through the opening. They appeared Human-oid, with black arms pulling them through the chamber hatch. All three were huge, like the seven-footer Kirk had seen attacking Gaila. But they crawled with a fluidity that gave Kirk a shiver of dread. This was inhuman, almost insectlike movement, light and weightless. As each figure cleared the chamber hatch, it crawled like a great fly away from the ladder and across the underside of the platform to the nearest lumenite wall. All three entities stopped suddenly and hovered there. They looked like vapory shadows on the spire's glassy translucent surfaces.

"I don't like this, Bones," said Kirk.

Then another head appeared in the opening above. And another.

"We're up to five," said McCoy.

Bogenn's voice barked in his ear. "Give me a sit rep, Cadet," he ordered.

"We've got five Doctors," reported McCoy.

"They're ... hanging on the inside of the spire," said Kirk.

"What?" growled Bogenn. "Repeat that!"

"Would you call this a fair fight, Jim?" said McCoy.

"Almost," said Kirk.

Suddenly another swarm rose up from the platform.

"Another damned booby trap!" cried McCoy as he whipped out his sound emitter and the cloud froze. But then, slowly, the swarm started swirling again, as if in slow motion.

"Good god, Jim, it's evolving a tolerance for the frequency!" yelled McCoy in alarm.

Above them, the dark figures clinging to the glass emitted their own cacophony of sounds, hissing and moaning as before, then adding a piercing, nails-on-a-blackboard screech as well.

McCoy winced at the sounds. He looked at Kirk. "This could be very bad for us."

Kirk raised his phaser and blasted the slow-swirling swarm into ash.

"But worse for them," he said.

Then he swung the weapon upward. One of the figures was creeping down the glass toward them.

"I have a hunch about these guys," he said.

Kirk fired again, vaporizing the approaching figure and burning a hole in the lumenite spire behind it. At this, one of the other figures seemed to explode, blowing apart in a puff of black smoke like an artillery air burst. Then the smoke began to swirl.

McCoy watched in horror.

"They're *all* swarms!" he said.

Kirk fired again, targeting the swirling smoke. A bright flash, not seen in the other phaser strikes, erupted as the shot hit. Again, the incinerated bits dropped to the platform. Two of the remaining three figures broke apart into swarms and mingled together into a single swarm. Kirk aimed and fired. This time, the phaser's nadion discharge seemed to flow like a fluid around the dark cloud.

"It's adapting again," said McCoy, "evolving some kind of shield." McCoy pulled out his phaser and twisted the settings knob. "Parag said a smart swarm might do that."

Kirk grimaced. "Did he say what we should *do* about it?"

"Yes, this," said McCoy. He fired a more focused blast that burned a large swath through the swarm. "Adjust your phaser modulation to a higher frequency, Jim. It may only work for a few shots before—"

Suddenly Kirk's backpack exploded.

A hissing swarm burst out. Kirk dove away and rolled hard into a wall. The swarm was all over him. He managed to activate his sound emitter, but it seemed to have little effect now. Meanwhile, the surviving bits of the swarm above dove like a downburst of wind in McCoy's face, blinding him. Both cadets were coughing hard. Kirk felt the crawl of subcellular bits creeping across his skin, penetrating and migrating into his chest and abdomen. A wave of nausea racked him. Next to him, McCoy was starting to convulse. Both Kirk and McCoy knew they had only seconds left. Kirk felt himself on the edge of consciousness.

Looking up, he saw the Doctor's face. The figure had descended, and stood over him. The "hood" was actually a swirling swarm, and from it a face appeared. It was the face of a woman he did not know. And then the face morphed before his eyes into ... his own face. A pale, waxy, masked version of his face. It was the creepiest thing Kirk had ever seen.

"James T. Kirk," spoke the figure. Just like the night by the Palace of Fine Arts.

What a lousy way to go out, he thought. *Mocked by my own face.*

He groped for his phaser, thinking to set it on overload. The massive explosion might tear off the top of the building, but at least he could take out this deadly mocking menace that was killing him now.

But his phaser was nowhere to be found.

And then he heard the voice again; the words were unintelligible. The last thing Kirk felt before blacking out was the reverse migration of nanites from his torso. The last thing he saw was a black torus of smoke hovering above his body.

Uhura, sitting next to Detective Bogenn at the command console on the thirtieth floor, heard the Doctor's voice in the console speakers via Kirk's microphone. The minute she did, she bracketed the coded clip and copied it to a sound file separate from the ongoing recording.

"We got that recorded," she said.

"Give me a report, boys," said Bogenn into a console mike. "Hey, Cadets! What's going on?"

Uhura immediately created a spectrograph of the statement and then ran it through her translation loops. The whole process took just forty-five seconds.

"Here it is," said Uhura. "The translation reads: 'Assimilation is not advisable at this time. More five-six-one-eight study required. Terminate process and proceed to recharging chamber.'"

Uhura and Bogenn listened to the silence coming through the console.

"Kirk?" called Uhura. "Do you read me, over? Dr. McCoy?"

Kirk struggled to his feet.

Directly above him, he could hear the whine of a propulsion system powering up. He looked frantically for his phaser—still no sign of it. He scrambled up the ladder rungs into the beacon chamber.

"He's running, Bones," he said, panting. "He's leaving."

"Kirk, what's happening?" called Uhura's voice in his earpiece.

"There's a flyer up here," reported Kirk.

Kirk could see the flashing red strobe of the aviation beacon glowing around the edges of the ceiling shield platform. But as the engine whine grew louder, the red flashing stopped. Then it hit him: *The beacon is a starship,* he thought. The swarm had somehow assimilated the aviation strobe—the perfect disguise.

"Uhura, call Starfleet Operations," said Kirk. "Get a sensor lock on that ship."

Below him, McCoy groaned on the landing. Kirk looked down and saw him grab a railing with one hand and pull himself up to his knees. Amazingly, McCoy still had his phaser.

"Bones!" shouted Kirk over the rising engine whine. "Toss me your phaser!"

Kirk reached out. McCoy swung and hit Kirk's hand with a perfect toss. Kirk cranked the phaser's setting knob to sixteen, full power, and narrowed the firing spread. Then he stepped back down through the opening, dropped five rungs down the ladder, aimed the phaser straight up at the starship, and fired.

It was a spectacular blast.

Kirk's shot blew off the entire top of the spire. The sturdy lumenite glass cone shattered like a delicate crystal goblet. Debris blew straight up . . . and then curved downward in fiery arcs as it tumbled in all directions.

Kirk clung to the ladder rungs and covered his face as the spire superstructure shuddered. Jagged chunks of cone glass dropped back through the blown-open top. Below him, McCoy was curled in a protective crouch against the wall on the landing. When debris stopped falling, Kirk glanced up through the jagged hole.

The west wind now whistled into the spire.

Directly above, a cube the size of a small hut hovered in the air, as if inspecting the damage. Its surface was textured with geometric patterns, and a ghostly, greenish light lit it from within. After a few seconds the cube slowly rose, rotating gently.

It looked so bizarre and unthreatening—a floating green cube—that Kirk just watched in fascination for a few seconds. Then he realized, *That's the swarm.* But before he could draw another bead, the cube suddenly zipped upward at unimaginable speed.

It disappeared in less than two seconds.

CH.12.12
After the Dust Settles

Two days later, Cadet Uhura laid her hands flat on her workstation console in the Institute of Xenology's xenolinguistics lab. A satisfied smile slowly spread over her face.

"Computer?" she said. "Please welcome me back."

"Welcome back, Cadet Uhura," said the console.

She felt good. This was home. Her participation in the hunt for the Doctor was rewarding. She'd helped crack the case. Now she could dive back into her work.

It was all good.

"Computer, please run a search for the number string five-six-one-eight," she said.

"In what database?" asked the console.

"All databases," replied Uhura.

"Acknowledged," said the computer.

The door hissed open behind her. She swiveled her chair around. Her satisfied smile grew slightly wider.

"Hello, Commander," she said.

"Cadet," said Spock. "You look pleased."

Uhura checked her smile. "Well, 1 am," she said, patting the console.

"You should be," said Spock. Arms folded, he stepped up beside her and noted what was on the monitor. "1 am told you performed most admirably in the police case," he said. "1 am not surprised."

"Well, 1 couldn't let you down, Commander," she said, folding her arms too.

"Oh, that is not possible." He waited a moment and then quickly said, "1 thought you should know about the results of the sensor trace, since you were the one who called it in."

"You mean on the alien starship, sir?" she asked. "Because actually, 1 just passed along the request. That was made by—"

"Search completed," said the console. "No significant results."

Uhura looked surprised. "Really?" she said. "You checked all your databases?"

"Yes," said the computer.

"Everything in the Starfleet neural network?" asked Uhura.

"Yes, everything that was not classified," said the computer.

"Hmm," murmured Uhura.

After a short pause, the console said, "We interpret that as a request for a verification search scan."

Uhura laughed. "You really have me figured out, don't you?"

"Beginning verification scan," said the computer.

Spock found the exchange amusing. He nodded at the screen and said, "If I may ask, why the interest in that number?"

Uhura looked at the screen: 5618. "The alien nano-swarm had this identifier," she said. "And my last translation from the swarm intelligence included the phrase 'Assimilation is not advisable at this time. More five-six-one-eight study required.' It communicated this immediately before withdrawing."

"Fascinating," said Spock.

"Do you have a theory, Commander?" asked Uhura.

"Regretfully, I do not," said Spock. "Clearly the alien entity is referring to that which it was sent to study."

"Well, it has a pretty nasty way of 'studying' folks," said Uhura. "So, you were telling me about the sensor trace on the alien ship?"

"Yes," said Spock. "Starfleet Operations managed to get a vector lock on the craft before it escaped. A remarkable achievement in such a constricted time frame."

Uhura brightened. "So where did it go?"

"Unknown," said Spock.

"But you said they got a vector lock on it," said Uhura, confused.

"They did," said Spock. "But then it disappeared, almost literally. The sensor readings at its last known waypoints indicated a transwarp velocity almost beyond comprehension."

Uhura shook her head in amazement.

"So do you think it's headed back to the Delta Quadrant?" she asked.

Spock tilted his head sideways a bit, considering the idea. "Could very well be," he said.

Their eyes met for a couple of seconds.

"Commander," said Uhura.

"Yes, Cadet?" replied Spock.

"I think I have some very interesting data on the phonology of Klingon aggressive-mode speech patterns you might enjoy reviewing."

"Excellent," said Spock. "I have fifty-seven minutes until my faculty meeting."

"Perfect," said Uhura.

And then they got to work.

● · ·˙· ·˙·✦ ·˙✦ ··˙

At the Brewsky's counter, Kirk cleared his throat a few times. Yes, the irritation was still there from his dust-storm encounters, two nights prior. But he had another motive.

"What's a guy gotta do to get some *service* around here?" he called out.

After a few seconds, Hannah stepped out of the back-room.

"Hey, you," she said, walking slowly toward him.

"Hello, barista," said Kirk. "I see you still work here."

"Apparently," she said. "They handed me this apron when I walked in." She gestured to her apron, which wasn't much longer than her little miniskirt.

"That's a good sign." Kirk tried not to focus on her legs.

She stepped to the espresso machine, dumped three big scoops of fine-ground coffee in the filter basket, and then rammed the handle of the metal portafilter into place to start the brew. She glanced over her shoulder and smiled at Kirk.

Kirk said, "Hey, I didn't say please."

"You don't need to anymore," she said.

Kirk just stood and watched her work for a few seconds. She wasn't self-conscious at all. He liked that.

He noticed that tonight she wore her hair up. He saw the hint of a tattoo on her neck, under the pile of hair scooped up, and was intrigued. He realized there was a lot he needed to learn about Hannah. "You changed your hair," he said. "I like it."

"I get bored easily," she replied.

"Should I take that as a challenge?" asked Kirk with a glint in his eye. "Do I need to do something special to keep you from getting bored with me?"

Hannah shook her head and laughed.

"So when do you get off?" Kirk asked, drumming his fingers on the counter.

"Hmm . . . ," she said, pretending to consider his question. Kirk held his breath and waited. "I just decided that it's now. *Jen!*" she called.

Jen stepped from the back room. Her hands were powdered with flour. "Yes?"

"Okay if I split a little early tonight?"

Jen gave a sly look at Kirk. "Why?"

"Pretty please," she begged.

"Give me five to finish up this batch of scones," said Jen. "Then I'll take the counter. And you owe me!"

"Thanks, Jen!" said Kirk and Hannah in unison.

Kirk strolled over to his corner table, feeling almost giddy at the thought of having a few hours of Hannah all to himself. He had a lot to tell her. He felt like a better man, thanks to her. Certainly a better cadet. He owed her, big-time. If he ever got to sit in the captain's chair of a Starfleet capital ship, his decisions would be informed by her way of looking at things. Plus she was so damn sexy. *Jen can't finish those scones fast enough,* he thought.

A few minutes later Hannah plopped down into the chair next to him.

"So what shall we do tonight?" he asked.

"Let's study," she said.

"Study?" repeated Kirk. *Seriously?*

"You got a test coming up?" he asked.

"No, I just like to study."

Studying wasn't what Kirk had in mind. He had been thinking moonlit stroll and then maybe a drink or two at a bar. Or dinner. Nevertheless, he agreed to her plan.

"But first," he told Hannah, "I was hoping we could take a walk."

"Okay," said Hannah. "Why?"

"Because it's really foggy and chilly out tonight," he replied. "Uncomfortably cold, in fact."

Hannah gave him an uncertain smile. "I like walks, but um, what's your angle here?"

Kirk pointed to her jacket, which hung on a coatrack behind the counter. "Your jacket," he said. "It doesn't really keep you very warm, does it? In fact, that jacket sucks. Or am I wrong about that?"

Hannah looked over at her jacket.

"No, you're right," she said. "It sucks."

"So, you will be freezing and I just can't have that . . . so it will be up to me to keep you warm!" Kirk grinned at his logic. "Let's go for a walk."

Hannah stood up and slid her arms around Kirk's waist. She pretended to be considering his idea. "So this walk is just a ploy to get a little closer to me?" she asked, looking up at him under lowered lashes. Kirk's head was spinning.

"Just for a few minutes, I promise!" He held up his arms in mock surrender. "Then we can come back here and study."

Hannah arched an eyebrow. "Cadet, who said anything about studying *here*? My apartment is just a few blocks away." She playfully pushed him away, walked over to the coatrack, and pulled on her jacket. "Coming?" she asked over her shoulder.

Kirk suddenly thought studying sounded like the best idea he'd ever heard.

"War is my life, my whole life," Thrand said.
*"It is what I have chosen.
There is nothing else for me."*

He stalked away, ending the conversation.
Cwenneth stared after him, weighing the jar in her
hand.

"Curiosity can get you killed, Cwenneth," she
muttered. "Treacherous Norse blood runs in his
veins. You have to think about saving your life and
escaping. Keep away from him. Stop trying to see
good where none exists."

The trouble was a small part of her heart refused to
believe it.

* * *

Saved by the Viking Warrior
Harlequin® Historical #1202—September 2014

Author Note

Some characters just decide they want to be written. *Lady Cwenneth was one of those characters. She* popped into my head and refused to go. Part of the trouble with writing this book is that the primary source documentation is not very good for Northumbria in the ninth century. It is a mixture of legend and fact. Sometimes the facts masquerade as legends and sometimes it is the other way around.

One of the inspirations for the story was an archaeological dig in Corbridge where they discovered a woman buried in the Viking, rather than the Christian, manner. The Vikings did not settle around the Tyne, rather they had the area as a client kingdom. Just how friendly everyone was toward the Vikings remains an unanswered question.

I do hope you enjoy Cwenneth and Thrand's story. In case anyone is wondering, Thrand is the grandson of the hero's stepbrother in *Taken by the Viking* and the sister of the heroine in *The Viking's Captive Princess.* This is why he knows how to make the healing balm that Cwenneth uses in the story.

As ever, I love hearing from readers. You can contact me through my website, www.michellestyles.co.uk; my blog, www.michellestyles.blogspot.com; or my publisher. I also have a page on Facebook—Michelle Styles Romance Author—where I regularly post my news. And I'm on Twitter as @michelleLstyles.

MICHELLE STYLES

SAVED BY THE VIKING Warrior

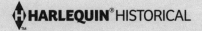
HARLEQUIN® HISTORICAL

Recycling programs
for this product may
not exist in your area.

ISBN-13: 978-0-373-29802-0

SAVED BY THE VIKING WARRIOR

Copyright © 2014 by Michelle Styles

HARLEQUIN®

Printed in U.S.A.

™ www.Harlequin.com

Did you know some of these novels are also available as ebooks? Visit www.Harlequin.com.

For my youngest son, Patrick,
who wanted a Viking story because there was
more fighting and who passed his A levels
and now is studying at university.
Sometimes hard work does have its own reward.

MICHELLE STYLES

Born and raised near San Francisco, Michelle Styles currently lives a few miles south of Hadrian's Wall with her husband, three children, two dogs, cats, assorted ducks, hens and beehives.

An avid reader, she became hooked on historical romance when she discovered Georgette Heyer, Anya Seton and Victoria Holt one rainy lunchtime at school. And, for her, a historical romance still represents the perfect way to escape.

Although Michelle loves reading about history, she also enjoys a more hands-on approach to her research. She has experimented with a variety of old recipes and cookery methods (some more successful than others), climbed down Roman sewers and fallen off horses in Iceland—all in the name of discovering more about how people went about their daily lives. When she is not writing, reading or doing research, Michelle tends her rather overgrown garden or does needlework—in particular, counted cross-stitch.

Michelle maintains a website (www.michellestyles.co.uk) and a blog (www.michellestyles.blogspot.com), and would be delighted to hear from you.

Chapter One

Spring 876—near the border between
Viking-controlled Northumbria and
Anglo Saxon-controlled Bernicia

'We've stopped again. How many times can the wheels get clogged with mud? Perhaps we should have waited until the spring rains stopped.' Lady Cwenneth of Lingwold peered through the covered cart's one small window. 'This journey to Acumwick has taken twice as long as it should have with all the stops Hagal the Red's men insist on making. Delay after delay. I want to prevent hostilities rather than be the excuse for them.'

Her new tire woman, Agatha, glanced up. 'Are you that eager for marriage to Hagal the Red? You went on about his unsavoury reputation only a few nights ago. About how your brother threatened you into the marriage.'

Cwenneth pressed her lips together as the cloying scent from the herbs Agatha had spread to help with the stuffiness of the cart tickled her nostrils.

In her loneliness, she had confided too much the other night.

'I spoke out of turn, Agatha. It doesn't do to remind me.'

'I was just saying,' the maid muttered, stirring the herbs and releasing more of their overpowering scent. 'Some people...'

Cwenneth concentrated on smoothing the fur collar of her cloak rather than giving a sharp answer back. Squabbling created enemies. She needed friends and allies more than ever now that she was about to live in a foreign land amongst people with a reputation for barbarity and cruelty.

Her marriage to the new Norseman *jaarl* of Acumwick would ensure her brother and the inhabitants of Lingwold would finally achieve peace after years of war. As part of the marriage contract, Hagal the Red agreed to provide protection particularly against Thrand the Destroyer, the berserker who enjoyed killing for the sake of it and exacted more than his fair share of gold from Lingwold.

Hagal's sworn oath to bring Thrand's head to Lingwold had ensured her brother had put his signature on the marriage contract's parchment.

'You look solemn, my lady. Are you that unhappy?'

Cwenneth hastily composed her face into a more cheerful countenance. 'I'm eager to begin my new life. A fresh start away from the unhappiness of the past few years.'

Cwenneth gave the only positive reason she could think of sharing with Agatha. Her brother had given her a stark choice when she had protested at the match—either marriage to Hagal the Red or a convent of his choosing with no dowry, nothing to look forward to except a barren cell and hard physical work for the remainder of her existence.

'It will happen if you please your new lord and master, my lady. It's easy if you know how.' Agatha gave a superior smile and arched her back slightly so her ample breasts jutted out. 'Men are such simple creatures. Easy to please, if you take my meaning.'

Cwenneth glanced down at her own slender curves. Positively boyish and flat in comparison. She had to hope Hagal the Red liked thin women.

'The journey was supposed to last a week. Thanks to the incessant rain, it has been twice as long.' Cwenneth frowned. Once the rain stopped and the mud dried, the raiding season would begin in earnest. If the marriage wasn't formalised, would Hagal the Red actually provide the promised protection? Would he end the threat of Thrand the Destroyer? 'What if Hagal takes the delay as an insult?'

'I am sure it rained in Viken where they came from. He will understand.' Agatha gave a throaty laugh and stirred the herbs another time. 'They appreciate a woman up north, and Hagal the Red will be all the more impatient for the wait. They say he is very vigorous in bed.'

The dusty dry scent of the herbs invaded Cwenneth's mouth, making her throat feel parched and her head ache.

'I hate travelling in a cart. It makes me feel ill with its swaying and bumps.' Cwenneth firmly changed the subject away from bed sport. She knew the rumours about Agatha's prowess in that area and how her sister-in-law had caught her cavorting with Cwenneth's brother.

She craned her neck, trying to see more, but there was nothing except for bare trees, raising their branches to the sky. 'My brother would have allowed me to walk for a little, but Hagal's man refuses even to discuss it. When I am officially his lady, things will have to change.'

'I'm sure it will,' Agatha said in that overly familiar way she'd recently adopted. Cwenneth gritted her teeth. She needed to assert her authority over the maid. 'Change is in the air. For everyone. You never know, you might not be cursed any longer.'

Cursed—the word pierced her heart. What else could you call a woman who had failed to save her husband and child from a fever? Who had lost her home to a stepson who hated her and blamed her for the death of the woman he had considered his mother?

'Repeating gossip is wrong,' she said far too quickly.

'Your husband died and then your child after that old crone died on your doorstep. What is that if not cursed?'

'It is unlucky and has nothing to do with my forthcoming marriage. We will speak no more of it.'

Cwenneth hated the lingering sense of guilt that swamped her. Her stepson's former nurse had been caught stealing gold from the local church. She had had to request her departure. The priest had threatened to withhold communion from the entire household if she continued to shelter her. The woman had gone muttering curses and predicting vile things including that Cwenneth should lose all she held dear and that her womb would remain barren for ever.

Although she had laughed off the words at the time, dismissing them as the ravings of a confused woman, less than three weeks later, the bad luck started. Aefirth had returned home wounded and died.

Six weeks after that, she had lost her young son and any hope she might be carrying another. She had returned to her childhood home unable to bear her stepson's accusations any longer. The whispers about her being cursed began in earnest. Even now the memory caused cold sweat to run down her back. What else did she have to lose before the curse lost its power?

Agatha kept silent, so Cwenneth adopted an innocent face and added, 'A wonder you want to serve under such a woman as me, then.'

Agatha fiddled with the dry herbs. 'There was no prospect for advancement at Lingwold. That much was made very clear to me. I've no wish to be a beggar woman. I have plans.'

Cwenneth leant forward. No prizes for guessing who had made her that offer—the same person who had delivered the ultimatum about her marriage when she had tried to stall: her brother. 'I expect my servants to be loyal, Agatha, and not to repeat old gossip. I expect them to speak with a civil tongue as well. Remember that or you will not remain my maid for long.'

Agatha's cheeks flushed at the reprimand. 'I beg your pardon. And I do hope for a bright future for you. Maybe you will find happiness...'

Happiness? Cwenneth hadn't expected to fall in

love with the much older Aefirth either, but she had.
Their marriage had initially been one of duty and the
joining of estates. She clearly remembered the instant
she'd known—Aefirth had put his hand on her belly
when she had said that she felt their baby stir. The
delight in his eyes had taken her breath away, and she
had known that she'd love him for ever. He said that
she made him young again. All that had gone in the
space of a few days. All because of the curse.

The interior of the cart with its overpowering
stench of herbs seemed small and more confining
than ever once she started to think about all she had
lost and would never have again.

'I'm going out to breathe fresh air. You may remain
here. I'll be back before you miss me.'

'Surely, you should stay here. The last time you
tried to leave the cart, things went badly.'

Cwenneth firmed her mouth. She knew precisely
what had happened the last time. Narfi, Hagal's stew-
ard with the shifty eyes, had shouted at her, calling
her all sorts of filthy names. She had retreated rather
than argue like a fishwife. But what was a name compared to a few final breaths of freedom now that the
marriage truly loomed? What if they never allowed
her out of the hall again? If she never saw the spring
flowers in the woods?

'Lend me your cloak. From a distance and if the
hood covers my hair, we look about the same,' Cwenneth said. 'No one will see that I lack your curves.'

'Yes but...'

'Hagal's man forbade me, but not you. I will take
full responsibility if anyone questions me. You won't
be beaten. I won't allow it.' Cwenneth touched her

maid's cold hand. 'When we reach Acumwick, I'll speak with Hagal and quietly explain that I dislike rough treatment and being shouted at. If that man, Narfi, can't learn to keep a civil tongue in his head, he'll have to go. Hagal the Red wants this marriage. He will have to respect my wishes.'

Agatha tapped her finger against her mouth, but did not meet Cwenneth's eyes. 'No one has shouted at me. Tell me what you want and I can fetch it.'

Cwenneth frowned. Agatha's bold manner grew the nearer they got to Acumwick.

'I *need* to go out and stretch my legs,' Cwenneth said, adopting a superior attitude and pinning the maid with her gaze. Agatha was the first to look away.

'It is on your head then.' Agatha fumbled with her cloak. 'Don't go blaming me. I did try to warn you. Do what you have to do quickly.'

The exchange of cloaks was quickly accomplished. Agatha stroked the rabbit fur collar of Cwenneth's cloak with an envious hand.

'I appreciate it. I'll return before anyone notices.'

'Just so you are.' The woman gave a great sigh and ceased stroking the cloak.

Cwenneth raised the coarse woollen hood over her golden blonde hair and quickly exited before Agatha found another reason to delay her.

The bright spring sun nearly blinded her after the dark shadows of the cart. Cwenneth stood, lifting her face to the warm sunlight while her eyes adjusted. All the worry and anxiety seemed to roll off her back as she stood breathing in the fresh, sweet-smelling air. The stuffy woollen-headed feeling from the herbs vanished and she could think clearly again.

Without pausing to see where anyone else might be, she walked briskly to a small hollow where the bluebells nodded. The rich perfume filled her nostrils, reminding her of the little wood behind the hall she'd shared with her late husband. Aefirth had loved bluebells because her eyes matched their colour. He'd even had her stitch bluebells on his undergarments, proclaiming that they brought him luck.

Always when she thought of Aefirth, her heart constricted. She had desperately wanted to save him when he returned home with his wounded leg, but the infection had taken hold and he'd died. Old warriors died all the time from wounds. No matter how many times she tried to remember that, her mind kept returning to the woman's curse. Aefirth had recovered from worse before. Why had the infection taken hold that time?

Impulsively, Cwenneth picked a bluebell and held it in her hand. The scent made her feel stronger and more in control—what she needed in the cart rather than evil-smelling herbs which made her feel tired and stupid.

She picked a large handful of bluebells, stopped and breathed in their perfume one final time before returning to her duty.

'I'll be brave. I'll be kind to Agatha and make her my ally instead of my enemy, but I will remember my position,' she whispered. 'I will make this marriage to Hagal the Red work because it is for the good of everyone. A new start for me and a chance to leave past mistakes far behind. I'm certain that is the advice Aefirth would have given me.'

A great inhuman scream rent the air before the dull clang of sword against sword resounded.

Cwenneth froze. A raid! And she was too far from the cart's safety. Her men would rally around the cart, thinking they were protecting her. No one would be looking for her out here.

She should have stayed where she was supposed to be. Her brother's men would defend the cart to their last breath. She wished Edward had allowed her a few more men, but he'd bowed to Hagal's wishes and had sent only a token force of six. Agatha would be fine as long as she stayed put in the cart and did not come looking for her.

'Stay put, Agatha,' she whispered. 'Think about yourself. I can look after myself. Honest.'

What to do now? She could hardly stand like some frozen rabbit in the middle of the bluebells, waiting to be run through or worse.

Hide! Keep still until you know all is safe. Aefirth's advice about what to do if the Norsemen came calling resounded in her mind. *Find a safe spot and stay put until the fighting has ended.* She was far too fine to wield a sword or a knife. She tightened her grip on the flowers. The same had to hold true for bandits and outlaws.

Cwenneth pressed her back against a tree and slid into the shadows. Hugging the rapidly wilting bluebells to her chest, she tried to concentrate on her happy memories of her husband and their son. Before she had been cursed. She whispered a prayer for the attack to be short and easily repulsed.

An agonised female scream tore the air. Agatha!

Cold sweat trickled down Cwenneth's back. The bandits had breached the cart's defences.

How? Hagal's men were supposed to be hardened warriors. He'd given her brother his solemn oath on that.

The pleas became agonised screams and then silence. Cwenneth bit the back of her knuckle and prayed harder. Agatha had to be alive. Surely they wouldn't kill a defenceless woman. The outlaws couldn't be that depraved.

The silence became all-encompassing. Before the attack, there had been little sounds in the woods and now there was nothing. Cwenneth twisted off her rings and hid them in the hem of her gown before gathering her skirts about her, sinking farther into the hollow beneath the tree and hoping.

Two Norseman warriors strode into the rapidly darkening glade. She started to stand, but some instinct kept her still. She'd wait and then reveal herself when she knew they had come to save her. They could belong to Thrand the Destroyer's band of outlaws rather than Hagal. He had every reason not to want this marriage. It must have been his men who attacked them because they knew what it would mean. Her heart pounded so loudly she thought they must hear it.

'The maid is dead. One simple task and she failed to do that—keep the pampered Lady Cwenneth in the cart. Refused to say where she'd gone. Claimed she didn't know,' the tall one said. 'Now we have to find the oh so spoilt lady and dispose of her.'

'Good riddance,' Narfi said. 'That woman was

trouble. She knew too much. She asked for too much gold and then got cold feet. Couldn't bring herself to be associated with murder. No spine.'

He put his boot down not three inches from Cwenneth's nose. She pressed her back closer to the hollow and fervently prayed that she would go unnoticed. Her brain reeled from the shock that Agatha was dead! And that she had been willing to betray and murder her!

'We spread the rumour it was Thrand the Destroyer who did this? Clever!'

'No, Thrand Ammundson is in Jorvik, attending the king. Halfdan keeps him close now that he fears death. More is the pity.' Narfi chuckled. 'The Northumbrians fear him more than any. Can't see why. He isn't that good. Sticks in my craw and Hagal's. Ammundson gets gold thrown at his feet without lifting his sword simply because of his legendary prowess on the battlefield. I could take him in a fight with one hand tied behind my back.'

'Why did Hagal want the Lady of Lingwold dead? Did he hold with the curse?'

'Revenge for her husband killing his favourite cousin three years ago. He swore it on the battlefield. Hagal is a man who settles scores. Always.'

A great numbness filled Cwenneth. Not an ambush because of the gold they carried for her dowry or a random act of banditry, but a deliberate act of revenge by Hagal the Red. She was supposed to die today. There was never going to have been a wedding to unite two peoples, but a funeral. The entire marriage contract had been a ghastly trick.

Her stomach revolted, and she started to gag, but

Cwenneth forced her mouth to stay shut. Her only hope of survival was in staying completely silent.

Cwenneth tightened her grip about the flowers and tried to breathe steadily. Why hadn't Edward questioned him closer? Or had the opportunity to get rid of the menace that was Thrand Ammundson tempted her brother so much that he never thought to ask?

All the while, her brain kept hammering that it was far too late for such recriminations. She had to remain absolutely still and hope for a miracle.

She had to get back to Lingwold alive and warn her brother. Why go to all this trouble if Hagal had only wanted to murder her? She had to expose Hagal the Red for the monster he was before something much worse happened.

'Gods, I wish that maid had done what she promised and slit the widow's throat at the signal. I was looking forward to getting back to the hall early like. Now we have to trample through these woods, find her and do it ourselves.'

The second man sent a stream of spittle which landed inches from her skirt. Cwenneth forced all of her muscles to remain still, rather than recoiling in revulsion.

'She won't survive out here. Soft as muck that woman. Pampered. Unable to walk far. Everything had to be done for her.'

'You only have that maid's word that the Lady Cwenneth had no weapons.'

'It doesn't matter if she does. Imagine that useless creature coming up against any wild beast! How would she fight? Boring it to death with her complaints about food or the slowness of our progress? The woman doesn't know one end of a sword from another. She wouldn't last more than a few heartbeats even if she does have a knife.'

They both laughed and started to search the undergrowth off to her right. Quietly, Cwenneth searched the ground for something sharp, something so she could defend herself if they did find her. She did know how to use a knife. The pointy bit went into the flesh and she should go for the throat. Her fingers closed around a sharp rock.

A solitary howl resounded in the clearing. Cwenneth's blood went ice-cold. Wolves. She didn't know which sort were worse—the four-legged variety who lurked in the woods or the two-legged variety standing not ten feet from her who had just slaughtered people for no good reason.

Narfi clapped his hand on the other man's back. 'Don't worry. Dead women tell no tales. By the time we reach Acumwick, the wolf will have done our work for us. We'll come back and find the body in a day or two. Hagal will never know. Now let's get to the hall. I want my food. Killing always makes me hungry.'

Making jokes about what she'd do when she met the wolf and speculating on how she'd die, the pair sauntered off.

Cwenneth hugged her knees to her chest, hardly daring to breathe. She was alive, but there were many miles of inhospitable country between here and Lingwold.

She screwed up her eyes tight. She'd do it. She'd prove them wrong. She wasn't minded to die yet and particularly not to suit thieves' and murderers' schemes. She would defeat Hagal and prove to everyone that she wasn't cursed.

The air after a slaughter takes on a special sort of stillness, different from the silence after a battle when the Valkyries gather the honourable dead. Then the birds pause, but the air continues to flow. After a slaughter, even the air respects the dead.

The instant Thrand Ammundson came around the bend in the road, he knew what had happened—a slaughter of the innocents.

'Gods! What a mess.' Thrand surveyed the carnage spread out before him. An overturned, smouldering wreckage of a travelling cart with six butchered and dismembered bodies lying about it dominated the scene. The sickly-sweet tang of fresh blood intermingling with smoke and ash hung in the air.

'You would think after ten years of war, people would know better than to travel so lightly armed,' one of his men remarked. 'Halfdan maintains the peace, but there are Northumbrian bandits. Desperate men do desperate things.'

'Surprised. They thought they were safe,' Thrand answered absently as he bent to examine the first body. 'Always a mistake.'

He gently closed the old man's eyes and forced his mind to concentrate on the scene. The bodies were cold, but not picked clean. And the fire had failed to completely consume the cart. It had merely smouldered rather than burning to the ground. Not a robbery gone wrong, but cold-blooded murder. And he knew whose lands they crossed—Hagal the Red's.

Hagal would be involved, but behind the scenes. A great spider waiting for the fly to blunder in.

Thrand pressed his lips together. Everything proclaimed Hagal the Red's handiwork, but he needed more proof if he wanted to bring him to justice, finally and for ever. Something solid and concrete. Hagal had had a hand in the slaughter of Thrand's family back in Norway. Thrand knew it in his bones, but no one had listened to his proof and Hagal had slithered away like the snake he was.

'How do you know they were surprised?' Helgi, one of his oldest companions-in-arms, asked, kneeling beside him.

'Look at their throats. Cut.' Thrand gestured towards the two closest bodies. 'And this lad and that man still have their swords in their belts. Whoever did this got in and got out quickly.'

'A dirty business, this. Who would dare? Northumbrian outlaws?'

'I have a good idea who our enemy is. He won't bother us. More's the pity.' Thrand knelt beside the second body, little more than a youth. No arrows and impossible to determine the type of blade used from a clean cut. Thrand frowned, considering the options. The intense savagery of the attack sickened him, but, knowing Hagal's methods, it failed to surprise him.

There was never any need to mutilate bodies. A dead man will not put a knife in your back.

He had only discovered Hagal was in Halfdan's employ after he swore his oath of allegiance to Halfdan and had agreed not to attack a fellow member of the *felag* on pain of death.

Hagal's time would come. Once his oath was complete, Thrand would ensure it. He refused to add the shame of being an oath-breaker to his titles.

Without his code, a man was nothing—one of the lessons his father had taught him. And he had to respect his father's memory. It was all that remained of him. Thrand had shown little respect for him and his strict rules the last few months of his life, much to his bitter regret.

'If they attacked this party of travellers, they could attack us,' someone said.

'Do you think they'd dare attack us?' Helgi shouted. 'You have never been on the losing side, Thrand. Your reputation sweeps all before it. They pour gold at your feet rather than stand and fight.'

'Only a dead man believes in his invincibility,' Thrand said, fixing Helgi with a glare. 'I aim to keep living for a while.'

At his command, his men began to methodically search the blood-soaked area for clues, anything that could prove Hagal was here and had done this. He didn't hold out much hope. Hagal was known to be an expert at covering his tracks.

'A woman,' one of them called out from beside the cart. 'No longer has a face. What sort of animal would do that to a woman?'

'Any clues to her identity?'

'High born from her fur cloak. Her hands appear soft. Probably Northumbrian, but then there are very few of our women here.'

Thrand pressed his hands to his eyes. A senseless murder. Such a woman would be worth her weight in gold if held for ransom. Or if sold in one of the slave markets in Norway or even in the new colony of Iceland, she would command a high price. Why kill her? Why was she worth more dead than alive to Hagal who valued gold more than life itself?

'See if anyone survived and can explain what happened here and why. Dig a pit for the bodies. It is the least we can do. Then we go forward to the Tyne! We need to return to Jorvik before Halfdan convenes the next Storting.' he proclaimed in ringing tones.

'And if the bandits return…they will know someone has been here.'

'Good. I want them to know,' Thrand said, regarding each of his men, hardened warriors all, and he could tell they too were shaken by this savagery. But he knew better than to trust any of them with his suspicions about Hagal. Thrand was well aware Hagal had used his spy network to escape in the past.

'This is Hagal the Red's land. Surely he will want to know about bandits operating in this area. He has sworn to uphold the king's peace,' Knui, his late helmsman's cousin, called out. 'Will we make a detour?'

'Leave Hagal the Red to me.' Thrand inwardly rolled his eyes at the naive suggestion. Hagal's way of dealing with this outrage would be to hang the first unlucky Northumbrian who dared look at him and be done with it. No one would dare question him.

'But you are going to tell him?' Knui persisted.

'We've not actually encountered any outlaws, merely seen the aftermath of an unfortunate occurrence.' He gave Knui a hard look. Knui was only on this expedition because it had been his late helmsman's dying request. Sven had sworn that Knui wasn't in Hagal's employ, but his words made Thrand wonder. 'Speculation serves no one. Our first duty is fulfilling our oath to my late helmsman, Sven, and ensuring his child will want for nothing. We gave our oaths on his deathbed. First the child and then... perhaps...once we have returned to Jorvik and the Storting is finished.'

'What do we do with her? Leave her for the eagles? Or put her in the pit with the rest?' one of his men called. 'They were far from kind to this one.'

Thrand stared at the woman's mutilated body with distaste. It reminded him of Ingrid, the woman who had caused him to betray his family and who had ended up murdered. One more crime to make sure Hagal was punished for. A senseless, wasteful crime. 'Lay out the dead before burial while I check to see if any more bodies are about. There may be some clue I missed. And we want to make sure we don't have to dig two pits.'

He left his men to their task. With a drawn sword, he went into the woods, circling about the site. He forced his mind to concentrate on the task rather than revisiting long-ago crimes. Any little signs which might give him a clue to where the attackers went, or if any of the party had survived.

He pressed his hands to his eyes. 'Come on, Thrand Ammundson. What are you missing? Concentrate instead of remembering the long dead.'

When he approached the end of his circuit, he noticed scattered bluebells rapidly wilting in the warm afternoon. Someone else had been there. The dead woman? Or...?

He frowned, annoyed with himself for not immediately considering it. Details mattered. High-born

Northumbrian ladies always travelled with at least one female companion.

Someone had survived. Someone who could bear witness to what happened here. Someone who could speak in the king's court and condemn Hagal. He gave a nod. The gods had finally given him his chance if he could get the creature to Jorvik alive.

Moving slowly and paying attention to little clues on the ground—a broken twig here, a scattered flower there—Thrand followed the woman's trail. He discovered a hollow where she must have hidden for a while. There was evidence of other feet as well. Kneeling down, he felt the soil. Cold. The attack had been this morning, so she could not be far…if she had survived.

He spied a single wilting bluebell on the far edge of the glade.

'Where are you? Come out! I'm here to help!'

The only sound was the wind in the trees.

He frowned, drew his sword and slowly picked his way through the undergrowth, looking for more signs. The trail was easier as if the woman had ceased to care about being followed. The far-off howl of a wolf pierced the stillness. Wolf or Hagal's men? He knew the sort of death he'd prefer. With a wolf, the woman stood a chance of a quick death.

He entered a clearing where gigantic oak and ash spread their bare branches upward. A shaft of sunlight cut through the gloom, highlighting the strands of golden hair which had escaped from the woman's coarse dark-brown cloak as she tried to free the fabric from a thorn bush. Her fine gown was immediately obvious.

Thrand breathed easier. The woman remained alive. He sheathed his sword.

'Are you hurt?'

She glanced up with frightened eyes, eyes which matched the few bluebells she still carried and pressed closer to the thorn bush. The cloak opened slightly, revealing a gold-embroidered burgundy gown. Her long blonde hair had come loose and tumbled about her shoulders like spun gold.

Thrand whistled under his breath. He found it hard to remember the last time he'd seen a woman that beautiful.

Had Hagal finally made a mistake after all this time?

He held out his hand and tried for a gentle approach rather than his usual brusque manner. 'I come in peace. I've no wish to harm you. What happened back there? Back with the cart?'

She gave an inarticulate moan, redoubled her efforts to free herself from the bush. The cloak tore and she started to run. Thrand crossed the glade to her before she had gone three steps. He caught her shoulders and gave her a little shake.

'If you run, you die. These woods are no place for a lone woman.' He examined the fine bones and delicate features of her face. She came up to his chin. Most women barely reached his shoulder. 'Particularly not one who is gently bred.'

He allowed his hands to drop to his side and waited. Had his words penetrated her shocked brain?

Her tongue wet her lips, turning them the colour of drops of blood on snow. 'I'm already dead, Norseman. Here or elsewhere—what does it matter?'

'Are you injured? Did they hurt you? How did you escape?'

She slowly shook her head and started to back away. In another heartbeat she'd run. Thrand silently swore. He did not have time to spend chasing this woman through the forest.

'Do you want to live?' he ground out. 'Simple choice.'

She stopped, hesitating. 'I…I…'

Forget gentleness. He had tried. The Northumbrian woman was stubborn beyond all reason. Action was required. He reached out and grabbed her wrist.

'You come with me.' He pinned her with his gaze. 'Whatever happened to you before, know that you belong to me hereafter. I'm your master now.'

Chapter Two

You belong to me. I'm your master. The words re-verberated through her brain. Cwenneth stared at the large Norseman warrior who held her wrist captive, hating him. After all she'd survived today, she'd ended up a slave to an unknown Norseman. And she knew what they were capable of.

Surely it would have been better to die a quick death at Narfi's hands than to suffer this…this torture!

She had been a fool to trust Hagal the Red and his promises in the marriage contract. She had been a fool to flee from her hiding place at the sound of this man's voice. She had been a fool to try to undo the cloak when it became entangled on the thorn bush.

Time to start using her mind instead of panicking like a scared rabbit! Aefirth would have wanted her to.

'I belong to no man, particularly not a Norseman.' Cwenneth brought her hand down sharply and twisted. 'I will never be a slave. Ever.'

He released her so abruptly that she stumbled

backwards and fell on her bottom, revealing more than she would have liked of her legs. Cwenneth hastily smoothed her skirts down.

'That's better,' she said in her most imperious voice, playing for time and ignoring the way her insides did a little flutter at his intense look. 'Keep your hands to yourself in the future.'

'If you want a race, so be it, but I will win.' The planes of his face hardened to pure stone. 'You are welcome to try. I will catch you before you go ten steps. And my mood will be less generous.'

He reached down and raised her up. His hand lingered lightly on her shoulder, restraining her.

'Will you strike me down if I run?' Cwenneth whispered. She'd survived Narfi, only to be killed for sport by this man? Her limbs tensed, poised for renewed flight, but she forced her legs to remain still.

'Where is the challenge in killing women?' he responded gravely. 'I'm a warrior who fights other warriors. Playing games of chase with a beautiful woman will have to wait for another day. I've other things to attend to. Give me your word that you will come meekly and I'll release your arm. Otherwise, I will bind you.'

Cwenneth concentrated on breathing evenly. Playing games of chase, indeed! As if she was some maid flirting with him in the Lingwold physic garden! She was a widow whose heart had been buried with her late husband and son.

She clung on to her temper and did not slap his face. This was about survival until she could return to Lingwold. Once she was safe behind the thick greystone walls, she could give in to sarcasm and her temper. Until then, she guarded her tongue and kept her throat whole.

'Let me go and I'll give my word,' she ground out.

'Satisfied?' He lifted his hand.

She stared at the large Norseman warrior standing before her. He had released his hold, but the imprint of his hands burnt through the cloth. Large and ferocious with glacial blue eyes, a man who took pride in fighting, and the last sort of person she wanted to see. Who was he? Was it a case of things going from bad to worse? How much worse could it get? At least Thrand Ammundson was in Jorvik. No one could be as bad as that man.

'You see, I keep my word. Now will you? Will you trust me?'

Cwenneth swallowed hard to wet her throat and keep the tang of panic from invading her mouth. Trust a Norseman? A Norseman warrior? How naive did he think she was?

'Say the words now.' He pulled a length of leather from his belt.

'I'll come with you…willingly. There is no need to bind me,' she muttered, despising her weakness, but she hated to think about her wrists being bound and marked. 'I give you my word. I won't make a break for my freedom.'

'And I accept it.' He refastened the length of leather to his belt. 'You see I'm willing to trust you, but then I can outrun you.'

'How do you know how fast I can run?' she asked, watching the leather sway slightly like a snake.

'You wear skirts.' His dark-blue eyes darkened to the colour of a Northumbrian summer's midnight, but held no humour. 'Skirts tangle about your legs and catch in thorn bushes and brambles. If I have to chase you or you disobey me, things will go much worse for you.'

Cwenneth lifted her chin. She had to concentrate on small victories. She remained unbound…for the moment. It would be harder to escape if he decided to tie her up. And she planned on escaping when the time was ripe. 'I will take your word for it. I've never worn trousers.'

'A modicum of sense in your brain. Not my usual experience with Northumbrian women.' His brows drew together. 'Why are you here? Why were you left alive? Why was your entourage attacked?'

She knew then he'd found the carnage that lay back there on the road. Silently, she named the six men who had died, thinking they were protecting her. They were seared on her heart. Someday, somehow, Hagal would be made to pay. Even faithless Agatha needed justice. In this darkening glade with the bare trees towering above her, she had half-hoped that it was a dreadful nightmare and she'd wake up to find Agatha softly snoring near here or, better still, in her tapestry-hung room at Lingwold.

'The attack came from nowhere,' she began and stopped, unable to continue. A great sob rose up in her throat, and in her mind she saw the images of the bodies where they fell and heard the unholy screams. She forced the sob back down. No Norseman would have the pleasure of seeing her cry. She straightened her spine and looked him directly in the eye. 'I'm sorry. I can't speak of it. Not yet. Please don't make me.'

'You're my responsibility, and I want you alive.' He

captured her chin with hard fingers, and his deadened eyes peered into her soul. 'As long as you do as I say.'

'My world has changed completely.' Cwenneth forced her eyes to stare back into his.

She knew she was a tall woman, but her eyes were merely on the same level as his chin. He made her feel tiny and delicate, rather than overgrown as she had in the past. Even Aefirth had been barely taller than her. Absently she rubbed where his hand had encircled her wrist.

'I give better protection than the men who died, the ones who were supposed to ensure you and the other woman came to no harm.' He released her chin. 'Was she your mistress?'

'My mistress?' Cwenneth hesitated. He thought her the maid! Her heart leapt. A tiny glimmer of hope filled her. This Norseman had made a fundamental error.

If he knew who she was, he'd return her to Hagal who would surely kill her. A wife, even a solemnly betrothed bride like she was, was a husband's property. And they were fellow Norsemen. She needed to get back to Lingwold and warn her brother of Hagal's treachery rather than be delivered with a pretty bow about her neck to that viper.

'Who was your mistress? Quick now. It is hardly a difficult question.'

'The Lady of Lingwold. She was on her way to finalise her marriage to Hagal the Red.' Feverishly Cwenneth prayed that her deception would work. 'I'm her tire woman. Cwen. I'd left the cart to gather blue-bells and hopefully improve the smell. After all the travelling we had done, the cart stank. The herbs in the cart gave my lady a woolly head.'

She gulped a breath of air as the words tripped off her tongue. So far, so good.

He pointed to the gold embroidered hem of her gown. 'A very fine gown for a maid to be wearing, Cwen.'

'One of my lady's cast-offs,' she said with a curtsy. 'I had it in honour of her marriage. She had many new gowns and no longer had need of this one. It was from her first marriage and quite out of date.'

He nodded, seeming to accept her word. The tension in Cwenneth's shoulders eased a little. Cwen had a good ring to it, reminding her of Aefirth's pet name for her.

How hard could it be to play the maid? It was far safer than being herself—the woman whom everyone wanted dead or believed cursed beyond redemption, destined never to have a family who loved her.

'And, Cwen, your lady did not wish to get out of the cart and sent you instead. Did she fear bandits?' His lip curled slightly as if he disapproved of such fine women.

'She knew about the possibility of outlaws. There are desperate men about these days.'

'Even though she must have known she was on her bridegroom's lands.'

'Even then. My lady was timid.' Cwenneth gestured about her. 'It is in places such as these that man-eating wolves lurk. Or so my…her nurse used to say.'

She winced at her near slip, but his face betrayed nothing. Perhaps he didn't have that good a grasp of the language. Or perhaps… Drawing attention to the mistake would only make matters worse. But she had to have convinced him. He looked to be more muscle than brain like most of the Norsemen. Certainly his shoulders went on for ever.

The ice in his eyes grew. 'If she was in the covered cart, how did she know about the woods, the wolves and most of all the bluebells?'

'My lady caught a glimpse of the outside through the slats in the window when the cart stopped so they could get the mud off the wheels. I went to fetch them,' Cwenneth improvised. 'She would hardly have let me go if she thought the attack was going to happen. My lady trusted her men and the promises her bridegroom gave.'

Cwenneth finished in a breathless rush. If she kept to the truth as much as possible, she should be able to fool him.

When she had her chance, she'd escape and return to Lingwold, like in the stories her nurse, Martha, used to tell. Her brother would see that justice was done. Enough warriors to make a formidable army would flock to Edward's banner when he put the call out to avenge this outrage.

'I find it hard to believe Hagal allowed his bride to travel without protection. Or did she intend to surprise him? This timid bride of his?'

'Hagal provided over twenty warriors. You would have to ask them why they fled. My lady was only allowed six of her own men.' She waited, heart in her throat, to see his response.

His stone-hard face betrayed nothing. 'Do you wish me to take you to Hagal the Red's stronghold? He will want to hear news of his bride's demise.'

Cwenneth's stomach knotted. The Norseman was leaving the decision up to her. Lingwold was a real possibility instead of a cloud-in-the-sky fantasy. She could almost see the comforting stone walls rising up before her.

'Her brother needs to hear the news first. He will give a reward for information about my lady. I know it.'

The Norseman remained implacably silent.

Cwenneth pressed her hands together and gathered her courage. 'I believe…I believe Hagal's men murdered everyone in my party.'

There, she had said it and had mentioned the possibility of a reward. Gold always motivated the Norsemen. Her stomach twisted in knots. In the silence which followed she could hear the flap of a wood-pigeon's wings.

'A strong accusation,' he said, his face remaining devoid of any shock or surprise. 'Why would Hagal's men want his bride dead? He will have spent time and effort negotiating the marriage contract.'

'Perhaps they are in the pay of Thrand the Destroyer and betrayed their master.'

'I think not,' he said, crossing his arms, and his face appeared more carved in stone than ever. No doubt he expected her to cower. 'Try again. Who attacked this convoy?'

Cwenneth glared back and refused to be intimidated. 'I speak the truth—Hagal's men did it under his orders. I overheard them speaking afterwards. He wanted her dead to fulfil a battlefield vow he made. I hope even Norsemen have a respect for the truth. The

Lord of Lingwold certainly will. He'll see justice is done and Hagal the Red is punished for this crime.'

As she said the words, Cwenneth knew she spoke the truth. Edward might have desired the marriage, but he wanted her alive. Blood counted for something…even with Edward. He would take steps to avenge Hagal's actions. Even a convent without a dowry currently sounded like heaven compared to being a Norseman's slave or, worse still, murdered.

'How did you propose to get to Lingwold? It is over a hundred miles through hostile wilderness and floods. The mud-clogged roads from the recent rain are the least of your problems.'

Cwenneth sucked in her breath. He knew where Lingwold was, but then it was one of the largest estates in southern Bernicia.

'Walk!'

'Wolves and bears lurk in these woods. Not to mention outlaws and other desperate men who roam the roads.'

'I know. I was waiting until nightfall before I returned to the…' Cwenneth's throat closed. What did she call it now that murder had taken place? 'To where it happened. I hoped to find something there, something I could use on my journey. I refuse to simply sit here and die.' She clasped her hands together to keep them from shaking uncontrollably. 'Will you take me to Lingwold? Help me complete my journey? The Lord of Lingwold will give a great reward for information about his sister. I promise.'

'I've no plans to visit Lingwold at present.'

Cwenneth blinked. He was refusing? 'What do

you mean? There will be a reward. A great reward. Gold. As much gold as you can carry.'

'The promise of a *small* reward for telling a man his sister is dead fails to tempt me. The great Lord Edward of Lingwold might even take a severe dislike to the man who brought him news of his sister's demise.' His mouth curled around the words as if her brother was anything but a great lord.

'You have a point. He is known to have a temper.' Cwen fingered her throat. She couldn't confess now. Not now that she knew this man disliked her brother so much that he refused to consider a reward. She'd have to come up with a different plan. That was all. 'Where do we go?'

'You go where I choose. You tell your story when I choose and to whom I choose. And not before. Like you, I know Hagal the Red did this.' A bright flame flared in his eyes, transforming his features. 'I have my own reasons for wanting him to face justice.'

Until he chose? To become his slave for ever? Cwenneth firmed her mouth and renewed her vow. 'Who are you? What shall I call you?'

He made a mocking bow. 'Thrand Ammundson.'

Thrand Ammundson. Thrand the Destroyer. Cwenneth gulped. The Norseman whose band of warriors raided Lingwold yearly. The man who loved killing so much that his name was a byword for destruction. The man who was supposed to be in Jorvik, but who was here and probably on his way to raid innocent Bernicians.

Her luck was truly terrible. Of all the Norsemen to encounter, it would have to be him, the one man other than Hagal the Red most likely to want her dead.

'You're Thrand the Destroyer?' she whispered, clasping her hands so tight that the knuckles shone white.

He was right—her brother had no cause to love him and every cause to kill him. As she had departed for Acumwick, Edward had crowed that he looked forward to having Thrand's head on a plate and his hide nailed to the parish church's door.

'Some have called me that, but they are wrong. I have never come to destroy, only to take what is rightfully mine or my liege lord's. The Norsemen of Jorvik did not start the last war, but they did finish it.'

'That makes it all right because you won,' Cwenneth remarked drily, trying to think around the pain in her head. Right now she had to put miles between her and Hagal, who definitely wanted her dead. Everything else could wait. Patience was a virtue, her nurse, Martha, used to say.

'The victor commissions the saga, as they say.'

A soft rustling in the undergrowth made Cwenneth freeze. She instinctively grabbed hold of Thrand's sleeve.

'Wolf or mayhap a bear,' she said in a hoarse whisper. 'My luck goes from bad to worse.'

Thrand put his fingers to his lips and pivoted so that his body was between her and the noise.

He started to draw his sword, but then relaxed.

'There, see.' He pointed with a long finger. 'No wolf.'

Cwenneth crouched down and found herself staring into the tusked head of a boar. The animal blew a hot breath over her face before giving her a long disdainful look and trotting off.

'That was unexpected,' she said, sitting back on her heels.

'Thor has shown you favour,' Thrand remarked in the quiet that followed. 'Good luck follows your footsteps in battle when Thor favours you.'

'I don't believe in the Norsemen's gods. And I know what those tusks can do. My stepson was gored once. It ended his fighting days and he walks with a bad limp. I wouldn't call that lucky.'

She gave an uneasy laugh. A god favoured her? Thankfully he didn't know about the curse she carried. He'd abandon her in these woods if he did. Pressing her hands together, she tried to control her trembling and breathe normally.

'You're married? What did your husband say about you travelling with your lady to her new home?'

'My husband died and…and I found myself back in my lady's service.' A fresh dribble of sweat ran down her back. The words rushed out of her throat. 'My luck has been dreadful these last few years.'

'You're wrong.' His searing gaze raked her form, making Cwenneth aware of her angles. Her sister-in-law was one of the plump comfortable women which men loved, but Cwenneth had few illusions about the attractiveness of her body—all hard angles with only a few slender curves. 'You survived the slaughter. That makes you luckier than the corpses back there.'

Her shoulders relaxed. He hadn't noticed her slip. 'I've lingered too long in these woods. Can we go from this place?'

He made a mocking bow. 'As my lady wishes.'

'I'm not a lady. I am a maid, a person of no consequence.'

A faint smile touched his lips. 'It is well you reminded me.'

She shook her head to rid it of the prickling feeling that he was toying with her. But Norsemen were not that subtle. They used brute force to destroy farms and steal livestock, rather than cunning to discover the hidden stores. She'd bide her time and escape.

'What have you found, Thrand? Anything? There is nothing to say who did this here,' Knui called out as Thrand emerged from the woods with his prisoner in tow. 'We thought the demons who must dwell in this place had found you and conquered your soul. But then they whisper that Loki has already determined your fate at Ragnarok.'

'A witness,' Thrand answered shortly, keeping a firm grip on Cwen's wrist. Binding a woman was always a last resort. He would use her to bring down Hagal and finally revenge his parents. What happened to her after that was none of his concern.

'Will you take her to Hagal?' Knui asked with an intense expression. 'The slaughter happened on his land. He will want to find the Northumbrians who did this and punish them. A direct assault on his authority can't be tolerated. Think about how Halfdan will react when he knows. These bastards want to start the war again. Do they never give up?'

'In my time,' Thrand answered, giving Knui a hard look. With each word, Knui proclaimed that he was indeed Hagal's creature. It was only Thrand's promise to Sven which stayed his hand and prevented him from running the man through. Sven had given his oath his cousin would be loyal with his last breath. 'I have promises to keep first, as you well know.'

'But won't she slow us down?' Knui continued grumbling, seemingly oblivious to the threat in Thrand's look. 'The last thing we need is a woman with us. It is going to be difficult enough to get in and out of Bernicia as is.'

Knui was right in one respect. The last thing he wanted on this journey was a woman, but Hagal, who loved gold more than life itself, wanted her dead. And that was more than enough justification for keeping her with them and alive.

'Let me worry about that.'

'We need to be back before the Storting starts,' Knui persisted. 'I want a say in Halfdan's successor, even if you don't.'

'You seek to challenge my authority, Knui, son of Gorm, kinsman to Sven Audson?' Thrand reached for his sword. If Knui wanted a fight, so be it. He had never walked away from a battle. He never would. 'Do so openly. I've no time for games and whispers. Are you prepared to chance your sword arm against mine? Shall we see who the victor will be?'

Knui glanced over his shoulders and saw the other men had moved away from him, leaving him isolated. The colour drained from his face.

Thrand waited impassively.

'Not I.' Knui hung his head. 'I have seen you on the battlefield, Thrand. I know what you can do. I am content for you to lead us.'

'I accept your judgement.' Thrand sheathed his sword and the rage subsided. There would be no need to do battle with Knui…today. But he no longer trusted him.

Sweat poured from Knui's forehead. 'Thank you.'

'I lead this *felag*. The woman comes north with us…unless any cares to fight me.'

'Do you think we can get a ransom for her?' Helgi called out.

'She claims to be the maid. When has anyone ever ransomed a maid?' Thrand answered, giving Cwen a significant look. Her pale cheeks became stained the colour of her gown and she kept her eyes downcast. 'What is a serving maid worth beyond her value at the slave market?'

'Yes, I am the Lady of Lingwold's maid,' Cwen called out. 'How could I be anything else?'

Thrand schooled his features as his men looked to him for confirmation. He inclined his head, not committing himself either way. Her voice was far too fine and her gown, under the coarse woollen cloak, too well made. He'd bet his sword and a good more besides that she was the true Lady of Lingwold.

'Indeed,' he murmured, releasing her wrist. She instantly rubbed it. 'How could you be anyone but the maid?'

'You are going to bury them here? After you have taken everything of value from them? They served my lady well. She respected them,' she said, turning away from him and not answering the question. 'They deserve better than being plucked clean by the crows.'

'They have no use for their swords where they are.' Thrand shrugged as his men busied themselves with completing the pit. 'The crows have enough to eat. No point in leaving them out in the open.'

Her brow wrinkled as she pleated her burgundy skirt between her fingers. 'I…I suppose not. But there must be a churchyard near here. They should have a Christian burial. Find a priest.' She gave a tiny sniff. 'The decent thing to do.'

He bit back the words that he had no decent bones left in his body. All he lived for was war. It had been a part of his existence for so long, he knew no other way of life. All finer feelings had vanished years ago on blood-soaked ground before a burning farmhouse in southern Viken. Burying them was the best way to make Hagal uneasy. 'This is a conversation you should have with the lord of these lands.'

She paled and took a step backwards. 'You mean Hagal the Red.'

Thrand watched her from under his brows and wondered if she knew the truth about how her bridegroom had acted in Norway and Northumbria? What had he promised her family to lure her out here so he could fulfil his vow of revenge?

'The Lady of Lingwold was meant to be his bride. Once he learns of the massacre, he will come here,' he said, willing her to confide the truth and beg for his assistance. 'He is a man who likes to see the aftermath of such things with his own eyes. Shall we wait?'

She tucked her chin into her neck. The action highlighted its slender curve and the way her golden hair glinted in the sun. He curled his hands into fists and concentrated.

The consequences of being distracted by beauty were deadly. He had learnt that lesson in Norway. No, the Lady Cwenneth in her way was just as black-hearted as Ingrid had been. And her earlier remarks about the dress being ruined showed how her mind worked—she did not care about people, but things.

'He wanted everyone dead and I'm alive,' she said in a low voice. 'He'll kill me if he finds me. He'll come after you as well once he knows.'

'I want him to wonder who is buried and who did the burying,' Thrand answered shortly. 'I want him unsettled. I want him to wonder if you are dead out in those woods or not. I want him to know fear for once.'

'Do you fear him?' She shivered and wrapped her arms about her waist, and her shoulders hunched. 'I do. What sort of man does what he did? Makes such orders?'

'Not in a fight.' Thrand's hand went instinctively to his sword. 'I have studied how he fights in battle. Utterly predictable. Always goes for the downwards thrust followed by a quick upwards one to finish his opponent off. Never varies. And he hangs to the rear rather than leading from the front.'

Her crystal-blue gaze met his—direct and determined. 'Hagal doesn't fight fair. Ever. He looks for the weakest point and goes for it. He did this with... with Lord Edward.'

'What did he promise Lord Edward to make him cough up his sister?' he asked silkily. 'What did the Lord of Lingwold hope to gain?'

'Peace and your head.' She lifted her chin, every inch the proud lady. 'Does it bother you to know you are hated that much?'

Thrand schooled his features. Despite everything he thought he knew about Northumbrian ladies and their empty-headedness, a reluctant admiration filled him. She might be beautiful, but she also had a brain which was full of more than feather beds, ribbons and embroidery.

'How did murdering you get the Lord of Lingwold my head? Everyone thinks I'm in Jorvik with the king.' He allowed a smile to play on his lips.

Her brows drew together and finally she shrugged. 'I don't know. Ask Hagal. He was hardly going to confide his intentions to me. Understandable in the circumstances, but aggravating as I'm sure you will agree.'

She inclined her head. Thrand fought the unexpected urge to laugh. Lady Cwenneth had more than a bit of grit to her. He sobered, but it didn't mean he should trust her one little bit.

Thrand turned the matter over in his mind. The more he thought about it, the more far-fetched it seemed. Marriages took a long time to negotiate. No one knew he would be in the area. He hadn't known until a few days ago that he'd be travelling north. But there was a method to Hagal's madness. He always played a long game.

Why did Hagal need the Lady Cwenneth's death? Why now? How would killing her bring Lord Edward Thrand's head? And what did Hagal get out of it? He drew a steadying breath.

The answer would come to him as he travelled north and before he arrived back in Jorvik for the Storting. Then he'd know precisely how to deploy Lady Cwenneth to destroy Hagal once and for all. For too long that particular Norseman had eluded him.

'Well?' she asked, tapping her slipper on the ground. With her set chin and fierce expression, he could almost believe she was descended from the Valkyries. 'Do you have the answer? It would make me feel safer if I did.'

'You will have your opportunity for revenge. I trust you will use it well as I doubt you will get a second chance.'

'One chance is all I will need. He will not rise when I am done.'

'And you are certain of that? What are you going to do? Plunge a knife in his throat? Are you capable of that?'

All fight went out of her shoulders. Instead of an avenging Valkyrie, all was naked vulnerability and confusion. Lady Cwenneth was no shield maiden. 'I have no idea. All I know is he should die for what he did. Hopefully you are right about this.'

'I know I am right...this time,' Thrand muttered and tried not to think about the unquiet dead he'd failed.

Chapter Three

Cwenneth avoided looking at the pile of bodies and instead concentrated on the smouldering remains of the cart. Smoke hung in the air, getting in her eyes and lungs. Her entire life, including the future she hadn't truly wanted but had been willing to experience for the sake of her people, was gone.

'Is there anything left? Anything salvageable?' she asked.

'Either burnt or taken,' came Thrand's reply. 'Did your lady only travel with one cart?'

'There was a baggage cart as well.' She frowned. 'I should have said earlier.'

'It is all gone then. Your lady's dowry. They took anything that wasn't nailed down and burnt the rest'

The words knifed through her.

'But my things? My mother's…comb.' Cwenneth clamped her mouth shut before she mentioned the mirror and her jewellery. Since when would a maid have her own mirror, let alone rings and pendants?

It wasn't the gold she missed, although she was furious about it. What she missed most was the lock of Richard's hair, his soft baby hair. She used to wrap her fingers around it when she needed comfort and normally wore a pendant with it in to keep him close to her heart. Stupidly, she had taken off the pendant this morning and put it in the iron-bound trunk to keep it safe because the clasp was almost broken, and now it was gone for ever.

'Time to go. There is no point in sifting through ash.' Thrand put a heavy hand on her shoulder.

Cwenneth resisted the temptation to lean into him and draw strength from him. She stood on her own two feet now, rather than leaning on anyone, let alone a Norse warrior. 'The sooner I am away from this place of death, the better.'

'Take some boots. You will need them.' The glacial blue in his eyes increased.

'Why?'

It was clear from his expression what he thought of her. A barely tolerated encumbrance. Cwenneth didn't mind. It was not as if she wanted to be friends. Somehow, some way she'd find an opportunity to escape.

Escape? Back to what? A brother who saw her as a counter to be used? And a sister-in-law who hated her? Cwenneth banished the disloyal thoughts. They were family. Lingwold was home and she loved its people. Whatever the future held, it wasn't being a slave to this Norseman.

'Why do I need boots?'

'Unless you wish to walk in bare feet, you need boots. Your slippers will be torn to ribbons within a mile,' he said with an exaggerated politeness.

'From where?' Cwenneth gestured about her.

'Where are the boots stored? Where am I going to find a pair of boots?'

He gestured towards the bodies. His men immediately paused and backed away from them. 'You are going to allow a good pair of boots to go to waste while your feet bleed?'

Her stomach knotted. He wanted her to rob the dead. 'It feels wrong. They died wearing those boots.'

He made a cutting motion with his hand. 'Do the dead care? Will they rise up and challenge you?'

A faint burn coursed up through her cheeks. She winced. He probably robbed the dead without a pang of guilt. Norsemen were like that. They took rather than respected the property of the living or the dead.

Cwenneth glared at him, hating his long blond hair, his huge shoulders and the fact that he was alive and her men were dead. 'I have never robbed the dead before.'

'Do you want to choose or shall I?'

'I'll choose.' Cwenneth walked over to where the youngest of her men lay. Dain's mother had been her nurse when she was little. She had asked for him because she thought he'd have a good future in her new household. Martha had readily agreed. 'Dain's boots. They are solid and new. His mother gave them to him before we departed. They are good leather to walk a thousand miles in, or so Martha proclaimed. She'd have liked me to have them.'

'And you think they will fit?' he asked in a casual tone. His eyes watched her as a cat might watch a mouse hole. 'Shouldn't you try them on first?'

She pressed her lips together. Perhaps she'd been too hasty at dismissing him as all brawn and very little brain. She needed to be very careful from here on out and weigh her words, rather than rushing to fill the silence.

'I have large feet for a woman.' She bent down and tore several strips of cloth from Dain's cloak. Luckily the material ripped easily. 'This should be enough to fill the toes.'

She knelt down and started to stuff the boots before she said anything more.

'You have done this before,' he remarked, hunkering down next to her.

Up close, she could see that his hair was a hundred different shades of yellow and that his features were finely made despite his overbearing size and manner. Their breath laced. Her hands trembled, and she redoubled her efforts. All she had to do was ignore her unwanted reaction to him. He wanted to unsettle her for his own perverse pleasure. Well, she'd disappoint him. She lifted her chin.

'Once at Christmas, I dressed up as a bard.' She gulped, rapidly shoving her feet into the boots before walking a few steps. 'I mean, my lady did and I helped her. She wore her husband's boots… When I get back to Lingwold, Martha will appreciate the gesture.'

'And you believe the boots will last that long?'

'I have to.' She rubbed her hands together, pushing the thought away that she might never get back. Lingwold for all its faults was her home. 'What shall I be riding in? Where is your cart?'

He appeared to grow several inches and his shoulders broadened. Barely tamed. Every inch the warrior. 'Playtime is over. You won't be riding, Lady Cwenneth.' Thrand made a low bow. 'Your ladyship will be walking. I am fresh out of carts and my horse is not overly fond of Northumbrians or women. And I'm not minded to inconvenience him for a proud Northumbrian lady like you. The only question is whether or not I have to tether you to my horse.'

She put her hand to her throat and her heartbeat resounded in her ears. He had called her Lady Cwenneth. Lady! 'You know. How?'

His lips turned up into a humourless smile. 'Did you think me an idiot? I've known since the first time you opened your mouth. It amused me to see how far you would push it and how many mistakes you'd make. You're a very poor liar, my lady, even if your voice is sweet enough to charm birds from the trees.'

Cwenneth stared at her hands. Each word knifed her heart. She had been certain that she had fooled him. Naivety in the extreme. It would have been better if she'd died in the woods. She was Thrand Ammundson's prisoner—worse than that, his slave. He knew her brother wanted his head and had been prepared to pay a high price to get it.

How could he be so cruel as to play this sadistic game? Giving her hope and then turning her over to the one man who would kill her? Her knees threatened to buckle. Summoning all her strength, she locked her knees and balled her fists.

'Will you deliver me to Hagal? Trussed up like a prize? Was that what you were always planning on doing? Why bother with the play-acting?' She stretched out her neck and attempted to seem fiercesome. 'Why not cut off my head and send it back to my brother as a warning? Go on. Do it now.'

'My enemy wants you dead. Why should I want to do that job for him?' Something stirred in his lifeless eyes—a flash of warmth and admiration that was so quickly concealed Cwenneth wondered if she had imagined it. 'The enemy of my enemy is my friend. I learnt that in Constantinople and it kept me alive.'

'We do share a common enemy, but we will never be friends. Temporary allies at best,' she said, tapping her finger against her mouth. *The enemy of his enemy...* She wanted to fall down and kiss the ground. They were on the same side. He needed her alive and unscathed.

'You take my point.'

Her heart did a wild leap. She was going to see Lingwold's grey walls again. She'd never complain about the tapestry weaving being done incorrectly again or the subjects her sister-in-law considered suitable for gossip, but which bored her senseless. She'd be back with her family and people who understood her.

'Then you'll be taking me to Lingwold.' She clasped her hands together to keep from throwing them about his neck. 'My brother will pay a huge ransom for me. I swear this on my mother's grave. He has many men pledged to him. He could send an army against Hagal, assist you in getting rid of your enemy. My brother hates being taken for a fool, and Hagal played him.'

She knew in her relief she was babbling like a brook. When the words had all flowed out of her, she stood, waiting for his agreement. The silence grew deafening. The bravado leaked from her veins as his stare hardened.

'We're allies,' she said in a small voice. 'It makes sense.'

He shook his head. 'I'll never go to Lingwold. Your brother's assurances aren't worth the spit it takes to say them. If I took you back to Lingwold, I would be truly fulfilling Hagal's promise to your brother. I know what will happen to me if I enter Lingwold with you even if Hagal has been destroyed. After I've finished with you, you may go where you please. Your fate is not linked to mine beyond that day.'

'I failed to consider that.'

Her brother could be every bit as ruthless as any Norsemen. War had brutalised the idealistic youth she'd known. He bragged about outsmarting them and leaving a band of them to die in a burning house. He proudly proclaimed that it was the only reason Thrand had left him alone for the last raiding season. Her brother might listen to her story, but only after he'd taken Thrand's head. If Thrand had acted on her advice, she'd have ended up betraying the man she depended on to save her life.

Thrand nodded towards the muddy track. 'Time to go, your ladyship. Walk—or would you prefer to have your hands bound and be tossed on the back of my horse? I'm in a generous mood after your display of courage. Not many women have asked me to take their life.'

'I'm not a sack of wool. I will walk. Where are we headed? South to Jorvik?'

'North to fulfil an oath to my late helmsmen. But I intend to return to Jorvik before the next Storting.'

'When is that?'

'Less than a month.' He made low bow. 'That will

have to satisfy you, Lady Cwenneth. And you had best keep up. I have no time for stragglers, particularly when they are pampered Northumbrian ladies.'

Cwenneth touched her neck, her hand automatically seeking the reassurance of her lost pendant and Richard's lock of hair. She forced her fingers down. 'I will walk until it is time to stop. Have no fear on that. I won't need special assistance.'

'I shall be interested to see you try.' He raised his voice so it rang out loud and clear. 'Lads, the lady is for walking and reckons she can keep up. Do I have any takers? Will she be able to and for how long?'

All about her, Thrand's men began to wager on how long she'd last. Several remarked on how all Northumbrian ladies were pampered and unused to hard work. One even predicted she would not make but a few yards beyond this place before she demanded to ride. Cwenneth gritted her teeth and silently damned them all to hell.

'Do you always keep at this pace?' she asked, trying to wring out her gown as she trudged through the mud. She must have blisters on top of blisters. Every fibre of her being longed for a warm hearth, a roof over her head and a soft bed to sink down in. But with every step she took and mile she passed, she took satisfaction in proving another Norseman wrong.

'Getting through the woods and putting distance between us and the massacre is a priority.'

'We've put miles between us and…and where the massacre happened. Surely it must be time to find shelter for the night.'

Every sinew in her body ached. She hurt even where she didn't think she had muscles.

Thrand half turned from where he led his horse through a muddy puddle and lifted an arrogant eyebrow. 'We need to make up for lost time. I want to get through these woods before night falls and the rain starts in earnest. We camp in safety. Does that suit your ladyship? Or has my lady changed her mind and now wishes to become a sack of wool?'

The exaggerated patience of his tone grated on her frayed nerves. She stopped and put a hand in the middle of her aching back. 'Leave me at a farmhouse. Do your raiding or whatever you are going north to do and pick me up on your return. I'll wait patiently.'

'How would I know that you'd stay there? Waiting *patiently*?'

'I'd give my word.' She fixed him with a deliberately wide-eyed gaze, but kept her fingers crossed. If the opportunity to go happened, she wouldn't linger, but she would send a reward once she made Lingwold. 'No one has questioned it before.'

He made a disgusted noise. 'If I had taken your word earlier, I would still think you the tire woman. Underestimating my intelligence does neither of us any credit.'

Cwenneth ground her teeth. Fair point. She forced her feet to start marching again. 'A necessary deception. I had no idea if you were friend or foe.'

'Once having deceived someone like that, how do you build trust? I'm curious to hear your answer, my lady.'

'I'm not sure,' Cwenneth admitted and concentrated on skirting the next puddle. 'But you should consider the suggestion if you think I am slowing proceedings down. A good commander thinks of all his men. My late husband used to say that.'

'Consider being left at the farmhouse.' He slowed his horse slightly and kept pace with her feet. 'Hagal and his men will begin hunting you once they suspect you live. They will not stop until you are dead or you have defeated Hagal. How will you ensure that farmer's loyalty when his crops are threatened? A good commander should think about all eventualities before coming to a decision.'

Cwenneth's stomach knotted. Hagal's men, in particular Narfi, knew every farmhouse in the area. They were bound to check once they discovered the buried bodies and that hers wasn't there. Her flesh crept. Thrand was right—why would any farmer shelter her? She wouldn't be safe until Hagal was dead and she was back inside Lingwold's walls. 'I failed to think that far ahead.'

'If you want to stay alive, let alone gain the revenge you want, you will have to start thinking ahead and you will stay with me. I'm your best…no…your only hope.'

'But we are staying at a farmhouse. The thought of a bed and a pillow has kept me going for a while.'

His face took on a thoughtful expression. 'People do remember travellers and when Hagal's men come, they will answer their questions.' He gave a half shrug, but his eyes were sharp as if seeking something from her. 'A lone woman travelling with a group of Norsemen… I doubt many fine ladies travel through this part of the country. If Hagal's men fail to find your body in the woods, they will check with the surrounding farms. It is what I would do.'

Cwenneth regarded the ground, rather than meeting Thrand's direct stare. To think she had earlier dismissed him as being all brawn and no brain. He had considered several steps ahead rather than thinking about immediate needs. She needed to start thinking smarter and stop giving in to prejudice. Thrand Ammundson was highly intelligent as well as a formidable warrior.

Some place deep within her chimed in that he was also good-looking when he wasn't scowling. She ignored it. She had not been interested in men since Aefirth died. Her very being had been encased in ice.

She narrowly avoided another muddy puddle and tried to think about what her next move should be in this real-life game of cat and mouse she was playing, rather than what Thrand looked like when he wasn't scowling. The only advantage she held was that Hagal thought her dead.

'You've fallen silent, my lady. Do we stop at the next farm? I can see smoke rising in the distance. There will be a welcome of sorts.'

Cwenneth hiked her gown up to keep it out of the mud and silently bid goodbye to all thoughts of a feather bed. The only thing keeping her out of Hagal's clutches was his belief that she was dead. 'You're right, we need to continue on and stopping at a farm is far from a good idea. The stress of today is addling my nerves.'

'Here you had dreams of a bed,' he said with heavy irony. 'Have you given up on your dreams so quickly? Are all Northumbrian ladies this weak willed?'

'Do you know many Northumbrian ladies?'

'I've met enough.'

'They weren't me.' Cwenneth made a show of placing her feet down, even as the pain from the blister seared up her right leg. 'I can keep going as long as you require it. There is no need to stop at a farmhouse or any settlement. The open air suits me fine.'

A hearty laugh rang out from his throat. 'You learn quickly.'

'Did you plan on stopping at a farm? Before…before you encountered me?'

He pulled his horse to a halt. All good humour vanished from his face. 'I've my reasons for not wishing to be remembered.'

'And they are?'

'My own.'

Just when Cwenneth was convinced they would be trudging through the dank mud all night, Thrand imperiously lifted his hand and pulled his horse to a halt. The entire company stopped. 'We will make camp here tonight. We should be safe. The ground is good in case of attack…from anyone or anything.'

Cwenneth sucked in her breath, giving silent thanks her walking for the day was done. But she was also pretty sure that she had beaten all wagers against her. It was strange—whenever she had considered quitting, she remembered the wagering and became more determined to prove them, particularly Thrand, wrong. 'Expecting trouble?'

'It is better to expect trouble than to encounter it, unprepared,' Thrand said before issuing orders to his men. 'Perhaps if your men had…'

'They were outnumbered. The outcome would have been the same,' she answered, placing her hands in the middle of her back, rather than giving in to the desire to collapse in a heap. Once down, she had her doubts about getting up again. 'I keep wondering if there was something more I could have done, but my brother was determined on the match. He threatened me with a convent of his choosing and no dowry. I considered being the wife to a Norse *jaarl* was the better bet. Without a dowry, I'd have been little better than a scullery maid. It shows how wrong a person can be.'

'And defeating me means more to your brother than his sister's life?'

She pressed her hands to her eyes. 'Edward had no part in this. He wanted to believe Hagal's assurances and saw the marriage as a way to gain a powerful ally. But he'd never have sent me if he suspected the truth. A dead sister is no use to him in his quest for power within the Bernician court.'

His level gaze met hers. 'There was nothing you could have done once the events were set in motion. The only mistake Hagal has made in this enterprise is to allow you to fall into my hands alive.'

'But…'

'He will pay for it. Now sit and rest. Women like you have no experience at setting up a camp and cause delays.'

'You have a very low opinion of Northumbrian ladies.'

'My dealings with them have been deliberately kept to a minimum.' The glacial blue of his eyes thawed slightly. 'However, you did better today than any of my men thought you would. You have earned your rest.' He shook his head. 'You are far stronger than even I thought you would be. You have made me revise my opinion of ladies. Not all are pale, puny creatures with less stamina than a mouse.'

'Good.' Cwenneth sank to the ground, rather than argue. Her feet throbbed and burnt. Sitting, being ignored, was bliss. But her journey home and back to her family had just begun. Somewhere along the way, she'd teach that arrogant Norse warrior that ladies from Lingwold were to be reckoned with. She clenched her fist and vowed it on her son's grave.

'Far from smart to provoke him, you know. His temper is legendary.'

She glanced up and saw a slender Norseman standing before her. She shaded her eyes. He'd been the one who had objected to Thrand bringing her along. Her own temper flared. 'His nickname gives it away—the Destroyer. I doubt he acquired it through being kind and gentle to his enemies.'

'Thrand is a great fighter. When a battle comes, he always wins. Halfdan's most potent weapon. They say rather than take the risk, people shower him with gold when he appears on their doorstep.'

'Have you travelled with him often?'

'First time.' The man leant forward and lowered his voice. 'I promised my cousin on his deathbed I'd come. Someone has to see right for his child as it is kin. And Thrand, he is the sort of man to lead an expedition into enemy territory and return, more than likely with bags full of treasure and gold. Sven had a good war because of his friendship with Thrand. There are iron-bound chests full of gold back in Jorvik.'

'That I can well believe.' Cwenneth said a fervent prayer that Thrand and his men would not be returning to Jorvik with more treasure looted from Bernicia.

'I want gold,' Knui stated flatly. 'Lots of it. But then you don't have any as Thrand will have already taken it. So I'm not sure why I'm bothering with you.'

Her hand hit her belt. Her rings. Aefirth would have understood. *Cwennie, survive*, he would have said. *Rely on no one but yourself.* Maybe this warrior would go to Lingwold and let her brother know she survived.

Edward would raise an army to free her if he thought Thrand the Destroyer had her. He'd march to Jorvik and make his demands heard. She had to have patience and think long term. Her hand started to fumble for the rings and her blood became alive with excitement.

A warning sounded in her gut. Why was a Norseman trying to make friends with her? Did he guess that she possessed even a little bit of gold? Why mention it otherwise?

Her hand stilled and dropped to her side. She had to proceed with caution and trust no one.

'Knui Crowslayer! Where have you hidden yourself this time?' someone called. 'I need some help with the firewood!'

'It was good to speak with you,' Cwenneth called after him. 'We must speak another time.'

She hugged her knees to her chest, oddly pleased that she didn't give up her rings at the first hint. If today had taught her anything, it was not to be blindly trusting. She would wait for her opportunity, rather than acting on impulse.

There was more than one way to get back to her old life. All she needed was patience and a workable plan. Thinking ahead rather than regretting mistakes.

'You have remained in the same place since we arrived.' Thrand's voice rolled over her. 'Is that wise? Surely my lady must have a complaint about the primitive standards of this camp.'

Cwenneth lifted her head. All of her muscles screamed with pain and the shadows had grown longer. She wasn't sure if she had slept or if her mind had become mercifully blank. Now everything came flooding back. She remained in the nightmare and it was about to get worse because they had stopped for the night. And she had no idea of Thrand's plans. He had claimed her as his woman.

Did he expect her to become his concubine? There had only been Aefirth. She knew how to be a wife, but she had little idea how to be a mistress. Refusing the position was out of the question, not if she wanted to live.

'I wait for my orders, to find out what I need to do, rather than presuming.' Muscles protesting at the slightest movement, Cwenneth struggled to stand, but he motioned she should stay seated. She gratefully sat back down.

'Are you capable of following orders?' Up close she was aware of his height, the broadness of his shoulders and the way his shirt tightened across his chest. There was power in those muscle-bound arms, but gentleness as well. She could clearly remember how he'd approached the wild boar—slowly and carefully, rather than scaring it. 'Doing whatever I ask of you?'

'If I'm going to stay alive, I have to learn.'

'Clever woman.'

'I've kept my word so far. There is no need to tie me up. I'm not going to run away tonight, not on these feet.'

His gaze slowly travelled over her, making her aware of how her hair tumbled about her neck and the way her gown was now hopelessly stained with mud. She must look like something the dog had dragged in.

His thin smile failed to reach his eyes. 'I doubt you'd have the strength.'

'I kept going today.'

He put a hand on her shoulder. Heat flooded her. She wanted to lean into his touch. 'My men wagered that you wouldn't.'

'I heard them when we started. Who won in the end?'

'I did.'

'You bet on me?'

The blue in his eyes deepened. 'My purse is heavier. But you lasted even longer than I thought you would. Impressive. I thought, back by the farm, you'd beg for a ride.'

'Giving up is not an option if I want to return to my old life. It is better to be unbound. It makes me believe that one day I will regain my freedom.' She kept her head erect. 'I have my pride. The lords and ladies of Lingwold never beg.'

'And you want to return?'

'Very much. It is my home.' Cwenneth looped a strand of hair about her ear. 'Life is good at Lingwold. The walls are strong. Food is plentiful and everyone sleeps soundly in their bed. I would even kiss my sister-in-law and stop complaining about her silly rules about how you weave tapestry.'

'If it is in my power, word will be sent after I have finished with you.' He balanced the pouch of gold in his hand. 'But you have presented me with another problem. You walked too slow.'

'I hate horses.' Cwenneth leant forward, wrapping her hands about her knees. There was no way her feet would harden by morning. 'There, I have admitted it. My fear of horses was stronger than my hurting feet. Tomorrow may be a different story.'

She had been wary of horses ever since Edward's stallion had bitten her arm when she was ten. All she had done was try to give it a carrot. Edward had laughed at her fear.

'Here.' He tossed a small phial of ointment to her. It landed in her lap. She twisted off the top and wrinkled her nose.

'And this is?'

'For your feet. An old family recipe. My grandmother used to swear by it. It heals blisters.'

She blinked twice as her mind reeled. She had thought he'd come to mock or worse. 'Why?'

A faint smile touched his features, transforming them. A woman could drown in those eyes, Cwenneth thought abstractly as a lump formed in her throat. She refused to hope that he was being kind. She doubted Thrand the Destroyer knew the meaning of kindness or simple human decency. He probably had another wager that he wanted to win.

'Put the ointment on. We will have to go miles tomorrow and I have no wish for you to hold the men back. Purely selfish. I need to be back from the north within the month.'

She weighed the small jar in her hand. The man she thought devoid of all humanity had shown that he wasn't and that made him all the more dangerous. 'I will in time.'

He made an annoyed noise in the back of his throat. 'It goes on now. Your feet need to have a chance to heal.'

Without waiting for an answer, he knelt down and eased off her boots. Her feet were rubbed raw with large blisters on the heels and base of her feet.

Cwenneth gave a moan of pain as the cool air hit them.

'You kept going on these? Impressive.'

'For a Northumbrian lady?' She held up her hand. 'Please, I did overhear banter when the men were wagering. I'm not deaf or daft. And, of course, Narfi thought I was a pampered pet who would not last the night.'

'What do you think of Norsemen?'

'That they are muscle and—' She clapped her hand over her mouth. 'And I have seen firsthand your intelligence.'

'You would do well to remember that.' He nodded towards her feet. 'And it is for anyone. I have seen young men in tears over less. And I think you do yourself a disservice. You have a stronger will than most other women I've met.'

'You met someone with a stronger will?'

His body went rigid, and the stone planes in his face returned. 'A long time ago.'

'I had no choice. You would have tethered me to that horse and made me run simply for the pleasure of it. I've heard the stories.'

'I would have slung you over the back with your hands tied behind your back to prevent you stealing my horse.' His brows drew together. 'Humiliating a woman ultimately humiliates the man more. My father taught me that.'

Cwenneth breathed a little easier. Thrand Ammundson was no nightmare of a warrior. 'I stand corrected.'

'Courage impresses my men. You never know when you will need allies. You impressed them today. Now let's see about these blisters.'

He ran a finger along the base of her foot. For such a large man, his touch was surprisingly gentle. Warmth spread up her leg, making her feel alive and cared for. She wanted him to keep stroking, keep kneading the ball of her foot. A sharp pain went through her.

She jerked her foot back. 'That hurt.'

'The blisters can be healed. Give me the jar.' He held out his hand. 'I will show you how and tomorrow you do it yourself. Morning and night until your feet toughen. Tomorrow we go quicker.' He took the jar from her unresisting fingers and knelt down before her.

A pulse of warmth radiated from his touch. He touched first one blister, then another, spreading the soothing ointment on. Cwenneth leant back on the green moss and gave herself up to the blissful relief of the pain vanishing.

A small sigh of pleasure escaped from her throat. Immediately, he stopped and dropped the jar beside her.

She glanced up at him. His eyes had darkened to midnight-blue.

'Why do you stop?' Her voice came out far huskier than she intended.

'Finish it. You have the idea.'

'Thank you for this,' she said, reaching for the jar. A liquid heat had risen between her legs. He hadn't even kissed her or touched her intimately, and she had behaved like…like a woman of the street rather than the lady she was. He was her enemy, not her friend. Her cheeks burnt with shame. Ever since Aefirth had died, she had been encased in ice. She had been so sure she'd never feel anything like that again and now this. With this man who should be the last person on the planet she was attracted to, her enemy but also her saviour.

To cover her embarrassment, she bent her head and pretended to smell the strongly scented ointment. 'An old family recipe, you said? It is better than anything the monks could provide, but it smells so strong.'

'It is good for burns as well. Thankfully my grandmother taught me how to make it before she died or it would have been lost for ever. She used to use lavender or dog-rose petals to make it smell better, but I have never bothered with it.' He gave an awkward cough. 'It has helped me many times. Now let me see you put the ointment on.'

Cwenneth breathed easier, grateful to get the subject away from how his touch made her feel. She needed to remember who he was and what he was capable of. They might have a common cause, but he remained her enemy. She couldn't be attracted to him.

'I can see where smelling of roses would not give

the right impression for a warrior.' She forced an arched laugh. 'Is it true that berserkers like you can't tell the difference between their own men and the enemy in battle?'

His face emptied of all humour and became a dark, forbidding mask. Her shoulders relaxed. A forbidding stranger she could deal with, the man who kneaded the ointment into her foot was the danger.

'I've never killed any of the men who serve under my banner, Lady Cwenneth. But then I'm no berserker, merely a warrior who has fought in many battles and proven his worth to his king.' He inclined his head. 'Can you appreciate the difference?'

Cwenneth examined a stain on her gown. She had made a mistake. 'They say... I had heard rumours. I thought it best to ask. I apologise. My ignorance about your customs is no excuse, but it is all I have. I'll try for better in the future.'

'Rumours are often lies,' he said gravely.

'They say in every rumour a kernel of truth hides,' she said quickly before she lost her nerve. 'Why are you a warrior in a foreign land, Thrand? Why did you follow that path? Why didn't you stay in the North Country?'

His hands curled into fists, but he stood absolutely rigid. 'Because it was the only way which was open to me.'

'People always have a choice.' Cwenneth concentrated on slathering the ointment on her feet. 'Do you enjoy killing? Is that what it is?'

'Killing is always a last resort. Intimidation works better.' He gave a half smile. 'But I am good at warfare. Very good at it. My sword is my fortune. I fight for gold, rather than a country.'

'But haven't you ever wanted to be something more?' she persisted. 'Both my husband and brother were warriors, but they also had another life which included lands, a hall and a family.'

'War is my life, my whole life,' he said. 'It is what I have chosen. There is nothing else for me.'

He stalked away, ending the conversation.

Cwenneth stared after him, weighing the jar in her hand.

'Curiosity can get you killed, Cwenneth,' she muttered. 'The same treacherous Norse blood runs in his veins as Hagal's. You have to think about saving your life and escaping. Keep away from him. Stop trying to see good where none exists.'

The trouble was a small part of her heart refused to believe it.

Chapter Four

Thrand concentrated on setting up camp properly in this inhospitable and rain-soaked place rather than thinking about Lady Cwenneth and the way with a few simple words she had caused him to remember long-forgotten emotions and people. But her questions kept hammering at his brain.

Why had she wanted to know his reason for becoming a mercenary? What did she hope to gain from it? Mercy? Pity? He doubted if he had any left. All the finer feelings had died when he had discovered his parents' bodies, despite Lady Cwenneth's insistence that she saw good in him.

War gave him life and a reason for being on this earth. When he knelt in the mud before the smouldering farmhouse with his parents' mutilated bodies at his side, he had known what he had to do.

'What are you going to do with the woman?' Knui called. 'Now that you have won your wager and proved your point. She managed today, I'll grant you that, but barely. We need to be back in Jorvik for the Storting and I want the question of my cousin's child settled.'

Mine. Cwen is mine. The thought came from deep within, shocking him slightly at its fierce possession.

Thrand filled his lungs with clean air. He lifted his brow. 'Do?'

Several of the other men turned pale as they recognised his tone.

'She struggled. The Tyne remains several days' walk in harsh conditions. Return her to her people and collect a ransom. They will pay nothing for a corpse,' Knui continued on, seemingly oblivious to Thrand's growing irritation and anger. Thrand forced a breath, forced himself to remember his promise to Sven that he would look after his cousin on this trip even though Knui had the reputation of being a big mouth and a braggart. Sven wanted his child welcomed by one of his family. 'Best sell her to some farmer if you do not wish to collect ransom for her. I've done that in the past. Not as much gold, but some. She won't make it to the Tyne.'

'My pouch of gold is heavier because you bet against her.'

'She will bring ill luck to our expedition,' Knui commented.

'Thor favours her and, if she has Thor's favour, she will make the Tyne and beyond,' Thrand commented, looking at the man in turn as he explained about the earlier encounter with the boar.

'Thor sent a boar to look after her in the woods?' Helgi gasped.

'What other conclusion can I draw? The boar blew on her face as if he was anointing her,' Thrand said, fixing Knui with a hard stare. 'One ignores a gift from the gods at one's peril.'

'You're a hard man, Thrand Ammundson,' Knui said, making a low bow. 'I'd thought to spare her life, but you are the leader of this *felag*. Your word and Thor's boar must hold sway. The lady will bring good fortune to this enterprise.'

Thrand clung on to his temper with his last ounce of self-control. Knui had kept to the right side of the invisible line which separated him from insubordination.

Once the *felag* had dissolved, he and Knui would settle their differences, but for now he needed him here where he could see him. The last thing he wanted was Knui running to Hagal with the news. Lady Cwenneth's survival had to be revealed at the time of his choosing and not before. Hagal had slipped away from traps before. This time he wanted to leave nothing to chance. 'Lady Cwenneth travels with us. She will not be sold to a passing farmer or merchant. My responsibility and mine alone.'

'Where has the lady gone?' Helgi asked. 'I wanted to ask her about the boar's tusks and how they curved. It makes a difference to the destiny.'

Thrand frowned, his gaze sweeping the camp site. The steady drizzle had stopped and the sun had come out. Then he saw her, curled in a small ball beside his pack. His shoulders relaxed. She was still here. And she was his. The gods had given her to him to avenge his parents' murder. And he would use her without pity or remorse.

He walked over and spread his cloak about her shoulders. She mumbled slightly and turned her face towards him. Her lips shone red in the pale oval of her face. Innocent. Beautiful—and her chances of living were slim. An unaccustomed stab of pity went through him. 'Leave her to sleep.'

Cwen's dream were confused—to begin with it was all blood and gore mixed up with Aefirth's corpse holding its skeleton arms out to her and she started running, but could not escape. She grew so cold that her limbs shook and she doubted that she'd ever be warm again. But she knew she wanted to live, not to die. But then a heavy spice scent combined with a life-giving warmth settled over her, making her remember sensations she thought were lost to her. A peace descended along with warmth. And she watched Aefirth mouth 'goodbye, go live'. She was safe. All would be well. She half opened her eyes and saw another cloak covered her, far finer than the one she had lent Agatha. A dreamless sleep claimed her.

In the pale grey light before dawn, Thrand sat, listening to the steady breathing. He never slept long and it was easier to allow other less troubled, dream-plagued men a chance for their rest.

A slight moan turned his attention to the cloak-wrapped woman. Cwen had barely moved since he had taken her half-eaten bread from her fingers and wrapped his second cloak about her. What was he going to do with her, this Lady of Lingwold?

'You are not what I wanted or needed in my life, Cwen,' he murmured.

Cwen began to thrash about on her makeshift bed. 'No, please, no!'

He put his hand on Cwen's shoulder. Even the simple touch to waken her from her dream had his body hardening. His mouth twisted. Cwen needed to sleep, rather than be enfolded his arms. She was a complication that he could ill afford. He had to use her, rather than care about what happened to her.

'Be quiet. You will wake the others.'

'Thrand?' she whispered, panic evident in her voice.

'The very same.'

'I'd hoped it was a dream. That I would wake and find myself in Lingwold. Or failing that, Agatha snoring beside me.' Her voice faltered and her bottom lip trembled, making him want to taste it. 'But I woke here, knowing what happened and knowing that I can't go back to the same person I once was. My life divided and there's no one to guide me.'

He removed his hand and moved away from her. Hell indeed. It had been months before he slept properly after his parents' murder. And then only because he'd killed two of their murderers. 'Unfortunately, there is no magic spell to make this go away. Lie quietly. Morning will come soon enough. You are safe here amongst my men. No dark riders will come and get you. Sleep. Close your eyes.'

He walked away from her and the temptation to hold her.

She followed him, his second cloak dragging on the ground. 'I want to talk to someone. Please. I don't want to dream. I want to know that other people are alive.'

Her words touched a long-buried wound. After his parents' death, he too had wanted company, but there had only been the sound of owls hooting in the night.

'You enjoy disobeying my orders.'

'Was that an order?' She ran her hands up and down her arms. 'It is no good lying there and pretending, knowing that you are awake.'

'You slept for most of the night.'

'You watched me?'

'I notice everyone,' Thrand ground out, annoyed he had revealed anything to her. 'Part of my job. Don't consider yourself special.'

She dipped her head, not meeting his gaze. 'I'll try to remember that.'

Thrand shifted uncomfortably. He had hurt her and it wasn't what he had intended. The words had come out far too harshly. All the more reason why starting anything with Cwen was bound to end in disappointment and heartache. He never felt comfortable around women. They either wanted too much or not enough. Even with Ingrid, the woman he'd betrayed his parents for, they had never really talked. It had been all physical.

'My men need their sleep, even if you don't.' He gestured towards his men. 'They were awake when you shut your eyes. You missed the songs and the fight when Helgi and Knui quarrelled over a game of tafl.'

'Will it always be like this?'

'Knui quarrels with everyone,' he said, pretending to misunderstand her question. 'I regret I ever agreed to his coming on this journey, but it was the only thing which would settle Sven. I wanted my friend to die easily, rather than ranting. I wanted him to...'

'You don't trust him.'

He gave her a sharp look. 'I trust very few people, but a good commander trusts his men.'

'And is Knui your man?'

'Trust is forged in battle. I've only travelled with Knui.'

She leant forward, and he could spy the pale hollow of her throat where his cloak gaped. 'Will I always see them—the corpses, I mean? I swore I could hear the sound of pounding hooves coming after me. Hunting me.'

He carefully shrugged, hating that he wanted to take the pain and suffering from her. 'Some men suffer and see the parade of the dead. Others sleep soundly.'

'And you? Do you sleep soundly?'

Her mouth trembled and it was all he could do to keep from dragging her into his arms and kissing her until the dreams fled. He clenched his fists. He made a point of not caring.

'Watching the stars helps. That and exhaustion.'

Her long lashes covered her eyes. 'Was that why you forced me to walk? You were doing me a service? I hadn't considered that. Thank you.'

'Don't go making me into something I am not. My reasoning was purely selfish. I knew my men would bet against you and I enjoy winning.' The muscles in his neck relaxed. There, he had told her a partial truth. He was not going soft or losing his edge, but there was something about this woman he admired. She had courage.

'If it helps me to sleep, then I'm grateful. It is better you didn't say or otherwise I'd have worried about the dreams.'

'You have a different way of looking at things.'

She stretched out a foot. He watched the high white

curve of her instep and struggled against the urge to hold it again. 'My blisters are much better. Your grandmother must have been a very holy woman to create such a miracle cure.'

'She learnt the recipe from her mother.' Thrand put his hand on her shoulder and felt her shiver. Her words brought back long-forgotten memories. This sense of disorientation and questioning was so familiar. The memory of sitting and staring at the smouldering heap that had once been his house, knowing that he too should have seen the signs, stirred deep within him. 'My grandmother used to say the past was written in stone, but the future is written in water. I never understood it until I was forced to grow up.'

She shook his hand off. 'Then I shall have to ensure Hagal pays for his crimes. It is something I can do to honour the dead.'

Thrand's muscles tensed. A small beacon of hope. A willing witness, rather than a scared, reluctant one, would give much better testimony. 'Do you mean that?'

'Yes, yes, I do.' She tilted her head to one side, her long lashes making dark smudges against her pale cheek. 'Is there a way?'

'I want you to make a statement in front of the Storting, tell them what happened. Loud and clear, looking them in the eye and never faltering.'

'And if the king chooses to believe Hagal and return me to him? Or if Hagal kills me? Once he knows…'

'Hagal already wants you dead. It is my job to keep you alive.'

'I have been thinking. There must be a way to disguise myself, make it less likely to be remembered if we encounter anyone before…before we reach Jorvik.'

'Then you will do it?'

'Ensuring Hagal and the men who committed the murders are punished for this must become my life.'

Unaccustomed pity stabbed his heart. A beautiful woman like her should have more than vengeance in her life. Annoyed, he pushed the thought away. Cwen had the right to live her life as she saw fit and what happened to her afterwards was none of his concern. 'You have courage, Lady Cwenneth.'

'A compliment, I think.' In the grey light, he could just make out the crooked half-smile, which changed her features from pretty to heart-stoppingly beautiful.

'What do you consider your most memorable feature?' he asked, rather than giving into the renewed temptation to kiss her.

'My long, blonde hair. One true asset, according to my sister-in-law.'

'Cut it. Having it short will make you like a thrall, a slave.'

'Will you do it?' Cwenneth stared directly at Thrand and willed him to understand. 'I am afraid my hand will not be steady enough even if I can get a sharp knife.'

'Right now?'

'Before we start travelling again. Before I become memorable to any traveller.'

'Hold your head still.'

He took a knife from his belt and with one swift motion, a lock of golden hair tumbled to the ground, swiftly followed by the next one, until all about her feet a golden carpet lay. Her entire being tingled with awareness of him, the way he moved and the gentleness of his touch for such a large man and his warm, spicy scent.

Cwenneth screwed up her eyes and tried to breathe slowly. It had to be a reaction to the day's events rather than a true attraction to a man like him. She had never felt this way about Hagal or any of the other North men she'd encountered. And she knew what he'd done, even if the rumours were exaggerated.

'With the right tools, the task is easily accomplished.' He stepped back and considered her from hooded eyes. 'Your hair was too heavy for your delicate features. Your eyes appear much bigger. You were wrong—your hair isn't your most memorable feature. Your eyes are.'

Her hands paused in their exploration of her shorn head. 'My mother used to call them the window to my soul.'

His face took on an intent expression. 'They are. Windows.'

'I will take your word for it. There is no mirror around here.' Cwenneth's heart thumped. Thrand's eyes were mostly iced over. What did that say about his soul? 'I had a little silver mirror that had belonged to my mother, but it is gone now. Burnt or stolen. Lost to me at any rate.'

She swallowed to get rid of the lump in her throat. It wasn't so much the mirror, but losing her connection with her mother.

'There is a pond where you will be able to spy your face. You can wash the dirty streaks from your skin while you are at it.'

Cwenneth scrubbed her face. 'I hate having a dirty face. You should have said.'

'You fell asleep before you ate the evening meal.' He put a hand on the middle of her back. 'Come and see the new you.'

He led the way to a small pond, keeping his hand on the middle of her back. A faint mist hung over the lake, and a solitary duck paddled.

'If you crouch down and lean out…'

'I know how to do it,' Cwenneth answered, going over to a flat rock and away from the touch which sent liquid heat coursing through her insides.

She leant out and looked, half expecting to see her usual reflection, but instead a woman with very short hair and enormous blue eyes stared up at her. Thrand spoke the truth. Her eyes were suddenly the most noticeable thing about her face. Her chin and jaw line were far stronger than she'd have liked. A very determined face, but with vulnerable eyes. Her, but not her.

She put out a hand, created ripples in the pond, destroying the image.

'Not to your liking. I can tell from the way you slap the water.'

Cwenneth concentrated on splashing cold water on to her skin before drying it. 'Far too fierce and determined. Here I always considered myself to look delicate. I wouldn't recognise me so that must be a start.'

'With short hair and the tattered gown, anyone we encounter will think you a thrall and not worth the bother of investigating your identity.'

'Until I open my mouth.'

'Keep silent.' In the pale light, the planes of his

face had relaxed, making him far more approachable. 'Thralls are supposed to be silent. It is part of their charm. Is that possible for you?'

'You are teasing me now.' A bubbly feeling engulfed her. How long had it been since anyone teased or joked with her?

His face instantly sobered. 'I never tease. Ask anyone.'

She bowed her head and plucked at a loose thread on her gown. The bubbly feeling went. 'Why are you helping me? Why are you willing to shield me from Hagal?'

'You asked me earlier why I became a mercenary,' he said slowly. 'Hagal made me into one. I was a barely bearded boy when he turned me into a killer.'

'How?' Cwenneth whispered, watching him. To become a killer at such a young age. Not a warrior, blooded in battle, but a killer. 'How did he do it?'

'Along with three other men, he murdered my family. I have dedicated my life to ensuring their murderers were punished. It was the only way I could honour my parents. I slew the first of them that night. It satisfied something deep down in my soul and I discovered I was good at it.' He stood with his feet apart and hands fisted. His eyes no longer held any light, but were as ice-cold as midwinter. 'What I have done since that day I do to calm that itch in my soul. I don't fight for country or king, but because I get paid. And I've killed men because I was ordered to.'

'Your family? Did you find them slain in a similar fashion?' Cwenneth placed her hands on her head. She was so wrapped up in her own misery that she had missed the obvious point—Thrand never questioned her accusation about Hagal, a man he must have fought alongside.

Her breath caught. Thrand's desire for revenge had nothing to do with what happened back in the woods and everything to do with past wrongs. She was to be a tool, much like he used a sword or an axe. He wasn't doing this because he was attracted to her or felt some connection with her and her plight. She pressed her nails into her palms, making half-moon shapes. 'You knew, before I opened my mouth and accused Hagal, who was responsible. Hagal was involved in your parents' murder.'

'Years ago.' Thrand's mouth twisted as he stared out at the pond. 'Justice goes by a different name in Viken now that we have the current king. I left with a price on my head as that king approved of getting rid of the thorn in his flesh who was my father.'

Cwenneth struggled to understand. 'We are far from the North Country. Hagal has been in Northumbria for years, serving Halfdan, the same king you serve. His elevation to a *jaarl* shows he has served him well.'

'My oath to Halfdan forbids me from harming any in the *felag* as long as they stay loyal.' He slammed his fists together. 'I was unaware of Hagal's presence in the *felag* or I would never have given my sacred oath. A bad bargain, but a bargain it remains. And simply putting a knife in Hagal's back would not do it. I want him to suffer.'

She struggled to understand. 'But surely—'

'I honour my father by keeping sacred oaths. A man becomes worthless if he breaks his solemn oath and I am unworthy enough as is. He was one of the finest men I ever met. Honourable to a fault.'

'But strict with those who did not obey him?'

'My father died for his code.'

'Fathers only want what is best for their sons.'

Thrand stood in the glade, head up and unrepentant, but underneath she glimpsed the young man who had wept bitter tears when he found his parents. A man who was determined on revenge, but who clung to his father's code because it was all that remained of his family…because it was the only thing which separated him from his family's murderers.

Giving into instinct, she cupped his cheeks so he was forced to look into her eyes. 'Your father would be proud to have such a man as you for a son.'

Their breath laced, caught and laced again.

'You never met my father. My father had little time or forgiveness for people who failed him.'

'But I've met his son.' Her mouth began to ache. She wet her lips, not knowing what she wanted, but knowing she was powerless to move away from him. Her hands pulsed with warmth. 'You gave me that ointment and covered me with the cloak. Now you have cut my hair to help me hide and keep alive.'

'Hagal wants you dead. It is enough reason to keep you alive. It is the first time he has left a witness. The first mistake he has made in a very long time. I've been waiting for it and I plan to use you to destroy him. That is the sole reason I have helped you.'

'But you *have* helped me.' She stroked his cheek with her palm. 'The action counts, not the reason.'

With a groan, he put his arms about her and his mouth descended on hers. He tasted of spring rain and fresh air, but with more than a hint of dark passion. And she knew she wanted that passion. He made her feel alive, rather than as if she was one of the walking dead, the way she had felt since Aefirth and Richard died.

She pressed her body closer to his hardness, seeking him. She wanted him in a way she had not wanted any other man. She wanted to drown in this kiss and forget everything that had happened to her. She moaned and arched her body nearer.

Instantly, he stepped away from her. The cool breeze fanned her heated cheeks while her body thrummed with liquid heat.

Cwenneth dropped her eyes. She had just pressed her body to a man who was a virtual stranger, inviting him to take her.

'Please say something,' she whispered, putting her hands to her head.

'Return to the others,' Thrand answered, trying to regain control of his body. He had not intended on kissing her, nor on his body reacting so violently to her nearness. He knew what out-of-control desire for a woman did to him, how he lost perspective and how easy it would be to care for a woman like Cwen.

If anything, with her hair short, she looked more desirable than she had with her long hair tumbling about her shoulders. Her mouth had become crimson from the kiss, and her eyes were dark blue. The memory of her honey-sweet taste invaded his body. 'Now! Go!'

He half turned to Cwen, knowing if she made a gesture towards him, he'd pull her into his arms and take her mouth again, plundering it for all its warmth, promised passion and the balm it brought to his soul.

His goodness had stopped years ago. He had been the one to disobey his father and to meet Ingrid secretly, even though his father had warned him against becoming involved with the woman. His desire for her had been too great, and he hadn't believed his father about her past behaviour.

All he'd seen was an ageing man who had hurt his leg in a fall and wanted to spoil his fun. It had been the first time that he had openly defied his father.

After he had found his parents, he had confronted Ingrid and she had admitted the truth—she had lured him away so that his parents could be killed, Hagal could acquire the land he coveted and she could be free of Hagal. He had left her on her knees, begging him to save her. Later her strangled and mutilated body had been discovered and he'd known if he had had an ounce of goodness in him, he would have saved her, but instead he'd left her to her fate.

Cwen did not need to know about that. Or the traps Hagal had managed to wriggle free from over the years. Or the people Thrand had failed to save.

She hadn't taken to her heels when he roared at her. She simply stood looking at him with those trusting, big eyes as if he could actually protect her.

Something twisted in his gut. He never wanted her to think him a monster. He wanted her to believe the impossible—that there was more to him than simply warfare, battles and killing.

'Did you hear me, Cwen? Go this instant!'

Her lips turned up into a sad smile, and her shoulders hunched. 'You called me Cwen. My late husband used to call me Cwennie.'

He released his breath. The crisis had passed. He had regained control of his body and pushed away all thought of drinking from her mouth. 'You can hardly be Lady Cwenneth with short hair. Cwen suits you.'

Chapter Five

The first rays of the spring sunshine broke through mist, warming Cwenneth's face and the back of her neck. Without the accustomed weight of her hair, her entire body seemed lighter. So far today, the going had been easier and her feet had hurt less.

The banter between the men bothered her less and she was beginning to figure out the individuals—which ones she liked and which ones were better avoided altogether. The thing which struck her was how little difference there was between these men and her brother's men or even the men who had served under her husband's banner.

From what she had seen this morning, she was very glad she'd followed her instincts and had not offered Knui Crowslayer her rings. He took the slightest opportunity to belittle and mock everyone. It made it easier when Helgi muttered that he had been forced on them by their dead friend.

'Today is going to be a good day. You can taste it in the air.' She inhaled a deep breath, savouring the tranquillity.

'Can you?' Thrand asked, coming to walk beside her as he led his horse.

A tingle ran through her body. After they had returned to the camp, there hadn't been any time to talk to him and explain about the mistake she'd made in kissing him like that. She had just hoped by ignoring it, everything would go away and they'd return to that ease they'd had before she'd made a mess of things.

'The air is perfumed with bluebells and the sun is shining.'

'And how do you explain the sound of horses, coming towards us? At speed?'

Nausea rose in her stomach, replacing her sense of well-being. 'Too soon. Tell me it is too soon.'

'Hands on swords.' He gave Knui a hard look. 'I speak. No one else, whatever the provocation. Farmers on the way to market, most likely. No point in borrowing trouble.'

'And me? What should I do?' Cwenneth fought against the rising tide of panic.

'Hunch your shoulders and keep your eyes down. It should suffice if you keep silent.'

Cwenneth bent down and grabbed a handful of dirt. Silently, she offered up prayers that her fears were unfounded. It was far too soon for anyone to be out hunting her.

The lead horse stopped in a cloud of dust.

The horseman lifted his helm, revealing his dark-blond hair and scarred face. Narfi. Her luck was out.

'Narfi the Black, fancy encountering you here and in full war gear,' Thrand said in a loud voice. 'Is there some problem with the locals? Not paying their tribute on time? And you are going to bully them into it? Nothing new there.'

Narfi curled his lip. 'Here is a sight that I did not expect to see today. Thrand the Destroyer and his band of merry followers. My master will wish to know why you are here.'

'No doubt.' Thrand stood in the centre of the road, his right hand casually resting on his sword.

'And your business is…? Be quick about it, man. I've things to do.'

'I travel on the king's business as usual,' Thrand said, concentrating on Narfi while he fought against every instinct in his body which told him to scoop up Cwen and ride away with her. 'What do I do but serve my king? Is there some war I need to know about? You appear dressed for battle.'

'We hunt bandits, Thrand Ammundson. There are many who refuse to accept our law. It is our task to keep the peace.' Narfi swung down from his horse. He was about half a head shorter than Thrand, stockier and with fists like ham hocks and a strut like a bantam cockerel's. 'Do you come to break it?'

'Keep a civil tongue in your head,' Thrand said, fixing Narfi with his eye. Off to one side, he saw that Cwen had obeyed his orders. She stood with her shorn head heavily bent. He released a breath.

'Hagal the Red is the lord in these parts, not you.'

'He has risen far under Halfdan's patronage. We both serve the same master…for now. Allow me and my men to go about our king's business as the land is at peace.'

'These Northumbrians need to learn a lesson.' Narfi scratched his nose. 'They grow bolder by the day—stealing sheep and cattle so that their children can be fed. Hagal has ordered me to take all measures necessary to ensure the Northumbrians understand they lost the war.'

'Halfdan desires peace in his lands for all his people. Taking food from children's mouths breeds resentment rather than loyalty. Halfdan made the same remarks only last week.' Thrand's fingers itched to draw his sword and knock the smug sneer from Narfi's face. Once he would have done so and accepted the consequences, but his years of warfaring had taught him to wait and allow his opponent to make the first and often fatal mistake. It was about taking the opportunity when presented. Narfi would give him that opportunity...eventually.

'The king would never have said such a thing in his youth,' Narfi remarked. 'We need a strong king who will put the needs of the Norse first.'

'Someone like Hagal?'

'You said it, not I.' Narfi openly smirked.

'Hagal does fancy challenging for the crown!' Thrand inclined his head. 'Thank you for the confirmation. It puts a different complexion on matters. I shall redouble my efforts to be there for the Storting.'

'I've seen you fight, Thrand. Too much the legend and too little the cold killer these days.' Narfi placed his hand on his sword's hilt. 'Your reputation as a warrior is exaggerated. Easier to have one demon than a thousand. You or rather your name does have its uses.'

His men nudged each other.

'Intriguing.' Thrand listened to the confirmation of what he'd long suspected. Others had used his reputation as a cover for their own deeds. A part of him was pleased Cwen had heard the independent confirmation. It bothered him that he wanted her to think of him as more than a mercenary.

'Hagal is worth ten of you,' Narfi muttered.

'Your words, not mine.'

Cwenneth forgot to breathe as she waited for the verdict which would allow them to pass unmolested.

Narfi stood not five feet from her, the man who supposedly had charge of her, the man who had murdered Agatha and the rest, and he challenged Thrand. She heard the genuine pleasure in his voice as he tossed off taunt after taunt. He sought a fight with Thrand.

This was going to end badly. She could feel it in her bones. Thrand and his men were outnumbered. She knew what these men were capable of and how they butchered innocent men.

Her knees threatened to collapse and the world started to turn dark at the edges. Cwenneth shook her head, trying to clear it. Fainting was a luxury she could ill afford. If she fainted, or even made a sound, Narfi would be bound to notice and recognise her. Her only hope was to remain like a statue, a statue of a thrall.

Cold sweat pooled at the base of her neck, her mouth tasted of ash and her back screamed from hunching over. The instinct to run and hide grew with each breath. She fought with all her might to keep still and hunched over. Her haircut and stained clothing had to be enough.

In her mind, she repeated Thrand's words over and over again—*Narfi would never equate a thrall with the missing Lady of Lingwold.*

Narfi cast his lifeless eyes over the group.

Pulling her cloak tighter about her, she hastily lowered her chin and hunched her shoulders even more. *Thralls kept their eyes to the ground.*

Silently, Cwenneth prayed for a miracle.

Suddenly, Narfi's shoulders relaxed and he beamed with false good humour. 'Next time call at the hall, rather than sneaking about like a thief, Thrand Ammundson. Hagal keeps a good table for men who belong to his *felag*.'

'Halfdan holds my oath.'

'It is the same thing.' Narfi made a dismissive gesture with his hand.

Cwenneth released her breath. He accepted Thrand's word. They might get through this without any bloodshed, or Narfi realising who she was.

'I'll remember for the next time, but today I decline.' Thrand gave a little cough. 'It never does to keep a king waiting.'

'What sort of bandits are you looking for?' Knui called out. 'I know Hagal the Red's reputation for rewarding those who assist him with gold.'

'Did I say bandits?' Narfi's eyes narrowed. 'We're searching for a woman. Hagal's bride has been kidnapped. Hagal wants her released. If any of you discover her and brings her to the stronghold, he will give you gold. You have my solemn oath on it.'

Cwen curled her fists and concentrated on the ground. Surely Thrand's men would keep silent. Thrand had made it clear that she belonged to him.

'We will keep it in our thoughts and, should we discover such a person, I will be sure to let Hagal know,' Thrand said smoothly as he gave Knui a hard stare. 'You will have to be content with my word, Narfi.'

'How much gold?' Knui called out.

'More than you could carry, Knui Crowslayer.' Narfi gave an evil smile. 'As you have given us information in the past, you know he is a man who keeps his words in these matters.'

Before Cwenneth could make a sound, Knui had reached her and shoved her forward. She stumbled and fell at Narfi's feet. 'Here you go. Here's your missing woman. Now I want my gold.'

Cwenneth concentrated on Narfi's mud-splattered boots, praying for a miracle. Thrand and his men were outnumbered and Knui had turned traitor.

The tip of Narfi's sword jabbed her cheek, pricking her and forcing her face upwards. Her gaze locked with Narfi's dark one.

'You thought, my lady, to hide. Pathetic disguise, cutting your hair. You should have stayed in your cart and had a quick death. Better for everyone.'

'Why?' Cwenneth asked in a trembling voice. 'Why better for everyone?'

'Because your husband slew Hagal's close kinsman two Aprils ago.'

'The woman belongs to me,' Thrand thundered and his sword knocked the blade from her cheek. 'I've claimed her. I'll not give her up easily. I will deal with the traitor later, but for now this is between you and me, Narfi.'

Cwen scrambled on her hands and knees away from Narfi. When she reached the other side of Thrand's legs, she stopped, put her fingers to her cheek and wiped a drop of blood away. Her stomach roiled. Thrand had come to her defence but for how long? Thrand was a warrior, a warrior like her husband and her husband had died of his wounds.

'This woman belongs to you? Since when?'

'You marked her. No one marks my woman.' Thrand concentrated on Narfi as he struggled to keep control of his temper. The small trickle of blood on Cwen's cheek nearly sent him over the edge and in order to survive a fight with Narfi, he had to remain in control. But Narfi would fight him or be branded a coward for ever. 'Given my mood and the brightness of the day, I was prepared to overlook your insolence about my mission, but not this. You will pay and you will pay in blood.'

'Make her a present to Hagal.' Narfi took a step towards where Cwen cradled her cheek on the ground. 'He will be most interested to know where his errant bride has been. He'll arrange a special welcome for you, Thrand, as you discovered her.'

'Over my dead body,' Thrand said, moving between Cwenneth and Narfi.

'That can be arranged.' Narfi lifted his sword. 'Shall we see if the man matches the legend after all?'

There was a hiss of swords as Thrand's men drew their weapons. Thrand held up his hand, checking their movement. They obeyed him in an instant. Knui looked over his shoulder, suddenly unsure. Thrand glared at him. Knui's reckoning would come. He would see to it personally, but first Narfi.

'A fair fight between you and me, Narfi, with Lady Cwenneth as the prize. Winner takes everything. No need for our men to fight.' Thrand paused, allowing his words to sink into Narfi's puffed-up brain. 'Unless you are all talk and no sword arm.'

'I welcome the opportunity to prove the man is much less than the legend.'

Instantly, the air became alive with the men making wagers on who would win. Thrand caught Helgi's eye and nodded. Helgi moved towards Cwen, helping to clear a space for the fighting, but being there to protect her if Narfi's men decided to act before the fight was through.

Narfi made a mocking bow towards where Cwen crouched on the ground. 'You should have stayed in the cart like you were supposed to, my lady. Your death would have been quicker. I intend to take my time after your so-called champion dies.'

Cwen paled to ghost-white. Hot rage poured through Thrand's blood. Narfi enjoyed baiting her and making her feel uncomfortable. The man deserved to die. 'Does your arrogance know no bounds?'

'When you lie dying, you will know what folly it is to believe in the legend of your greatness.' Narfi lifted his sword.

Thrand thrust his sword downwards, catching Narfi on the thigh. 'I defend what is mine!'

Narfi responded with a swift blow which Thrand easily deflected. The two men circled each other, trading blows, but nothing decisive. A probing of strength and skill to learn as much as possible about his opponent.

In the early days, after his parents' death, Thrand had engaged in many of these fights. It had been the only way to get to two of his parents' murderers. And he had nearly lost his life by being too quick and impatient. He had learnt to sit back and wait for the opportunity. They always overreached in time.

Thrand crouched, tossing his sword from hand to hand, enjoying the faint thrill of combat against a good opponent.

Thrand moved to his right. Narfi stuck out his foot. Thrand rolled, avoiding the blow, and rose to catch Narfi's elbow.

'That passes for fighting, Narfi? My grandmother would have done better.'

'Is that who taught you? I had wondered.'

Thrand narrowed his eyes, watching the movement of the sword. Narfi would try again. He fought dirty, relying on the trip and trick, rather than any real skill. But Narfi also left himself exposed every time he tried it. A question of patience and not giving in to frustration or anger.

Thrand gave Cwen a quick glance. Her face except for the streak of blood was completely white. Thrand's blood boiled anew. He choked it back with difficulty and blocked another blow from Narfi, but Narfi also kept his distance, preventing Thrand from delivering the killing blow.

Sweat streamed down Thrand's eyes, blurring his vision. The time was right. Risky, but he could force the issue. He pretended to sway and stumble as if he were disoriented and tired.

Unable to resist, Narfi came closer and once again stuck out his foot. Thrand deliberately crashed down. Narfi's sword caught his back, sending a pain jolting through him but Thrand forced a roll and jammed his sword upwards.

With one fluid motion, Narfi fell, gave a gurgle. Thrand kicked the body to free his sword.

His men and Narfi's were arranged about in a circle, silently watching. Thrand pointedly turned his gaze from Knui. Promise or no promise to Sven, the man had betrayed him and defied his leadership. A swift death was too good for him.

'Lady Cwenneth is mine. Mine. Does anyone else fancy trying their luck?'

The cowards who passed for Narfi's men started to back away, looking to save their hides. Thrand concentrated on breathing. Get them gone, before he dealt with Knui. And he wanted to know how many other of his men might betray him. In the silence which followed, the others began to beat their swords against their shields and proclaim their loyalty to him. The noise grew until the woods rang with sound and Narfi's men had taken to their heels and fled.

'Watch your back!' Cwenneth called out. 'Knui!'

Thrand pivoted and swiftly dispatched Knui, who had crept up on him with a drawn sword. Knui gave a soft gurgle and fell on top of Narfi.

'I owe you a life debt, Cwen,' he said, looking straight at her. The bleeding had stopped on her cheek. He wanted to enfold her in his arms and taste her lips again. 'You saved me from having to execute him. Sven was blind to his defects.'

'We are even, then. Narfi would have killed me, and the death he had planned would not have been quick or easy.'

'We're even,' Thrand confirmed, bending down and cleaning his sword, rather than reaching out to her. Little things to occupy his mind and hands. He

had come far too close to losing control and it had
been his anger at what could happened to Cwen which
spurred him on, rather than his desire for revenge or
the knowledge that his men depended on him to get
it right. And that scared him half to death.

Cwenneth rose unsteadily to her feet. Somewhere
in the top of the tree, a bird started singing again, fill-
ing the air with joyous sound.

Knui and Narfi lay dead on the blood-soaked
ground. They were the first men she had ever seen
die violent deaths. Knui had betrayed her and would
have killed Thrand. And Narfi would have tortured
and murdered her.

Several violent shivers went through her. She lived,
but the man who had started the slaughter breathed
no more.

'Are you all right, Cwen?' Thrand asked. 'You
seem miles away. We need to get going before they
return with reinforcements. Narfi will be left for the
crows to pick over.'

'And Knui? What happens to his body?' she whispered, keeping her eyes averted from the bodies.

'I regret that I ever allowed Knui on this expedition. I thought to honour my friend's request, but
Knui had the black heart of a traitor and deserved a
traitor's death.'

'He tried to kill you.'

'He knew that he had to or I would have killed
him.' Thrand's face became hard. 'Once he had allowed his greed to get the better of him, he was
doomed.'

'You suspected him.'

'I distrusted him, but I never expected him to

betray me or my men in this fashion. Sven would never have asked me to have Knui on this *felag* if he had suspected the full extent of his treachery. Some would say that Knui's death was far swifter than he deserved.'

'He had betrayed others?'

'Hagal pays gold for betrayal, not out of the goodness of his heart. You heard Narfi the Black. They had done business together before.'

'Narfi took pleasure in killing,' Cwen said slowly, concentrating on the bodies rather than on Thrand's hard face. 'He spoke about getting a large meal after the slaughter. Do you ever feel like that? That killing makes you hungry? Do you need to eat?'

She wasn't sure why she asked except Narfi's statement yesterday had truly revolted her. Maybe if she knew Thrand was like Narfi, then this longing for Thrand would go. Maybe she would feel like she should find a way to escape from Thrand and get back to her old life, instead of having this small thrill that he had claimed her as his woman and had fought for her.

'My appetite goes for days,' Thrand replied. 'The last thing I feel right now is physical hunger. All I feel is sorrow that two warriors are dead and all because of the greed of one man.'

Cwenneth nodded. A small piece of her rejoiced. He was not as depraved as Narfi. But it still did not make him safe or any less her enemy…her very temporary ally. 'I'm trying hard to find pity in my heart for them, but I can't. Goodness knows what sort of person that makes me.'

'The line between revenge and justice is as fine as a hair.'

She bit her lip, hating that part of her had rejoiced at Narfi's death. She never considered that she would be someone who enjoyed another's demise.

'I should be better. The priest at Lingwold would tell me I was wrong and any death diminishes me, but Narfi needed to die.' She shook her head. 'I suppose at least the worst one is dead. Justice of a sort for my men.'

'No, the worst one remains alive,' Thrand corrected with a stern gaze. 'Do you think these men would have done what they did if Hagal hadn't ordered them to? He keeps his hands clean, but his heart is black. I've no idea how many other warriors he has corrupted with his gold, but I can make a guess.'

'Have I put you and your men in danger?' she asked, putting her hand on Thrand's sleeve. 'They know you are in the area now. When I overheard Narfi and the other man speaking back in the woods, it was mentioned that they could not spread the rumour you had done this because you were in Jorvik with the king. But now Hagal will know before night falls. They will say you did it, not Hagal. They will make you into an outlaw.'

'Only if we fail to make the Storting.' Thrand slammed his fists together. 'When they have reinforcements, they will come looking for us, in particular you. We go now.'

'Why would they listen to me? All Hagal has to do is proclaim it was Narfi acting on his own and—'

'Narfi would have slit his own mother's throat

if Hagal asked him to,' Helgi called out. 'Everyone knows whose creature he was. There are many in the Storting who reckon that he'd never bed a woman without asking his master's permission.'

Cwennneth pressed her lips together. 'Is that supposed to be reassuring?'

'You are more of a threat to Hagal then ever. You know too much. You're the proof that Hagal planned this. The king will listen to you and hear the truth in your words.'

'I heard Knui say that he had taken Hagal's gold previously for information,' Cwenneth said. 'There must be others who have taken gold. Surely they should be exposed.'

'Exactly!' Helgi said. 'This woman of yours, Thrand, is more than a pretty face. She has a quicksilver mind. Thor has favoured us indeed.'

'The proof of what?' Cwenneth stared at him. 'What does Hagal intend?'

'The proof he intends to move against the king. Or rather the king's chosen successor when the king dies. Halfdan is gravely ill. Hagal knows that most of the inner circle distrust him. It is why he was sent to Acumwick, rather than being kept close in Jorvik. I suspect he intends to use your brother and his men in some way to assist his cause.'

'My brother made peace with the Norsemen so he would not have to go to war again. This was what my marriage was about—a weaving of peace. He wants to remain at Lingwold for the birth of his child.'

'Your brother is no stranger to war, though. The Lord of Lingwold can command an army. Hagal wants that army.'

'Or maybe just the dowry he stole to pay off his bribes.'

'If he needed that, he would have kept you alive so he could have had you beg your brother for more gold. How big was your dowry?'

She sucked in her breath. Norsemen politics sounded as precarious as Bernician. But Thrand was wrong. Edward had more respect for his men than to move directly against Halfdan. He still counted the cost of the last war.

'More than it should have been,' Cwenneth admitted with a sigh. 'My sister-in-law grumbled about it, but my brother thought it was a small price to pay if he no longer had to worry about paying Danegeld every year to you.'

'Your brother has never paid me Danegeld.' Thrand leant down and picked up his sword, cleaning it on Knui's cloak. 'We met in battle and that was all. I went south and killed for my king there. It is where I collected my gold.'

'He swears he pays it to Thrand the Destroyer. Grumbles every single time. "That misbegotten Norse raider" is probably the kindest thing he has said about you.'

Thrand frowned. 'Hagal has held the north since the end of the last war. If anyone demanded payment, it will be one of his men. They simply used my name to extract money.'

'Yes, that bothered Narfi.' Cwenneth shook her head. 'And my husband would have slain Hagal's kinsman in battle, rather than in cold blood. It is the fortune of war. There is a difference.'

Thrand stilled, listening. 'Our time grows short.'

He turned away from her and barked several orders in Norse. His men looked unhappy, but agreed. Two quickly mounted their horses and rode off in the opposite direction. Another three followed suit going another way. Within a few heartbeats she and Thrand stood alone in the glade with the bodies and two horses—Thrand's and Narfi's.

'What is going on?' Cwenneth asked as her stomach knotted.

'Change of plan.' He put a hand in the middle of her back. 'You stay with me. My men have other jobs to do. If we split up, there is more chance they will follow one of them. Hagal will think that I will make straight for Jorvik and that is where he will concentrate the search. We need to go north. I will fulfil my oath.'

Cwenneth regarded the deep and menacing woods, rather than leaning into his touch. She had no idea how she was going to run, let alone walk. Her legs were like jelly. But if they stayed, Hagal would return with more than enough men to deal with Thrand.

'How far do we have to go before we can stop? Before we are safe?' she asked, moving away from his touch.

His face grew grave. 'You won't be truly safe until Hagal is defeated. It would be wrong of me to lie to you, Cwen. Helgi and Ketil are going to Jorvik to tell the king what happened here. Halfdan will listen to them and stall any request for blood money for Narfi the Black and Knui Crowslayer's families until the Storting begins and I have returned. He owes me that much. The others go to warn various other warriors whom I know are loyal to Halfdan. They need to be on the lookout for the traitors, men who have accepted Hagal's gold and are prepared to forsake their oaths.'

A great hard lump of misery settled in her breast. She pushed the thought away and concentrated on her immediate problem. 'How far do you expect me to walk?'

'I don't.' He leapt on his horse. 'Your walking days have ended. They will expect me to take you south, but we are going north. It is the best way to keep you safe.'

'But I can't ride!' Cwenneth gasped out. She looked at Narfi's horse. There was no way she could do it. The brute bared its teeth at her. 'I've no idea of how to ride and now isn't the time to start.'

'Your education has been singularly lacking then. We remedy it—now.' He caught Cwenneth by the waist and hauled her up on his horse, setting her in front of him. He kept her in place with one arm while the hand held the bridle. He made a clicking noise in the back of his throat and his horse lunged forward.

Under her bottom, Cwenneth felt the power of the horse. It amazed her that he could handle such a big animal with ease, but it was as if he and the horse were as one. Liquid heat rushed through her. This man had fought for her.

'Would Hagal beat you in a fair fight?' Cwenneth gave an uneasy laugh and tried to concentrate on other things besides the warm curl in the pit of her stomach. She'd get over this attraction to him. He had made it very clear where his feelings lay. His interest in her was as a weapon against his enemy. He did not care about her as a person, or more importantly as a woman. 'Or is he like Narfi? All talk and pride.'

He increased his grip on her waist. 'Hagal fights better than any man I know. But he prefers to play the spider and allow his victims to blunder into his web.'

Cwenneth gulped and concentrated on the horse's ears. She'd hoped that Thrand would dismiss Hagal as not very good and overrated, but Thrand respected his skill.

'Where are we going if not to Jorvik?'

'To the north. Near Corbridge.'

The north. Corbridge. In Bernicia. Still many miles from her home, but reasonably close to her stepson's lands. Cwenneth's breath caught.

Only yesterday, she would have been trying to figure out a way to escape and get to her brother. Everything had changed now. She had seen the personal risk Thrand had taken to save her life. She knew what Narfi was capable of and she had to believe that Hagal was a thousand times worse. Hagal had to be stopped before he caused the whole of Lingwold to be destroyed.

'What is in the north?'

'I made a promise to my best friend. I will ensure his child is well looked after. Before all things. I owe Sven my life many times over. He was the closest thing I had to a brother. If something should happen and my life were to end before this was done, I know Odin would forbid me entrance to Valhalla.'

Cwenneth bit back a quick retort. Thrand knew he might not survive the coming battle and he wanted to do right for his friend. More proof if she needed it that he was very different from Narfi and Hagal. He was a good man.

'Will you be taking the child with you?' she asked.

Her mind reeled as she thought about how a child would cope amongst the Norsemen.

'Why would I want to do that?' Thrand sounded genuinely shocked and surprised.

'Because it is your friend's child.'

'The child has a mother. I will make sure the child is looked after, but my life has no room for children or any sort of family.' This time there was no mistaking the finality in his voice. 'Until my vengeance is complete, I don't have room for anyone in my life.'

Cwenneth hated that her heart ached.

Chapter Six

Thrand concentrated on keeping his body upright and in the saddle and ignoring the increasing pain in his back. Narfi's final blow had cut deep into his back. With each pound of Myrkr's hoof, the wound protested. Years of battle had taught him to bury the pain and attend to the task at hand—escape.

Cwen was a weapon, nothing more. His destiny was not to have a family. He'd lost his family through his own mistakes. He wouldn't risk it again.

He shifted in the saddle. White-hot pain shot through his back. An involuntary moan escaped his lips. He tightened his grip on the reins and on Cwen's waist.

'Something is wrong!' Cwen half turned in the saddle. A frown came between her delicate brows. 'Are you well?'

'I'm perfectly fine,' Thrand answered between gritted teeth. If they stopped, he doubted if he could get back on Myrkr and be able to lift Cwen up as well. Already his vision was hazy. 'Far too soon to stop. Myrkr has a good few miles left in his legs. He is just slowing because of the extra burden.'

She put her hand against his chest. 'Do you really think that or are you simply saying it, hoping I will believe it?'

He concentrated on the road ahead, rather than how Cwen's curves felt against his body. 'Few dare question me.'

'Perhaps more should. Stop being arrogant and inclined to believe the legend of Thrand the Destroyer.' She gave an uneasy laugh. 'You're really Thrand Ammundson, a seasoned warrior, but still human.'

'You are wrong. We are the same.'

'I beg to differ.'

Cwenneth glanced back at Thrand's face when he didn't give a quick retort in turn.

Over the past few miles, all the colour had drained from his face, making it more like a death mask than a living countenance. His arm about her waist now resembled a dead man's grip.

She gasped. She should have checked Thrand for wounds before they left. She knew how quick Aefirth had been to dismiss any wound as trivial. Why should Thrand be any different?

Even Myrkr had sensed something was wrong. The horse was moving slowly and kept glancing back at Thrand.

'We need to stop,' she said. 'Right now. You must stop.'

'Go farther.' Thrand drew a shuddering breath. 'Need to keep you safe.'

'May God preserve me from stubborn warriors.' She reached for the horse's bridle. 'We stop now!'

The horse halted immediately. Thrand listed to one side, and his arm abruptly loosened. Cwenneth made a wild grab for Mrykr's mane and barely stayed on the horse.

'What do you think you are playing at, Cwen?'

Cwenneth let go of the mane and slid off the horse. She mistimed it and fell to the ground. Not the dignified dismounting that she'd hoped for, but it would suffice.

'Making sure we stop before you collapse and die.' Cwenneth stood up gingerly and stretched out her hands and legs. Nothing seemed to be broken. Her heart beat so fast that she thought it would burst out of her chest. 'Measures had to be taken. You're badly injured. Stop playing the legend and pay attention to the man.'

'Leave it.' His jaw jutted out, making him look more like a stubborn boy than a fearsome warrior. 'I don't need any of your help. Anyone's help. Now are you getting back on the horse? Or do I leave you to fend for yourself?'

'An empty threat.' Cwenneth tapped her foot on the ground. 'You need me alive.'

'Cwen!' He slid off the horse and winced, putting his hand to his back. His mouth was pinched white with a bluish tinge.

'The fighting was intense. Two men died. My price for continuing on is examining your wound.' She held out her hand. 'Please, before you get us both killed.'

'I can take care of myself,' he muttered, not meeting her eyes. 'I have been doing it for long enough. And if I have survived this many battles, I reckon that I will survive a bit longer.'

She held her hand. 'I can help. Together we can

bind the wound so you can travel. You look half-dead.'

His brief look of longing nearly took her breath away but before she could actually register it, the mask had come down. 'Far too stubborn.'

Cwenneth put her hand on her hip. She had always deferred to Aefirth and her brother, not wishing to risk their wrath, but Thrand was different. He was not the sort of man to use his fists on a woman whereas her brother had always been quick with his if he didn't get his own way. 'My late husband died because he ignored his injuries. I won't allow you to do the same.'

'Why would you do that for me?'

'Self-interest. I need you alive to keep me alive.'

He gave a great sigh. 'If you insist…but no fussing.'

'I do insist. There seems to be a deserted hut over here. Shelter, as the sky threatens rain.' Cwenneth pointed to a little building with its roof in desperate need of repair. A small stream ran alongside it. Shelter and water—what more could she want? Providence. A small boar was carved on the lintel over the door.

Cwenneth's heart leapt. If she ever returned to her old life, she'd make sure she incorporated the boar in any device she might have. Did women in convents have devices? Her brother was likely to make good his threat and send her to one. Whitby, if she was lucky. Or further up the coast if she wasn't. But she'd deal with that once it came about. Right now, there was no guarantee she'd reach Jorvik.

Thrand lifted a brow. 'You have no idea who uses it. Or when they might return.'

'We'll stop here for the night.'

'We need to get up north and back to Jorvik as swiftly as possible. Time is of the essence. I promised my men.'

'Your men will wait for us.' She marched towards the hut. 'Are you coming? Or do you leave me to die? Your one weapon against the man who killed your family?'

'How do you know my men will wait?' His smile was more like a grimace of pain. 'They are mercenaries. They will go with whosoever pays them the most amount of gold. There is adventure for the taking at the moment. Ireland, Iceland, even the trading routes to the east require men with strong backs and stronger sword arms.'

'You would wait for them,' she said with sudden certainty. Thrand would wait because he was that sort of person, because he honoured his word. 'Only Knui spoke out. The rest remained silent. And none bet against you.'

He tilted his head to one side. 'You appear to know my men very well.'

'They're men of honour.' As the words left her mouth, she thought of the irony. Two days ago, she would never have thought she'd utter those words about any Norseman, but she knew they were the truth. Honour didn't only belong to the Bernicians. 'I am going into the hut. You may follow if you wish, but we are not leaving this place until I say.'

She marched into the hut. Her heart thudded in her ears as she heard Thrand's horse whinny. She clenched her fists and hoped that Thrand would not challenge her any more.

'The hut appears derelict, but it has been used in the recent past,' Thrand said from the doorway. 'Whoever used it will be back.'

'Take off your top and stop being difficult.' She put her hand on her hip.

'A masterful woman. How refreshing. Most of the Northumbrian ladies I've encountered faint at the sight of blood.'

She rolled her eyes. 'I make no comment on the women you might have encountered previously.'

'I spoke of ladies. Northumbrian ladies.' His soft words skittered over her flesh.

'Then as you know I am no longer a lady. I am a woman. You claimed me.' She snapped her fingers, hating the sudden flash of jealousy which struck at her core. Which other ladies had he known? It wasn't any of her business. Truly. She wasn't interested in him. Not in that way. She was only with him because she wanted to survive.

A voice deep within her called her a liar.

'I will have no more of this nonsense about me being a gently bred lady who faints at the sight of blood. I am a widow and have seen the male torso before. I attended my husband during his last illness.'

'You are wrong there, Cwen. Your breeding oozes from your pores.'

'Stop stalling. Strip.'

He pulled off his top and exposed his torso. His skin was a golden hue except where a network of scars gleamed white.

Cwenneth sucked in her breath and hastily averted her eyes from the faint line of hair that led down his chest and disappeared into his trousers. She'd had enough humiliation with his rejection of her kiss earlier that morning.

'Have you seen enough, my *lady*?'

'I'll let you know.'

She walked slowly around him, hoping that he didn't notice the flame in her cheeks. The removal of his shirt had dislodged the slight scabbing. Fresh blood oozed from the cut on his lower back. It was a wonder that he had remained upright, let alone was able to ride a horse, hanging on to the both of them. Cwenneth swallowed hard. The debt she owed him grew with each passing breath.

'Before I take another step that wound will be cleaned and stitched,' she said, opting for a practical tone. Her stomach roiled. 'Hopefully Narfi's sword was clean.'

'Can you stitch wounds?'

'One thing I can do is sew. I embroidered my gown, not that there is any gold left on it,' she commented drily.

'But have you sewn flesh?' His fingers brushed hers. A jolt of fire ran up her arm.

'I've seen worse,' she said, avoiding the question. She had watched the monks sew up Aefirth three times—the first time he came home after a battle, after an accident in training, and the final time. But now wasn't the moment to confess her lack of practical experience. 'The wound doesn't gape and no vital organs are touched or you wouldn't have been able to ride for so long. You have lost blood and the wound still seeps. Sewing rather than burning. A simple enough task for me.' After what had happened with Aefirth and Richard, her confidence in her abilities to heal were next to nil. She had promised her sister-in-law to always call for the monks and never to attempt anything on her own again. But Thrand needed help immediately before he lost more blood or the wound festered.

His hand captured hers. 'You tremble.'

She pulled away from him. 'I can do it.'

'We could find a monastery. A monk would stitch me up. They have in the past. Honour bound, even to help a pagan sinner such as me.'

'Once Hagal knows you fought Narfi, he will check every church and monastery in the vicinity just in case. He is not a man to respect sanctuary.'

He closed his eyes for a long heartbeat.

'My husband died from a wound that went putrid.' She kept her gaze on the walls of the hut. Her nails made half-moons in her palms as she felt moisture gather in the back of her eyes. 'He should have gone to a healer straight away, but he was eager to get home. By the time the monks and I had a chance to look at the wound, it was too late. The poison had spread. They tried to burn it out, but failed.'

He placed a heavy hand on her shoulder. 'How would you have felt if he had died elsewhere?'

She spun around and looked into his face. His mouth was pinched and his lips were more blue than red. 'Do you have a choice?'

He closed his eyes and his pallor increased. Sweat now cascaded down his face and his arms began to shake.

Cwenneth clamped her lips together and waited, silently praying that he would see sense and stop being stubborn. Men.

He bowed his head. 'I give in. Tomorrow morning we go. My pack and saddle will need to be brought in. Myrkr stabled. I've no wish for some thief to take them while we are messing with my back.'

'Remain here.' Without waiting for him to reply, she walked out of the door. Myrkr bared his teeth at her. Normally, she'd have backed away and not even tried. But that wasn't an option. She advanced forward and gripped his bridle.

She tugged, but the horse remained still and unmoving. He gave a low whinny and shook his head, determined to wait for his master.

'Move it,' she growled and shoved her shoulder against the horse. 'You have to so I can save his life. Do this for Thrand.'

To her astonishment, Myrkr allowed her to lead him to the small lean-to she'd spied at the side of the hut. There was a manger with the remains of some oats in the bottom. 'You see—food.'

While the horse ate, she rapidly undid the saddle and removed Thrand's gear. 'I'll return later. Let you know how it went. Give you some more food.'

The horse lowered his head and pawed the ground twice as if he understood. She pressed her hands to her head. Talking to horses and expecting them to understand—she must be losing her mind. But her nerves eased slightly to think she was not alone.

She staggered back into the hut and dropped the pack down with a thump. 'Myrkr is safely stabled and your pack is here. Your saddle can wait.'

In her absence, Thrand had started the fire. The flames highlighted the increasing pool of blood on his shirt.

Cwenneth clenched her fists. God save her from self-sufficient men. She put down the pack with a loud and satisfying thump.

'Be careful with that. If it was too heavy you should have said.'

'What is in there? The takings from your latest raid?' she bit out.

'Enough gold to provide for Sven's child as well as healing herbs and a little food.' He sank down to the ground. 'I think I might have overdone it after all.'

'What healing herbs do you have?' Cwenneth's mouth went dry. 'My late husband always used to have a few supplies, just in case there was no monastery available. Hopefully you use the same herbs.'

He motioned towards his pack. 'There are some. Valerian root, knit bone and a few others. No poppy seeds. Those who have served in Constantinople swear by it, but it gives me strange dreams. And I do have silk for sewing up. Linen stitches do not hold as well. And there is some ale for washing the wound. Or drinking. I don't have any linen for bandages. My shirt will have to do.'

The tension in her shoulders relaxed slightly. She would have preferred wine or something stronger, but ale would do. She simply had to hope that he would either keep still or pass out once she started sewing. 'Valerian is good. It will help you to sleep if it is mixed with alcohol.'

'Afterwards. I'll drink it afterwards.' His eyes burned fiercely into her soul.

'Can you hold yourself steady?'

'I've withstood worse.' He raised his chin, and his blue gaze pierced hers. 'Our healers are not known for their gentleness. When I can, I go to a monastery as the monks are better at healing than our so-called healers. They are as apt to murmur a spell as to sew you up.'

'Interesting, since you have sacked monasteries.'

'I've never made war against the monks. There is no sport in killing an unarmed man.'

Her eye bulged. 'And you fight for the sport?'

'That and other things.' His eyes blazed. 'It is what I am good at. The only thing I am good at…in case you hadn't heard.'

Cwenneth concentrated on the hollow at the base of Thrand's throat. Narfi had made it clear that he had spread rumours about Thrand, but Thrand was also a seasoned Norse warrior with all the horror it entailed. He was her brother's enemy, but there was more to him than just being a warrior. He could have easily turned her over to Narfi for gold, but he hadn't. He had made sure that they put miles between them and any pursuer. And he valued his friends. He was keeping his promise to Sven. 'I had heard.'

'Good.' He closed his eyes. 'Whenever you are ready…'

Cwenneth bent her head and concentrated on threading the bone needle. 'I'm ready now.'

'Get on with it.' Thrand lay down on the pallet on his front, exposing his back.

'Please let the curse be gone. My life depends on him,' she murmured as she started cleaning the blood from his scarred back.

Cwenneth sat back on her heels and examined her handiwork. Once she had started sewing, the rhythm had begun to flow and her stitches had become neat, pulling the flesh together. The wound wasn't as deep or complicated as she had first feared.

The main problem had been its length. Thrand would bear the scar for the rest of his life. Another one to add to the series of silver and purple lines that criss-crossed his back. Unable to find any rags, she sacrificed the bottom third of her gown to make a satisfactory bandage. His shirt was far too bloodied for any purpose but feeding the fire. She had enough for two changes of the bandage before she would have to start finding more cloth.

That was a problem for another day. Right now, it was about making sure the blood stopped.

She reached over and gave the coals a stir. The fire blazed brightly for an instant, consuming the last of his shirt before subsiding into a pile of coals.

'Thrand,' she said softly, ignoring the tighter and tighter knot which had taken up residence in the pit of her stomach. 'I've finished. But I'm cursed, you see.'

Silently, she prayed that Thrand would answer. He lay so still that she had to wonder if he even lived. She wished she had her mother's mirror to check his breath. She pushed at his shoulder and turned him onto his side.

Thrand gave a soft groan and then started to splutter. 'I don't believe in curses.'

Cwenneth brushed away an errant tear from her cheek. He lived and now all she had to do was to keep him alive.

She went to the fire and retrieved the potion of valerian root and ale she had made. 'Drink this.'

Chapter Seven

⚬⚬⚬⚬⚬⚬

The world about him rose rugged and unspoilt, tall snow-covered peaks and dark rich soil, lit with a flat, unnatural light. A hard land, but a good one. Thrand knew without being told where it was. Iceland, the new colony where Sven had once joked that a man could be free to live his life as he saw fit.

Thrand had visited it several years before when he had signed on to a trading vessel for a season. He had arrived to discover the man he sought had died two months before. Thrand had silently marked the name off as one less he had to kill and had left. But this was the first time he had dreamt of the place.

He knew he was dreaming by the light and the lack of breeze. But he also knew he wanted to remain there. He knew he could remain if he wanted to. Thrand bent down, running the soil through his fingers, like he had seen his father do a thousand times. A simple action to determine if planting time was near, but one he'd never done as an adult. The earth felt good in his hand, a living thing rather than the cold, hard, lifeless touch of steel.

His eyes were unfocused. He grabbed her hand.

'Is it over? Have we won? Tell me that.'

'Yes, we've won,' she confirmed softly and prayed that she spoke true. This time she would defeat the infection or die in the attempt.

The longing to have a place of his own struck him deep in his soul. Once he had thought he'd spend his life planting and harvesting, rather than earning his keep by his sword arm, as his mother had longed for him.

He looked back towards the longhouse with its gabled roof. It reminded him of his boyhood home, but it was set back on a hill, not too near the water. To the right sat a pen filled with horses. Their different-coloured manes shone in the light. One pawed the ground as if to say, *come, train me, if you are man enough.*

He gave a crooked smile. As a boy, he had thought he'd spend his time training horses for a living. His father had laughed and told him to pay more attention to his fighting skills. His gentle mother, though, had smiled and quietly encouraged him.

Thrand's heart ached. He missed his mother's sweet smile and the way her long fingers were always busy with something, from spinning to weaving and even shelling peas. She had never sat still and she had always taken time to help others in their hour of need. For many years it had hurt too much to remember, especially the cruel way her laughter had been silenced. But here, the memories made him long for something else. Here he had hope.

A woman came out of the house with two children clinging to her skirts. Her face was turned from him, shadowed. She held out her hand, beckoning him in, welcoming him. He started to go towards her and ask her name and if those children could be his. He wanted to know who else was there. Somehow, he knew if he went further, he'd be part of a family again.

'Thrand, Thrand, wake up.' A hard hand shook his shoulder. He fought against it, wanted to stay and see if he could have a family again, if he could find peace at last. 'Thrand! I know you can hear me. Give me a sign. One little sign.'

He fought against the voice, fought to remain in his dream land, but the woman and her children had vanished, leaving him all alone on a windswept plain. He was at a crossroads. A great part of him longed to rejoin the woman, but the clear voice kept calling him, making it impossible for him to go farther.

'Thrand, wake up! Make some sign! Show me that you live. You have to live!'

The dream had vanished as if it had never been. Leaves and straw poked through his cloak, and his nose itched. But most of all he was aware of the woman beside him.

He opened one eye and saw Cwen crouched down beside him, a worried frown between her perfectly arched eyebrows. Her slender hand hovered above his shoulder. The flickering light of the fire highlighted her cheekbones.

He would have almost considered her a goddess or one of those angels that the Christians believed in. But she wrinkled her nose and sneezed. And he knew she was real. Angels or goddesses did not sneeze.

Cwen had called him back from the dream land. He swallowed hard, remembering how Sven had spoken about a journey to an empty country before he died. How he looked forward to starting a home there with his wife and child. To having a life beyond war.

'Cwen?' he whispered between cracked lips. His entire body was drenched in cold, clammy sweat and his arms felt as weak as a newborn babe's. 'You stayed. I thought you might go. Escape back to Lingwold.'

'Where would I go? I gave you my word.' She put a hand on his forehead. 'Your temperature has broken. It is a good sign. I think you will live to fight Hagal after all.'

Her blue eyes sparkled in the firelight. Had she been crying? He dismissed the idea as impossible. No one cried for him…not since his mother died.

His mother had spent most of the year before her death weeping over him and his imagined failures, as his father raged and predicted dire things. Until in the end, he had figured that he might as well be as bad as they both seemed to think. He started to take pleasure in goading his father and getting a reaction. His dalliance with Ingrid had driven his father wild and that had been part of the fun.

To his eternal shame, he had proved worse than either parent had ever imagined. His actions had led directly to their deaths. He had tried to change and to become the sort of man who would was worthy of his parents. But still he failed; he had not been able to take his revenge. So far, Hagal had always slipped away.

'It will take more than a little wound like that to kill me,' he said to distract his mind from the past and his failure.

Instead of Cwenneth answering him, her eyes turned unbearably sad and her bottom lip trembled.

Something inside Thrand broke. He had meant to give her a compliment and he had made a mess of it.

'Cwen, what is wrong?'

'Nothing is wrong.' A single tear trembled in the corner of her eye.

He started to lift his hand to cup her face, taste her lips and kiss the shadows from her eyes. Then he remembered what she had said about her husband and his death. His hand fell back.

He'd been foolish. She wasn't weeping for him. She was weeping for her dead husband. It should have made him feel better, but the thought was like a hot knife in his stomach.

In that instant he hated the man and that his widow should weep for him so long after his death. If he died, no one would weep. No one would ever weep. He wanted it that way, didn't he?

'Then why are you crying?'

She hastily scrubbed her reddened eyes. 'Smoke from the fire.'

He nodded, allowing her lie. 'I told you—you are stuck with me for a while yet. I have had worse wounds and have lived to tell the tale.'

'Are you suffering any pain? I can get you some more valerian.'

Only around his heart. His hand fell back to the makeshift bed, rather than bringing her head down to his lips.

'I heal quickly. The wound isn't deep.' His mouth tasted foul and his body ached with new pains with each breath he took. His life was supposed to be very different, but protesting about it would not change his destiny.

It bothered him that he wanted her to feel something for him. When had a woman ever felt something for him? Like Ingrid, they had all wanted something from him.

It was fine. It was the way he wanted things. His life held no room for the gentler aspects of life—a woman's loving touch or a family. The longing from his dream was the product of a fevered mind. The thought failed to ease his pain.

'I need to change your bandage. Your thrashing about has loosened it.' Her hands pushed him down. 'Lie still. On your side. Allow me to work.'

His fingers picked at the linen bandage. The cloth was far finer than his shirt. 'Where did you put my shirt?'

'I have had to burn your shirt as it was blood-soaked beyond what a simple wash could do. We should never have ridden as far as we did. Are you always this reckless?'

'What did you use?' He clenched his fist and tried to think of the garments in his satchel. The most likely cloth was Sven's last gift to his former mistress—a fine linen shift. It annoyed him that he was bothered. 'What did you use?'

'A bit of my undergown. It is strong linen and clean. I had no idea where the clothes in your satchel had been.'

He forced his body to remain still as her cool hands worked. She had sacrificed part of her undergown for him. She had not taken Sven's token to his former mistress, the woman who had borne him a child. Sven had insisted that his woman must have it, with practically his last breath. It made him feel worse—

beholden to Cwen, rather than angry with her. 'I will replace it when we get to Jorvik.'

'The wound has stayed shut. I used the remaining blister ointment on top of the stitches.'

'It helps with healing,' Thrand confirmed.

'As long as it keeps infection at bay…' She didn't pause in her ministrations but continued to tighten the bandage.

Her fingers brushed his skin, causing an agony of a different sort. Thrand practised breathing steadily.

Impersonal. She probably would have done it for anyone. He had to stop hoping that she harboured some feeling for him. Or that he could have a future which was very different from his past.

The dream had been simply valerian-induced with no hidden meaning.

He tried to get up. To his shame, he seemed to have no more strength than a kitten. A wave of tiredness washed over him. He collapsed back down on to the pallet, rather than resisting it as he would have done normally. He rubbed his hand across his jaw. He sported some bristles but not many and not too long. 'How long have I been asleep?'

'The entire night, most of a day and all evening.'

The clouds from his mind vanished and his muscles were suddenly on high alert. 'Entire day and night? Why did you let me sleep that long? Has the fire been on all this time?'

'I gave you valerian root mixed with the ale. The infection… You had to be kept warm.'

'We need to travel. We've stayed here far too long.' He redoubled his efforts to stand, but her hands pushed him back down.

'You need to sleep.' Her voice soothed him. 'Who travels during the night? Drink some more valerian and ale and take the pain away.'

He shook his head. The scar under his eye itched. The first time it had happened, Ingrid had just told him to sleep in her arms and then two armed men had burst into the barn. His instinct never played him false. They had tarried far too long here as it was.

'No, we go.' He heaved himself up from the pallet and his back screamed in agony. 'Now, before morning.'

'No one has passed by. I heard some jangling of a cow bell last evening, but there was nothing more. No one knows we are here. Whoever used this in the past is long gone.'

'Smoke from the fire will have been visible. For miles. Particularly if you had the fire going during the day.' He put his hands on her shoulders and steadied himself. The room swam slightly before righting itself. The hardest part was always the getting up. Thrand focused on the smouldering coals.

Two bright patches appeared on her cheeks. She stepped away from his touch. 'You said Hagal would search to the south, towards Jorvik.'

'We've no idea where they're searching. And the smoke has been rising long enough for someone to take notice. Smoke from a deserted hut always attracts attention.' He ran his hand through his hair. 'It was only supposed to be for the operation in case you had to burn the wound to stop the bleeding.'

'It kept you warm.'

'You were supposed to smother the fire once the operation was done!'

Cwen pursed her lips. 'Obviously, I missed that instruction in my concern for your health.'

'Sarcasm fails to alter the situation.'

'Neither will yelling at me.'

Thrand kept his back rigid and took three steps forward. The pain nearly blinded him, but he could move. 'We go now, before we have to entertain unwanted visitors.'

'Will you be able to get on your horse? You can barely stand.'

She put her hand on his arm. It took all of his willpower not to cling on to her for support. She had to think he was fine if he was going to save her life.

'All the more reason for departing.'

'My late husband used to say…'

'Preaching your late husband's words won't alter the situation.'

The way her face fell twisted his gut. Thrand pressed his hands to his eyes and attempted to regain control. What was it about Cwen that made him want to obliterate any man who had touched her? She wanted her late husband, not him. Natural. Why would a lady like her care about a Norse warrior like him?

He gulped a mouthful of life-giving air and regained control of his emotions. Task at hand, not longing for something which could never happen.

'We walk very slowly, but we put a distance between this place and us,' he said with exaggerated patience.

'I am a lady, not your slave. I dislike being ordered about.'

'Humour me, Cwen. Please.'

Cwenneth pressed her lips together, hating that Thrand was being logical. They had stayed here for far too long, but she had not had a choice. Keeping him drugged had been the right thing to do. She could not face losing him to an infection, not after seeing how Aefirth had suffered.

She watched as Thrand kicked dirt over the fire, extinguishing it, then tested it for heat and putting more dirt over. A hard lump settled in her stomach.

She wished she had thought of the risk of being seen, instead of staring into the flames and thinking about Aefirth's last days.

She picked up her cloak and concentrated on shaking it out. 'I will bow to your superior wisdom—after all, you must have experience at escaping.'

He turned back to her. 'If you give me the pack, I will see about Myrkr.'

'I will handle the pack and the horse,' she said between gritted teeth and shouldered the heavy bag. 'I'm hardly some useless lady who can't lift more than a feather.'

Thrand slowly turned back towards her. The planes of his face softened, making him human. 'I have never considered you weak.'

A warm glow infused her body. He thought her strong. Aefirth had always considered her helpless. She hated the disloyal thought.

'We take frequent breaks. I refuse to have you act like a martyr.' She glared at him. 'Do you understand? I can give orders as well.'

A muscle twitched in the corner of his cheek. 'Few would dare order me about like that. My reputation precedes me.'

'I know the man, I don't fear the legend.'

'Truly?'

'The only thing I care about is getting to Jorvik and making my statement to Hagal. You are a means to an end. That is all.'

Her heart protested at the necessary lie. She wanted him to live because…he'd saved her life. Cwenneth balanced the pack on her shoulder and refused to think beyond that reason.

'It is good to know where your priorities lie.'

'There. Is the pack on Myrkr to your satisfaction this time?' Cwenneth's entire being was aware of Thrand standing directly behind her, watching her every move, but he had listened to reason and allowed her to put the pack on the horse. He had just made her do it three times until he was satisfied.

He put a finger to her lips. 'Hush. Listen.'

A faint jangle of a bridle sounded on the early-morning breeze.

'Sounds travel far in the mist,' she whispered as her muscles froze. 'They are not coming this way…'

'Caution saves lives.' He placed his hand on her shoulder. His breath tickled her ear, causing her stomach to swoop with an altogether different emotion. Cwenneth concentrated on breathing steadily.

'Caution?'

'We hide until they leave.'

'How do you hide a horse like Myrkr?'

Thrand led the way farther into the woods, stopping beside a small knoll. He gave Myrkr a slap on his hind quarters and the horse obediently trotted off. 'Like that. He will come when I whistle.'

'What's your secret?' she asked in a low voice.

'My secret?'

'Myrkr obeyed you instantly and without question.'

'He trusts me. You should try it some time. It could be a good habit to get into.' Thrand turned back to her. 'Get down and wait. Whatever happens, keep your head down and keep silent.'

Her heart thudded in her ears. 'I can be quiet.'

'With any luck, they will ride on past without investigating if the fire remains warm now that the smoke is gone.'

'And if they don't?'

'We face it when it happens. But my sword arm has never failed me yet.'

Cwenneth gulped hard. 'We need to stay together. Going off scouting will increase our chances of being seen.'

His large hand covered hers. The simple touch eased her and she found she could breathe again. 'There is no need to give in to panicked fear.'

'I'm not afraid,' she lied, hoping he'd believe her.

'That makes one of us then. It is fine to be afraid, Cwen, but use it, rather than panicking.'

Cwen pressed her lips together. 'I'll remember that.'

He lay down in the hollow, stretched out, but his hand hovered over the hilt of his sword. 'Let's hope Thor still favours you.'

Cwenneth manoeuvred her body so that their shoulders were just touching. Even that innocent brush sent a pulse of warmth throughout her body. 'Aren't your gods supposed to be fickle?'

He put his finger to her lips. 'All will be well, Cwen. It is far too dark for them to want to go into the woods.'

The cold dew seeped up into her body as they lay there in the grey mist of dawn, waiting. The jangling of the bridles came louder and stopped.

'Anyone there?' a Northumbrian voice called. 'Answer us or we are coming in.'

Cwen glanced at Thrand, who quickly shook his head.

She crouched lower, tried to make her body smaller.

'I don't know what your lad saw,' came another voice, rougher but with a lazy authority. 'But nobody ever uses this hut, not since Simon the Fat died. His ghost haunts it.'

'There was someone,' a young boy's voice protested. 'I saw the smoke when I brought the cows in from the far field. Ghosts don't cause smoke.'

'Do you think it was him? With our new lord's lady?'

'Wherever Thrand the Destroyer is, it won't be here,' an older, rougher voice said. 'Why would he be going north? There ain't nothing for him. You've roused me from a warm bed and a willing wench for this! Your lad thought he saw wolves circling the sheep the other week and it were nothing.'

Several men agreed with him. Cwenneth risked a breath. In the grey light, she counted five shapes. Five against one. The odds were terrible.

'We should check,' the first voice said. 'My lad knows what he saw and where.'

The door of the hut creaked.

'The coals are warm…barely,' someone called.

'But they ain't here. No telling who it was. Could have been the Destroyer and his men.'

'In your nightmares!'

The uneasy laughter followed the swift retort.

'Only one horse,' someone else shouted. 'Doesn't the Destroyer always travel with more men?'

Cwen and Thrand exchanged glances. Thrand eased his sword out of the sheath. She nodded and resumed praying, more in hope than expectation.

'We should search for them. They won't go far.' The boy started towards where Cwen and Thrand hid. Cwen shrank deeper into the hollow. Her muscles tensed, ready for flight.

'I didn't see anyone as we rode in,' someone shouted and the boy halted inches from their hiding place. 'If the Destroyer has left here, our farms are in danger. Our women.'

'They will have left before it became dark. Stands to reason.' Rough Voice gestured to the boy, calling him back. The boy scampered back to the others. Cwen breathed again.

'And if it is the Destroyer, he won't be alone. He will have his men with him. Hardened warriors, not farmhands. And more than one horse. Do you want to face them?'

'But we should let the Norseman know. He promised a substantial reward.'

'And you are a Northman's lapdog now?'

'I know what is good for me and mine.'

'What do you think will happen if they find him here? Do you think they'd reward you with gold? Or take all your crops like they did last year?' Rough Voice snorted. 'I know what Norsemen's rewards are like. He is as likely to rob you blind as fill your pockets with gold. Best to keep your head down and out of their affairs. You don't want them to have any knowledge of treasure you might have.'

'He'll come back to it later!'

'I hadn't considered that. I don't want any trouble.' The man drew his boy closer.

'I'm not minded to do any Norseman's bidding,' Rough Voice said. 'Even if he was here, what business is it of mine as long as he leaves my crops and gold alone?'

Others murmured their agreement.

'Let them find the Destroyer themselves, I say,' Rough Voice proclaimed in ringing tones. 'A plague on all greedy Norsemen.'

'And if they return?' the boy piped up.

'If they return and ask, we tell the truth—we checked but no one was here. But why bother trouble if trouble ain't bothering us? I have lambs to birth and cows to milk.'

After a pause which felt like a lifetime, they all agreed with Rough Voice.

The tension in Cwen's shoulders eased as Thrand released his grip on his sword.

Discussing the perfidy of Norsemen, the likelihood of an early raiding season and the state of lambing, they departed.

Cwen rolled over on her back and stared at the rose, dawn-streaked sky. Her blood fizzed as she drank in mouthfuls of life-giving air.

'They have gone. Truly gone.'

He put his hand on her shoulder. 'I told you—you

have Thor's favour. It could have gone either way and it went in ours. Thanks to you and your luck.'

She propped herself on one elbow and regarded his face. His dark-blonde hair streamed out across the ground and bristle shadowed his jaw.

'I'm pleased you didn't have to kill that boy.'

'I'm a warrior, not a suicidal maniac. I only fight when I have to.' He expelled a long breath and stood up without touching her. 'The odds were not in my favour and as long as our hiding place remained undetected, there was no need. But I wouldn't have hesitated.'

'I know.' Cwenneth stood up and brushed the dirt from her skirt.

Thrand gave a low whistle which sounded more like an owl than a human. True to his prediction, the horse returned within a few heartbeats. Thrand leaned over and rubbed the horse's nose.

'They've no appetite for the search. You heard the one with the rough voice. Do you think we will be safe on the road?' she asked.

He raised a brow. 'No more roads. And we skirt all settlements. The fewer people who know about our business, the better. We've no idea how far Hagal's rumour has spread.'

She held back the words saying that, despite everything, she had found a little bit of peace in this hut. She had proven that she could heal, that some of the more damning things whispered about Aefirth's and Richard's deaths were untrue. Not everyone she tried to heal died. But that would be revealing too much of herself to this man. 'And your stitches? Are they up to a long ride?'

'You sew a fine seam. I'd expect no less from you.'

'A compliment?'

He shrugged. 'You're a strong woman, Cwen, and a lucky one. Never allow anyone to tell you differently.'

Their gazes caught and held. She cleared her throat. 'How do you propose me getting on that horse?'

Her voice was far more breathless than she would have liked.

He jerked his head towards a stump. 'Use that as a mounting block. The sooner we are away from Hagal and his men, the better. Every day we delay is another day that Hagal has a chance to spread his poisonous lies about me kidnapping you. And the next time, the farmers might not be as wary of Norsemen as that lot was.'

Cwenneth hugged her arms about her waist. She had been foolish to think that he might want an excuse to hold her. And she had nearly embraced him after the men left. What sort of person was she that she needed to face the humiliation of rejection more than once?

Chapter Eight

*D*esire. What he felt for Cwenneth was nothing more than desire. He had been without a woman for months now. He had intended finding a willing woman the night Sven had died, but after that there had not been time. He had learnt his lesson after Ingrid—not to allow his heart to become involved. Purely physical and avoid complications.

Cwen was not the sort of woman one used and discarded. She was the other sort, the sort his father had told him that you protected and looked after, a woman like his mother. Strong and full of integrity. Thrand pushed the thought away. Cwen was his means of achieving revenge for his mother's death. That was all.

'Shall we stop here?' Cwen said, half turning. Her delicate brows puckered into a frown. 'Here beside this stream is as good as any place to camp for the night. Stopping before it gets too dark.'

The small wooded glade with a stream running through it would serve for the night. And his back was on fire. 'You have a good eye. It will meet our needs.

I will take the first watch. You look exhausted. We've gone far enough away from any pursuers.'

She put her hand on his arm. 'And if you think to fool me by saying your back doesn't hurt by agreeing to my request, I must warn you, your brow is creased with pain and you winced when you mounted Mrykr the last time. You need to sleep. After all we've been through I won't lose you to an infection.'

Thrand drew his upper lip over his teeth. She had noticed his discomfort. He struggled to remember the last time anyone had noticed how he was, rather just accepting his bland words. Probably his mother. What would she have thought of Cwen?

Thrand shook his head, trying to clear the thought. He knew what his mother had hoped for him—a wife and children—but that would have to wait until he had avenged her death. He couldn't do both. He'd seen the terrible things that happened when men became distracted.

'The last thing I need to do is sleep.' He gave a crooked smile as she slid down from the horse. 'I spent enough time the last few days asleep. Someone has to keep watch.'

'I can take the first watch.'

'When were you trained in swordplay, my lady? It will be safer for all if I remain alert.'

'I never had the chance to learn.' Cwen tucked her chin into her neck. 'My late husband considered it beneath my dignity, or rather beneath his wife's dignity. Perhaps I should have questioned his authority, but he was much older than I and much wiser in the ways of the world.'

'He made a mistake.'

'How hard can it be to use a sword? All you have to do is to remember which end to strike with.'

'There is more to it than that.' Thrand paused and silently vowed that he would teach her to fight before they reached Jorvik. For her own safety, she needed to learn. He didn't want to think about her being alone and vulnerable, dying like his mother had done. She, too, had not known how to use a sword and believed that there would always be someone there to protect her. 'My dreams are troubled ones. I'm used to getting by on little sleep.'

'I hate dreaming.' A vulnerable light shone in her eyes. 'I worry about your wound becoming infected. I lost my husband to one and if I lose you...how will I survive?'

A sudden stab of jealousy went through Thrand. He only hoped her much-older late husband had deserved her. 'It wasn't your fault he died. Destiny. We can't chose the date of our birth or the date of our death. Warriors die of infections all the time. I'm very tough.'

'Aefirth said the same when he lay there. He absolved me of all guilt. He was old, and I had my whole life ahead of me. It didn't make it any easier.' Her fist balled. 'And you're wrong about me being lucky. Any who seek my help will die. My stepson's nurse called out a curse when I put her from the hall and now I'm destined to lose everything I love.'

'And because your husband died, you believe an old woman's words?'

'More people died.'

'Who?'

'Our son. He was two,' she said, turning from him.

Her shoulders hunched. 'He died days after Aefirth. Of a fever. I wanted to die as well, but it didn't happen. I have had to live with the knowledge of how I had failed. If I'd been a better person, I would have saved them both. But I'm wicked and so was punished. My stepson didn't even allow me to lay flowers at Richard's grave. He was afraid of the curse spreading.'

Thrand sucked in his breath. Cwen had had a son. She had had a life before now. She had been a mother. She had had a child. The emptiness of his life grated. Never once had he had the joy of holding his own child. In the stillness of the evening he envied her.

He shook his head, trying to rid himself of the feeling of wanting something more to his life. He knew what he did and why. It was the only life he had known since his family was slaughtered. It had to be until he had disposed of Hagal. Longing to have anything else led to a dulling of his sword arm and his appetite for fighting. There was no room in his life for anything but hate and killing.

'You're not cursed,' he muttered.

'You've never lost a child. It was as if my heart had been torn from my body. I prayed to God to let me die, but here I am. In the woods that first day, I found that I wanted to live. Even the thought of being with my son held no comfort.'

'We cannot control when people die. The Norns of fate are tight-lipped crones and only they know what sort of thread they have spun for a man's life. You are a good person who experienced bad times.' He knew the words were inadequate and far too harsh. He had never been good at the soft words. Even Ingrid had teased him about that. Actions for him were always more important than words. 'But it is how you respond to those times which is important. My mother used to say that to me.'

At Cwenneth's anguished look, he ran his hand through his hair. He hated having to provide comfort. He always said the wrong thing. 'What I mean is that it is a tragedy when a young child dies. Far harder than when a man does. But to think we have a say in it is wrong. Outrunning your fate is impossible. Whatever words I say, it won't make your burden any easier.'

She bowed her head. 'Richard was the light of my life and my husband's. He was such a bright thing, always into mischief, and his laughter… I wanted to take his place, but here I am.'

'How did it happen?'He hesitated. 'If you want to talk about it…'

'One moment, he was alive and well, laughing and having a game of tag with the cook. I was grateful for a little peace as Aefirth's funeral had been two days earlier. The next he complained of a stiff and hurting neck. He had a high fever and a rash. I had gone to get a poultice and when I returned, all the life had vanished. And to make matters complete, I lost any hope that I might be carrying another child. Before it started, I'd been so sure that I'd felt the baby quicken. When I had confided in Aefirth in those final hours before he died, he seemed so happy.' She looped a stray tendril of hair about her ear. 'And then…I felt like such a fool.'

'Why did your stepson behave as he did?'

'My stepson accused me…well, we never were going to be close in any case…he said that his nurse's curses were strong. He told me that I had destroyed his family, but they were my family as well.'

'Old men and children die all the time.'

'But they were my family, not strangers. I wanted them to live. Desperately.'

He reached out and laced his hand with hers. Inside him, something curled up and died. Cwen had lost not only her husband, but her son. He couldn't imagine the pain she must have gone through. It had been hard enough to leave his parents' grave. 'It was wrong, that. Not allowing you to lay flowers or mourn your son properly.'

She pulled her hand from his. 'I think of him every day. I nearly came to blows with my sister-in-law when she said that I'd get over it. Why would I want to forget my son?

'Not that it is any help…people said that to me, but there wasn't anything anyone could do to take away the pain.

'At least you could fight against someone. How do you fight against an illness?' She stood up. 'The priest said…that…it showed I'd done something wrong. A punishment from God…but I was following his orders. He had told me if I didn't dismiss the nurse, he'd withhold communion from everyone.'

'It seems to me that the priest should be blamed rather than you.' Thrand reached over and covered her hand with his. This time she kept her hand in his. 'He was trying to deflect his guilt when he blamed you.'

She raised shimmering eyes to his. 'Do you think so?'

'I know so.' He tilted his head to one side and saw

the diamond gleam of a teardrop on her cheek. 'Some day you may have another child. After this is over.'

'Drink the tea,' she said shoving the cup forward. 'I don't want to talk about it any more. My heart was buried with Richard. No more children for me. Ever. I can't take the pain.'

'Why did you agree to the marriage with Hagal?'

'Not to regain a family.' She crossed her arms. Her eyes threw daggers, all sorrow vanished. 'If you must know, I was taking the lesser of two evils. My brother had threatened to send me to a convent of his choosing without a dowry. I doubted if I'd last long there. What can a cursed woman do in a convent?' She shrugged. 'Now the only future I know about involves destroying Hagal. Sometimes I want to think beyond that moment. I want to believe that there is more for me.'

'Do you want another marriage?'

'I want a life. I want to believe that I'm not cursed.'

He stared at the tea, suddenly desiring the oblivion it would bring. Maybe when he woke, he'd stop longing for things he had no business wanting—a family, a life without war and the taste of Cwen's mouth.

He drained the cup in a single gulp. 'Keep the sword across your knees. Sit over there as it will give you the clearest view. Scream if you see any movement at all.'

She sat down with the sword awkwardly placed on her lap. 'Like this?'

'You need to learn to defend yourself,' Thrand said, closing his eyes. At last a way to repay the debt he owed her. He could ensure she knew how to defend herself. 'We begin tomorrow at first light.'

'And you won't make it easy for me? Make concessions?'

Thrand opened his eyes. 'Why would I?'

'My husband used to make things easy for me... even when I told him that I may be a lady, but I wasn't a child.'

The orange light from the sunset highlighted her height and the slenderness of her build. She certainly did not look the type, but she was tough, far tougher than he had first imagined. His eyes grew heavy. Already his mind was slipping back to Iceland and its possibilities. Somehow Cwen and Iceland were connected in his mind, but he couldn't figure out how or why.

'Your husband probably would have bet against you walking all that way on the day we met.'

'He would never have allowed me to attempt it.' She gave a laugh. 'For too long I have depended on other people. I want to stand on my own two feet. I've finished cowering. I'm tired of feeling helpless and dead inside because of something which I could not stop. You're right—some parts of your destiny you can't change.'

'Knowing the difference can be difficult.'

'Thank you for saying you will teach me how to use a sword. We're friends now.'

He raised himself up on his elbow and fought against the wave of tiredness. Friends. He wanted her friendship. He wanted to see her come back to life and not be one of the walking dead. And it scared him. 'I've never been friends with a woman before.'

She spun back around. 'And I want to learn to ride. Properly. Aefirth never allowed me to do that either.

How hard can it be? I managed to stay on today without falling off. A start, yes?'

Thrand released his breath. The dispassionate part of his mind told him that he should be rejoicing. She was going to do what he wanted. He was finally going to be able to destroy the person who had been involved in his family's slaughter. He would fulfil his oath to his father. And if it meant her death…he'd lose a friend. It bothered him that she had become important to him and that his desire for her showed no signs of abating.

'Most people are afraid of me and my horse,' he said, not bothering to hide his bitterness. All the women who had shied away from him crowded his mind. All the whispers which followed him throughout the years. 'Why not you?'

He had to lance this hope before it started. He'd seen too many men lose their focus over a woman. He needed to keep his mind on what was important— revenging his family. He pressed his lips together and struggled to ignore the pain in his heart.

She stood and turned away from him. The curve of her neck highlighted her vulnerability, but also hinted at her strong backbone. 'What do they fear?'

'They fear my reputation,' he explained as gently as he could.

She stared directly back at him. Her tongue wet her lips, turning them a dusky pink in the sunset. 'I stopped being afraid and became your friend.'

He caught her hand and brought her knuckles to his mouth. A simple touch which nearly undid him. He could understand why her husband had wanted to keep her safe. Trouble was, if he was going to honour his pledge to his parents, he was going to have to risk losing her. 'Stay that way.'

Cwenneth sat with the heavy broadsword balanced on her knees. The night was far too cold. She brought her cloak tighter around her body and tried to watch for anyone who might harm them. Enemies. Even Northumbrians who might have once been her friends, but who would not be friendly to Thrand.

The irony stuck in her throat. Thrand had become more than a temporary ally. He thought enough of her to give her the first watch and he was going to teach her how to use the sword in the morning. Aefirth would never have done that. He preferred to keep her…as a child. Cwenneth frowned, hating the disloyal thought. But it was true and she had fought bitterly with Aefirth about it, before he had left the final time. But she had discovered that she liked being treated like an adult, like an equal.

Never again would she allow her brother or anyone else to bully her. Or proclaim it was for her own good.

Her teeth chattered slightly. She looked over to where Thrand lay, seeming sound asleep. She ran her hands up and down her arms and stamped her feet. The sword started to tumble off her lap, but she grabbed it before it hit the ground.

One of his eyes opened. 'Come here.'

'Why?'

'You are cold and don't deny it. The sound of your teeth woke me up. The last thing I want is for you to catch a chill.'

'I'm fine, and you should be asleep. I'm taking the first watch.'

'Be sensible, Cwen. How can I sleep if you are making that noise?'

'Fine.' She picked the sword up and brought it over to him. 'Do you truly think I can learn to use a sword? Properly?'

'You can do anything, if you set your mind to it.'

She blinked. 'How…how do you know that?'

'You are the woman who walked.' He took the sword from her and indicated where he had been lying. 'My turn to stand guard. Close your eyes and sleep.'

She snuggled down into the warm spot. Her limbs immediately stopped shaking. She faked a yawn to keep from asking him to hold her. 'I hadn't realised that I was so tired.'

He put his cloak over her. His spicy scent wafted up, holding her. Cwenneth's blood thrummed. She concentrated on breathing steadily, refusing to beg. If he wanted to touch her, he would have done so. They were friends, not lovers.

'Do you have someone waiting for you in Jorvik?' she asked. 'Some woman?'

'There is no one. I travel alone. I live alone. Always.'

'You are travelling with me now.'

'Only through necessity.' He cleared his throat. 'You will be returned to Lingwold after you give your testimony. But my house is fine enough for any lady.'

Cwenneth balled her fists. 'I was just curious.'

'Less curiosity, more sleep.'

'And if I can't sleep?'

'Watch the stars. It is what I plan on doing.'

Thrand watched her in the grey light, intensely

aware of her every move, fighting the urge to gather her into his arms. His body throbbed to the point of agony. Deep within his soul he knew he was the wrong man for her.

If he seduced her out here, it would lead to complications. She was not the sort of woman you bedded and walked away from. He had not really understood what his father had been saying about Ingrid until now—there were women you wanted to spend a few hours with and others who deserved to have a man's entire life. Cwenneth deserved eternity, but he had no room in his life for such a woman. His entire life was war and killing.

He reached out and smoothed her cropped hair. She gave a soft sigh and turned towards him, her lips gently parted, eyes firmly closed.

It was going to be hard enough to forget her when the time came as it was.

'What are you doing to me, Cwen?' he asked. 'I need to remember who I am and what I want in this life.'

'You want to start teaching me how? Lifting the sword over my head?' Cwenneth asked. She had woken up to Thrand on the other side of their camp, full of plans of how he could teach her to use the sword, rather than holding her as he had in her dream.

She was instantly glad that she hadn't begged him to hold her last night when she was so cold. He had made it very clear: they were companions. He wasn't interested. Aefirth had taught her not to be bold and not demand. A man liked to be the pursuer, not the pursued.

'Is there a problem, Cwen?' Thrand said, coming over to where she stood. 'You have been standing there for a long time, looking at the sword. You would have been cut down a dozen times over. In order to fight, you need to be able to lift the sword. Concentrate on lifting with your stomach.'

'Is there anything lighter?' she asked as she lifted it gingerly in front of her. The sword slipped from her grasp and fell to the ground with clunk.

'You can lift this one if you concentrate.' Thrand gave her an intent look. 'You are capable of more than you think. Lift it over your head while I count to ten. One last try before we go.'

Capable. Thrand believed she could do it. She spat on her hands and redoubled her efforts. This time, she lifted the sword above her head.

Sweat pooled on her forehead and the back of her neck, but she kept her arms straight. All of her muscles screamed, and she wondered if she could hold it for more than a count of five.

Slowly, Thrand counted to thirty. Each number seemed to take longer than the last. 'You may let go now. Try not to drop it, but let it down slowly. Controlled. You can do this, Cwen.'

Rather than dropping the sword as her muscles screamed they wanted to do, Cwenneth forced her arms to relax and placed the sword at her feet. 'I did it. For a count of thirty. You said I could do it and I didn't believe it. But I really did it.'

His eyes reminded her of the summer sky. 'That I did. You will be able to use a sword in next to no time. Your arms will get stronger. But you have to be able to use a sword like mine. You never know what might be to hand when the time comes.'

'Perhaps we can use something lighter until my arms get strong enough.' She swung her arms, trying to get the feeling back. 'Standing there with a sword over my head as Hagal's men attempt to cut me down won't do me much good.'

Myriad blue lights danced in his eyes. Cwenneth sucked in her breath. When his face was relaxed, he was so handsome. She banished the thought. The last thing she wanted to spoil was this new-found ease with him.

'I doubt I've ever met a woman as determined as you,' he said, returning the sword to its sheath. 'We'll make a legend of you yet.'

'For too long, I have let other people take charge and have been content to hide if trouble came.' She made a stabbing motion with her hand, banishing all thoughts of his looks and the shape of his mouth. 'I have no wish to be a lamb to Hagal's slaughter. If that makes me legendary, I will take it. Is the lesson over with?'

His gaze darkened. 'We start with a stick. When you are practising, you don't want to injure the person so you use wooden swords.'

Something in his tone made her pause. 'Did you ever hurt anyone in practise?'

'I didn't start with the intention of hurting him. He was the one who chose to use real blades. He thought to end my life.'

'Were you an experienced warrior?'

'No. It was only a few months after my parents' death. And he sought to make an example of me.'

He handed her a stick, ending the conversation. 'Remember to keep it between your body and the other person.'

'I'm not sure.'

He put his hand under her chin and raised her face until he looked deeply into her eyes. 'You can do this, Cwen.'

Her breath stopped in her throat. Her heart started to beat wildly. 'I want to, but I'm not sure I'm holding it right.'

He adjusted her grip with a cool impersonal touch. She forgot how to breathe. Did he know how much he affected her? She swallowed hard and concentrated on the stick.

'Do your worst, shield maiden. See if you can land a blow on my body.'

'Shield maiden?'

'Occasionally women fight with us for one reason or another. They are called shield maidens. The best of them become Odin's Valkyries.'

She moved her stick upwards, and he easily blocked it. The impact shuddered through her arm. Cwenneth redoubled her efforts, but each time he easily blocked the move. A bird started singing right behind her, making her jump and breaking her concentration.

Thrand's stick hit hers and sent it spinning out of her hand.

'How did you do that?'

'You left yourself open. First rule of swordplay is never to be distracted. Block everything out except for your opponent and where his sword is moving.'

'That must be impossible.'

'You have to do it in order to be any good. Concentration grows as you get better.' His eyes softened. 'With practice, you can be aware of other things but your main focus has to be on where that next move is going to come from. A heartbeat's lapse is all that stands between life and death.'

'What should I be doing? How can I improve?' Cwenneth put her hands on her knees.

His brow knitted. 'My father used to say that it just happened, but my mother suggested that I empty my mind and concentrate on my opponent's shoulder. Where the shoulder goes, the arm must surely follow.'

'Was your mother a shield maiden?'

'Her mother had been, but my mother had different skills.' His mouth took on a bitter twist. 'Neither my father nor my grandfather considered the skill necessary.'

'And all the Norsemen have this focus?' she asked, wanting to learn more about his family. 'Or is it something unique to your family?'

'Sven used to swear that Hagal lacked concentration, but he has won far too many bouts.' Thrand's full lips turned up in a reflective smile. 'Sven liked to talk nonsense after he had taken ale.'

'And Hagal has always avoided fighting you.'

'Despite my challenges, he has found reasons to decline.'

'Are you ready to try again?' Cwenneth lifted the stick, watched his shoulder and blocked the downward thrust of his stick. Once. Twice. Three times. With each successful block, her confidence grew and she noticed that Thrand made it more difficult.

Sweat gathered on her brow. She glanced at Thrand.

A faint sheen of sweat glistened on his forehead. 'We should stop. We need to travel today and you are injured despite what you think. Someone needs to be sensible.'

He caught her sleeve. Her entire body tingled with an awareness of him. Her lips ached to be kissed.

'I am not used to being looked after,' he said finally, making no any attempt to capture her mouth and moving away from her. 'War is all I know, Cwen. It is all I will ever know.'

Cwenneth's heart felt an odd pang. His eyes were so sad when he said it. 'You must know about other things like planting crops and keeping livestock.'

'The last time I helped with the sheep, I was fourteen. My father sent me up to the meadows for the summer.' He gave a half smile. 'It was the last peaceful summer I knew. When I returned, the problems began.'

'Did you give up singing and dancing as well?'

'I can feast with the best of them, but I don't want you harbouring any illusions.'

'Why would I harbour illusions about you? Your reputation is well known.'

He caught her sleeve and pinned her to the spot. 'You're right. You are more dangerous. Hagal has underestimated you. We will win, Cwen.'

In winning, she was going to lose him. What they had right now, the ease between them, was temporary. Cwenneth pressed her aching lips together. It was wrong that she wanted more. 'We need to get to Corbridge and fulfil your vow before we can destroy Hagal.'

If she told her heart enough times, maybe she'd stop thinking that there had to be another way.

Chapter Nine

'This is as good a place as any for the night,' Thrand said, gesturing to a small cave in a hillside. In the distance, Cwenneth could hear the faint gurgle of water.

They had not encountered anyone, and Cwenneth felt more hopeful that they would reach their destination without any trouble. Surely Hagal would not risk sending his men this far into Bernicia.

'Shelter and water. What more could a woman ask for?'

'I'm pleased you approve.' Thrand slid off Myrkr.

Cwenneth had noticed that today he had kept his body from touching hers as they rode. Whenever he could, he found reasons to walk.

The ease of this morning's sword lesson had vanished and Thrand seemed preoccupied, answering her questions in as few words as possible.

'If you can gather some firewood, I will go and fetch the water.' Thrand stretched. 'I could do with a wash and Myrkr a drink.'

Cwenneth froze—half on and half off Myrkr, the image of Thrand's naked skin gleaming wet imprinted on her brain. She forced her feet down, nearly tripping.

'Do you have a problem with that?' he asked, taking the pack and Myrkr's saddle from the horse.

'No, no problem. I am perfectly capable of tending to Myrkr. We have reached an understanding.'

Cwenneth carefully set the pack and saddle inside the mouth of the cave before she went about finding some firewood. Anything to keep from finding an excuse to check on Thrand and see if he was truly bathing. He had made it very clear that he did not think of her in that way. They were friends, not lovers.

When would she learn that he wasn't interested in her, not in the way she wanted him to be?

He probably saw her as a skinny stick of a thing with very little sex appeal, the same as her sister-in-law's assessment of her charms right before she departed from Lingwold. And since then he had been careful not to touch her. She had thought he might kiss her when he taught her this morning how to use the sword, but he hadn't. And she refused to be pathetic and beg. Men disliked pushy women. Aefirth had told her that enough times, but her mind kept whispering that Thrand was not Aefirth.

She gave a wry smile. Only a few days ago, she had worried that he might force her, now she worried that he wasn't touching her. She was being ridiculous.

'Come on, Cwenneth, stop stalling,' she muttered. 'You need to find dry wood, instead of dissecting what Thrand might or might not feel for you. Maybe if you are lucky, he will catch some fish and you can have a hot meal instead of the hard bread.'

She gathered three more armloads of firewood and started to lay a fire in the entrance to the cave.

There was a distinct rustling inside.

'Thrand?' she said. 'That took you much less time than I thought it would.'

The rustling stopped, but there was no answer.

From somewhere behind her, she heard a snatch of song in Thrand's off-key voice. Thrand was clearly still at the stream.

Cwenneth pinched the bridge of her nose. Whoever was inside wasn't Thrand and they could easily take Thrand's sword and the gold before she returned from fetching him.

'Come out right now!' she called. 'We mean no harm, but we will not let you rob us blind.'

She waited in the afternoon sun. The only response was more rustling.

Her hand gripped the knife she now always wore in her belt. There wasn't time to wait for Thrand. She had to act.

'Stop being a coward,' she muttered. 'Whoever it is, he doesn't have a horse. You just need to keep him there until Thrand arrives.'

A large owl flew out, beating its wings against her face. Cwenneth screamed. The owl did not stop, but kept on going, flying high into the sky.

She sank down on the ground outside the hut and started to laugh. An owl. She had been frightened of an owl.

'What do you think you are playing at, screaming like that? You could have let half the countryside know where we are.' Thrand towered over her, the thoroughly enraged warrior. His hair gleamed dark gold in the sunlight and a few drops of water from his bath in the stream clung to the strong column of his throat. Enraged, but still breathtaking.

Silently, she cursed her attraction to him. She smoothed her skirt down so her limbs were covered before twisting over.

'What is your explanation for this?'

'I heard a noise and thought someone might be trying to rob us. But it was an owl, only an owl.' Cwenneth rose and tried to brush the dirt off her skirt. She concentrated on the blossom on the nearest plum tree. 'I overreacted.'

'What did you intend to do with that knife?'

'I was going to make sure whoever it was did not run off with our gear. All I had to do was to keep them in the cave.'

'You should have come for me first when you suspected something.'

'I wasn't going to lose our things.'

'I forbid it.'

Cwenneth blinked twice. 'You forbid?'

'Next time, you get me before you attempt anything foolhardy. Your life is too valuable. After we are finished, you can do what you like, but until then you obey me.'

'I finished with being a cosseted lady, Thrand, when Narfi murdered everyone in my party. It is why you are teaching me to use a sword. I can defend myself.'

He stepped closer to her. She knew if she reached out a hand, she would encounter his broad chest. 'Most people think twice about provoking me, Cwen.'

'I am not most people.' She made the mistake of

glancing up into his dark forbidding face. It could have been carved from stone, but she saw something more in his eyes. Concern? Caring? It was gone so quickly she couldn't tell. 'Your temper doesn't bother me. Shouting and standing there with clenched fists will do nothing.'

'Cwen!'

'I deemed it necessary. Time was running out. I acted.' She ran her hands through her hair, plucking bits of grass out. So much for looking desirable or attractive—she undoubtedly looked a mess. 'You were having a wash.'

'Overconfidence can kill.'

'So can sitting around and waiting to be rescued.'

He grabbed her arm. The touch sent a warm tingle coursing through her. She slipped out of his grasp and glared at him.

'The key to this exercise is to stay alive, not go confronting anyone,' he continued in a quieter tone.

'I confronted an owl!'

She glared back him. His angry face was inches away from her. Their breath interlaced and a warm curl started in the middle of her stomach. Every particle of her was aware of this man.

'Do not do it again!' he said, giving her shoulders a little shake. 'You could have been hurt.'

'Or what?' she asked, her heart beginning to race. 'What will you do?'

She moistened her lips with her tongue. She knew she was playing with fire, but it was also hugely exciting. The last time he had been unbalanced, he had kissed her. And she wanted him to kiss her. Badly.

She advanced towards him, but he retreated until his back was against the side of the cave.

'Cwenneth!' The word was torn from his throat as he stood rigid. The muscles on either side of his neck bulged. 'You go too far.'

'Thrand, I haven't gone far enough,' she whispered, not moving away from him and lifting her mouth towards him. 'That is part of the trouble. I need to go further. I am strong and it is time I started acting like it. Or else I might as well have died in the slaughter. I'm tired of waiting, Thrand. I want you.'

'You don't know what you are asking.'

'I do know. I want to feel alive, Thrand. Make me feel alive.'

With a long groan, he lowered his mouth to hers. The kiss was savage in its ferocity, demanding and taking. She returned the kiss, looping her arms about his neck and pulling him closer. This time she was not taking any chances that he might pull away. She wanted to see what would happen when the kiss ended.

She could not remember if Aefirth had ever kissed her this passionately. There was something about the wildness of the kiss that called to a dark place deep within her soul—utterly new and unexplored. What was more—she wanted to be kissed like this, like he was branding her with his mouth and stamping his possession on her.

Their tongues met, tangled and teased. With each passing heartbeat she knew one kiss would be too little. She needed more, much more.

His hands came about her body and pulled her close. She felt every inch of his hard, muscular body.

He wanted her. A bubble of happiness infused her. After what happened she had been worried that he had no desire for her, but he had, and she intended to use it to assuage the heat which had built up inside her.

She tightened her grip on his neck and tilted her pelvis towards his as her tongue delved deeper into his mouth. His hands slid down her back to cup her bottom and hold her there, unmoving against the hardest part of him. She wriggled slightly, feeling him press against the apex of her thighs and knowing she needed more.

His tongue slid round and round in her mouth, gently pulling and tugging. Warm and wet. What had been a curl of heat in the pit of her stomach grew to a wildfire in the space of a few breaths.

She found it difficult to remember when she had felt this alive. Her whole word had come down to this man. And she knew she needed more than a simple kiss. She wanted to feel his skin against hers. She wanted to feel alive. His tongue drove deeper into her. She pressed her body closer and felt his arousal meet the apex of her thighs. She rocked against him.

'You are playing with fire,' he murmured against her lips as his hips drove against her again.

She answered him by arching towards him, allowing her breasts to brush against his chest. 'I'm a grown woman. I know what I am doing.'

He groaned in the back of his throat and switched their positions so that her back was against the wall as his hands roamed over her body, cupping her breasts and teasing her nipples to hardened points. First over her gown and then, after he tugged slightly, slipping inside the cloth and touching her bare skin.

The ache within her grew.

His mouth nuzzled her neck as his hands played. Hard-working hands sliding over the smooth skin, pulling and squeezing. Each fresh touch sent a wave of fierce heat through her, melting the ice which had encased her since Aefirth's death, leaving her molten and quivering, but alive. Oh, so alive.

Giving in to instinct, she tugged at his trousers and encountered the hardened length of him. Hot, but silk-like smooth. She closed her fist around him and felt him, knew she needed more. She wanted him in her, giving her the release she knew her body craved.

'Please.'

His mouth returned to hers as he moved her skirts, picked her up and settled her on him, driving in deep.

Her body welcomed him in. Fire meeting fire. Hot and fierce. She tightened her legs about him, held him within her as he drove deeper.

Their cries intermingled.

Slowly, slowly, she came back to earth. She touched his face. Droplets of water still clung to his hair. Tiny diamonds shining in the light.

He withdrew from her and pulled up his trousers. Her skirts fell about her limbs.

'Say something, Thrand. Tell me what you are thinking.'

'That should not have happened. I didn't mean for it… Cwen, did I hurt you?'

'Why not?' Her hands went to her top and automatically began to readjust it. 'What was wrong with it?'

'Nothing was wrong.'

'Then what is the problem?' Her heart drummed so fast in her chest that she thought he must hear.

'Because,' he said, putting his hands on her shoulders and pinning her to the spot, 'someone has to be sensible. I have no idea what you want, what you expect from this.'

'I wanted you to do this. I was a willing participant.' She put her hand on her hip. 'You might have the courtesy to say you enjoyed it.'

He ran his hand through his hair. 'That goes without saying. You were... You are amazing. Cwen, I always get these things wrong.'

She breathed easier. He did want her, but for some reason he was treating her like she was a fragile object. Or a lady with marriage prospects. She drew in her breath sharply. That was it. Her heart expanded a little. He still thought of her as someone who mattered. The truth was that she didn't. Not to her brother and certainly not to Hagal. The only person she had to worry about pleasing was herself.

'We are both adults, Thrand. Not every coupling ends in marriage. I'd have to be very stupid if I remained in ignorance about that. What is between us...it is about the here and now, not some far-off future. I'm asking for no more than today. This afternoon.' She forced a crooked smile. 'The last man who wanted me for a bride wanted to kill me. The whole experience has made me question the value of marriage.'

He groaned in the back of his throat. 'Don't do this to me, Cwen. I am trying to give you a choice. My self-control is in tatters where you are concerned. If I lose it, I may lose you.'

'Why?'

'I may frighten you. I have frightened women in the past. I may mark you without meaning to. Other women have complained about me being more interested in war than them. I am not good at making small talk about gowns and hairstyles. I get bored at feasts. I like blood-soaked sagas rather than the romances which have the women sighing. And…and I value your friendship.'

Relief flooded through her. He was trying to protect her and worried about appearing less than a hero in her eyes, rather than not desiring her. She hated the unknown women who had made him like this.

'You found my touch unpleasant? My kiss distasteful?' She pretended to consider the possibility before running her hand boldly down his front. 'Is this why you are so hard again? So quickly? I have only known my husband and he was a great deal older than you, but he was never aroused like this after we made love.'

Her breath caught at her audacity. Proof if ever she needed it that she had changed. She would never have dreamt of touching Aefirth like this, but it felt right with Thrand. With Thrand she could be who she wanted to be. She allowed her hand to linger for a heartbeat.

'Cwen…' he said, standing completely still.

'I believe your body, not your mouth.'

'I can't make you any promises. I…I have seen women turn away from me before. I don't want to hurt you, Cwen, but if you only mean to tease, tell me now and neither of us will get hurt.'

'Who hurt you, Thrand? Who made you doubt all women?'

'Her name means nothing.'

'It means something to you.'

'Ingrid,' he admitted. 'She made me all sorts of promises when I was young. That summer before my world changed. I had slipped out to meet her that day my parents were killed.'

'Go on. Tell me the whole story. I want to know.' Cwenneth hated how her mouth went dry.

'There is little to tell. It was a young man's lust. I refused to listen to my father's commands or my mother's entreaties. I wanted to marry her. I thought we had something special. I went to where we were supposed to meet, intending to ask her, but was met by Hagal's friends. They beat me and left me for dead. But not before Ingrid had told me the truth. Rather than thinking I was the love of her life, I was a monster in the making. Ingrid had used me to get back at Hagal because she knew he feared my prowess at fighting. He had seen it as an opportunity to ruin my family.'

'Did you love her?'

'I thought I did.'

'What happened to her?'

'I found her hanging in the barn where we were supposed to meet. The day after my parents' funeral. There have been other women, but…always war called to me. I needed to fight.'

Cwenneth struggled to hang on to her temper. Suddenly she knew what Thrand was doing and why. 'I'd walk away from you now, but that is what you want me to do. And I am in no mood to oblige you.' She put her hand on his chest and grasped his shirt. 'I'm staying. I want to explore this thing between you and me if you are willing. Not a wild windswept passion, up against a tree, but something where we both take our time and enjoy it. I'm a widow, not some blushing maid. Pretending this attraction between us isn't there won't make it go away.'

'I have no room in my life for anything but my work.'

She closed her eyes and knew what he was saying—purely the physical, no pretence towards finer emotions. She needed to feel his hands and mouth on her. She wanted to feel alive in the way that his kisses made her feel. She couldn't remember feeling this alive ever.

'There are no promises in life,' she whispered, putting her fingers over his lips and gathering her courage. Doubts were for the woman she used to be. 'If anything, the last few days have taught me that. And I have not seen a monster. I have seen a very brave man who risked his life to save others, including me.'

'You talk too much.' His mouth descended and drank from hers, long and hard, sending pulses skittering through her body. And she knew that her passion was definitely not spent.

She tore her lips from his. 'This time, we should be more comfortable.'

He ran his hand down her back, sending a wave of fire coursing through her. 'A woman with authority. I like that.'

'That is good. I have discovered that I like being independent. It means I can do this without having to wait.'

She captured his face between her hands. In the afternoon sunlight his eyes had become deep pools of blue.

'Why did you think you had to wait?'

'My husband…' She shook her head. 'You bring your ghosts, Thrand, and I bring mine.'

'Hush. A woman who participates makes it more interesting than a woman who lies there, hoping it will be all be over.'

Slowly, she brought his face down to hers, taking her time and tracing the outline of his lips with her tongue. 'Good to know.'

'You smell of grass and sunshine,' he murmured against her hair.

'Here I thought I might smell of horse.'

'Always the practical one.' He lifted her chin. 'We can take a bath together…later. There is a pond. I left Myrkr tethered there…'

She raised his hand to her lips. 'Later. He can enjoy the grass.'

He ran his hand down her back, stopping to cup her bottom. 'You appear to be overdressed. I have longed to see what you look like unclothed, but…'

'My choice?'

'Precisely. You do have a choice, Cwen. I want you to enjoy this.'

She stared at him. No one had ever seen her naked. Not even Aefirth. They had been very conventional in their lovemaking and she had always waited for him in her bed. She had never shed her clothes in front of any man, let alone shedding them in the sunlight, but Thrand was very different from Aefirth.

Cwenneth assessed Thrand under her lashes. He

was asking, and she knew she did want him to see her naked. She wanted this relationship to be different. She wanted to be the new Cwen, rather than the old restricted Cwenneth. 'Undress me.'

'My pleasure.' He slowly undid the laces of her gown, loosening it, then raising it above her head. Then he took off her under-garments.

She stood in the mouth of the cave, naked with the afternoon sunlight warming her shoulders and back. She crossed her arms over her breasts and hid her puckering nipples.

'You should not be shy.' He ran his hands lightly along her arms. 'Far better than my imagination.'

'Do you mean that?'

'I lied.' A smile split his face. 'Much, much better than my imagination.'

For such a large man, his touch was incredibly gentle. He made her feel cherished. Her insides twisted. Cherished as if he actually cared about her.

'Now you,' she said, pushing away the thought. Finer feelings were unwelcome. Purely physical was what she had agreed to.

She undid his shirt and lifted it above his head, exposing his golden flesh. The linen bandage stood out from his smooth skin.

She reached out and touched his shoulder, mimicking his move, exploring the contours of his skin. With Aefirth, she had always been the passive one, waiting for him to be the first as she thought a proper wife should. But with Thrand those considerations counted for nothing. There were no rules or customs. She was free to do as she chose.

She wanted to touch him and be an equal participant. She wanted to explore every muscle and sinew of his body. She wanted to feel him moving inside her again.

She let her hand explore the line of hair which ran down to his groin.

He groaned in the back of his throat and pulled her to him. 'Slow this time. If you go further, it will be the same as last time and I want to give you pleasure.'

'I liked it fast and furious.'

'Then you will like it even slower.'

Their bodies collided, skin touching skin, and he drank deeply from her mouth as his hands roamed freely over her back. Gently, he lowered her to the cloaks he'd quickly arranged on the ground. For a brief heartbeat he loomed over her, but she reached up with a hand and pulled him down beside her.

She tangled her fingers in his shoulder-length hair, pulling his face to hers, reclaiming his lips and probing the depths of his mouth with her tongue.

He moved his mouth down the column of her throat, nibbling and tasting, sending fresh licks of fire coursing throughout her body. She tried to tell her heart that he was vastly experienced and knew how to play a woman's body the way a bard would pluck a tune from a lute. But her heart refused to believe it. There was something more, something which had been missing from her couplings with Aefirth.

His fingers captured one of her breasts and rolled the nipple between his thumb and forefinger. A gasp burst from her mouth.

'You like?' he rasped in her ear as he played with her nipples, pulling and stretching them.

She tugged at his shoulders, needing him inside her again. 'Please…Thrand.'

'I want to make it good for you. Please allow me to do this. I want to show you how good slow can be.'

She gave a nod. His mouth went lower, following the trail his fingers had blazed. He captured first one nipple and then the other, making swirling patterns with his tongue and licking them into hard pointed peaks while his fingers played between her folds, sliding in and out of her, making her warm, wet and needy.

Her body bucked upwards as wave after wave of pleasure rolled through her until she thought she could stand no more, but also knowing she had to have more. She wanted the ultimate release.

She tugged once again at his shoulders, needing to feel him inside her. This time he relented and settled himself between her legs, driving forward. She opened her thighs and welcomed him in, feeling her body expand to take the length of him.

They lay there for a timeless moment, joined, and then she began to move her hips, giving into the ageless rhythm.

He responded and they were swept together on the crest of a wave.

Much later, Thrand came back to earth and regarded the woman now sleeping in his arms. She had given herself to him unstintingly. Twice. Once fast and furious up against the side of the cave and the other slow, an exploration of their bodies and how they could move in time with each other. Even now, his body hardened at the mere thought of having her again. He wanted to experience all her possibilities. Amazing. He frowned, unable to remember if he had ever felt this way before with a woman whom he barely knew.

He ran his hand over her short hair. For the first time in a long time, he felt at peace, as if the hungry wolf inside him had become tame and no longer looked for revenge. He remembered how his mother used to caution his father against revenge and where it would lead. She used to say that there were other ways of punishing a man. He'd never been able to think of one, but now he wondered. Could there be?

'What have you done to me, Cwen?' he whispered softly. 'I want to believe in a future which holds only peace. I have stopped only having hate in my heart. Do you know how impossible that is for me? My family needs to be honoured. Fighting is my life. I lose my edge and I lose everything.'

The soft sound of her sleeping was the only reply.

He made a face. It was dangerous to hope or to think beyond the next day. Battle and war kept him alive. He'd seen good men die because they lost their concentration. And Cwen wanted to return to her former life. She didn't want his sort of life.

When his revenge was complete and his time of battle done, then he could think about acquiring a family. Until then he travelled light. What was the point in complications and roots when the ghosts of his father and mother still begged him to do the right thing? And the right thing had to be killing Hagal. A life for a life.

He hated how his insides twisted. He wanted to be worthy of her and protect her for ever, but he knew what he was like and what lurked inside him. How everyone he'd ever loved had ended up dead because of his actions. He envied Sven's simple solution of starting again. Cwen would need another reason than just him.

Cwen said that she saw good in him, but there was also the warrior who killed and the boy who had failed his parents. She needed someone better than he was or could ever be.

'I'm sorry,' he whispered. He gently removed her head from the crook of his shoulder and slid out.

Cwenneth woke to an empty cave and a cloak covering her nakedness.

'Thrand?' she called out. 'Is there a problem?'

'Getting things ready to leave,' came the answer from outside. 'We need to go, Cwen. Sooner rather than later. Time is slipping from our fingers. There is a full moon tonight. We can start once it rises.'

She gulped hard. They were going. He had slaked his pleasure and now he was ready to go. What had passed between them was in the past. Had she expected anything different? He was a Norse warrior.

'I thought we were staying the night. Or was that just pillow talk?'

'Instinct.' His bulk appeared in the mouth of the cave, but the shadows made it impossible to see his face. 'If I ignore it, we are both dead. It served us well in the hut.'

She wished he would come over and touch her. Was he disappointed in what had passed between them?

A tiny knot started in the pit of her stomach. She

had made a fatal mistake and had started caring about a Norse warrior, the sworn enemy of her family. In his arms, she had dared to dream that they might make a more lasting alliance. Funny how the dreams went when she woke.

'Do you regret what happened?' she asked before her courage utterly failed her. 'Be honest with me, rather than feeding me some lie about following your instinct.'

His eyes widened. 'Regret? How could I regret something like that? You were magnificent. Better than that—a healing balm.'

Her breath came a little easier. She had to follow her instinct and not lose her temper. Thrand was panicking about something.

'You left me to wake up on my own.'

'I never sleep very much. I went out to watch the stars.' He shrugged. 'I wanted to let you sleep. You needed it. But we have to go. We can cover miles before the sun comes up.'

'The countryside remains still. It is at least another day's journey to the Tyne and your friend's child. We can spend more time together…more time for…' She made a little gesture with her hand.

'I've been thinking. It might be best if we forget this.'

'Why?'

'As pleasant as it was, it should never have happened. You and I. I can't give you what you want.'

Cwen put her hand on her hip. 'How dare you presume to know what I want!'

His voice became cold. 'I've had enough women.'

Cwenneth flinched, but then she clenched her fists. He wanted her to turn away. 'Stars.'

'What?'

'You told me to watch the stars if I couldn't sleep and I have spent most nights watching the stars, willing the sleep to come.'

'What does that have to do with anything?'

'Being in your arms beats watching the stars. I actually slept. It is a start, Thrand. I felt alive, rather than one of the walking dead and I've been one of them for so long.'

She wished his face wasn't in shadow. She wished he'd walk over and take her in his arms. Anything to stop the terrible pounding of her heart. A faint breeze rippled over her skin.

'There is a chance you will survive. A very good chance.'

'Hagal wants me dead. There is no getting around that. He knows I live and made his vow to avenge his cousin's death through mine. I fear closing my eyes. Why watch stars when I can find peace in your arms? I'm asking for no more than that.'

'I'm tired of watching stars as well.' His arm went around her. 'And when we are done, no regrets.'

'No regrets. This is about the here and now.' She put her hand on his cheek. Her insides felt hollow. Her heart had been buried with Aefirth and Richard, hadn't it? What she felt for Thrand was desire, not love, not something lasting and true. When they parted, she would remember the time with fondness, but would live the sort of life she was born to. She would return to being a Northumbrian lady.

She hated that her old life no longer held any attraction.

Chapter Ten

The farmstead stood unobtrusively near the river Tyne. It was not much to look at, but Cwenneth could tell with a brief glance that it was prosperous. The walls were well maintained and the sheep grazing in the meadow looked fat.

'This is where the child is,' she said to break the uncomfortable silence which had grown up between them over the past few miles.

'So I am given to understand,' Thrand replied, pulling Myrkr to a halt.

Without waiting, Cwenneth slid off. They had stopped briefly to sleep beside a stream. Her dreams had featured death and destruction. Only when she woke and had Thrand's arms about her did she relax. It had felt right to wake up in Thrand's arms. But she also knew that the farm marked a turning point. Every mile after this took her closer to her destiny and near-certain death. Was it wrong of her to wish for a reprieve? And to hope that Hagal could self-destruct without her being involved? Did she have to appear in person?

'What is the woman's name?' she asked, trying to stop thinking about the future and her own cowardice.

'Maeri,' Thrand said slowly. 'Sven was wild about her. He wanted to marry her once he found out about the child.'

'What are you going to do?'

'Make sure the child is well looked after. I will make sure Maeri knows that he should be brought up as a proper Norseman and that several men have volunteered to foster him when the time comes. Knui would have formally welcomed him into Sven's family, but I will have to perform the ceremony instead.'

'The child is a boy?' Cwenneth asked.

'The message gave no clue to the sex. It has been passed from Norseman to Norseman.'

Thrand got off the horse and started to walk beside her. Cwenneth noticed how he evenly matched her stride. There was a steady companionship between them now. Her heart clenched. What was between them was temporary. Temporary allies, friends and now lovers.

Believing otherwise was to slide back into the same fool's paradise she'd inhabited when she thought marrying Hagal the Red would bring peace. Even if he wanted to marry her, where would they go?

'How old is the child?' she asked, trying to keep from examining her feelings.

'A year or so, I believe.' Thrand looked straight ahead, watching the curl of smoke from the farmhouse rise in the crystal-blue sky. 'We have been in the south, keeping peace, not the north. It took a while for the message to reach Sven.'

'Then do you know if the child is even alive?' she asked gently. Someone had to say it and prepare Thrand for the worst. The farm appeared peaceful and prosperous. The last thing they would need was a rampaging Norseman bent on destruction simply because something had happened which was beyond everyone's control. Children were fragile blessings. Her hand went instinctively to where her pendant had been.

She shook her head. Why was it so easy to believe this about another's child and not hers?

'Sven wanted to know his child was looked after. He wanted to make it right for the mother and the babe.' He stroked Myrkr's mane. 'We had gone out to wet the babe's head when the fight occurred. He took a knife in the back which was meant for me.'

Cwenneth reached out her hand. It made sense now why Thrand felt such a sense of responsibility towards this child and its mother. Even if he refused to see it, there was much that was good and honourable in him. She would be hard pressed to name other men who would do as much for a fallen comrade. Aefirth possibly; probably not her brother, Edward. 'Sven's death wasn't your fault. You couldn't know. Were you the one who started the fight?'

A muscle jumped in his jaw. 'I finished it. They were drunken fools who objected to Sven looking at their women. But he wasn't the one interested in getting his leg over. I was. I often have a woman when I am in Jorvik. A different one each time. The black-haired woman had been flirting with me. Nothing had been decided. No coin had passed hands.'

'Then you're not to blame for another's fit of temper,' she said, trying to keep her voice light. 'I, for one, am very glad you didn't die. Who would have saved me otherwise?'

She waited for his laugh. His face settled into its old harsh planes.

'Sven had so many plans for the future. He wanted to go to Iceland and start afresh with his Maeri. He thought they could be free there to live the way he wanted to live. There is land for the asking and no king. Iceland had become an obsession with him. He'd half convinced me that I ought to go, but I've promises to keep.'

'Had he talked about Maeri before he knew about the baby?' Cwenneth enquired gently. Iceland where people could be free had nothing to do with her. Like Thrand, she needed to destroy Hagal. 'The message took a long time to reach him. Surely if he felt deeply about her, he would have gone to see her. He had to have known how babies were created and that there was a possibility.'

'On and off. And it is not that easy. We had a job to do in the south.' Thrand gave a little shrug. 'We used to tease him about it. He nearly had me killed when he left her the last time. He used to say he owed me for saving his life that day, but he was my comrade-in-arms.'

'He sounds like he was a good friend.'

Thrand's face became set in stone. 'He was like the brother I never had. If not for him, I would have lost my life a dozen times over on the battlefield.'

'And how many times would he have lost his life?'

'That is not the point. I failed to save him. And I've killed the man he sent to welcome his child into his family.'

'You're far more of his blood than his cousin could have ever been.' Cwenneth shuddered, remembering the way Knui had talked. 'He would have sold that child for gold.'

'I'll make it right for Maeri. There is enough gold to give her a comfortable life and I have Halfdan's promise that the child can enter the king's service when the time comes, if it is a boy. If it is a girl, a suitable marriage partner will be found.'

'And she will be content with this?'

'She will have to be.' Thrand frowned and a muscle twitched in his jaw.

'What is it, Thrand? What is wrong? You've been worse than a bear with a sore head today.'

'You will help me break the news? I can't stand a woman's tears,' he admitted, running his hand through his hair. 'I'd far rather face a horde of angry Northumbrians armed to the teeth than one woman's tears. And Maeri is a weeper. The way she clung to Sven the last time…'

'I shall have to remember to keep my eyes dry when we part,' Cwen said, forcing a smile. She knew the instant they parted for the last time, the tears would flow, but she would refuse to cry in front of him. She wasn't going to stoop to trying to hold him. Allies, friends and lovers, but they would go their separate ways.

'Cwen!'

She reached out and gave his hand a squeeze. 'I will be at your side, but you'll find the right words. I have faith.'

He nodded with thinned lips. 'That makes one of us.'

* * *

Thrand fixed the farmer with a hard stare. He was hiding the woman, or at the very least knew where she could be found. His refusal to meet Thrand's eyes and shifting feet gave him away.

Years of experience collecting Danegeld from men who wanted to cheat had taught him to pay attention to the little clues. He would get there without actually resorting to violence, but the farmer would understand the consequences for his continued refusal.

'I wish to speak to Maeri, the woman who used to work on this farm,' he repeated the words slowly, taking care to emphasise each word. 'Fetch her.'

The farmer went red and then white. Thrand flexed his hand close to the man's face. 'She…she isn't here. You are wasting your time.'

'Where is she?

The old woman standing behind the farmer shifted uneasily, but remained silent. Thrand gave Cwen a helpless glance. He didn't want to beat the information out of the farmer, but he had little choice if they continued to defy him like this. She shook her head and mouthed *no violence*.

'Where is her child?' Cwenneth asked, moving between him and the farmer. 'Can you tell us that much?'

'Aye.' The burly farmer clicked his fingers. 'Fetch Maeri's brat.'

A rat's-tails-for-hair girl raced across the farmyard towards where the animals were kept. After a few heartbeats in which the farmer and his wife looked more and more uncomfortable under the heat of his glare, the girl emerged with a little boy dressed in rags and covered in dirt. His fetid stench wafted towards them.

Thrand frowned. Children should smell of fresh air and sunshine, not reek of manure.

But he immediately saw a likeness to his old friend in the boy's nose, chin and hair. He had the mother's dark brown eyes, but there was a definite look of Sven about him.

A wave of sorrow passed through Thrand. It should be Sven standing here, viewing his son, not him. His friend lived in his child. Sven would have loved this moment and would have known what to do and how to put this right.

Could he trust these people, including the absent mother, to look after Sven's son?

He dismissed the thought as pure folly. He had done what was right by coming here. And Sven had always proclaimed what a wonderful mother Maeri would be and how she longed for children. Perhaps these people's idea of looking after children was different from his own.

'And the boy's name?' Cwen asked, kneeling down and holding out her hands to the children. 'Come here. There is no need to be afraid. This man knew your father. He is here to make sure you are properly looked after.'

The girl came hesitantly forward, half carrying and half tugging the little boy. Closer, the boy appeared more like a wild animal than a child. 'Pretty lady, is that Aud's father?'

Thrand's heart thudded and he leant forward to hear what Cwen might say about him.

'His father's friend. His father sent him because

he was prevented from coming. But he'd intended on coming and claiming the child as his own.'

Thrand's heart twisted. Trust Cwen to come up with the right words. She seemed to possess the knack of it. When the time came, she would say the right words to Halfdan and destroy Hagal for ever. She had to. He couldn't bear the thought that she might die or worse, be under Hagal's control. He pushed the thought away and concentrated on the girl. Focusing on the far-off future was never a good idea.

'His mam's dead, pretty lady,' the girl said with a curtsy. She jerked her head towards the couple and whispered. 'They didn't want to say on account of what he might do. They know his reputation. He wintered in these parts afore like.'

Cwen gave him a warning glance over the boy's head as the news thudded through Thrand's brain. The boy was an orphan. It changed everything and nothing.

He gave Cwen a nod and made a gesture that she should continue with the questioning.

'What is the boy's name?' Cwen asked.

'Maeri called him Aud.' The old woman made a clucking noise in the back of her throat. 'Too unchristian for the priest. We call him Adam when necessary.'

Thrand nodded. Maeri had named him after Sven's father. She'd expected Sven to come back. That was a good sign at least. Once again, he wished that he had taken the knife, instead of Sven. Pure luck. A little voice in his mind whispered *but then he'd never have met Cwen and would never have experienced peace in her arms*. He silenced it. Sven was a good man.

He didn't deserve to die in the way he had. And now the proper arrangements for the child had to be made.

'Is there a reason for the child's filth?' he asked, eyeing the child warily. Although he was used to the stench of war, he knew the difference between a battlefield and a farm.

'He sleeps with the pigs,' the girl said, releasing Aud and coming to stand in front of him. Her dress was dirty, there was a smudge on her face and she was far too thin. 'I'm not afraid to tell the truth. He sleeps there because it is the warmest place and he can get a few scraps.'

'Keep quiet,' the old woman scolded. 'Please, sir, Hilde works in the kitchen for the scraps. We took her in as a charity…when…my niece died…' Her voice trailed off at the farmer's look.

'Pigs,' Aud said proudly, lifting his chin and looking in that instant precisely like Sven. 'Pigs. Pigs. Pigs.'

Thrand frowned. Sven's son should not be sleeping with the pigs. Once his temper would have exploded, but with another warning look from Cwen, he struggled to contain it. Her soft words appeared to be yielding the information required. 'It certainly smells like he has rolled in pig dung.'

'We can clean him up, sir,' the young girl said. 'He is a good boy. Does what he is told most times.'

'Do that!' he ground out. He pointed to the old woman. 'You help. That child smells of manure and rotten food. Children should be clean. They should smell like children, not dung heaps.'

The old woman rushed off, dragging the protesting child with the girl not far behind, chattering about how they were going to bathe and look proper for the Norseman.

Thrand breathed deeply, urging away the feeling that he wanted to tear the farmer limb from limb for treating children like that. 'I wait for an explanation.'

The farmer's colour rose, and he refused to meet Thrand's eye. 'We had given up hope of anyone coming. It has been such a long time since Maeri sent the message.'

'When did she die?' Cwenneth asked, placing herself between Thrand and the farmer as her mind raced. Anyone with half an eye could see the child was neglected. Something had to be done, but Thrand had refused to consider taking the child when they had spoken about it earlier. And she didn't trust the farmer to look after the child or the little girl. But Thrand losing his temper and striking the farmer would inflame things, rather than improve them.

'Two months ago,' the farmer admitted, his cheeks becoming ever redder under Thrand's fierce gaze. 'Maeri died two months ago. Very sudden like.'

'From what?' Cwenneth fixed the farmer with her eye. 'Why did she die? Sickness? An accident?'

'She'd just married.' The farmer tugged at the collar of his shirt as if it was suddenly too tight. 'A good man. It was a good match in the circumstances.'

'What happened?' Cwenneth placed her hand on Thrand's sleeve. He put an arm about her and pulled her close. She laced her hand through his, and he clung to it as a drowning man might cling to a spar.

'She miscarried.' The farmer adopted a pious expression. 'The priest said it was a judgement from God as she'd lived a loose life. There is nothing you can do if someone strays from the path of righteousness.'

Cwenneth longed to crack the priest over the head. It was easy to pontificate and make judgements. Miscarrying a child had nothing to do with piety. Her sister-in-law spent hours on her knees praying and still she had lost two babies. And Cwen had thought she'd been doing God's work when the old woman cursed her and she lost any hope of a baby. It still hurt.

'But this *good* man she married didn't want to look after her child.' Thrand's nostrils flared.

'Can you blame him for returning the child here?' the farmer answered with a shrug. 'He only took Adam because he wanted Maeri. She was a good cook and kept a tidy house. She wouldn't be parted from her son. So after her death, my wife pitied the poor bairn.'

Cwenneth went rigid. *So sorry for him that she allowed him to sleep with the pigs.*

'Did she have any family?' Cwenneth asked when she trusted her voice. 'Did they turn their back on the child as well?'

The farmer shook his head. 'Her parents died a few years ago. Her mother had been my late wife's sister, which is why we took her in. Adam will be a good worker in time.'

'Thrand,' Cwen whispered, tugging at his sleeve. 'You have to do something. That child will die if you do nothing. If you simply give gold and walk away. There has to be a way of giving him a better future than what he will have here.'

Thrand said nothing, simply looked straight ahead.

But his face became ever more thunderous and his fingers clenched even tighter.

'I will leave you two,' the farmer said, flushing red. 'I need to see how the boy is getting on. When he is cleaned up, he is a right bonny lad.'

He scurried off, leaving them alone in the farm-yard.

'Before you say anything,' Thrand said, holding up his hand. Every particle of him bristled with anger. 'What you are about to ask is impossible. Keep quiet and we won't fight. We remain friends. I have no wish to quarrel with you over this, Cwen.'

'How do you know what I was going to ask?' Cwenneth tapped her foot on the ground. Thrand had to see that the child needed their help. She refused to leave, knowing the child might die. Somehow, she'd find a way to save that innocent little boy.

'My life doesn't have room for anyone else, let alone a child who is little more than a babe. That child needs a mother.' His jaw jutted out, and his shoulders broadened, making him look every inch the fierce Norse warrior that he was. 'Do I look like a mother? Do I look like the sort of person to wipe his nose or his tears? Or to clean up his sick? Or even make sure he is properly fed?'

Cwenneth's heart thudded, sinking to the pit of her stomach. He didn't want anyone in his life. He wasn't willing to change to save this boy. 'No child.'

'No child. No one else. I've seen the sort of life camp followers and their children lead. What is more, I have seen what happens to them when their warrior dies. I would not wish that on my worst enemy.' He placed his hands on her shoulders, and the harsh lines of his face softened. 'I am a warrior, first, last and always. Have I ever said anything to make you think differently?'

'The war is over. Others are settling. You could ask the king…' Her voice faded as she realised what she had said… Her cheek grew hot under his stare.

'A man such as me? With my reputation? Who would want me for an overlord?' He shook his head. 'Halfdan heaved a sigh of relief when I took gold over lands. I've no desire to have a large estate or be a great lord. Forget it. I know what a snakepit Jorvik politics are. They are nearly as bad as Viken politics. And it was precisely because my father angered powerful lords that Hagal was able to murder with impunity.'

Drawing on years of experience, Cwenneth schooled her features, but in her heart she mourned. Against all logic, she had been hoping that he would say something about her staying with him and perhaps asking the king for Hagal's lands once he had been unmasked as the villain.

'You can't leave him, Thrand Ammundson,' she said around the lump in her throat. 'It would be tantamount to cold-blooded murder of an innocent child. And whatever else you are, you're not a murderer of children.'

His look would have made a lesser woman faint with fear.

She clenched her fists. She had been so stupid asking. It wasn't as if she had asked him to marry her. She understood there were no guarantees in their relationship. It was temporary. But this was not about them, it was about the child. She had to get past the battle-hardened warrior and reach the man who had held her in his arms last night and who had whispered encouraging words when the nightmare had woken her.

She closed her eyes, gathered her thoughts and started again.

'I know what happens to bastards, particularly if the priest has taken against them,' she said slowly. 'That he has survived this long is a testament to his mother and his own robustness.'

'What would you suggest?' he enquired with narrowed glacial eyes. The ice in his voice cut through her heart.

'We could take him to Lingwold.' Cwenneth wrapped her arms about her waist and tried to keep her insides from trembling. That child needed her protection, but she had no power. 'I know the priest there. He will make room for him and will treat him with honour. He is a good man. He will ask few questions. Aud will thrive with enough food and he will get an education.'

'You want me to send Aud to Lingwold with a message—please look after this child?'

She held up her hands and willed him to understand. 'It would save his life. I…I could take him. I would return. I give you my word.'

'No!'

'No?' Anger coursed through her. Even now, he failed to trust her. 'What is wrong with my idea? Father Aidan will educate him. He has done so with many orphans in the past. They've become monks, useful members of the community.'

'Sven's son is not going to go into a monastery. He hated monasteries and monks.'

Cwenneth rolled her eyes. 'You don't want him to go to a monastery. You won't have him with you and leaving him here is not an option. What do you intend to do with him? How do you intend on honouring your friend?'

Thrand put his hands on either side of his head. 'I know this! Give me time!'

'We have little time! You must decide!'

Their quarrel was interrupted by the farmer returning with Aud in his arms. 'You see the boy can be made to be tidy.'

Aud had been hastily washed and dressed in clean clothes. His damp white-blond hair curled in little ringlets and his big brown eyes made him look like an angel.

'There,' the young girl said with a pleased air as if Aud were her own. 'He cleans up right lovely.'

She too had changed into clean clothes and her hair was neatly brushed.

'Yes, he does,' Cwenneth answered softly, thinking about Richard and the fresh smell he had always had after his wash. She wanted to smell that again. 'You both look lovely. May I hold him?'

The farmer started to hand him over, but Aud wriggled free and toddled over to Thrand, holding up his arms.

'Up!' he cried.

Cwenneth started forward to take possession of the boy before Thrand rejected him and the wailing started. If Thrand disliked a woman's tears, he'd like a toddler's even less.

However, rather than shying away or pretending he hadn't noticed like Aefirth had once done with Richard, Thrand knelt down so his face was near to the boy's. He stuck out a finger and ran it down Aud's cheek.

'You look remarkably like my friend, your father, Sven, Aud Svenson,' he said in a tender voice. 'With you alive, he lives on. My old friend would be so proud to be your father. He wanted the best for you.'

Aud threw his arms about Thrand, and Thrand hugged him back. Cwenneth bit her lip, wondering if this was the first time any child had ever been that open with the warrior.

'We would like to invite you to eat with us. My man and I discussed it,' the old woman said, coming forward. 'Maeri would have wanted it. She always said that her man would return for her. I feel so guilty now for having pushed her into that marriage. It brought nothing but trouble.'

'We would be delighted,' Cwenneth said quickly before Thrand had a chance to refuse. There had to be a way of giving that little boy a life, but she needed time to think of an idea which Thrand could embrace.

The remains of the simple meal lay on the table. The pottage had not been fancy, but it was nourishing and there was enough for all.

A huge lump rose in Thrand's throat. He found it difficult to remember the last time he had sat down to a supper with ordinary people. The taste of the stew and rough wheat bread brought back memories of sitting down with his parents and eating after a day working in the fields.

Aud sat next to him, seemingly oblivious to the fact that children generally feared him and kept away from him, hiding their faces whenever he approached. Throughout the meal, Aud kept jumping up to get one of his treasures such as a bird's feather or an interesting stone.

With each new offering, Thrand was aware of his hollow words to Cwen earlier. He couldn't leave the boy and walk away. He, too, knew what Aud's fate would be, even if he left gold—ignored at best and actively abused at worst. Aud would be used like an animal, not treated like the bright boy he was.

A monastery was not going to happen, not for Sven's child. Lingwold would mean he could not maintain contact with the child. Cwen's brother wanted his head on a platter. The battlefield was no place for a child. But he could hardly bring up a child on his own. Where would he leave him when he had to go on the king's business? In Jorvik? Who could he trust?

He slammed his fist against the table. The conversation ceased. Everyone turned toward him with a mixture of apprehension and fear in the farmer and his wife's faces. Cwen's showed mild irritation. Only Aud seemed oblivious to the tension. He jumped up again and toddled off.

'It is all right,' Hilde said with a bright smile. 'He does it because he likes you. He doesn't mean to get you angry.'

'I'm not angry with him,' Thrand mumbled. 'I enjoy his company.'

'Then what is the problem?' Cwen asked, lifting a delicate eyebrow.

Thrand swallowed hard. How could he confess the agony he was going through? After he told her that he didn't want anyone? How could he confess to caring about the boy's future? And caring about her future, but knowing his current life had no room for either?

'Nothing is wrong.' He pushed his trencher away. 'I suddenly missed Sven. He would have liked to meet his son. He liked children. They never hid their faces when he appeared.'

He patted Aud on the head as he returned bearing yet another gift. The boy beamed up at him and handed him another feather. This time from an owl. He released another breath. The boy hadn't shrunk from him despite his thumping of the table.

'For you,' Aud said.

'He likes feathers and birds,' Hilde said helpfully. 'That one was one of his very favourites.'

'I'm sure Thrand will treasure it,' Cwen retorted with a determined look on her face.

Thrand forced a smile, but all the while his heart ached in a way that it hadn't for years. He wanted a different future.

'Aefirth often ignored Richard's offerings,' she said in a low voice as she leant towards him.

'I'm not your late husband.' Thrand carefully tucked the feather in his belt. 'I'm honoured the boy has given it to me.'

Cwen stood and straightened her gown. 'We should leave these people.'

'Leave?'

'They will have chores to do and we have a long way to go.' There was an incredibly sad dignity to her bearing, reminding him of the statues he'd seen in Constantinople. Thrand found it hard to reconcile this closed-off and dignified woman with the vulnerable one he'd watched over last night in case the bad dreams returned, the one who had turned to him with a soft sigh as she nestled her head against his bare chest.

Thrand frowned. He wanted to spend more time with the boy and get to know him. But it also seemed like he had reached a turning point in his life. What he did next had the power to alter his life for good or ill and it frightened him far more than the prospect of facing a horde of angry warriors.

'Please stay,' the farmer's wife choked out. 'It is good to see Adam…Aud so content and happy. He has spent weeks crying for his mother and driving me to distraction. The pigs were the only creatures which stopped his tears.'

'It won't be long before dark,' the farmer said. 'Stay here where it is safe.'

'Only tonight. We can sleep in the barn,' Cwen said, her look challenging him to say differently. 'We will need to be off at first light. Thrand has fulfilled his oath to Sven Audson.'

'We will stay,' Thrand said, touching the feather Aud had given him.

Somehow he'd find a way to solve his dilemma. Fresh air always made him think better, particularly when the sands of time slipped through his fingers. He needed to make the right decision, rather than one he'd regret for the rest of his life. 'Cwen, will you come for a walk around the farmyard with me? I should like to investigate Aud's home and the animals they keep here. Sven would expect that of me.'

She gave a small nod.

He held out his arm. By the end of the walk, he knew he had to have a workable plan for Aud's future.

Chapter Eleven

Thrand led Cwen out into the low afternoon light. Together they made a circuit of the farmyard and its buildings. He noticed how he automatically adjusted his pace to suit Cwen's. He could remember how his father had done the same for his mother and how they too had walked about the farm at this time of day.

The sky was beginning to be streaked orange and crimson. A certain peace hung over the place, but Thrand's thoughts kept circling back to his future, one which currently did not hold Aud or even Cwen. The prospect of not having Cwen depressed him, but how could he make her want to stay with him? She'd been very clear on the boundaries of their relationship. A tiny voice nagged that he had forced them on her. He frowned and tried to silence it.

'If he had lived, what was Sven planning on doing?' Cwenneth asked as they stopped beside the large barn for the second time. 'If Maeri had been free?'

'Does it matter? It is useless to speculate.' The words came out harsher than he'd intended.

She pleated her travel-stained gown with her fingers. 'I suppose not. I was curious. Sven Audson sounds like a man who always had a plan.'

'Iceland. He wanted to take his family to Iceland.' Thrand abruptly let go of her arm.

The lowing of the cattle, mixed with the snuffling of the pigs, took him back to his boyhood. He went into the barn and breathed in the straw-scented air. He shook his head. He had no business remembering that easy time.

The last time he had been in a barn like this one was when Ingrid had led him there. He knew what had happened afterwards and he had avoided them ever since. But now he suddenly realised that he had missed the utter peace and tranquillity that went with them.

'What did he want to go there for? Surely he could have started a new life in Northumbria.' Cwenneth asked, putting her hand in his.

He closed his fingers about hers, grateful that he did not have to explain. She seemed to understand his distress. She led him away from the barn and towards the green pasture. In the distance he could see the blue-grey waters of the Tyne.

'He wanted to leave this place of war and go to a land that had never seen conflict,' he said when he trusted his voice.

Cwen frowned. 'And there is no war in Iceland?'

'A man can be free from his past there, or that was what Sven claimed. He was tired of the political intrigue that surrounds Halfdan now that he is ill. He had no great love or loyalty for any of the rivals. He wanted out.'

'If the other Norsemen are like Hagal, I can understand that sentiment.' Cwen's mouth turned up into a sad smile.

'Halfdan is an excellent warrior. He looks after his men, but the others? They are after their own glory.'

'Why not go back to the north where you all came from if he had made his fortune?'

'He had no wish to return to Viken. I never enquired too closely why he left. We all had our reasons. He wanted a life free from his past where his child could grow up innocent of all feuds.'

She tapped her finger against her mouth, and her eyes turned thoughtful. 'A life free from your past. Is that something you would want?'

Thrand stopped. His entire being stilled. Iceland! He had been blind. It was the perfect solution. But would she agree? Did he dare ask? He knew what they had agreed, but the more he knew Cwen, the more uncomfortable he was about having her face Halfdan and the pit of snakes which passed for the Storting. Anything could happen, particularly as Hagal had started spreading rumours blaming him for the events.

He wanted to keep her with him, rather than sending her back to Lingwold where she could be used again as a pawn in her brother's quest for power.

'A man can have his reasons,' he said cautiously, trying to think how best to put it without making it seem like he cared for her. 'Thor knows Sven must have had enough. He saw it as a chance for a fresh start and the opportunity to show Maeri the man he could be.'

'Is it a good land?' He detected a slight note of

wistfulness in her voice. 'A fertile land where you could grow crops free from…well…free from the threat of war and the necessity of paying Danegeld? It sounds silly. Ever since Aefirth died, I have spent nights standing at the window, longing for such a land. I didn't think it existed.'

'It is a hard land, but it can be good. The valleys are fertile. Trade is good with Norway.' At her questioning glance, he added. 'Sven and I visited it a few summers ago. There are crystal waterfalls and springs which run hot. One of his cousins settled there. Now he tends his sheep and horses instead of risking his life on the eastern trade to Constantinople.'

'It sounds lovely.'

'Would you like to see it?' he asked before he lost his nerve. The meaning of his dream when he woke from the fever suddenly became crystal clear. It was not about dying alone, but living with a family. He could have a family again. He could protect them. He would not repeat his father's mistakes or his own. He could outrun his past. All he had to do was to emigrate with Cwen.

Travelling to Iceland would give him a chance for a new start in a fresh, clean land. He could leave his past behind him just as Sven had planned to. He could stop being a warrior and become a farmer.

'What did you say?' Cwen stopped pleating her gown and stared at him.

'I am willing to take you there. You would like it, I think. Boats take some getting used to, but the journey is done in stages. You will adjust.'

Her eyes widened as his words sank in. 'You want to take me to Iceland? Why?'

He gathered her hands between his. He had to get the words right. He wanted to put them in such a way that she could not refuse. If she refused, he didn't know what he would do.

He knew she did not want him for ever. She had made that perfectly clear the other day when they had first made love. What woman would? He had too much darkness inside him. But she was a natural mother. He'd seen the longing in her eyes when she held Aud. Once in Iceland, he'd prove to her that he was worthy of her. 'Cwen, come with me. Let's go to Iceland and take Aud with us. Fulfil Sven's dream because he can't. Aud is an innocent child. Why should he have to suffer for something which has nothing to do with him? Are you going to allow Hagal to destroy another life?'

'What are you asking me?' she gasped out.

Thrand took heart from the fact that she didn't attempt to pull away. He tightened his grip about her slender fingers. 'Marry me, Cwen, and provide Aud with a mother. That little boy needs a mother desperately. He needs you.'

Marry him? Thrand wanted to marry her, move to Iceland and put their pasts behind them. He wanted her to go to Iceland with him and be Aud's mother.

Cwenneth stared at the large Norseman standing before her, holding her hands as the giant sky began to darken all around them. The ground tilted under her feet. She forgot how to breathe. She had to have heard wrong. Had that innocent child with his treasures touched his stone-cold heart in a way she couldn't? She'd seen how they were together. It was wrong of her to wish that it had been her.

'Please say something, Cwen. Have you lost your voice?' The raw note in his plea tore at her heart.

'Did you just ask me to marry you?' she whispered finally before he turned away from her and this chance slipped away.

He put an arm about her shoulder, bringing her close to his body. 'Yes. You can be Aud's mother. You saw how he was at dinner. A little care and he will blossom. He has the makings of a fine warrior. Did you see the treasures he kept bringing me at supper?'

'Aud's mother.' She shook her head. It was wrong of her to even offer when she knew she was almost certainly facing death in Jorvik. 'But I'm the wrong woman. I let my child die alone. I should have stayed with him. Aud deserves better. He deserves a mother who will stay with him.'

'Your son died because it was his time. And this boy's mother died also. Are you going to say it was his fault?' Thrand's lip curled. 'The priest implied it was. Maybe you believe it too, but don't wish to say. Do you believe the boy is cursed?'

'Of course not! You are being ridiculous.'

'It is you who are being ridiculous.' He put both hands on her shoulders, and his summer-blue eyes looked deep into her soul. 'You have a great capacity to love, Cwen. You need to lavish it on someone who will appreciate that love rather than waste it.'

Cwenneth broke away from him and pressed her hands to her temples, trying to think around the sudden pain in her heart. Capacity to love and not wasting it. 'Are you saying that I am some sort of lovelorn female who wears her heart on her sleeve, just hoping for any creature to love me back?'

'I am not worthy of your love!' Thrand's words echoed round and round the pasture.

'You think I love you?' White-hot anger coursed through her veins. She couldn't love Thrand. What they shared was passion. She knew it would end and had planned for it. She had kept her heart out of it. 'Of all the arrogant, pig-headed assumptions! Simply because we have shared passion, I am supposed to love you? Have feelings for you? What utter rubbish!'

'My mistake.' Thrand inclined his head, which once again wore his warrior's mask. 'I thought I had best warn you…in case you agreed to the marriage. What love and finer feeling I had died years ago. It is futile to hope. I don't even know how to begin to care for someone. I've no practice in it. You are right. The women over the years have blurred. I find it hard to put a name or face to one of them. But I know I will always remember you. If you want to call it caring, you can.'

'Why are you telling me this?'

'It is important that I'm honest with you, Cwen, in all things. I wouldn't want to marry you under false pretences. Or have you become disappointed in me. But I know that Aud will never let you down. Like you, he hungers for someone to love.'

Her heart shattered into a thousand pieces, hurting in a way that it hadn't since Richard's death. She had not realised until he said those words how much she did care for Thrand.

Over the past few days, she had come to like him—no, *like* was too mealy-mouthed of a word. She had kept telling herself that it was desire and passion but it was more than that. She admired his courage, his ability to think on his feet and the way he reacted so calmly to each new threat. And how he gave her confidence to try new things. She considered him more than a friend. But what she felt for him was very different from the quiet and uncomplicated love she had had for Aefirth.

Cwenneth drew an unsteady breath and moved away from the comfort of his body. She wrapped her arms about her waist. She had to get this right and understand what he was offering, not be seduced by the nearness of his body. 'You mean after Jorvik and speaking to the king about Hagal. Things have to be done in their proper order, Thrand. It is foolish to speak of such things until then. Aud has already lost one mother.'

The words *if I remain alive and am not returned to Hagal* hung in the air between them.

Thrand's eyebrows drew together. He made a cutting motion with his arm. 'I mean not bothering to speak to the king about Hagal and departing immediately for Iceland to begin a new life. The rumour of the kidnapping will work against you. Hagal would claim I seduced you and a woman's words are not to be trusted. I can see the purpose in his rumour now. He seeks to discredit your testimony. And we have become lovers, Cwen. How could I lie about that?'

Cwenneth closed her eyes. He was right. She should have considered Hagal would seek to blacken Thrand's name once he learnt who had rescued her. He certainly had wasted no time in spreading the rumour that Thrand had kidnapped her. 'Will he try to get you blamed for the slaughter as well?'

Thrand made an annoyed noise. 'He can try, but Halfdan knows what I am like. I've never kidnapped a woman before, nor have I murdered in cold blood.'

'But those murders need to be avenged.'

'Narfi, the man who committed the murders, is dead. Is it necessary for you to risk your life for something which will not change the course of history or bring the dead back to life?'

Cwen pleated her gown between her fingers. 'And when we are in Jorvik, waiting for the ship to be ready? Hagal knows that I am alive and with you. He wants me dead because of what Aefirth did to his cousin.'

'Hagal would have to fight me, something he has avoided doing for years, despite my attempts at provocation. Your brother has me gone. Everyone is happy. Just not in the same way we had planned. Plans can change, Cwen. For the sake of the child, they should.'

His words thudded through her. 'But the marriage contract? My dowry?'

'Betrothals are put aside all the time.' Thrand made a cutting motion with his hand.

'It seems a shame just to allow Hagal to have my dowry. He will use the gold for bribes.'

'Your brother can sue Hagal for it. It is what the courts are for. I've more gold than I could ever spend in ten lifetimes.' He put his hand on her shoulder. 'We have to think about saving an innocent child's life. It is what my mother would have wanted.'

Cwenneth stared at Thrand as the enormity of what he offered washed over her. Her dreams lately had been full of what would happen once she reached Jorvik. The only thing which had calmed her was waking to have Thrand's arms about her and watching the rise and fall of his chest.

She knew deep in her heart that she'd never truly relax until she had proof that Hagal was dead. But Thrand was right—Edward could try pursuing Hagal through courts for the dowry. She could send word once she was in Iceland.

A tiny smile crossed her lips. Edward would not be able to do anything about her living the life she wanted to lead. No more threats of a windswept convent. Or marriages to further Edward's power.

'It is very tempting to believe we could do this.'

Thrand stepped closer and laced his hand through hers. He brought their knuckles up to his lips. 'Seize this chance to give that boy the perfect mother and a new start in Iceland away from all the politics and killing.'

'Flattery. And you have no idea what I was like. Far from perfect.' Cwenneth's cheeks flamed, and she pulled away. If he touched her again, she'd agree to everything. She scuffed her boot against the packed dirt of the barn floor and tried to stop her imagination from building longhouses in the clouds. 'Sometimes I was far too impatient, too concerned with running Aefirth's estate, rather than attending to my child. I should have done more when I had the chance... There are nights I wake up in a cold sweat, remembering all the chances I once had and neglected.'

'You need another child in your life. If you and your husband had had another child, you would not have proclaimed you could not mother that child because Richard had the misfortune to die. Whatever else happens, Aud needs a mother and he likes you. Even I could see that.'

Cwenneth's throat closed. Somehow it had felt right to be holding a little boy again. She had savoured his little-boy smell and the way he kept finding things for Thrand to look at. It made her remember Richard, but in a good way, rather than in the heavy regretful way she had fallen into. 'I like him very well. I could come to love him.'

Thrand's face clouded and his shoulders hunched slightly. 'Then it is me who is the problem. You have no desire to be married to me. I understand. War and battle have made me, but I will try to be a good fa-ther. I swear it on my parents' grave.'

'I never said that!' Cwenneth protested before he had a chance to leave. She knew if she let him walk away, her one opportunity for a life would slip past. He might not be offering marriage for the reason she had hoped, but he was offering. And he was right. Jorvik could be very dangerous for the both of them. Thrand might dismiss Hagal's threat to him, but she couldn't. Iceland could save his life.

He turned back to her. His eyes grew wide. 'Then you will do it? You will go to Iceland with me and allow Hagal to dig his own grave.'

She swallowed hard and did not give herself a chance to think.

'Yes, I will do it. I will marry you, Thrand, and be Aud's mother. We will leave for Iceland as soon as possible.'

He caught her hands and twirled her about, lifting her off the ground.

Round and round until she was dizzy.

All the ice vanished from his face. He seemed years younger, eager and excited. The way he looked caused her heart to turn over. It was no good telling her not to love him because she already did.

'We should bring the girl Hilde with us,' she said when he set her down and the world had stopped spinning.

'Why?' he asked. 'Why should we take her? She seems well settled here.'

'She looks after Aud and I don't think they look after her very well either,' Cwenneth explained with a smile. 'It will be good to have another female to balance the two males in the family.'

He turned his face to her palm and kissed it. A great warmth flooded through her, but it was also tinged with regret. She wanted him to kiss how he'd kissed her at night, as if he desired her and only her. She knew he only asked because of the children.

'Then it is decided. We will go to Iceland,' she said briskly. She refused to mourn things she couldn't have. 'You, the children and I. We will live our life away from kings and politics. We will be free. Our freedom and a life well lived will be the sweetest revenge.'

He threw his arm about her shoulders and hugged her close again. She leant her head against his chest and savoured his warm, spicy smell. 'Sounds like a good plan to me. Freedom to be the person I am is something I have always sought. My father refused to bow before an usurper. I could never return to Norway as long as the current king and his heirs are on the throne.'

'What happens next?' she asked, trying to be practical and not think about the thousand reasons why this might be a bad idea. 'How do we get to Iceland? I have never considered it before. There must be a way.'

'We will go to Jorvik and meet my men. Some of them may wish to join us. Helgi has often expressed a wish to settle in Iceland. He had made plans to go with Sven. It is only right that I extend the offer to him. I will buy a boat and hire any men we might need. It will be done before you might think. We will be there by midsummer at the latest.'

She laid her head against the broad expanse of his chest and listened to the steady beat of his heart. She tried to keep the sudden wild leaping of her heart at bay. Somehow against the odds, she might actually live to see another Christmas and then the new year and the spring beyond that. She had a future. It felt good—better than good.

He pulled her close, resting his chin on the top of her head. 'It is time I rested my weary body and found another occupation for my arm. My father farmed after spending years as a warrior. I can do the same. My mother would be proud of me.'

'But…but…'

'We will buy a large tract of land and build a fine house as well as getting the right sort of boat for the voyage. Not a dragon boat, but a trader, a sturdy one which can carry livestock as well as people. I refuse to leave Myrkr behind. The horse has been a faithful companion for many years.'

She looped her arm about his neck and pulled his lips down to hers. 'You talk too much, Thrand.'

'Most people say I hardly speak.'

'They don't know you like I do.'

His mouth descended on hers, and she drank from it. Their tongues met and tangled. She allowed her body to say things that she knew she could never admit. His arms tightened about her and she could feel his arousal. A part of her rejoiced. He did desire her. She would make this marriage work. Even a mother like her was better than no mother. She wasn't sure she could love them, but she could give them a better life. She had to stop wishing on clouds for things that were impossible, like Thrand actually loving her.

Thrand wanted her to look after the children. And she shared his bed. Many marriages started on a far worse basis.

A small cough sounded in the back of the barn, bouncing off the walls. They jumped apart. Cwenneth silently gave thanks that the interruption had not been a few heartbeats later. Even now, she knew she looked well-mussed and thoroughly kissed.

She turned her head towards the sound. Hilde stood there, with the rough shawl thrown over her shoulders. She had a worried look on her face and carried a torch. Her intent face relaxed slightly when she spied them.

Cwenneth gave Thrand's hand a squeeze and went over to Hilde.

'Aud wanted to know where you had gone. I promised him that I would look out for you. He likes you both. Aud doesn't like many people. He misses his mother dreadfully.' Hilde gave a disapproving frown. 'Too many people have gone from his life. It isn't right. He is a good boy. He tries hard. Was he born unlucky? Is that the problem? Father Athlestan says it is.'

'Hilde.' Cwenneth knelt down and took the girl's cold hands in hers. 'We have decided to take Aud and you, too, if you like. We will give your master some gold to compensate him for the loss of two such fine children.'

She glanced back at Thrand. He gave a brief nod. 'Your master will be well compensated,' he confirmed.

The young girl's face broke into a wreath of smiles. 'Where would we be going?'

'To Iceland to start a new life.'

'I don't know where that is, but I would like that very much,' Hilde said without hesitating. 'I am a hard worker. Everyone says that about me.'

Cwenneth put her hand on the bony shoulders. She had wanted to have a little girl for such a long time, someone to teach to sew and to do so many things. She had never anticipated it ending like this. 'I am sure you are.'

'Shall we go and inform your master?' Thrand said.

'And Aud? Can I tell him?' the girl whispered. 'He never liked sleeping with the pigs. He is going to be part of a real family.'

Cwenneth regarded the stall where Mrykr was tethered. Real family. She had given up hope and suddenly Thrand had given her more than she'd ever dreamt. He might not love her, but she couldn't help loving him.

'Shall we let Thrand do it?'

The girl nodded rapidly. 'That would be best. He

will think it is another of my games otherwise. We play what will happen when his father comes to claim him. Only I never thought it would be like this. Or that I would get to go as well.'

'And this is what does happen,' Thrand said. 'Is it better than a game?'

Hilde's eyes glowed. 'Much better. It is a dream come true.'

'I have never been anyone's dream before. Nightmare, possibly. It feels good to be a dream.'

The little girl ran out of the pasture.

Later as they waited in farmyard for the farmer to get Aud's things, Cwenneth slipped her arm through Thrand's, breathing in the scent of straw, the final warmth of the evening sunshine and animal. She used to think barns were ugly things, but this one had a certain grace and charm to it.

She closed her eyes and made a memory. She opened her eyes with a snap.

'How will we get to the coast? We can't all ride on Myrkr's back. Aud is far too young to walk any great distance.'

'The farmer has agreed to sell us his cart and a horse to pull it.' Thrand gave a husky laugh. 'Did you think I lacked sense?'

'But the roads…' Cwen attempted to think her way around the problem. 'It took us far longer to reach Acumwick's lands than it should have.'

'The roads may be muddy, but I've a strong back and can get it out of any ruts. I suspect Narfi wanted to go slowly for his own reasons.'

She shook her head in amazement. She hadn't considered that. 'How long have you have been thinking about this?'

'When something is right, instinct guides you.' He put his hand on the small of her back. 'I'm well skilled at moving armies. Getting you and the children to the coast is little different.'

'A family is very different to an army. You are going to be those children's father, not their commander.'

'We need to go to Jorvik by another route,' Thrand said, changing the subject.

Cwen frowned and allowed it to go. But she silently resolved to make sure he understood his new role. 'Another route?'

'I hardly want to take the two children near to Hagal's holdings. We know they are looking for us and we barely managed to slip through their net. It will take a little longer and we will have to go closer to Lingwold than I would like, but it is either your brother who does not know we are there or facing Hagal who is looking for us.'

'Go past Lingwold, but never stop?'

'Do you trust your brother with the children? With me? We both know he wants my hide nailed to a church door. You send the message just before setting sail for Iceland.'

Cwenneth pursed her lips. Thrand was right. They couldn't take the risk. Her brother wanted Thrand's head. He'd act and then ask questions. He might even believe the rumours about the kidnapping. 'The last thing I want is Edward making trouble. I'll trust your judgement on this.'

'Spoken like a true wife.'

'They won't take you for Thrand the Destroyer.' She linked her arm with his. 'You will have a wife and two children. Something the Destroyer would never have.'

'Then it is good that I am the man and not the legend.'

His laughter rumbled in the quiet evening. Cwen found it hard to equate this man with the silent stranger who had arrived at the farm only a few hours before. She had to hope his instinct was correct and that they would be safe.

Chapter Twelve

'Please, sir, what is Aud to call you?' Hilde tugged at Thrand's shirt after they had travelled a few miles in the grey early-morning mist.

The cart went little faster than a slow walk, but it allowed the children to rest. They had also been able to take some bedding and a bit of food. Progress was slow but manageable.

'Why are you asking?'

'He is worried and too shy to ask.'

Thrand looked down at the little girl. His experience with females was limited and with girls he had next to none. There had been only him and a few male cousins when he was growing up. He glanced at Cwen to see if she would answer, but she was occupied with readjusting Aud's pack.

The boy had wanted to take all of his treasures and Cwen had managed to get it down to his most precious feathers and stones, but he wanted to carry it rather than storing it in the cart. Both Aud and Hilde had decided at the last stop to walk for a little ways. Thrand hadn't objected as the going was muddy and it took all his concentration to keep the cart going.

'Call me?'

The girl dropped her voice and glanced over her shoulder. 'A special name. People in families have special names for each other. And we're a family now.'

A family. The girl's words caused the enormity of what he'd done on impulse to wash over him. The warrior who had resolutely resisted any complication or entanglement had voluntarily saddled himself with two young children and a woman. These people depended on him for their survival.

He frowned. He just had to approach it as though they were members of his *felag*, rather than his family. He had kept his men safe in the past.

'It all happened so fast that I haven't given it much thought.' He gave Cwen a questioning glance. She nodded encouragingly. He found it impossible to get rid of the impression that she had put Hilde up to this. She wanted to test him. 'Most people call me Thrand. And Cwen answers to Cwen. It is best to keep things simple.'

Hilde's face fell and she let go of his shirt. 'I wanted Aud to have a special name for you. It will make it more like Aud and I are truly brother and sister.'

'We're going to Iceland,' he said, watching Aud struggle slightly with the pack. 'It makes more sense to use the Norse words rather than the Northumbrian words. You are Norse now. Use those.'

'And the proper words are…' Cwen lifted both the protesting Aud and his pack into the cart. 'The children won't know the words and I don't either. Maybe you can teach us all Norse so we can speak the language before we get to Iceland.'

He clenched his fists, feeling his own inadequacy. He should have said the words to begin with. And he should have thought about lifting the boy in the cart. '*Mor* for mother and *Far* for father.'

'Yes, they can use those words,' Cwen said. Her brow puckered. 'It is silly, but...I'm pleased they are not the same in Northumbrian.'

A knife went through Thrand's heart. She still clung to her dead family.

'Can you practise, Hilde?' he asked deliberately turning from Cwen.

'Yes, *Far*.' The girl gave a little curtsy and laughed. Aud laughed as well and took up the chant—*far, far, far.*

'No, you have it wrong. One *far*, not two.'

'Did they go too far with the *fars*?' Cwen asked with an innocent expression on her face.

Her pun sent the children off into fresh peals of laughter.

'Just one *Far*,' Thrand explained, trying to keep a straight face. He knew he should strive to be like his father—dignified and remote so he could instil discipline, but a large part of him wanted the ease that Cwen had. '*Far-far* means something else.'

'What does *Far-far* mean?' Cwen asked. 'Or don't I want to know?'

'Grandfather. My father.'

Thrand paused. His father had been a remote figure and had left most of the child rearing to his mother. Thrand knew in that instant that it was not what he wanted. He didn't want to be the person who always laid down the law and seemed perfect. He knew his imperfections too well. It was one thing to be called *Far* and quite another thing to actually be a father. He remembered vowing that when he had been punished for some minor misdemeanour.

'Is it the same for all grandfathers?' Hilde wondered.

'No, Cwen's father would be *Mor-far*. It means mother's father.' Thrand frowned as the girl continued to look perplexed. 'It is how you tell who belongs to whom. *Far-mor* would be my mother, while *Mor-mor* would be Cwen's mother. It is very simple really. Logical.'

'Shall we play a game, children?' Cwen asked. 'You say a word and then Thrand will give us the Norse word. It can help to pass the time.'

'If we are going to play, I had better have Aud on my shoulders so he can see properly.' Without giving the boy a chance to protest, Thrand swung him up. It felt natural to have the boy grab hold of his hair and cling on.

They continued that way for a little while, but then Aud decided he wanted down and began to kick hard. Thrand stopped and took him down. The boy ran to hold Hilde's hand and they started chatting away.

Cwen quickened her steps until she was level with him. 'Thank you,' she said in an undertone.

'What, for picking Aud up? It is the best solution. He doesn't weigh much and he can see better from up here. Carts used to make my stomach ache when I was little.'

'No, for giving them a special name for me which isn't *mama*. I had been racking my brain, and you came up with the right answer.'

'Cwen, I can't imagine the heartache of losing a child, but I do know that these children are not seeking to replace your son in your heart.'

'How did you become so wise suddenly?'

'I've served under different commanders over the years. Some good, some not so good. There is always a period of adjustment. Our group is like a *felag*.'

'A *felag* rather than a family. Do you see yourself as our commander?'

'I see myself as a father. I know the difference.' Thrand looked straight ahead. 'I wonder if my own father did.'

She put her hand on his sleeve. 'I'm determined to keep my end of the bargain and be a good mother.'

'You will find a way.' He cupped her cheek. 'I believe in you.'

'And I believe in you and finding a way to be a father rather than a commander.'

'Can someone help? *Mor? Far?*' Hilde called out. 'Aud has fallen in a muddy puddle.'

Thrand turned towards where the little boy stood, rubbing his eyes and covered in mud. He rolled his eyes as Cwen gave a long sigh.

'Problem?'

'I had forgotten about this part of parenting,' Cwenneth said and waited for Thrand's explosion. Aefirth had always hated it when Richard was deliberately naughty and if the way Thrand had reacted yesterday when he first met Aud was any indication, she was in for a long day.

Thrand raised an eyebrow. 'Aud seems to attract dirt. He can bathe when we stop. For now take some of the cloth I planned to give Maeri and wipe the worst off.'

She stared at him dumbfounded. 'I thought you would be upset about it.'

'It was hardly Aud's fault. He didn't ask to fall into a puddle.'

'I think the pair were fooling around,' Cwenneth confessed. 'I heard giggling just before it happened.'

Thrand stopped. 'Is that true, Hilde?'

She scraped her toe in the dirt. 'It was an accident, but we were playing.'

Cwenneth watched a variety of emotions cross Thrand's face. Finally, he gave a rich laugh. He stopped suddenly and shook his head a little.

'Before I knew you, I barely laughed. Some questioned if I even could. I see now that I had simply forgotten how to.'

Her heart expanded at the words. She did mean something to him. She put her hand to his cheek and felt the faint rasp of bristles. 'I hope you will laugh often in Iceland, but what are we going to do about this deliberate naughtiness?'

All merriment vanished from his face.

'I can't do this,' he confessed in an undertone. 'If I lose my temper, I'll frighten the children.'

She stared at him and knew what he was asking and how much it must have cost to ask.

'He will have to ride in the cart if he is naughty. If he is good, he can walk or ride on your shoulders.' Cwen patted Myrkr's neck and tried to keep her voice sounding practical. But her stomach churned. It was wrong that she wanted more of him than he was willing to give.

The faint stench of smoke hung in the air. Cwenneth wrinkled her nose. It was far more than chimney smoke from a farm or village.

She glanced towards Thrand. His easy-going stance of a few moments ago had vanished.

'Can you take Myrkr's bridle?'

'What is going on?' Cwen asked, keeping her voice low. The last thing she wanted to do was to frighten the children.

'Impossible to say.' Thrand nodded. 'We keep going forward but be prepared to go into the woods on your left.'

Cwen nodded. They went around a bend and saw the remains of what had been a farmhouse. The small plume of smoke rose in the air. Cwenneth's stomach clenched. Someone had burnt the entire farm including the barns to the ground, and there was the distinct smell of cooked meat. Whoever had done it had not bothered to take the livestock.

'Was it raiders?' Hilde asked, sitting bolt upright.

'Why would there be raids here, honey?' Cwen said. 'We are near the borders of Lingwold and the lord signed a peace treaty with the Norsemen.'

'Not all raiders are Norse,' Thrand commented. 'Even if the Northumbrians would like to think they are.'

'Well, what do you think?'

Thrand shrugged. 'Wrong season.'

'A tragic accident, then?' Cwenneth put her hand to her throat.

'Stay here with the children.' Thrand unsheathed his sword. 'I will check and see if there are any clues. If there are raiders about, it is better we know about them and plan for it.'

'And if anyone needs help…'

'If you hear me shout, get the children away from here. Leave the cart.'

'Off to the left.'

'Correct. I will find you.'

'Will you?'

'I'll always find you, Cwen.'

He went towards the farm. Cwenneth lifted the children down from the cart and stood with her arms about them. Aud stuck his thumb in his mouth and stood watching with big eyes as Thrand cautiously made his way over to the smouldering remains. Silently she prayed that he would come back and say that it was just a fire, probably started by a cooking pot.

'What is *Far* going to do?' Hilde asked, leaning into her.

'He is going to make sure that everyone is all right. And that we can travel on past without a problem.' Cwenneth silently willed Thrand to return.

'Who did this?' Hilde whispered. 'Bad men?'

Every instinct in Cwenneth's body told her that it was Hagal's work, but it made no sense. He should be well to the southwest of here. Edward would never do such a thing. He would not burn people's houses and claim it was the Norse.

'Everyone has left.' Thrand returned far quicker than she had thought he would.

'No…no bodies…'

'A fresh grave in a little graveyard. I reckon the attack happened about two days ago.' His deep-blue gaze met hers. 'And it was an attack, Cwen. I found the marks of a double axe on the door and several arrows. Whoever lived here didn't stand a chance.'

'We were supposed to be at peace.' Cwenneth

shook her head in disbelief. 'Things like this were not supposed to happen any more. We wanted time to recover from the war.'

'We don't know who did this.'

'The Norse warriors are the only ones who use double axes. It is supposed to be the hallmark of Thrand the Destroyer.'

A faint dimple shone in the corner of his mouth. 'Funny that. I believe he was otherwise occupied.'

'I know that. You know that, but the villagers around here will not know that. This slaughter will add to the legend of Thrand the Destroyer.'

'We will be keeping away from villages, then.' Thrand gave Hilde and Aud a significant look. Cwenneth knew precisely what he was thinking. It would be very easy for one of the children to blurt out his name. Hilde seemed particularly loyal.

'It would be for the best.'

'The last thing we want is someone recognising me and blaming me. I'm not saying that I am proud of everything that I have done, but I did it in battle against a known enemy. Yes, I have raided, but we were at war. You understand the difference.'

Cwen's stomach knotted, and she gave a small nod. 'You think Hagal did this, but why would he? He signed a treaty with my brother.'

'He broke it when he tried to have you murdered.' Thrand put his sword back in its scabbard. 'I don't pretend to know what is in that man's head. It is none of my concern now. All this...' he gestured about the ruined farmhouse '...all this is someone else's problem. If your brother can't tell honest men from rogues, I pity his people, but I feel no pity for him.'

'I think we had better get going. Put some distance between us and this.'

Aud's stomach gave a loud rumble.

'Aud is hungry,' Hilde announced with great importance.

'As soon as we can we will get you some food.' Cwen placed Aud and Hilde up on Myrkr, glad to have something to do. Concentrating on getting the children fed would keep her mind from worrying about why Hagal had decided to torch that farmhouse.

A hard knot appeared in the pit of her stomach. If Hagal had torched this farmhouse, how many other people had he killed, and worse, had he used her supposed murder as an excuse to do it? Thrand might think they were safe and had no further part to play, but she knew that farmhouse would haunt her.

'The sooner we are in Iceland, the sooner you can stop worrying about this sort of thing,' Thrand remarked.

'But it might still be happening.' Cwenneth picked up Aud. She didn't want to think about the danger to the farm where they had lived.

'It won't be your concern. It is not your concern now. We have chosen a different path. The children will be safe.' He put his hand on her shoulder. 'You can only look after your family, Cwen, not the whole world.'

Despite the wild flower–strewn glade where they camped, Thrand's nostrils still quivered from the stench of the burnt livestock. He put his cloak over the two sleeping children. Aud and Hilde at least seemed unconcerned by the slaughter they had encountered earlier. Cwen remained a bit pale and subdued.

The children had eagerly eaten the duck he'd caught, which Cwen had cooked with a few herbs and greens she'd gathered, but neither he nor Cwen had eaten much. And the children had waited until Cwen told them they could eat. How Cwen knew these things was beyond him. Looking after children was a whole new world where he had little skill or experience, but he wanted to learn. It surprised him how much he wanted to.

Thrand tore his mind away from the children and attempted to concentrate on the problem at hand, namely who was behind the burnt farmhouse and did it matter to his future? Were they in danger?

Hagal had to be behind it, but it made no sense. But there again, his attempted murder of Cwen made no sense either. At least Cwen lived. He doubted anyone had survived at that farmhouse. It annoyed him that the Northumbrians would say he had done it, but what was the point of worrying about his reputation in a place that he never planned to visit again.

'Do you want any more duck?' he asked, going over to where Cwen sat quietly mending a hole in Aud's trousers. 'You barely touched your food earlier.'

Cwen shook her head. 'I'm not hungry.'

'Can we have a song, *Far*?' Hilde's sleepy voice asked.

'I thought they were asleep,' Thrand said in an undertone.

'Sometimes putting a cloak over a child can wake them.'

'I did it carefully,' he protested.

Her hand stilled. 'Are you going to sing for her? Music used to settle Richard, and she asked for you.'

'The only songs I know are war ballads. You sing, Cwen. You do it. You must know a lullaby or two.'

She pushed the needle in and out of the cloth. 'My voice isn't very good and I haven't sung properly… not since…'

Thrand stilled as the memory of the dream washed over him. 'You do yourself a disservice. You sang once for me.'

She tucked her chin into her neck. 'Special occasions only.'

'Very well. I will try.' He searched his mind and started to sing one of the less violent sagas.

The little girl gave a sigh and turned over. Within a few heartbeats, there was the sound of her soft breathing.

'There, you did it,' Cwen said. 'You sang her to sleep.'

'Why did you sing in the hut?'

'I didn't think you heard me,' she replied. 'A bit of foolishness my nurse Martha told me when I was little. Some people can be brought back from the brink of death if the song is sweet enough. Luckily, as you pointed out, you were never in danger.'

Thrand took the cloth from her hand, put it to one side and laced his fingers through hers. 'You have a lovely voice. Can I hear it again?'

'When we get to Iceland and everyone is safe, then I will sing. It will be a special occasion.' She released his hand and stood up, wrapping her arms about her waist. 'I will be far happier and in better voice when we get there.'

He leant his forehead against hers and put his arms about her. 'Forget about the farmhouse. Forget about everything but these children.'

She laid her head on his chest. 'What if Hagal did it? What if he did it because of me? I spent my life preparing to run a large house and I know the responsibility a mistress has for her people. I wanted to be a peace-weaver, not a death-bringer.'

Thrand closed his eyes and forced his breathing to be steady. 'What-ifs play no part in our future. Going to Iceland is the best way to protect you and the children. What happens in Northumbria is no longer any of our concern. And you will be bringing peace— peace to my life and the children's.'

'But his reach is long. Knui proved that. How many other people have taken his gold? Who else might be lurking in the shadows?'

'Everyone will be on their guard now that it is known. Bribery only works when people are not looking for it.' He put a finger to her mouth. 'Hush now. I want to enjoy you and this moment. The children are asleep and there is only us. Who knows what tomorrow will bring?

'Make love to me, Thrand. There are no stars to count tonight.'

His head descended. She responded fully, greedily pulling at his mouth.

Afterwards when Cwen lay in his arms, sleeping with her lips softly parted, Thrand watched the faint light of the stars. Only yesterday he would have sworn that vengeance drove him and there was room for nothing more. But now he knew it could contain more. It could be richer than he ever dreamt.

Silently, he prayed, using words he remembered from his childhood, prayers his father used to say—that his sword arm would be strong and not falter. He tightened his arm about Cwen and smoothed her shorn hair. This time, he vowed, he would not fail his family. And he knew who his family was.

He sat up straight. Cwen! There was something he could do for her.

'Tomorrow we go north.'

'North?'

'You need to make your goodbyes…to your son.'

The ice coldness of the crypt hit Cwenneth as soon as she walked in, taking her back to Aefirth's funeral. The lingering scent of incense tugged at her nostrils. She braced her body for tears, but none came.

She walked briskly over to Aefirth's tomb, wanting to get it over with. She hadn't anticipated Thrand would make this gesture. Despite his dismissing the danger, she knew he took a grave risk in coming here.

Thankfully the young priest had not been present when she was last here. Maybe Thrand was correct. Maybe luck was finally on her side.

When she'd imagined coming back here, she'd always anticipated that uncontrollable sorrow would overtake her. Instead, an overwhelming sense of peace filled her as she slowly traced Richard's name on the tomb.

'I'm going to Iceland,' she whispered. 'I will make sure Aud and Hilde learn all the games you used to play. But know my heart is big enough to hold everyone. Loving them won't make me love you any less.

She allowed her hand to linger for a few heartbeats and then turned away. She was no longer the woman who had loved these two so fiercely. She'd always love them, but they belonged to her past. And her future was more important.

'Finished so soon?'

'I'm ready to go.' She touched her chest. 'There is no need to say goodbye as I carry them in my heart. But thank you for bringing me here. It was unexpected, but the risk was far too great.'

He put his hand on her arm. 'The risk was worth it.'

'We need to go now.' Cwenneth glanced over her shoulder. The priest had left them alone. 'Confronting my stepson with you and the children would be less than ideal.'

'The lord is away,' Hilde piped up.

'How do you know?'

'I asked the kitchen boy when he was giving the scraps to the chickens,' the little girl answered.

Thrand beamed. 'If you want to know something, Hilde will find out the answer.'

'Did you find out where he had gone?'

'The kitchen boy said that he was going off to war.'

Cwenneth shook her head as a shiver ran down her spine. Now that she thought about it, the hall seemed devoid of its usual life. 'He will have that wrong. My stepson has a limp. He is no warrior. Kitchen boys the world over like to sound important.'

'Did he say where?' Thrand asked.

Hilde shook her head. 'He wasn't sure. A long way from here. The kichen boy's brother went as well.'

'We need to go to the coast by the quickest way.' Thrand picked Aud up. 'Once we are in Jorvik, I will let Halfdan know. Your brother may be massing an army.'

Cwenneth swallowed hard. She had to think logically. They only had the kitchen boy's boast to Hilde. Her stepson could be anywhere. The Scots could be massing in the north and then there was Mercia to the west. 'Thrand…it will have nothing to do with us. My stepson would never lift a finger to save me. He believes I cursed his family.'

'I won't leave my king blind. If there are problems in Bernicia, he needs to be aware of them.'

'And Iceland?'

His warm hand curled about hers. 'I'm giving the king information. We will still go to Iceland. War is in my past.'

Cwenneth nodded, choosing to give the appearance of believing him. 'Iceland before autumn.'

Chapter Thirteen

The spring rain pelted down incessantly, soaking and chilling them to the bone. Cwenneth tightened the shawl that the farmer's wife had insisted on giving about her shoulders. They had made good progress after leaving Aefirth's crypt without anyone challenging them.

Without prompting, Thrand had set Aud on Myrkr while Cwenneth and Hilde walked beside him to keep the load light on the cart. Hilde kept up a steady stream of chatter which helped keep her mind from the niggling worry of which war her stepson had gone off to fight. It would not be anything to do with the rumour Hagal had spread. The one thing she knew for certain was that her stepson would never lift a finger to save her.

'You have become awfully quiet, Cwen,' Thrand remarked, lifting a tired Hilde up alongside Aud. 'Do you wish to ride as well? Or should we find shelter?'

Cwenneth's heart turned over. For the thousandth time since they had left the farmhouse she warned her heart not to care or have hope. But her heart had long ago stopped listening to her and it frightened her. She could so easily lose him. And the last thing she wanted was a war between the Norsemen and the Bernicians.

The needle sting of hail attacked Cwenneth.

'We should find shelter. Aud is being very brave, but hail hurts.'

'You must know of somewhere which will take travellers in and not ask too many questions. The children need a hot meal and to thaw out in front of a warm fire.' His brows drew together. 'Like you, I know we are near to Lingwold.'

'There is no point in trying the hall or any of the monasteries or inns. They are sure to inform my brother.' Cwenneth wrapped her arms about her waist. 'The last thing I want is my brother chasing after me, thinking I've been kidnapped as Hagal claimed. Time enough to send a message when we are in Jorvik.'

She took a step and her boot slipped slightly in the pile of hailstones. Thrand put his hand under her elbow, holding her upright. She met his midnight-blue eyes and saw the concern and something more which was instantly masked.

'Are your boots losing their grip?' Thrand asked. 'Go slower and watch where you put your feet. How would we cope if something happened to you?'

'They will last. They are good…' Cwenneth's voice trailed away as her shoulders suddenly became much lighter. There was a place they could stay! Safe with no fear of Edward or Hagal knocking at the door.

'There is somewhere we can stay.' Cwenneth fought to keep the excitement from her voice. 'Someone who would keep our presence a secret until her dying breath.'

'Are you sure of that? Gold and fear can be mighty big inducements. Do you know of any abandoned huts around here? Ones that a shepherd might use?'

'You remember Dain—the boy who had these boots before me. His mother lives near here. On her own. She won't ask too many questions. She was my nurse, my second mother before my marriage and she has no great love for my brother. She rightly blames him for failing to find Dain a place amongst his men. I would like to return the boots.' Cwenneth winced at the sight of the mud-splattered boots. 'Or at least pay for them. She deserves to know her son died bravely.'

When he said nothing, she added, 'The children need shelter from the rain. Somewhere warm where they can dry off in front of a fire. They are far too wet and cold. If one of them gets sick, we'll be forced to delay our journey. And we want to get to Jorvik as soon as possible.'

'I am aware of that. The question is where.'

'I would trust my life to Martha.' Cwenneth paused. 'And I would trust the children's lives to her as well.'

'If you are sure…'

'Very sure. She is my oldest friend.' She put her hand on Thrand's sleeve and felt the comfort of his muscular arm. 'When I was a young girl, she used to hide my misdeeds from my family and most particularly my brother. I would not be standing here if she had told. Edward did threaten bodily harm on more than one occasion.'

'What did you do? I find it hard to credit you were ever naughty. Or behaved foolishly.'

'Once I arranged it so an old bird's nest fell on Edward's head and showered him with spider's webs. Edward had been overly proud of his new ermine cloak. It was ruined beyond repair. And despite Edward offering a reward, Martha kept my secret.'

'This is another matter entirely, Cwen.'

'You did not hear the threats my brother uttered. Or the rewards he offered. I know which side Martha would choose.' Cwenneth concentrated on brushing the hail from Hilde's cloak. 'The children need to have some shelter and hot food, and the area around Lingwold is too built up to risk a fire.'

She waited in silence as Aud began to softly cry as the hail pelted down again, pricking like a thousand needles.

'I trust your judgement on people,' Thrand said, pulling her hood more firmly on her head. 'You took a chance on me, but keep silent about my name unless absolutely necessary.'

Cwenneth threw her arms around his neck and kissed him, drinking from his mouth. 'You won't regret it.'

His arms came about her and pulled her close. 'I plan on making you pay later.'

'Who goes there on a day like today?' an elderly voice asked in answer to Cwenneth's knock. 'I swear it became black as midnight at noon. Does it mean the devil is out on his rounds?'

Cwenneth gave a quick glance at Thrand. She motioned for him to be quiet. If Martha heard a Norseman's voice, she might bolt the door and lock it. The bone-chilling hail and sleet had only increased in the time it had taken to get to the farm.

'Travellers in need of shelter.' Cwenneth hated how her stomach knotted. 'Martha, please open the door and allow us to come in.'

The door creaked open and an eye peered out. 'Lady Cwenneth? By all that is holy, what are you doing here? Do ghosts walk abroad today? Is that why it is so dark out?'

Cwenneth winced. She hadn't realised her voice was that recognisable. 'The very same, but I am no ghost or apparition. I am real. Touch my hand. There are children, Martha. It is bucketing down. May we come in? Please, for the sake of my mother's friendship with you.'

Martha's eyes narrowed and she ignored Cwenneth's outstretched hand. 'We heard you'd been kidnapped. Owen the Plough even went so far as to predict that you were dead. No lady could withstand what happened to you.'

'Owen the Plough always did love to make dire predictions. I've brought Dain's boots back. You can see the mark he made on the back.' Cwenneth lifted up her gown to display the mud-splattered boots. 'You were right. They are excellent boots. Open the door properly and look.'

The door was flung wide open and the elderly woman rushed out. She clasped Cwenneth to her breast before leading them back into the small hut where a fire roared. The smell of warm stew and freshly baked bread perfumed the air. Aud and Hilde instantly went to the fire and started to warm their hands, rather than begging for a taste as she would have done at their age. In the firelight, Cwenneth could see the colour in their cheeks coming back. She breathed easier. Coming here and begging for shelter had been the right thing to do.

'You must tell me all your adventures and how you managed to be here with two children and this…warrior. After you have had something to eat. Those children are too thin by half.' The old woman put out a trembling hand and touched Cwenneth's cheek. 'You are real. You are alive. Did my…?'

Cwenneth shook her head slowly, hating the eager look which had come on to the woman's face.

'Slain before they had a chance to draw their swords. Betrayal of the most cowardly sort. Cold-blooded murder,' Thrand said in a low voice, 'or otherwise your son would have acquitted himself well.'

Cwenneth rapidly explained what had happened and how Thrand had rescued her. However, she was very careful not to give Thrand a name as she knew how people in Lingwold felt about him.

'I would be dead if not for him.' Cwenneth squeezed Martha's hand as the old woman wiped away a tear. 'Surely you can see the folly in saying it is worse than death to be rescued by a Norseman when the only reason why I am alive and breathing is him and his sword arm.'

The woman's eyes narrowed. 'And he is? You are avoiding the question, my lady. What is this man's name? He must have a name.'

Cwenneth swallowed hard. Lying was out of the question, but there was no telling how Martha would react when she knew, particularly after Thrand had been blamed for the torching of the farms. 'Does it matter who he is? He saved my life and travels with me. We will only be staying the one night.'

Martha tapped her foot on the floor. 'I think it does if I am going to welcome him under my roof. And I want his real name, my lady. I know how you try to cozen people.'

'Thrand Ammundson,' Thrand answered, stepping forward and holding out his hand. 'Thrand the Destroyer in flesh and blood and at your service. I'm grateful you have taken my family in.'

'Then the rumours are true. You did kidnap my lady and seduce her.'

Martha backed up. In another breath she'd run. Cwenneth readied herself to usher the children out. They could get a good few miles on them before Martha had the chance to raise the alarm.

Thrand lowered his hand on Martha's shoulder, keeping her from moving. 'Lady Cwenneth stays with me voluntarily. Initially she wanted to see justice served, but she stays now for the sake of these two children.'

The woman blanched. 'But they said it was all the Destroyer's work. Your bridegroom swore it on a bible.'

'We've been duped for the last few years. And my so-called bridegroom is a pagan. Christian oaths have no meaning to him.' Cwenneth pressed her fingers together. 'I was there. I know who killed your son and who rescued me. And while I don't know who torched those farms, I do know it wasn't Thrand. And I am prepared to swear that oath on any bible.'

Martha sank down on to the bench. 'But they said…

your brother said… I'm only a widow who has lost her only son and whose daughter won't speak to her.'

Cwenneth knelt before Martha, gathering the older woman's cold hands within hers. 'Edward must never know I was here. We only stopped because of the children and the weather. We needed shelter. I will let him know where I am when I reach Jorvik and the children are safe, but right now they need me.'

'My old lady, your mother, would bar me from heaven if she knew I'd refused to shelter her only daughter. Or had betrayed her. Your brother is much altered from the young man he once was.' Martha screwed up her face and appeared to think for a long while. 'For her sake, I will accept you under my roof, Thrand Ammundson, and keep your secret.'

'We accept with gratitude,' Cwenneth said quickly before Thrand exploded. 'We will be gone by morning.'

'Where are you going?' Martha asked.

'We head to Jorvik and then to Iceland,' Thrand replied, a muscle jumping in his jaw. 'Lady Cwenneth is coming with me to look after the children. It is the safest place for her.'

'Iceland! Have you been bewitched, my lady? It is the end of the earth. Surely your brother will protect you…from Hagal the Red.'

'He failed to before.' Cwenneth could hear the warning note in Thrand's voice. 'If he had heeded the warning signs, your son might be alive today. But instead he allowed himself to be blinded by a legend.'

'This is a bad business,' Martha said, shaking her head.

'Why is it a bad business?' Cwenneth asked.

'So many men dead. Your brother is baying for blood, my lady. He is raising an army to rid this land of Thrand the Destroyer for ever. He wants to free you.'

'How did he learn about my kidnapping?' Cwenneth asked. 'It puzzles me how the news travelled so fast. It took weeks for me to travel there. The roads are nearly impassable with the spring rain. We've had great trouble today with the cart.'

'Hagal the Red arrived a few days ago, swearing vengeance for your kidnapping, but he needed your brother's support.'

Cwenneth froze. Hagal was at Lingwold with her brother. Play-acting. Hagal obviously expected her to make for her old home and would act the contrite bridegroom when she did arrive.

'The best way to avoid a trap is to stay well clear,' Thrand said in a quiet but firm undertone, putting a heavy hand on her shoulder. 'There are so many reasons why we hold to our agreed course of action and the two main ones are sitting across from you right now.'

Cwenneth pressed her hands to her eyes and tried to will the sick feeling in her stomach to go. Hagal was here! Not in Jorvik. 'Did I say anything?'

'We will be on our way tomorrow. First light,' Thrand said, leaving no room for dissent. He went over to where the children sat and scooped Aud up. 'Aud is sound asleep in his stew and Hilde is not far behind. After a rest they will be ready to continue on. They are good travellers for ones so small.'

Cwenneth's throat caught as Aud's head lolled against Thrand's shoulder. Thrand looked every inch the father. To think he had proclaimed that he could never look after the children. He was a natural. And he cared for them. It was the way he carried Aud as if he was worth more than all the gold in the world combined.

She pinched the bridge of her nose. Caring for the children was one thing. Caring for her was another. She wished she could stop her heart from longing and from wanting to keep him safe.

Martha pointed to the loft. 'Put the children up there. It'll be warm enough and there is plenty of space for everyone to sleep.'

'I'll do it,' Thrand said. 'You stay here with your friend, Cwen. It will be a long time before you see someone from your birthplace again.'

Hilde went up the ladder first, and Thrand followed with Aud.

'It is quite the family you have there, Lady Cwenneth,' Martha said when the noise from the loft had died down a little.

Cwenneth laced her hand with Martha's. 'I'm glad you agree. I fear my brother would not. He would be beyond all reasoning, but know that I am happier than I have been in a long time. It feels right. I'm needed in a way I never was at Lingwold. Or indeed with Aefirth.'

Martha gave a reluctant nod. 'If you say he is a good man, I'll believe you. And he is the right age. Aefirth was far too old for you. He treated you like a child and never allowed you to make any important decisions.'

'Aefirth was good to me,' Cwenneth protested. 'He sought to protect me.'

'He wanted to play at being young. He should never have gone to war the last time he did. He should have stayed and looked after his estate. When he left you, he never trusted you to make the right decisions.'

Cwenneth pressed her lips together. What Martha said had merit. She had admired Aefirth and had liked being looked after, but he had never encouraged her to think for herself in the way Thrand did. He had left advisors for her. But Aefirth had only wanted her because he felt he needed another heir, one who could be a warrior instead of a cripple, and she was an ornament to his house. 'The woman I was loved him.'

'And the woman you are now? Who do you love?'

Was it wrong of her to keep hoping that Thrand would see her as more than the person who could help him fulfil his promise to his friend? Cwenneth fiddled with her eating knife. Now was not the time to reveal her problems with Thrand.

'There is something more,' she said instead. 'Something you kept from me because Thrand was in the room.'

'Your brother means to march to Jorvik and demand Thrand's head. He has called for all men who hate Thrand Ammundson to flock to his banner. He means to take Jorvik if the king won't listen. Even your stepson has come with men. You could have knocked me over with a feather when I saw his banner fluttering in the breeze the other day.'

'My brother is foolish if he thinks the king will listen. And insane if he thinks he can take Jorvik. Others have tried.' A pain developed in the back of Cwenneth's head. How could her brother be that foolish!

'Hagal has guaranteed safe passage through his lands to Jorvik in time for the Storting. He says that it will be your brother's last chance to get rid of the menace for ever and get you back as his bride.'

'Hagal wants me dead. Aefirth killed his cousin in battle. Unless my stepson is very careful, he too will end up dead.'

'He has never mentioned that. And your stepson is one of the ones yelling the loudest.' Martha tapped a finger on the side of her nose. 'But you always did say that he wanted easy glory.'

'That's because he has never been to war.' Cwenneth clenched her fist. She hated to think about the lives her stepson risked, men she knew and respected. 'Why does Hagal need an army of Bernicians?'

'According to Hagal, the Norse oath of fellowship forbids weapons and private armies during a Storting. My nephew was in the room when he said it. A great cheer went up. Finally a way to defeat the menace.'

A cold prickling went down Cwenneth's back. This was what Hagal had been up to—he was going to use her brother and his men to provide the army so that he could take over Jorvik and become king. And they would not be Norse. He would not be condemned as an oath-breaker.

She leant forward and gathered Martha's hands between hers. 'There is more to tell me.'

'Your brother was not inclined to move as your sister-in-law is pregnant and begged him not to leave her side. But then the burning of the farms started. They all swore it was Thrand the Destroyer. Old John's son watched his father being killed.'

'Thrand was with me.'

'It is better that you are leaving tomorrow. Your brother has a hard lesson to learn. He should listen to his wife and stay put. But since the farms were attacked, there is no reasoning with him. He wants Thrand Ammundson destroyed. Hagal has assured him that Halfdan will listen as he has kidnapped a fellow *jaarl*'s bride and made off with her dowry. And if not, your brother is prepared to take on the entire Norse army.'

Cwenneth closed her eyes and knew she had been living in a dream world. Hagal was not going to stop if they went to Iceland. He was going to take that army south. People would be killed. Other farms would be burnt to the ground. People she cared about. Everything in Lingwold would change. Men would lose their lives, women their husbands and children their fathers. And in Jorvik, there was no saying what would happen if Hagal actually did gain power. Would they even be safe in Iceland? Or able to reach it?

All because she was willing to let people think she was dead.

Hagal had to be faced, shown for the bare-faced liar he was, and stopped. Jorvik would be too late. Hagal needed to be stopped before he acquired an army.

'You appear ill, my lady. Shall I fix you a sleeping draught?'

Cwenneth quickly shook her head. She knew what she had to do and there was no point in arguing with Thrand about it. He'd only refuse to let her go alone or insist they wait until Jorvik. If Thrand accompanied her, they'd kill him. And she wanted to spend the rest of her life with him. The children needed him and his sword arm. She, on the other hand, could count on her brother's men to keep her safe. Her brother had no reason to seek her death. Once he knew the truth, his army would turn against Hagal.

'I'm a bit tired, Martha,' she said, a plan beginning to formulate in her brain. She wanted the comfort of Thrand's arms one last time and then she'd do it. Only she could stop this madness before it began.

'You go up and see that man of yours.' The old woman gave a huge smile. 'If I was a few years younger, I would give you a run for your money. Not that he'd notice—anyone with half a brain can see that he is devoted to you.'

'He's not—' Cwenneth responded too quickly and thought better of it. Let Martha believe in the romance. She knew the bitter truth—Thrand was currently interested in sharing her bed and he wanted her for the children. 'What made you change your mind?'

'No monster would take such good care of children. He handles them as if they are made of glass. And they are not even his own. I've misjudged him for years. And no man could ever have conducted as many raids as your brother claimed the Destroyer did.'

'Why do it then?'

'It gave him more power and more men. Your brother could always tell a good tale, particularly if it made him look the better for it. I've known him for a long time.'

Cwenneth reached out and grabbed the woman's gnarled hand. 'I'm glad we came here tonight.'

'Are they asleep?' Cwenneth peered into the moonlit loft. Through the tiny window at the gable end she could see the first stars in a sea of midnight-black.

Typical, she thought. They found shelter because the weather was awful and it had cleared. If only they had continued on, she'd never have known.

'As soon as their heads hit the straw. I was watching them for a little while.' Thrand reached out a hand. 'I was about to come down.'

Cwenneth caught his hand and brought the knuckles to her lips. He had purposefully stayed away so she could have time to talk to Martha. 'I came up instead to see where we would sleep. Aud and Hilde have that side of the loft and we can have this one.'

He tilted his head to one side. 'Did that old woman say something to make you upset?'

Cwenneth gave her head a quick shake. 'Nothing. She approves of you in case you wondered. She thinks you are exactly what I need. Apparently she thought Aefirth too old for me.'

He pulled her into his arms. 'Does she? I'm glad. I'll leave her some gold when we go. Or one of my brooches if you think the gold will offend her.'

'What were you thinking about while you were making yourself scarce?'

'When we are in Iceland, I'll build you a long-house. It will be little bigger than this house, but I want to have something of Bernicia for you and the children. The configuration is different from the house I grew up in in Viken, but it can be done.' He described it all so vividly that Cwenneth could see it take shape in front of her. The lump grew in her throat.

Iceland was an impossible dream after what she'd learnt from Martha. She could not walk away and allow men to die in her name, trying to rescue her. Making sure Edward understood the truth and acted in his own best interest was imperative. And as Thrand taught her—she made her own luck. She was the only person who could stop this madness before it started, before it did turn into a war.

If things happened how she planned, she'd be back before Thrand and the children woke. Then they could continue on to Iceland as if nothing had happened. As long as Edward knew the truth, he would not send men after Thrand. Once he saw that she was alive and unharmed, he would destroy Hagal rather than march to his doom in Jorvik.

'Are you cold, Cwen?' Thrand's breath tickled her ear.

'Today took more out of me than I thought it would.'

He brushed her temple with a featherlike kiss which sent pulses of heat through her. 'Are you going to tell me what is wrong, Cwen? What you intend to do?'

'Nothing is wrong. Everything is right. I simply have no idea when we shall next have a soft place to lie. And both children are sound asleep. We are alone together.' She pressed her body up to his and felt him harden. 'I want you, Thrand, and I believe you want me as well. Here. Now.'

Her hands entangled in his hair and pulled him closer.

He groaned in the back of his throat.

Slowly she pushed him down the straw. He fell easily back and pulled her on top of him.

'I'm in charge tonight,' she whispered against his throat. 'And I intend to take my time.'

'A threat or a promise?'

'Both.' She put her fingers to his lips. 'The time for talking has ended and the time for pleasure has begun.'

She slowly lifted his tunic, revealing his warm skin underneath. And then, allowing her hand to trail down his muscular chest, she undid his trousers and took them off.

He lay silver in the pale moonlight, naked and watching her. There was something very powerful about having a warrior such as him at her mercy.

She bent her head and tasted the hollow of his throat. Slowly, she moved her lips down his body, taking her time to taste and sample. So far most of their encounters had been about him taking charge—this time she wanted to be the one.

He groaned in his throat as she lapped at his nipples, enjoying the rough texture.

She cupped his erection and felt how he grew harder and longer in the palm of her hand. Giving in to impulse, she bent her head and tasted the tip of him. Silk smooth, but hard underneath. Ready for her. She moved her mouth lower on him and his body bucked upwards. His hands gripped the straw as if he was struggling to maintain control. She lifted her head and ran her thumb over the tip of him.

'Too much?' she asked.

'You are too dressed,' he gasped. 'Want you naked.'

He caught the hem of her tattered gown and brought it up over her head. Then his hands cupped her breasts and flicked the nipples, sending rivulets of pleasure throughout her body.

'Now we can both enjoy,' he murmured. He lifted his mouth and his tongue flicked her core. She ground her hips into him with each new sensation as she tried to concentrate on stroking him.

Finally, when she knew she was about ready to explode, she tore away from his pleasure-giving mouth and impaled herself on him, opening her hips to take his whole length in one fluid movement.

She started to rock back and forth, allowing her body to say all the things that she dare not whisper and to offer up promises for the future.

Thrand slowly came back down to earth. Something tonight had been different between Cwen and him. He couldn't put a finger on it, but for the first time in a very long time he felt as if he belonged to other people. She was in truth a part of him. She was the keeper of his heart, the sort of woman his father had told him that he would find one day.

'Cwen,' he rumbled in her ear when they were still joined. 'Thank you.'

She lifted herself up from his chest. Her entire body thrummed. 'I should be the one thanking you. I never knew it could be like that. It is much more pleasant to share.'

Thrand released his breath. He was tempted to tell her how much he loved her, but the last time he had said such words he had ended up fighting for his life. When they were in Iceland, when he had built a house for her, then she'd understand what she meant to him. How she was at the heart of the new family he planned. He could confess his dream then. 'It feels good to be part of a whole again. I had not realised that I missed it.'

'Part of a whole?'

'You, the children and me. They need parents.' Thrand knew his words were weak, but they were all he dared admit. He worried if he said anything more before they reached Iceland, he'd spoil everything. He wanted a family. His family. People he had ties with. He had lost one family and now it would appear he had gained another.

She struggled out of his arms. 'Always the children.'

'Someone has to look after them. You said so yourself.'

'I know, but…'

Thrand put his hands behind his head and looked up at the blackened beams. 'Once we arrive in Jorvik, it should take less than a week to find a boat. Many boats make the passage in the summer. Soon we will have both begun a new life and will be able to give those children the future they deserve. And I will let Halfdan know about Hagal's scheme. He will end it.'

Rather than wrapping her arms about his neck and thanking him, Cwen reached for her gown. 'And if your old life calls you back? If Halfdan needs you to rout Hagal?'

'It won't.' Thrand slammed his fists together. 'My focus is you and the children. I'm through with war, battles and revenge. Let someone else do it. But I'm also no traitor. I'll not allow Hagal to use the Bernicians to seize power.'

'Why do you think this?'

'Hagal is here and plotting something with your brother. Your brother can command an army, but it would be suicide to move against the Norse. Once Halfdan knows of Hagal's plotting, he will act. There is no need for either of us to do anything yet. When we are in Jorvik, I will set things in motion, but then we go to Iceland. Trust me.'

He hoped she understood what he was saying and how much she meant to him and how scared he was of voicing his feelings out loud.

With a sigh she laid her head back on his chest. 'It is good to know.'

He tightened his arms about her and bid the feeling that somehow he was about to lose her to go.

Chapter Fourteen

Cwenneth waited, wrapped in Thrand's arms until she was certain he was sound asleep. She pressed a gentle kiss on his mouth and slipped out from his arms.

In the moonlight she swiftly dressed. And then she kissed each of the children. Their little faces looked like angels. Tears welled up in her eyes. She wiped them away with fierce fingers. She was going to see them again. All of them. They wouldn't even know she had gone.

'I will return,' she said. 'I refuse to allow Hagal to destroy any more families. I refuse to allow Hagal to destroy you. I'll be back before you wake.'

She stole away downstairs.

'So you are truly leaving?' Martha said from the shadows.

Cwenneth stopped. 'You waited up. You should have gone to bed hours ago.'

'I wondered if your man had talked some sense into you. I hoped he had.' Martha came forward. 'I know what you are like, my lady. Meddling will get you nowhere.'

'Meddling? My brother is about to be tricked into a war which he will lose. And while he may deserve to lose his life for being a fool, the men of Lingwold deserve to live. One of the reasons I agreed to marry Hagal in the first place was because I wanted peace for my people. I don't want to be the cause of destroying lives. I am the only one who can stop this madness. How could I live with myself knowing people died to avenge my supposed kidnap?'

'Your man agrees?'

Cwenneth covered Martha's hands with her own. There was little point in telling of Thrand's decree. Jorvik would be far too late. 'I kept it from him. What can he do except get killed? My brother wants his head. It is why he agreed to an alliance with Hagal the Red in the first place. It is why he will march south—to put an end to Thrand the Destroyer.' She tightened her grip on Martha's fingers and willed her to understand the future. 'None of those men will make it back to the north. Hagal then will really be able to pillage this land. I'm the only person who can stop this.'

'You might want to believe that, but your man will have other ideas once he learns where you have gone. You belong to him now.'

'I don't belong to anyone,' Cwenneth said quickly. 'I have worked it out in my head. I will go in by the side entrance and through the kitchens. Once I'm there, I will send one of the servants to quietly fetch my brother. We will have a brief conversation and I'll leave a free woman. I will be back before anyone awakes.'

Martha's face turned mulish. 'You should discuss

it with your man first. He is supposed to be a great warrior, which means he understands strategy far better than you. Even I can see your brother could have you followed.'

'I want to spend the rest of my life with him and the children, Martha.' Cwenneth pressed her hands together to keep them from trembling. Always people treated her like a child, rather than recognising that she did have a mind. 'Hagal needs to be exposed for the lying murderer that he is before he can ruin all of Lingwold. I'm the only one who can do it. Once Edward knows I'm alive, this nonsense will stop. And he won't keep me. Even if he tries, I know all the ways out of the hall. I grew up there. Remember how I used to escape to visit you on baking days?'

Martha squeezed Cwenneth's hands. 'Your mother despaired.'

'There, you see. You should have some faith in me.' She patted Martha's shoulder. 'If I could escape my mother, I can escape from the hall.'

'And what shall I tell him if he wakes and you have failed to return? Confronting an angry Norseman is a fate I wish to avoid.'

Cwenneth stared at the dying embers of the fire. Martha's question was something she preferred not to think about. Thrand would be furious with her when he found out what she had done. She had to hope that he'd listen.

'Before the cock crows, I'll be back. Edward will listen to me and heed my advice. He has in the past.' Cwenneth straightened her shoulders and refused to think how long in the past it had been since Edward had listened. She would make him listen if she had to tie him down and beat him about the head. 'Failure is not an option.'

'If you haven't returned by mid-morning, I will tell him where you have gone, and if he is half the man I think he is, I won't be able to hold him.' Martha waggled her finger. 'Think on that, my lady. Think on that.'

A few stars faintly twinkled in the sky. Cwenneth raised her hood and stepped into the darkness.

A black shape stepped in front of her. 'Where do you think you are going?'

She missed a step and nearly fell. 'Thrand? You are supposed to be asleep.'

'Once Martha told her tale, it was obvious what you were going to do.' He lifted a brow. 'I asked you to stay with me and to confide in me. You refused.'

She dipped her head. He was making her out to be in the wrong, but it wasn't that way at all. 'I wanted to save your life.'

'How? By running away?'

'By going to my brother and telling him the truth?' She held out her hands and willed him to understand what she was doing was for him. 'It is the only way to stop this madness. If he knows the truth, my brother will stop Hagal. His interest is in saving his people rather than having a vendetta against you.'

'And what do you think he will do? Just let you go? Allow you to return to me? The kidnapped bride?'

She glared at him. 'Once my brother knows the truth and sees how he was duped, he will understand he owes you a life debt. Do you really think Hagal will be planning on keeping him alive?'

She waited for him to agree.

He ran his hand through his hair. 'You should always say goodbye when you go, even when you think you will only be gone for a short while. One of the things I always regret is that I never said goodbye to either of my parents. I slipped away to meet Ingrid. I was supposed to be working in the barn, mending a byre as punishment for disobedience.'

'I'm sure they knew you meant to,' Cwenneth said quietly.

He clenched his fists. 'My mother's body was in the barn. She'd left her hiding place and had gone searching for me. If she had stayed hidden, she would have survived. If I had said goodbye, she would have lived.'

Cwen went cold. His quest for vengeance made more sense now. Why he blamed himself. All the self-loathing and naked longing to change the past was written bare on his face. 'She should have trusted you were old enough. You were hardly a baby. You knew what to do in case of attack.'

His mouth twisted. 'You didn't know my mother. She was always fussing. I was her one chick. She knew my father's rules. She would have stayed hidden if she thought I was safe. But she didn't. She came to get me and I wasn't there. She died because of my lust for a faithless woman. I have regretted it every day of my life.'

Cwenneth breathed deeply. She had to get it right. Her instinct told her that Thrand had carried his guilt close to his heart and had never confided it before. 'We all make mistakes. You were barely more than a boy. How could you have foretold the future?'

His mouth twisted. 'It is nothing I am proud of, knowing that my actions caused my parents' death. But the children should know where you are going. Think about them and stop. They need a mother. They have bonded with you.'

'And if I do nothing, if I continue on to Iceland, what am I guilty of?' She held out her hands and willed him to understand that her decision had not been an easy one. 'People will die. Other boys will be left without their parents. Hagal needs to be stopped and I am the only one who can stop him. Here. Now. Before he has a chance to murder more innocent people.'

'And you think going to Lingwold will make a difference?'

'Doing nothing will allow Hagal to get stronger. If he leaves Lingwold with an army, he might succeed. Are you prepared to take that risk?'

Thrand looked down at her. His brow creased. 'Hagal wants you dead.'

She put her hand to his cheek. 'I can stop this madness before it starts, Thrand. I can expose Hagal's lies.'

'Then go to Jorvik and tell the king. Halfdan will listen, particularly as we know the true extent of Hagal's treachery. We will get there before any army.'

'I want to avoid more death, not destroy a generation of Bernician men.' Cwenneth wrapped her hands about her waist. 'One of the main reasons I was willing to marry Hagal was that I didn't want another woman to go through what I did when I lost Aefirth.'

'I…I…care about you, Cwen, and want to save your life. Throwing it away like this is madness.'

Her heart soared. Thrand cared about her. But then she forced herself to think and Cwenneth's heart shattered. Too little too late. She had settled for Aefirth caring for her. She had settled for a lot of things, but no longer. She wanted Thrand's love. She deserved more than lukewarm caring. She deserved his whole-hearted love.

'Part of you remains that boy who found his parents murdered.' She raised her chin. 'We need to stop Hagal while we can…unless you are afraid?'

'I've lived my life, hoping for the opportunity to destroy Hagal.'

Thrand waited in the silence. Inside he felt a great hollow open as if his heart was being ripped from his chest. He was a liar. Cwen was his life. Without her, he was nothing. And she did not love him enough to put him first. He might have confessed that he cared for her, but she didn't care for him. Her loyalty remained with her old family.

'Fine. I'm glad we have that settled. Now if you will let me go so I can return to *my* home…'

He gasped her upper arm. She might have rejected his love, but he couldn't allow her to stumble blindly into whatever trap Hagal had laid for her. 'You are not going alone, Cwen. I forbid it.'

Cwen took his fingers from her sleeve. 'You forbid it? You forbid nothing.'

Thrand clenched his fists. He ought to turn his back on her, but he couldn't. She might not believe in his love for her, but he knew it was fierce and strong.

The reason he lived now was to protect his family—his new family.

'I will go with you. In the background as insurance in case your brother does not behave how you'd expect.'

She arched her brow. 'What shall we do with the children?'

'Take them with us, of course. We are a family. We stay together. If it is safe enough for you, it is safe enough for them.' He glared at her, daring her to say differently. 'And who would think Thrand the Destroyer would be travelling in the company of two children? How many people have actually seen me? I will wear a cloak to cover my hair and will keep silent unless you actually need my help.'

'You are willing to do that? To let me speak first? To keep silent if necessary?'

Thrand put his hand on his sword. What he was about to was the hardest thing he had ever done—allow the woman he loved to go into danger. But he knew she was right, not because he needed vengeance for his long-dead family but because he needed to protect the family he had acquired. Looking over his shoulder and worrying was doomed to failure. Hagal had to be stopped now before he had an army on his side.

'Shall we put your theory to the test?' He raised her hand to his lips.

She bowed her head. 'I didn't expect you to agree.'

'So you could go off all indignant and lose your life?' Thrand put his hand on her shoulder. The faint stain of colour told him everything he needed to know. 'If you are going to face Hagal, then I'll be there, ready with my sword.'

'Thank you.' She laid her head on his chest. Thrand enfolded her in his arms and knew he'd protect her with his dying breath.

Cwenneth stared up at the grey stone walls of her old home. They had made good time from Martha's and had arrived before the main gate opened. Once she had dreamt of this moment, but now, instead of the welcome comfort, she knew it was potentially her prison and a death trap for Thrand. However, she could not turn her back and walk away. She had to stop Hagal, for good. And this was the only way she knew how to do it.

It meant a lot to her that Thrand walked at her side, carrying a sleepy Aud as Hilde held her hand. Each step she took, she was reminded of why she was doing this. These children deserved to grow up free from the menace which was Hagal.

Cwenneth hoped the children along with the cloak they had borrowed from Martha would provide enough of a disguise for Thrand. They had discussed the plan several times on the way over. Thrand reluctantly agreed that he needed to stay in the background until her brother learnt the truth.

'I will go through this back passage. You will go through the main gate and stay in the main hall. Once I have spoken to my brother, I will join you and we can walk out together. Slowly and carefully. If I am not there by the time it is noon, you must go back to Martha's and I will get there as soon as possible.'

Thrand's eyes glittered. 'I hope you are right, but if there is any trouble, I will be there. I will protect you.'

Cwen gave Aud a kiss and then knelt beside Hilde, rather than answering Thrand.

'I wish I had something…' She stopped and remembered the rings she had hidden in the hem of her skirt way back when this adventure first began. She rapidly extracted them. 'If anything happens to *Far*, you are to take these to the Lady of Lingwold and tell her what has gone on. Show no one but her.' Cwen looked over Hilde's head at Thrand. 'My sister-in-law may be many things, but she has a soft heart for children. She knows my rings. She will find a place for them…if the worst should happen.'

'Hilde, if there is trouble, we discussed what you do.'

Hilde nodded. '*Far* told me that I was to go to Martha. He showed me where he has hidden some gold for us. But it won't come to that, *Mor*. *Far* trusts you and your judgement.'

At Cwen's sceptical look, Thrand nodded. 'I have trained her well.'

She stood awkwardly, not sure what she should say to Thrand. There was far too much she wanted to say. 'I will see you soon.'

His hand curled about hers. 'I am counting on it.'

He turned with the children and didn't look back.

Keeping to the shadows, Cwenneth crept over to where the hidden passage ended and pulled the covering open. It smelt danker than she recalled, and she wished she had a light. The woman she had been when she'd left this place would never have dared to do this. Thrand believed in her and moreover had taught her that she was capable of far more than she dreamt.

Everything had seemed clear back at Martha's and indeed on the path here. But standing in front of the walls, it seemed a much harder proposition. Edward hated being duped. He always reacted badly. She had to hope that he turned on Hagal quickly and never discovered his most hated enemy was on his lands. She'd slip away quietly.

'There is no hope for it.' She spat on her hands and felt for the knife Thrand had insisted on her wearing. It remained securely strapped to her calf. 'I have to begin before I can be finished.'

She crouched down and began to crawl. Spiders' webs entangled in her hair, and she bumped her knee against a particularly hard rock. When she had nearly given up hope, she saw a faint crack of light. She pushed against the door, and it gave way.

She tumbled out on to the hard stone with a clatter which seemed to echo.

She froze, waiting, but there was no sound of anyone stirring.

A wild excitement filled her. She might just do it. She started towards the kitchen. Someone there would know where her brother slept. It would be safer. Edward would understand, she told herself for the thousandth time. He would let her go when she asked.

A hard hand descended on her shoulder. 'Who goes there?'

'I am Lady Cwenneth of Lingwold,' Cwenneth said with as much dignity as she could muster. 'Unhand me and take me to Lord Edward. There is much I want to say to him. There is much he needs to know before he makes the biggest mistake of his misbegotten life.'

'Not so fast, my lady,' the man replied with a thick Northman accent. 'Hagal the Red has business with you first.'

Chapter Fifteen

'Unhand me.' Cwenneth struggled against the re-straining paw of Hagal's henchman as he dragged her to where Hagal was holding court in a small room at the back of Lingwold. Hagal gave her a look which was pure evil. 'I am perfectly able to walk. I demand to see my brother. He is the lord here, not you.'

Hagal gave a nod. 'Release her. You will have your time later with the lady. You wish to see your brother, do you, wife?'

Cwenneth hated how her scalp crawled. She tore her arm away from the great hulk and silently vowed that he was never going to have any time with her. Thankfully, she still had the knife and she would not hesitate to use it.

'If you will take my arm, my lady.' Hagal held out his arm in a parody of a gentleman's pose.

'Where are we going?'

'Where else but to see your brother?' Insincerity dripped from every feature. 'We have all been wor-ried sick about you, my lady. Thrand Ammundson has a fearsome reputation. Your brother will rejoice to see you unharmed.'

'I am sure he will.' Cwenneth forced her feet to keep moving. All of her muscles tensed. Somehow she had to find a way to escape and warn Thrand. Hagal was not acting as though he suspected that Thrand was in the hall. She breathed a little easier and tried to hang on to that.

'Look who has returned, Edward!' Hagal crashed open the main door to the hall and propelled her forward into the tapestry-lined hall. She could remember how she used to play a game of echoes when she was little. If she stood in the right spot, just about where Edward now stood, her voice would bounce off the walls. In the wrong spot, it was as quiet as the grave.

The force of the blow made Cwenneth drop to her knees. She gritted her teeth and slowly rose to her feet, concentrating on the red and gold of the tapestries. The stench of sour wine intermingled with ale hung in the air. Her father would be spinning in his grave. She did not dare look around to see where Thrand and the children stood. If they had made it this far...

She lifted her chin. 'Brother, it is good that you have given me such a warm and heartfelt reception.'

'Cwenneth!' her brother said, rising from where he sat discussing something with several of his followers. Her sister-in-law was nowhere to be seen, but her former stepson sat beside him.

Edward's face was puffy and his nose red. He had the air of a man who preferred to drink and carouse rather than to lead an attack of any sort. In any fight with Hagal, he'd lose. Cwenneth's heart sank. Edward was blundering about like a fly unaware that he was caught in a web.

'You are alive.' He held out his arms. 'Thank God, you are alive. That monster let you live. And you've returned unharmed to us. Hagal is willing to overlook everything. We can still have the wedding.'

'I survived the attack, yes,' she said cautiously and remained where she stood.

Cwenneth looked at each of the men at the high table, including her former stepson. Her heart sank. There was not one she could fully trust to believe her story, not with Hagal and his men camped inside the gate.

'My sister is more resourceful than you predicted, Hagal the Red,' Edward remarked.

'A great relief to us all,' Hagal said with a bow. 'Thrand Ammundson does have a certain reputation with women. Back in Norway, he caused the death of my beloved Ingrid.'

'Still, my sister has returned to us after her ordeal. And she will give witness to what happened. Your king will have to listen to her. A delegation can be sent, rather than an army.'

Hagal's face turned crimson. 'One hopes that she is not a traitor.'

Cwenneth kept her gaze trained on her brother and willed him to believe her. 'Thrand Ammundson rescued me after Hagal's men slaughtered everyone else. Edward, you above all people should know my love for Lingwold is without question.'

'Why would Hagal want you dead?' her stepson asked.

She directed her gaze to him. 'Because your father,

my late husband, killed his close kinsman. And Hagal made a battlefield vow. Narfi took great pleasure in informing me of it before he challenged Thrand Ammundson.'

Her stepson blanched.

'Where is Thrand Ammundson now?' Hagal asked, muscling forward. 'How did your ladyship escape?'

Cwenneth's stomach clenched. If she lied, her brother would know. He had always had the uncanny knack of knowing when she lied. She had to keep to the truth as much as she could. There remained a possibility that Thrand would not be required to rescue her, that she could walk away from this unscathed and Thrand undetected.

'Where I left him, I presume.' She batted her eyelashes and hoped. 'He was badly injured in the fight with Narfi. Luckily I found the right track and made my way here.'

'And you are asking me to believe that you made it across country on your own? Cwenneth, you can barely make it across the castle yard.'

Various people laughed. She raised her chin and glared at her brother. 'I stand before you. Surely your eyes tell the truth.'

'Where did you get those clothes?'

'From Martha. Dain's mother. I stopped there to return Dain's boots. My slippers would not have held up on the long march home.'

Hagal snapped his fingers. 'She lies. Tell me where this Martha creature lives. Ammundson will be there. Let me send my men. Let me prove this to you. Your sister will be in league with your enemy. He has seduced her. She is damaged goods.'

'Do you take orders from a Norseman now?' Cwenneth poured all the scorn she possibly could into her voice. 'Why should you doubt my word?'

Her brother looked from one to another. 'What am I going to do with you, Cwenneth?'

'Allow me to live my life in peace. I've no wish to be married to him.' Cwenneth pointed a finger at Hagal. 'Nor do I wish to enter a convent. And I want my dowry returned to Lingwold's coffers, the dowry that his men stole from the baggage cart. It is all I ask.'

'We have an agreement, Lingwold. Honour it.' Hagal slammed his fist down. 'Or it will go the worse for you.'

'And what was that agreement?' Cwenneth argued. 'To call your followers and march to Jorvik, demanding Thrand's head? Did you truly think Halfdan would give it? Thrand is his man.'

'Thrand Ammundson has ravaged our lands!' her stepson shouted and the rest of the high table beat their hands against the wood in agreement.

'He has been in the south for the last two years,' Cwenneth retorted, meeting his gaze straight on. 'Thrand has been in the south these past two years. Hagal and his men used Thrand's name to extract the gold.'

'Who told you this? Ammundson?'

'Narfi. He was determined that I should understand and despair before I died.'

Her brother frowned. 'You know little of politics, sister, but you speak very boldly.'

'I tell you that if you leave Lingwold, you will never see it again. Hagal will ensure it. All of you.' Cwenneth walked over to the table and dumped her brother's wine goblet out on to the rushes. 'Our father would be disgusted with you.'

'Hey, what are you doing?'

'Hagal will claim you were a drunken sot, brother, and that is why you ended up with a knife in your back. And there would be some truth to this assertion. Start acting like the lord of these lands instead of some Norseman's lapdog.'

'You need to put your tale to Halfdan. He is the only one who is able to tame that mad dog Ammundson.' Hagal pounded his fist on the table, making the goblets jump.

'And you wish to go to war with the Norsemen? The entire Norse army? The Storting is amassing and they will defend their own. You only have Hagal's word that they will leave their weapons. You and I know what happened in the second siege of Jorvik,' Cwenneth said softly, training her eyes on her brother. 'Surely we have had too many years of war recently. You first considered this marriage contract because you wanted to plant crops and see your children grow up to honourable manhood. It can still happen, Edward, but not if you blindly follow Hagal the Red, Hagal the False.'

Her brother swayed where he stood and he looked at her. For the first time in a long time, she saw his eyes soften and the brother she had once known return. 'My sister has returned, unharmed. There is no need for me to go to war with the Norsemen. I will send a message of protest at the kidnapping.'

'You will do what?'

'My sister's claims must be properly investigated before I take further action. And once the truth is known, then I will move against the culprit.'

The high table stamped their feet in agreement.

Cwenneth pressed her hands to her eyes. It was over. Edward had seen sense. Hagal had nowhere left to turn. Edward had the greater army.

'Of all the weak-livered, mealy-mouthed responses!' Hagal strode over to her brother and jabbed him in the chest. 'You can't do that!'

'Can't I?' Her brother reached for another jug of wine. 'I believe I have done it.'

'Then you're surplus to requirements.' Hagal withdrew a knife and stabbed her brother in the side and twisted.

Before Cwenneth had a chance to scream, her brother collapsed to the floor, clutching his side. Hard hands captured her and dragged her to where the triumphant Hagal stood.

The reality of the situation slammed into her. Her only brother lay bleeding on the floor, possibly dying. Whatever wrongs he'd done her in the past, he'd cared enough to muster an army and, when confronted with the truth, he'd believed her. She'd never been more proud of her brother than when he stood up to Hagal. Somehow she'd find a way to get him help.

Cwenneth clenched her fist. The old woman's curse had no power. She made her own luck.

'Next!' Hagal called, stepping over her brother's body and giving it a contemptuous kick as he stared directly at her former stepson. 'I claim the right to lead as Lord Edward is incapacitated. I'm his anointed successor, his brother-in-law and I say we march to Jorvik. Does anyone dispute me?'

'I do!' Cwenneth cried. 'You cannot murder in cold blood and get away with it. A marriage contract does not a marriage make. I repudiate it! Get out, Hagal! Go!'

She regarded each of her brother's loyal followers, but they remained seated, pale-faced and immobile. Fear. They feared Hagal more than they wanted to avenge Edward's stabbing.

'You are a monster!' Cwenneth tore her arms from the restraining hands. She fumbled for her knife and lunged towards him.

'Shut up and learn your place, woman!' Hagal's hand hit her face with a crack. 'Be grateful that you still live. You will tell me where Thrand Ammundson truly is.'

The blow would have once set her reeling, but Cwenneth stood her ground and lifted the knife. A great calm settled over her. Panic and running away were not the answer. 'Never ever raise a hand to me again! You don't frighten me, Hagal the Red! I know you for what you are—a coward and a bully.'

With a hard blow to her wrist, he sent the knife spinning through the air. She stared at him in dismay. Her only chance gone. He captured her face. 'There will be payment, Lady Cwenneth. You will die slowly and painfully. Who will lift a finger to save you?'

'I will!' A large man stepped from the crowd and threw back his hood.

Cwenneth's heart gave a leap. Thrand! She wasn't going to die without seeing his face again. She gulped hard. But it meant he was in danger. The children were in danger.

'Thrand Ammundson. An unexpected pleasure.' Hagal made a slight bow, keeping hold of Cwenneth's face. 'You will see I have no need of your assistance, Old comrade.'

'Unhand my woman.'

'Your woman?' Hagal shook his head. 'My wife! To do with what I will!'

'The marriage has never been consummated!' Cwenneth yelled, tearing her face from his fingers. 'I will never be your wife. But I am proud to say that I'm Thrand Ammundson's woman!'

The entire hall gasped. Edward struggled to sit up. 'Ammundson is here?' he rasped out, holding his side. 'Seize him!'

'No, keep your places! I'll deal with him on my terms,' Hagal said.

No one moved except for Aud, who toddled out towards her. Cwenneth gave a cry and picked him up, holding him close.

'Bad man,' he said, touching her face and pointing towards Hagal. 'Bad.'

'Stay here with me,' she whispered. 'Your *Far* will beat the bad man.'

'Will you fight, Hagal the Red?' Thrand banged his sword against his thigh. 'For the possession of this woman? And the right to command these lands?'

'You will fight a fellow member of the *felag*?' Hagal gave a pitying smile. 'I can get you safe passage back to Jorvik or wherever you want to go. Leave now. This is none of your concern. You and I share a fellowship. I'm merely seeking to subdue the north.'

'My oath permits me to fight for a woman. And even if it didn't, I would still fight. Some things are beyond codes. Some things strike at the heart of a man's existence.' Thrand's face showed no emotion. 'It is time, Hagal, that we tested our strength. Man to man. Sword to sword.'

'You won't get out of here alive, Ammundson.' Hagal drew his sword. 'You know that. They will fall on you when I am gone. Lord Edward, you may die, knowing that I do keep my promises.'

'Neither will you. I guarantee it.'

They circled each other, testing and probing. Hagal was a worthy opponent who seemed to have studied Thrand's strengths and weaknesses.

Cwenneth put her hand over her mouth. Thrand couldn't lose. Could he? He had said that Hagal was better than good. She started to inch over towards where the knife had fallen.

Thrand went on his back foot and stumbled to one knee.

'This is the best the great Thrand Ammundson can do?' Hagal raised his sword over his head, preparing to deliver the death blow.

Cwenneth's hand closed about the knife. What was the first law of sword fighting? Never be distracted. Had Hagal learnt that lesson as well as Thrand? She had to try. She was in the right spot.

'Justice! I want justice for all who died in the wood!' she shouted.

'Justice! Justice! Justice!' the walls echoed back.

Hagal half-turned his head towards the noise. His sword checked. That heartbeat was all Thrand needed. He drove upwards with his sword and connected with Hagal's throat.

Hagal gurgled as he fell backwards.

'First rule of sword fighting—never allow anyone or anything to distract you.' Thrand stepped over the body. 'Do you understand what I was trying to teach you now, Cwen, back at the hut?'

'Completely,' she answered, going towards him. 'And we have nothing to fear from Hagal any longer.'

'Yes, you are a free woman.'

His arms encircled her and held her tight. For a long moment, neither spoke.

'Where is Hilde?' she asked, looking about her for the young girl.

'She will be here,' Thrand said. 'As soon as I suspected all was not going to go as you planned, I sent Hilde to fetch your sister-in-law. Let's hope she succeeded.'

'What is going on here?' her sister-in-law's voice resounded in the hall. 'Edward, this girl brought me Cwenneth's—' Her sister-in-law rushed towards where Edward had propped himself up against the table. 'What happened here? Cwenneth has returned…unharmed?'

'I made a mistake and believed the wrong man,' her brother gasped out, clutching his side. 'Hagal the Red was the problem, not Thrand Ammundson. I made a mistake because Ammundson had bested me in battle and now I owe him my life. My sister saved us. She saved Lingwold.'

'Hush. You have been stabbed. You need a healer.'

'My *mor* is a good healer,' Hilde said, tugging on

the woman's skirt with her free hand. 'She healed my *far*. He told me. Aud will tell you that as well.'

'Where is she?'

Hilde pointed to Cwenneth and with a doubtful frown her sister-in-law beckoned to Cwenneth. 'Cwenneth, I can see you have returned a changed woman. You have acquired two brave children. Can you help my husband?'

Thrand gave her a little push. 'Go on. Show them what you can do. Show them that you are not cursed.'

Cwenneth went over to her brother. The wound was less serious than she first feared. Rather than hitting his middle, the knife had glanced off his side and the cut was less deep than the wound Narfi had given Thrand. Yes, there was blood, but her brother should live once he sobered up.

'Can you do anything?' Her sister-in-law wrung her hands. 'I don't know how long it will take a monk to get here.'

'I can try. I make no promises, but I suspect it is his destiny to live.'

Her sister-in-law narrowed her eyes. 'You've changed, Cwenneth. I can hear it in your voice. The woman who left here would not have been able to stand up to Hagal the Red, nor would she put herself forward to try to heal anyone. You used to believe you were cursed. What happened?'

'There came a time for me to take charge of my destiny, and I have. You make your own luck, sister dear. Thrand Ammundson taught me that.'

Edward grabbed Cwenneth's hand. 'Will you forgive me, sister, before I die?'

Cwenneth resisted the urge to roll her eyes. She

had forgotten that her brother hated any sort of pain. 'If I dress it, it will be fine until the monks arrive. Goodness knows you have enough wine to pickle yourself, Edward. Some of this mess is from your spilled wine.'

'What…what are you saying?'

'I suspect you will live a long time, but hopefully less foolishly. And Hagal the Red is to blame for what happened here, not you.'

Her brother closed his eyes and his words slurred. 'It is good to have you home, Cwenneth. It is where you belong, with your proper family. I have felt so guilty about sending you away. It was wrong of me. Do you forgive me?'

'Of course I forgive you. Hagal fooled us all.'

Cwenneth worked quickly and bound up the wound. When she had finished, her brother gave a soft snore.

'Cwen, will he live?' Thrand asked, coming to kneel beside her.

'That wound won't kill him, but I say nothing about the alcohol.'

Two monks arrived. The elder one praised the neatness of her bandaging, making Cwenneth absurdly happy. But with the monk's arrival, Cwenneth became aware the mood in the hall had altered. The faces of the men and women showed little relief or friendship. In the time she had been treating Edward's wound, they had closed ranks, sealing off not only Hagal's men's retreat, but Thrand's way out as well.

'May I have a moment with Lady Cwenneth in private?' Thrand asked before Cwenneth could mention the danger he faced. 'I have no wish to outstay my welcome.'

Her brother nodded, his face creased with pain, and whispered something to her sister-in-law, who nodded.

'You may use my husband's private chamber. You may take as long as you wish to say goodbye.' Her sister-in-law laid a hand on Cwenneth's sleeve as she went past. 'Take care. We are family and we're delighted to have you with us again.'

'I make my own decisions, sister.'

'Yes, yes, but I don't want you to feel obligated to a man like that. He is reputed to have a stone for a heart.'

'You needn't worry. Obligation is the last thing I feel towards him.'

Cwenneth followed Thrand with a sinking heart into her brother's private chamber. Thrand was going to leave. He could see she and the children would be looked after. She felt the walls of the room press down on her. Hagal was dead and there was no longer any pressing need for her to go to Iceland. She should be rejoicing, but all she wanted to do was find a way to keep him with her and hold fast to the dream they once had.

He closed the heavy door with a loud bang and crossed the floor to her. 'Your sister-in-law lies. I do have a heart and I do care. I care passionately about what happens to you. I used the wrong words earlier. Can you forgive me?'

'Forgive you for what? You saved my life. You were right. I needed your help.'

His arms came around her. 'We defeated Hagal

together. Together we are far stronger. It was right
to act as you suggested. Waiting until Jorvik would
have been wrong.'

'My sister-in-law has offered me a home. The children as well,' she said moving out of his embrace.
There had to be a way of getting him out of here alive.
Later, she'd find a way to join him, if it was what he
truly desired. 'We will be safe here…in case you were
worried. You can go in peace.'

'Hagal has ceased to threaten you. You can live
here in safety and without fear of reprisal.' His face
began to look like it was sculpted from granite. 'I will
ensure that. Lingwold will be safe from Norse raids.'

Cwenneth put her hand to her mouth and tried to
hold the sob back. Thrand's dream of a farmer's life
in Iceland seemed to have vanished like the mist on
a spring morning. She raised her chin and refused to
beg. 'Then I must wish you a good life. You will be
able to go back to doing what you love best.'

He put his hands on her shoulders, preventing her
from moving. 'Without you, I have no life. I wanted
to say that before you started on about you staying
here so I can get free or some such nonsense. It is not
going to happen. We are a family now and families
stay together. The children, you and me. Together.'

She completely stilled. A lump rose in her throat.
'Together because of the children?'

'No, because of you. You are the heart and soul of
my existence. Until I met you, I was so preoccupied
with my need to revenge my family that I forgot to
live. You showed that there is more to life than vengeance and war. You made me want to live.'

Cwenneth's heart began to thump so loudly she

thought he must hear it. 'I made your family? You fought today to fulfil your vow.'

'Earlier I got the words wrong and I am making a mess of it again.' He gathered her hands in his and held them tight. 'The next time you even think about throwing your life away to save mine, think about this—without you, I am nothing. Before you, I only had hate in my heart and with you, my life has begun again. I was able to fight today not because I wanted vengeance for my parents, but because I wanted to protect my family. And the heart of my family is you and always will be. You're my everything.'

'Always?' She stared at him.

'I tried to show it to you, but I will say the words, if you need to hear them. Believe me, please.' He went down on one knee. 'I love you, Cwen, and I won't leave here without you.' His eyes softened, and she wondered that she ever thought them dead or full of ice. They were warm; they were eyes she could drown in. 'With you I have discovered what it is like to live again. I had become one of the walking dead, and my parents never wanted that for me. They wanted me to have a life as full as theirs was.'

Her breath caught in her throat. Thrand loved her. Truly loved her. 'I love you as well, Thrand. Very much.'

He gave a half-smile. 'You love me? How could you?'

Cwenneth's heart opened. 'Very easily. I want to go with you, to be your woman, to follow you about even though I will have no dowry, nothing to recommend me. I want to be a part of your family. Our family.'

'No, not my woman, my wife,' Thrand corrected. 'We will marry, Cwen. Come with me to Iceland, sit by the fire and grow old with me. I need you beside me for the rest of my life.'

'I would like that that very much.' She leant her head against his chest, breathing in his familiar scent. 'I have loved you for a long time. I believe I fell first when you healed my blisters. I had thought my heart was buried alongside Aefirth and Richard, but I see now that I was wrong. A small part of me will always love them, but hearts expand and grow. You and the children have become my family, the people I want to spend the rest of my days with.'

'The first time I saw you when you were caught in the thorn bush, you made me feel something beside the deadened dull emotion which had been my fate for so many years. I thought I had banished all feelings years ago and you taught me to love again.' He put a gentle hand to her cheek. 'You taught me to believe.'

She laced her fingers with his. 'Shall we go out and let them know our decision?'

'Together.'

'Yes, together.'

Cwenneth walked out of the room, holding Thrand's hand. Her sister-in-law raised her brow in surprise as the entire hall fell silent. Even the monks tending to her brother stopped.

'We are leaving. You may try to stop us if you wish, but I hope you don't. I am going to Iceland to be with the man I love. I have made my choice.' She held out her hands and both children ran to her. Thrand picked up Aud and put him on his shoulders. 'I have chosen my family, my true family of the heart.'

As the crowd parted they walked out of Lingwold together without a backward glance.

Epilogue

A farm in the east of Iceland a year later

The late-evening sun shone down on the newly constructed longhouse. Although it was mainly in the style of Norse longhouses, there were a few Northumbrian touches here and there. It had taken several months of hard work for Thrand and his men to build it once they arrived in Iceland, but Cwenneth thought it well worth the wait.

Cwenneth drew a deep breath, enjoying the rare moment of calm. Aud and Hilde were tucked up in bed. The household chores were done.

Thrand had allowed her to select the spot for the house and had been surprised at her choice. When she asked why, he said that the situation reminded him of something he'd seen in a dream once and then he confessed about the dream he had had in the hut when he had lain injured the previous year.

'Here you are,' Thrand said, coming out of the house, carrying a bundle. 'There is someone who wants to see you and show what she can do.'

She smiled and reached for their daughter Sinriod, who had been born a month ago. They had named her after Thrand's mother. If she had had any lingering anxieties about the curse, it had been laid to rest the first time she felt Sinriod kick in her womb. But Cwenneth knew even if she had never had Sinriod, she would still have felt blessed. She had her husband and her two children of her heart. Sinriod simply added to her happiness and contentment.

The baby opened her eyes, blinked and gave a huge smile at both her parents.

'She's smiling. Properly smiling. What a very clever girl. How long do you think she has been doing that?'

Thrand put an arm about her waist and pulled her and Sinroid close. 'After I finished my chores, I went in to check that our children were all asleep and this little one smiled at me. She wanted to come out and see her mother.'

'If she had smiled at Aud or Hilde, you would have heard the excited shouts from here to Reykjavik and possibly even to Bernicia.'

Thrand laughed, sending a warm tingle down her spine. 'They are both very proud of their baby sister.'

Cwenneth leant back into his embrace and looked up into his summer-blue eyes. Over the past year, the shadows had slowly faded from his expression. 'And why shouldn't they be?'

'You were looking pensive earlier this evening. Is there some reason why?'

'It has been a year since my caravan was attacked.'

'Only a year? It seems like a lifetime ago.' His arm tightened about her shoulders. 'It is hard to believe that I once thought my life should consist solely of war and vengeance. Through you, I learnt the best revenge is a life well lived with people who love you.'

'My thoughts exactly.'

They stood there, watching their baby daughter smile up at them, and knew that all was right in the world because they had each other and their growing family.

* * * * *

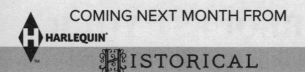

REQUEST YOUR FREE BOOKS!

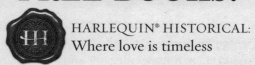

HARLEQUIN® HISTORICAL:
Where love is timeless

2 FREE NOVELS PLUS 2 **FREE GIFTS!**

YES! Please send me 2 FREE Harlequin® Historical novels and my 2 FREE gifts (gifts are worth about $10). After receiving them, if I don't wish to receive any more books, I can return the shipping statement marked "cancel." If I don't cancel, I will receive 6 brand-new novels every month and be billed just $5.44 per book in the U.S. or $5.74 per book in Canada. That's a savings of at least 16% off the cover price! It's quite a bargain! Shipping and handling is just 50¢ per book in the U.S. and 75¢ per book in Canada.* I understand that accepting the 2 free books and gifts places me under no obligation to buy anything. I can always return a shipment and cancel at any time. Even if I never buy another book, the two free books and gifts are mine to keep forever.

246/349 HDN F4ZY

Name _____ (PLEASE PRINT) _____

Address _____ Apt. # _____

City _____ State/Prov. _____ Zip/Postal Code _____

Signature (if under 18, a parent or guardian must sign)

Mail to the **Harlequin® Reader Service:**
IN U.S.A.: P.O. Box 1867, Buffalo, NY 14240-1867
IN CANADA: P.O. Box 609, Fort Erie, Ontario L2A 5X3

Want to try two free books from another line?
Call 1-800-873-8635 or visit www.ReaderService.com.

* Terms and prices subject to change without notice. Prices do not include applicable taxes. Sales tax applicable in N.Y. Canadian residents will be charged applicable taxes. Offer not valid in Quebec. This offer is limited to one order per household. Not valid for current subscribers to Harlequin Historical books. All orders subject to credit approval. Credit or debit balances in a customer's account(s) may be offset by any other outstanding balance owed by or to the customer. Please allow 4 to 6 weeks for delivery. Offer available while quantities last.

Your Privacy—The Harlequin® Reader Service is committed to protecting your privacy. Our Privacy Policy is available online at www.ReaderService.com or upon request from the Harlequin Reader Service.

We make a portion of our mailing list available to reputable third parties that offer products we believe may interest you. If you prefer that we not exchange your name with third parties, or if you wish to clarify or modify your communication preferences, please visit us at www.ReaderService.com/consumerschoice or write to us at Harlequin Reader Service Preference Service, P.O. Box 9062, Buffalo, NY 14269. Include your complete name and address.

HH13R

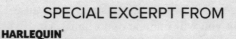
Zachary raised his head to look at her with mercurial
grey eyes. There was a flush to the hardness of his cheeks
and his dark hair was dishevelled. "I have forgotten nothing, Georgianna," he assured huskily. "If anything, I find
that edge of danger only makes you more intriguing.
Besides which, if you are a spy, then you are currently
an imprisoned one. My imprisoned spy." He smiled his
satisfaction with that fact.

Georgianna drew her breath in sharply as she once
again felt the soft pad of his thumb caress across the hardened tip of her breast.

"Perhaps that was my plan all along?" She tried to
fight the sensations currently bombarding her senses:
pleasure, arousal, heat. "Has it not occurred to you that
maybe my plan is to stab you at the dinner table with
a knife from your own ducal silver dinner service?" she
persisted breathlessly even as she found it impossible not
to arch once again into that marauding mouth as it continued to plunder the sensitive column of her throat.

"No." Zachary smiled against the fluttering wildness
of her pulse. He might have become slightly blasé these
past few months, but he was nevertheless positive his

self-defence skills were still as sharp. "Because I very much doubt you will find the opportunity. Or, if you did, that my strength would not far outweigh your own."

"Then perhaps it is my intention to hide one of the knives and take it back upstairs with me, so that I can stab you later, while you sleep?" There was now an edge of desperation to Georgianna's voice; she simply couldn't allow this to continue.

Zachary deftly released the first button at the throat of her gown. "Then I will have to ensure that the door between our two bedchambers remains locked at night."

"I do not believe you are taking me seriously."

"When I am holding you in my arms and about to kiss you? No, you may be assured I am not taking your threats seriously at all, Georgianna," he acknowledged gruffly.

"Zachary!"

"Georgianna," he chided gently as he released the second button and revealed the top of the silky smooth skin above the swell of her breasts.

"I cannot… This is not—" She broke off abruptly as Zachary claimed her mouth with his and silenced her protest.

Don't miss
ZACHARY BLACK: DUKE OF DEBAUCHERY
available October 2014 wherever
Harlequin® Historical books and ebooks are sold!

HARLEQUIN®

HISTORICAL

Where love is timeless

COMING IN OCTOBER 2014

Wild West Christmas

by

Jenna Kernan, Kathryn Albright and Lynna Banning

Curl up with a cowboy this Christmas with these three heartwarming tales:

A Family for the Rancher
by Jenna Kernan

Two years ago, Dillen Roach fell for wealthy debutante Alice Truett.
Now she's at his door with his orphaned nephews in tow!
Could Alice be the perfect Christmas gift for this solitary rancher?

Dance with a Cowboy
by Kathryn Albright

Kathleen Sheridan is determined to leave the tragedy of her past
behind her—including brooding cowboy Garrett. But with
Christmas magic in the air, can she resist the warmth of his touch?

Christmas in Smoke River
by Lynna Banning

Gale McBurney is an utter mystery to rich "city girl" Lilah Cornwell.
But to make Smoke River her home by Christmas, she'll have to let this
rugged cattleman take the reins…

Available wherever books and ebooks are sold.

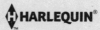

HISTORICAL

Where love is timeless

COMING IN OCTOBER 2014

The Truth About Lady Felkirk

by

Christine Merrill

The wife he doesn't know…

When William Felkirk opens his eyes, the past six months are blank. What happened? And who is this beautiful woman claiming to be his wife and caring for his broken body?

Justine will do anything to protect her sister, even if that means pretending to be a stranger's wife. She must guard the reasons for her deception with her life. But with every passing day, William unlocks her heart just a little more, and Justine knows she won't be able to hide the truth forever…

Available wherever books and ebooks are sold.

www.Harlequin.com

HH29805

HISTORICAL

Where love is timeless

COMING IN OCTOBER 2014

Betrayed by His Kiss

by

Amanda McCabe

In a city of shadows…

Orlando Landucci knows all too well what darkness lies beneath Florence's dazzling splendor. And when his beloved sister is torn from him, he will stop at nothing to avenge her death.

…only a kiss can light up the darkness

But from the moment he lays eyes on innocent Isabella Spinola, something inside him shifts. She is the kin of his sworn enemy, yet he feels compelled to protect her. With every forbidden kiss, Orlando's sense of betrayal deepens, so when the time for vengeance comes, will their bond be enough to banish the shadows forever?

Available wherever books and ebooks are sold.

Love the Harlequin book you just read?

Your opinion matters.

Review this book on your favorite book site, review site, blog or your own social media properties and share your opinion with other readers!

Be sure to connect with us at:
Harlequin.com/Newsletters
Facebook.com/HarlequinBooks
Twitter.com/HarlequinBooks